ANDREW M. GREELEY

WARNER BOOKS

A Warner Communications Company

Warner Books, Inc., 666 Fifth Avenue, New York, NY 10103

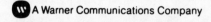 A Warner Communications Company

Printed in the United States of America
First printing: July 1988

10 9 8 7 6 5 4 3 2

Library of Congress Cataloging in Publication Data

Greeley, Andrew M., 1928-
  Angel fire.

  I. Title.
PS3557.R358A74 1988   813' 54   87-40605
ISBN 0-446-51437-3

Book design by H. Roberts
Map by Heidi Hornaday

*For Donna Colbert, Bob Colbert, Anne Fallon,
and in memory of Al Menarik.*

note

This story, about grace in creation, is not a doctrinal treatise on angels (such as Ladislaus Boros's *Angels and Men* or Dr. Billy Graham's *Angels, Angels, Angels*) and should not be interpreted by the norms appropriate for such treatises. It is rather speculative fiction based on two premises: evolution is directed toward mind; and, *pace* St. Bernard and St. Augustine, angels have spiritual bodies.

Hence Gabriella Light is a purely fictional entity and is based entirely on my imagination as guided by these two premises. Any similarity between her and any angel (or seraph) living or dead is purely coincidental.

Yet to paraphrase somewhat a remark of the fictional King Karl Gustav in this story, it would be a shame if somewhere in the *cosmoi* there were not someone like her.

I am grateful to my good friend Professor Oscar Hechter of Northwestern University for advising me about the biology in this story. He is not, however, to blame for either my mistakes or those of Sean S. Desmond of the University of Cook County.

—AMG
Tucson
St. Patrick's Day, 1987

There must be many places in the cosmos ... where evolution for various reasons has made more headway than here on earth, many places where it has by now pressed its efforts beyond generating life, consciousness and knowledge to new heights, enlarging the realm of subjectivity by annexing regions of which we are still ignorant.... These creatures would be equipped with brains which would help their owners to a much larger share of that mind which has just now begun to shed some light, though as yet a relatively faint one on our own heads.... We ourselves may have descendants as genetically distant from us as we are from *Homo habilis*.... We might constitute a bridge to nonbiological descendants of an entirely different sort....

—Hoimar von Ditfurth

Let us remember that the citizens of that country are spirits, mighty, glorious, blessed, distinct personalities, of graduated rank, occupying the order given them from the beginning, perfect of their kind, having ethereal bodies....

—St. Bernard of Clairveaux
De Consideratione, v. 4

Outside the open window
The morning air is all awash with angels.

—Richard Wilbur

More than in the Devil, I am interested in the indications of Grace.

—Flannery O'Connor

In all reflective species males and females tend to be attracted to one another and to fear one another.

—Desmond's Fourth Law

Something is afoot in the universe, something that looks like gestation and birth.

—Pierre Teilhard de Chardin

Grace is rampant.

—Gabriella Light, Ph.D.

Angels can fly because they take themselves lightly.

—G. K. Chesterton

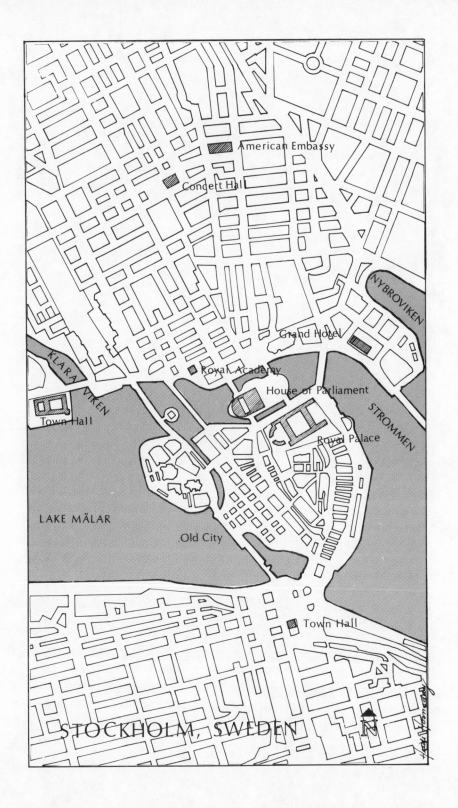

STOCKHOLM, SWEDEN

"It might be useful," said the rich womanly voice, "to model me as your guardian angel."

"I gave up guardian angels after Sister Intemerata's class in grammar school," said Professor S. S. Desmond, standing on the elegant queen-size bed of his room in the Helmsley Palace Hotel so he could search for a hidden speaker behind the expensively framed print that hung over the headboard.

"There are no speakers," the disembodied voice said casually, "though there is a microphone hidden in the television. I wouldn't worry about it. They can't hear me. . . . And it was shabby for you and your friends to eat garlic at lunchtime to torment Sister Intemerata's sensitive nose."

Sean Seamus Desmond gave up on the print and bounced to a sitting position on his bed. That was pretty clever. Not many people knew of the Great Garlic Caper. He thought about examining the TV and decided against it.

"You called your guardian angel Josephine, as I remember. Josie for short."

"Goddamnit, how did you know that?" he exploded.

I must have told someone. My sister?

There was a knock at the door. "Room service," said a muffled voice.

"Don't let them in," said the invisible woman urgently.

"Go to hell," Desmond told her, "I'm hungry," and to the door, "Come in, it's open."

The two men who pushed the door open did not have a room service cart with them. Nor did they look like waiters. Rather, they seemed to be longshoremen or perhaps merchant seamen. They wore dark pea coats, collars turned up, black trousers, and black ski masks pulled down over their faces.

And they had ridiculously tiny guns in their hands with absurdly long silencers.

I am going to be "hit," Sean Desmond told himself in stunned astonishment. He noted with abstract interest that his misspent life did not race before his eyes as they pointed the guns at him.

Twenty-two's, he thought, Mafia specials. My last thought—

A burst of flame flared at the muzzle of one of the guns, something like an angry insect buzzed by Desmond's left ear.

Missed the first one, he thought ruefully. I don't even rate skilled hit men.

Colored lights twinkled, briefly, in front of him, like a high-school-science animated film, the kind he had on occasion denounced as misleading.

The forehead of one of the longshoremen seemed to explode. A large red spot appeared on the chest of the other and then spread, as blood gushed out of his pea coat and cascaded down to the soft green carpet. Both men fell to the floor, as though their legs had been knocked out from under them.

"Wonder Woman trick," said the womanly voice ruefully.

As Sean Desmond watched incredulously, the two men decomposed before his eyes: flesh, muscles, blood, bones vanished in an almost instantaneous putrefaction process. Without the smell. Then their blood disappeared from the rug as if someone had cleaned it with an incredibly powerful solvent, one that did not damage the rug fibers.

He realized that he was going to be very sick. He rushed to the sumptuous bathroom and barely made it in time. His United Airlines first class lunch was quickly ejected, as was most of his breakfast. His empty stomach, not understanding that there was nothing left to give, continued to react violently.

The one luxury trip I'm likely to have in my whole life, he thought, reveling in self-pity, and I get mixed up with ghosts and gorillas.

He was conscious of a cool reassurance touching his forehead and a sympathetic embrace consoling him, as his mother had done when he was a very sick little boy.

"It'll be all right, Jackie Jim," the voice said tenderly. "Only next time, please do what I tell you."

He had not been Jackie Jim since he was five. Thirty-eight years ago. When he graduated from college and gave up his Catholicism, he'd decided to compensate by becoming even more Irish and had changed his name from John J. Desmond to Sean S. Desmond, almost to Sean S. O'Desmond. He decided against that because there was an upper limit to how much you could twit the biological fraternity and still expect to win a Nobel Prize. As it was, his incorrigible Irish wit had delayed the prize for several years.

The Royal Swedish Academy did not have much of a sense of humor. Well, his research on evolutionary "punctuation" finally forced the damn Swedes to give him the prize regardless.

And he'd get even with them in his acceptance speech.

At first he was too sick to challenge the womanly presence that had enveloped him. Then, as his stomach decided that it could go along—on an ad hoc basis—with her ministrations, he began to feel better.

He staggered out of the bathroom and collapsed into a chair. Across the street the massive gray transept of St. Patrick's testified that he was still in the real world.

"I need a drink," he said shakily.

"Give it a few minutes," she spoke again.

"Who the hell are you?" His hand rested on the phone to summon room service, but he was not quite ready to ignore her suggestions.

" 'We exist in a cosmos of unfathomable enigmas and mysteries,' " she replied, a touch of amusement in her sensual voice, " 'but it does seem likely that humankind is at a crossroads, at an ontological turning point. We may well have come to another

"punctuation" in the human evolutionary process. There is no reason to think that such times of great leaps forward are limited to
the drosophila, the notorious fruit flies on which I have done my
research. It may be a matter of hundreds of thousands or even millions of years, a relatively short time in the evolutionary dynamics
that began with the big bang. . . .' "

"That's my acceptance speech," he said, beginning to feel
a little frightened, "which no one else has read. . . . How could
you. . . ?"

She chose to ignore his question. "A little pompous, but it will
certainly stir them up. They'll think a long time before they give
the prize to another Irishman. And, yes, you're the only one to
have read it, but you talked to too many people about it. That's
why your late friends wanted to kill you."

"Why would anyone want to kill me because I engage in outlandish speculations about the direction of evolution?"

"That," she said, "is what we want to know."

He was talking, quite casually now, with a woman who lacked
a body but seemed to be able to save his life. An uncanny feeling
crept through his body, as if he was in a haunted house.

He often told his students that he rather doubted there was a
God but was quite sure there was a devil. Good spirits were problematic. Evil spirits were a given.

"And who are you?"

"We are the kind of being about whom you rather pugna-
ciously imagine in your Nobel acceptance speech: the products of
a different evolutionary process, which happens to be in a more
mature state of development."

"You're not!" he insisted flatly, slipping back into his mother's
brogue.

"We are." She laughed lightly. "Your satirical dreams turn out
to be true."

She really wasn't an angel, was she?

Angels didn't exist. Except in Sister Intemerata's classroom in
fifth grade.

And in his acceptance speech. But in theory.

"It's only a theory," he pleaded irritably.

"A theory," she murmured, "that could get you killed."

Biologist with Leprechaun Eyes and Angels on the Mind

Sean S. Desmond

Chicago. The secret of the Nobel laureate in biology, according to one of his colleagues, can be found in his eyes. "Only a man with Sean's playfulness and wit could imagine such an original contribution as the prediction of major leaps in the evolution of drosophila. But don't let him fool you. Sean Desmond is considerably more than an Irish stand-up comic."

Man in the News

A slender man with pale green eyes that twinkle with a hint of comedy, and the sandy hair and freckled face of a stage Irishman, Professor Sean Seamus Desmond seems to enjoy the controversy that has followed his career. With mock surprise, he shrugs. "They say I was lucky that my theoretical predictions were accurate. The poor old fruit flies in my colony just happened to grow smarter and live longer when I said they would. But I didn't make the prediction, my computer did. Lucky computer. Maybe we should send it to Stockholm."

Some of his colleagues are inclined to agree. Others say that it required not a computer but an extremely gifted biologist to apply the work on the genetic changes in maize done by Barbara McClintock to the evolution of fruit flies. They add that more than mere talent was needed to make predictions about when "punctuations"— sudden evolutionary leaps—in the fruit fly would occur.

"Computer?" says Dr. Joshua Hechter of Northwestern, a friend of Dr. Desmond. "It was only a tool to test Seano's theories. The real secret of his success is brilliance of insight matched by spectacular flair."

Dr. McClintock demonstrated that the genetic lines are constantly rearranging themselves in new patterns, which she called transpositions. These mutations do not seem to be the random variations described by an earlier laureate, French biologist Jacques Monod. Rather the changes appear purposive and perhaps under the direction of the organism itself. Dr. Desmond has argued for several years that if one attends carefully to the patterns of transpositions, one can predict both major and minor mutations in species as their evolutionary development continues and their environment changes. Fruit flies are ideal for testing such hypotheses because there is a new generation every ten days. A thousand human generations would require 25,000 years. The same number of drosophila generations would require only a quarter century.

Working with computer models, Dr. Desmond predicted "medium-size" leaps every 1,000 generations, plus or minus 100, and "major leaps" every 15,000 generations, plus or minus 1,000.

"It's almost as though the organism is experimenting with different transpositions," Dr. Hechter observes, "and then when it finds a novel environment or ecological niche that fits its purpose, it jumps, just as humankind did from *Homo habilis* to *Homo erectus*. Only a genius like Seano could have devised a schedule to predict such leaps."

Dr. Desmond himself is at first reluctant to compare the "punctuation" he predicted and then observed in fruit flies to phases in the evolution of humans. Then his pale green leprechaun eyes glitter. "Well, it might be something like the change when our bunch replaced that Neanderthal fellow. My superflies are stronger and smarter. They're harder to catch, better able to avoid traps and the normal predators, and so they live longer, only twenty percent longer, but that's enough for them to occupy the whole colony in a few generations. Put a business suit on the earlier fly and you'd hardly recognize him on the subway."

Such facetious comments about serious debates among biologists are part of the reason why some of his colleagues disapprove of Dr. Desmond. "Calling that mutated drosophila a superfly was a ploy to gain media attention," a distinguished colleague complained tartly, "and it proves that Sean really isn't serious."

A Chicago newspaper announced the decision of the Royal Swedish Academy with the headline, "Superfly Prof Wins Nobel."

Dr. Desmond dismisses such complaints with a wink. "What's the point in being Irish and a quarter leprechaun on your mother's side unless you can laugh at yourself?"

But he becomes serious when he is asked about his use of the word "intelligent" to describe the evolutionary dynamics he has observed. What else do you call it, he demands, when you observe direction and purpose, however mysterious the origins may be?

"Every organism is 'intelligent,' " he says briskly, "so long as you put the word in quotes and define it to mean 'processes external information and makes decisions, as between alternative courses of behavior, that serve to direct its own evolutionary mechanisms.' I'm not being a metaphysician. I don't know whether there is intelligence outside the organism. I don't know whether there is Intelligence—with a capital I—beyond the cosmos. I only know that the organism knows damn well what it is doing. Our task is to figure out how it does it. I'll leave the 'why' question to the Jesuits who teach my daughters."

Dr. Desmond was born on the South Side of Chicago—in the Irish ghetto as he calls it—in 1944. He attended parochial grammar schools and St. Ignatius High School, the same school that his daughters now attend. After graduating from the University of Notre Dame, he studied for his Ph.D. at the University of Illinois in Urbana and was appointed an assistant professor at the Chicago campus of the university. In 1975 he became a professor at the University of Cook County. "They really had to bend a few rules," he says with a grin, "to let a South Side Irishman in, even if I had stopped going to church."

While at Illinois, he met and married his wife, Mona Kelly, also from the South Side of Chicago. Dr. Desmond and his wife are now separated. Their two children live with Dr. Desmond in an apartment overlooking Jackson Park. "I amuse them," he says. "At least I think I do."

Dr. Desmond swims every day and hikes in the Lake Michigan dunes in the summer. He also runs in the Chicago Marathon—"toward the very end." He reads mysteries and science fiction and enjoys Woody Allen films. "I kind of identify with him," he remarks. "Like him, I sometimes think that my only wish is that I was born someone else."

Will he speculate on the next phase of the fruit fly evolution?

"It will be a long time before they're ready to study us."

And for humans?

Serious for a moment, he replies, "I hope there is enough 'intelligence' in the human organism to make a small leap toward more cooperation between peoples and nations. Otherwise we won't be around for the next really big leap."

And what will that be?

"Maybe," he winks again, "toward something like angels."

—*The New York Times*

"Trying to make up your mind whether I'm real, Professor Desmond?" she asked lightly. "Or merely the result of the second vodka martini you had before lunch?"

Her accent was mostly middle western urban like his own, but not perfect. Occasionally there were intonations that were a little bit off key, as though she'd learned his accent quickly.

"I won't talk any further unless you let me see you," he said stubbornly.

Next to one of the thick green satin drapes a neat hole had been drilled into the wall. Exactly 22 millimeters, Sean supposed. That hole was real. Not the voice, but the hole.

One must cling to the evidence.

"Your own arguments say that the energy patterns of our organisms might be so simple and yet so complex as to be imperceptible to minds still limited by the primitive energy patterns of the early stages of the human evolutionary process."

She was enjoying herself enormously.

"I still want to see you."

Lights flickered and blinked in front of him, like an enormous and graceful multicolored CRT screen. Intense, highly focused, and extremely elaborate energy patterns, mostly shades of red—all the way from crimson to pale pink—with a mixture of greens and blues and an occasional dash of maroon.

Patterns which, for all their attractiveness, were like nothing that Sean Desmond had ever seen before or ever imagined.

"Dazzling and lovely," he said, with an edge to his voice, "but I can't talk to a terminal screen."

The patterns changed colors, whirled feverishly, and then seemed to condense into the shape of a woman, sitting calmly on the green and gilt chair at the other side of the window. Her smile was as amused as her voice.

St. Paddy's was still across the street.

Sean Desmond reached out to touch her arm. It felt quite solid, and the beige cashmere sweater she was wearing was smooth and soft.

"You didn't think I would transmit electromagnetic waves, as you would call them, for your eyes without also transmitting for your sense of touch, did you? I can even produce parts of the spectrum you can't see or touch. How about some heat?"

Her arm became as hot as a blazing fireplace. He pulled his hand back quickly.

"I wasn't planning on being fresh," he said, his humor returning.

"But you like my appearance?" She smiled, with just a touch

what in his species would be considered vanity. "The appearance of my analog to be precise?"

Hell yes. She was just the kind of woman that Sean Desmond admired the most. Silver hair, smooth girlish face, full voluptuous classical figure, neatly encased in sweater and skirt, smooth skin, flawless facial bones, elegant and slender legs, soft brown eyes with long lashes, somewhere between thirty-five and forty-five: youth and maturity combined in a perfect blend.

Too perfect, like a manikin.

And, on closer examination, the skirt and sweater were not only simple. They were very expensive.

Why the hell not? If you're an angel, probably you can afford it.

Was she wearing a ring? Dumb question.

But he somehow couldn't quite focus his eyes on her ring finger.

"You'll do," he said.

"I'm glad." She relaxed on the chair, still greatly amused. "If I must travel with you to Stockholm and back to protect you, I would not want to be an eyesore."

"Travel with me?"

"Surely, I am your assistant. I will always be in an adjoining room." She nodded in the direction of an open door that Desmond was sure had not existed a half hour before. "Don't worry, you won't have to pay for me. And I'll be charming and intelligent, a credit to your importance and prestige."

No doubt about that. I'll be given all the credit for sleeping with this beauty without having to take any of the risks.

"To protect me from whom?"

She frowned, an empress asked a question she did not want to answer.

"The point is, Sean—you don't mind me calling you by your first name, do you?—not from whom but why. We know who they are but we do not understand why. We cannot read your minds. We are rather good at guessing, but your brain patterns elude us. Just as ours patently elude you."

"So Stacey's experiments..."

"Are quite entertaining."

"Was that you, er, folks singing?"

"Sometime during our little adventure, I will sing for you, Jackie Jim, and you will learn how we really sing."

Only later did Sean realize that she had not answered his question about whether Stacey had actually captured some of the conversations of her kind of being. She was very skillful, this woman angel, at not answering questions. Almost as if she were Irish. Or one of his daughters.

And she had perfect breasts, large but exquisitely shaped. They're not real breasts, only analogs. But they sure are gorgeous, especially when she breathes a little bit deeply and gets that maternal look in her eye.

Analogs to what?

Mind you, he was feeling no lust. He hadn't felt that since the night at Stacey's. He was merely admiring. As he would a marble statue.

That's what she was, a statue.

Too perfect, he told himself again.

"You peeked over my shoulder when I was writing my talk," he said, trying to put her on the defensive.

"I did not!" She blushed. "We respect the privacy of other species. I do not read your mind. I do not peer over your shoulder. It is not my fault that you tell everyone about what you wrote!"

"As we don't peer over the shoulders of chimps?"

She drummed her slender fingers on the ivory-colored handle of her chair, her high forehead drawn in an impatient frown. "I did not say that. You are not an inferior species, merely one at a different state in your evolutionary process than we are in our process, as you yourself have suggested in the talk which, I repeat," her voice rose slightly, "I did not read."

"So you're not really a guardian angel?"

"My kind does not intrude," she insisted, still flushed, still speaking as a human woman would when she was angry. "If you wish to have any little relationships with women like Stacey during our trip, I will not be a voyeur."

"But I'll hear about it afterward, like I am now?"

She grinned, her angelic anger spent. "That's what guardian angels do, isn't it?"

She thinks I'm inferior, though. A likable chimp.

"Roughly the same relationship as between me and the Irish

wolfhound I would have if I didn't live in the Cloisters."

"That might not," she said, smiling lightly, "be altogether fair to the wolfhound."

A joker.

"That puts me in my place, I guess."

The bullet hole was indisputably still in the wall near the window. So maybe it was a fantasy too.

"Come now, Sean Desmond." She smiled again, most affectionately. "You can't expect to joke with others and not have them joke back. Besides, that adorable little priest explained all about us, didn't he?"

"You think he's adorable too, huh? Most women do. Just the same, I'm not sure I want a guardian angel with a sense of humor."

"The alternative"—she continued to absorb him in her smile—"would be a guardian angel without a sense of humor, an absolutely intolerable relationship in your case."

Point for you, pretty lady.

"Well." He had survived his relationships with women by putting them on the defensive. "What rank are you?"

"Rank?" She chuckled.

"Yeah, like maybe a throne?"

"Oh, the nine-choir myth?"

"Not true?"

She waved an elegant hand. "Not relevant."

"You seemed a little offended when I suggested that you were a throne." He tried to drive home what little advantage he had. "I bet you're someone higher. Like a seraph, one of those alleged to stand before the face of God."

"Do you think, Jackie Jim, that you're that important?"

Nice put-down.

Later he told himself that again she had not answered his question.

"All right." He sighed the way his grandmother sighed. "Since you are going to call me 'Sean,' I'd better have a name for you."

She colored faintly. "I can be called 'Gabriella.' 'Gaby' if you wish."

The "a" in "Gaby" was pure South Side Irish. But when she said "Gabriella," the name sounded Italian. Her accent was still not perfect.

Sean relaxed. Thank goodness he was more flexible than most academics. He could adjust to a lovely extraterrestrial with minor strain. Even chat easily with her.

"No relation to the fella in the New Testament, are you?" He dialed room service and prepared to ask her what she wanted to drink. "Gabriel, I mean?"

It was his turn, he thought, to laugh lightly.

She was not amused. "I would remind you, Professor Desmond," she said grimly, "that Saint Luke was a male. Characteristic of the patriarchy of his time and very unlike the man about whom he wrote, he was a chauvinist."

Sean Desmond hung up the phone before room service answered. The loon thinks she's the angel Gabriel. With considerable difficulty he overcame his impulse to make the sign of the cross as his grandmother did.

To ward off banshees, leprechauns, pookas, and redmen.

And other dubious spirits.

2

Angels had been on Sean Desmond's mind for the last several months. It had all started when Stacey played her tapes for him the night his Nobel Prize had been announced.

Mind you, it was only a theory, and a satirical theory as the womanly voice had charged, a trick to get even with his own profession and his colleagues at the university.

A theoretical chicken that now seemed to be coming home to roost.

Sean had hoped that his off-and-on lover would reward him for his coveted (the adjective favored by the national media) prize with a bit of a playful romp. Candlelight, rare roast beef, an expensive California Cabernet, some lacy garments, and then playful passion.

Playful with Stacey? You have to be out of your mind, Sean Desmond.

Instead, there was Lite beer, a Weight Watchers' TV dinner, and jeans and a university sweatshirt on Stacey's thin and unwashed body.

And her tapes. You receive the top prize in all the world and you celebrate by listening to someone else's work.

Sean Desmond felt sorry for himself, a normal enough condition, and wondered what he had ever seen in Stacey, also a normal enough reaction to the woman who had briefly attracted him since Mona had walked out on him and the kids.

"We use Fourier analysis," Stacey droned on, "our sophisticated computer programs search through the white noise, break it down into sine waves, and seek for single frequency sound as the first step."

"White noise? How can noise be white?"

"The functional equivalent of white light—waves that occupy all the spectrum."

"I see." Maybe he could write one of his irreverent haiku about white sound. Let's see ...

> *sound snow white and dirty*
> *fell from the sky one day*
> *angel fire angel song*

"There's more beer in the fridge." Stacey was fussing with her reel-to-reel tape player. "Help yourself now if you want some. I won't tolerate any interruptions when my aliens are talking."

Stacey was a research associate at Argonne Lab; she had walked out on her psychologist husband and children at Berkeley so that she could be her own person. Everyone seemed to want to be their own person these days.

"Aliens, is it?"

"Your phony brogue bores me," she said as she put the rubber caps on each reel. "You know that."

At the university no one would dare to talk about aliens, especially at the round tables in the faculty-club dining room, a place where reason, sobriety, and three-piece gray suits were the rule. But at Argonne out in Westmont, with its vast accelerator and its secret government contracts, different rules were in force. You could investigate weird notions and think dangerous thoughts that would not be tolerated in the faculty dining room.

So long as you were deadly serious about the project. The trim young men from Langley who served as contract officers on Stacey's project could not, Sean suspected, cope with playfulness.

No more than could his own departmental chairman.

"If there are aliens among us, they must communicate with one another." Stacey's eyes, already too close together, drew even closer to one another as she adopted her professorial frown. "We take it that radio waves are the basic means of communication in the universe. Therefore, they would use radio waves—on a very different frequency, of course, from the ones with which we are familiar."

"Of course." Sean thought he had kept a straight face.

"Therefore we experiment with extremely powerful listening devices, highly sensitive tape, and recorders moving at a variety of very slow and very fast speeds. Then we enhance the resultant recordings by computer—fitting models to the sounds. Finally, we examine the enhanced tapes with yet another series of programs that selects out for us those which most probably represent communication, and ranks them in the order of the probability that they are indeed communication as we know it."

"Ah."

Sean knew about ghostly voices on tape recorders. Despite his professed agnosticism, he was profoundly superstitious. So he read an occasional book or article on occult phenomena. Moreover, he argued, a scientist should keep an open mind. This generation's occult, he had told the group at the round table, might be the next generation's science.

He had said that after he received tenure, on a split vote in his last chance.

Even before he had lured Stacey into his bed—or was it the other way around—he had read about the psychic "investigators" who put tape recorders in gardens at night and then played them at various speeds the next day until they found a "message." Not much different from Stacey's technique—except for the legitimating use of a computer model and the eagerness of the contract officers from Langley, who wanted to dialogue with the aliens in the hope that they would go to work for us against the Russkies.

"How many communications do you have?" he asked, trying to sound innocent.

"An enormous number." "Enormous" was one of Stacey's favorite words. "We're working on a program that will select for us the ones which offer the best probability of translation. Then we'll be able to reply to them in what is essentially their language and on their radio waves."

"Essentially" was another one of her words.

Training a computer to interpret ink blots, Sean thought. He had heard some of the "psychic" tapes collected by one of his students who was "into" such phenomena. It was easier in the biology department to admit to such interest than it was in the social sciences or the humanities.

Pure gibberish. But if you worked over gibberish long enough—with or without a computer—you were bound to find something. Usually that for which you were looking.

"First, we will play the unenhanced sound, speeded up, naturally," Stacey pushed down the play button. "It is a bit annoying."

A mild participle, Sean thought. It sounded like a rapid scratching of a metal ruler edge across an old-fashioned blackboard, the sort of activity in which he used to engage in Sister Mary Intemerata's class in fifth grade at St. Praxides grammar school.

Thinking about Sister Mary I. was probably what brought the memory of angels to his mind. 1954. The good old days.

"Interesting," he muttered.

"Hardly," Stacey sniffed, removing her thick glasses so that she could more effectively gesture. "Now," she stopped the player and adjusted the speed, "we turn to the computer-enhanced and -selected pattern, played at the slowest speed on this machine, essentially converting the enormously long waves into patterns that are intelligible to our ears."

"The patterns we were looking for," he muttered skeptically.

"Precisely." She missed his skepticism. "I merely push this play button, and you will be one of the first humans to listen to the conversation of aliens."

It sounded rather like the conversation of sophisticated Moog synthesizers, rich, deep, melodious, powerful.

"Amazing what they can do with computers." Sean sighed, as if he were not a user of advanced programs himself.

"What does it sound like?" Stacey asked, jabbing her folded glasses at him.

"Angels," said Sean Seamus Desmond without reflection. "The harmonious conversations of choirs of angels."

"Angels!" Stacey exploded. "Everyone knows there are no such things as angels. Please be serious for once in your life. Those are the voices of aliens! Extraterrestrials!"

"Interesting." A word which always impressed academics. "And you propose to learn their language and, uh, sing back to them."

The tape player stopped automatically when the sound faded.

"Naturally." Stacey brushed her stringy hair away from her eyes. "We have what is essentially a sophisticated translation program working on that dimension of the project now. It is, in effect, a code-breaking algorithm."

Aha, the boys from Langley. Or perhaps their counterparts from the National Security Agency.

"But what—"

"We *will* break their code," Stacey interrupted him, gesturing wildly with her glasses. "You can count on that."

"That assumes"—Sean reached for his empty beer can and then thought better of it—"that they do not have other modes of communication and that their language patterns are fundamentally the same as ours. How can you be so sure of either assumption?"

"The universe"—Stacey was now pacing up and down like a caged lioness, caged and hungry—"is essentially binary in its patterns. If these are rational beings, and it would be chauvinism to think they are not, then their communications will be essentially binary, no matter how enormously different from ours."

"Ah. But where are they?"

"Why all around us, presumably, if we can pick up these signals."

"Not light-years away?"

"Most improbable."

The young men from Langley, the next generation of Oliver Norths, would be quite upset to learn they were monitoring alien conversation that was millions of years old.

"They are smarter than we are?"

"That should be obvious."

"Then why don't they talk to us?"

Stacey flopped into her battered gray mohair couch, an exhausted but satisfied searcher for truth. "Honestly, Sean, how could one win a Nobel Prize and still be so unreflective? Presumably they are waiting patiently, as superior species do, for us to open up the communication links."

"We try to talk to chimps. . . . Maybe they don't want to converse with us."

"Then we will force them to." She jabbed her glasses at him again. "We have no choice. If we don't, the Russians or arguably the Chinese will do essentially the same thing."

"Interesting." Sean paused. "Play it again, Sam."

"What?"

"Er, I'd like to hear them again."

"Certainly."

The second time around the music was even more lovely. Ethereal yet somehow strong and solid. Pure spirits? The nine choirs of angels doing a sing-along?

Why not?

Arguably, to fall back on Stacey's third favorite word, angels or angelic-like ETs might sing that euphoniously. Or maybe the program was merely a sophisticated, enormously sophisticated, variant of the Macintosh program that turned computer sounds into music. Perhaps the Palestrina-like elegance of the singing was in the program and not in the essentially computer-enhanced noise.

You could force creatures like that to dialogue with you? What kind of an angel would it be that humans could control? The next thing they'd try would be to expropriate God.

The superstitious demon within him almost forced him to make the sign of the cross at that blasphemous thought.

Madness. But it provided grants and tenure. Which was what the academy was all about.

"Won't the Russkies"—he resumed his catechism—"have a hard time matching our computer programs? I thought they lagged behind in that field."

"When something is important to them"—she smiled triumphantly—"they catch up. Their rockets have much more powerful throw weight than ours."

"Ah. Interesting. . . . Would you play it yet again. I am candidly"—one of his words, always effective with academics—"fascinated."

While he listened to the thrones and the dominations respond to one another with antiphonal chant, he decided that he would escape quickly from the apartment. He would not, on the night his Nobel was announced, engage in passion with a woman who thought she could force thrones and dominations into dialogue.

What were the nine choirs about which Sister Intemerata had babbled?

Angels, archangels, virtues.

Thrones, dominations, powers.

Cherubim, seraphim . . .

One missing. The seraphim were the big deals, weren't they? The ones who stood before the face of God? What would God think of someone trying to force the crowd that stood before His face into dialogue? If there were a God . . .

Sean Desmond was a card-carrying academic agnostic, not that it did him much good. If you were Irish at the university and from the South Side of Chicago, particularly from Beverly, you were Catholic and that was that.

Especially if your daughters went to St. Ignatius after eight years at the University Lab School.

Well, all right, would you believe a Catholic agnostic?

God, however, was not merely a hypothesis for which there was no proof. He was also a profound scandal at the round tables during the lunch hour, as sex would have been when the faculty were all Baptist ministers. So naturally, Sean Seamus Desmond, being what he was, raised the God hypothesis at least once a week.

"Arguably, however," he said as he rose to leave, "the tradition of angels in primitive societies might reflect some archaic intuition into the existence of the creatures whose choruses you have recorded."

That would give her something to think about.

"Interesting," she murmured as they walked to the door. "I hadn't thought of that possibility."

'Course not.

One more failed assignation, he thought as he walked down the stairs of the apartment to 53rd Street. I sure do know how to pick them. What a great end to a day I've dreamed about for years.

Part of the fun of winning the Nobel, he reflected happily as he walked rapidly toward the Cloisters—as his apartment building on Dorchester was called—was that it embarrassed the university.

If they had to choose between a Nobel for Desmond and no Nobel, the university elders would have undoubtedly voted for the latter option. Fortunately for Sean S. Desmond, the franchise belonged to the Royal Swedish Academy and not to the faculty senate—or the round-table lunch eaters.

He heard footsteps on the sidewalk behind him. Only a dummy would walk five blocks through this neighborhood at night. He could see the headline:

Nobel Winner
Knifed in Mugging

Well, maybe he could run faster than they could. He had always been the fastest kid in the class at St. Prax's—useful for getting out of the trouble into which he usually managed to get himself.

I can run the marathon, kids, and you can't!

The footsteps faded away and Sean's heart began to beat more normally.

There had been rumors of his prize, but the wise men at the round tables dismissed these as preposterous. The university kept careful count of its Nobels—more than any other institution in the world. But it believed with a faith as uncomplicated as Sister Intemerata's that the prizes should go to those whom it deemed appropriate recipients. Like Congreve. Undoubtedly some senior faculty members were muttering to the press, off the record naturally, that "*Really* Congreve's work is more important than Desmond's. Mind you, Johnny is good, very good, quite clever in fact, but Congreve is one of the greats."

"Is your name, Sean or John, Doctor Desmond?" one of the reporters had asked at the press conference this morning. Deirdre and Fionna, more popularly Dee and Fee, his teenage daughters, giggled at the question.

"Sean Seamus"—he had beamed—"that's spelled *S, E, A, N.*"

In the mysterious way in which institutions create for their members two- or three-word imaginary catalogue listings, which then become even more infallible than papal documents, he had been labeled almost upon arrival as "clever, but not serious."

As in: "Oh, Johnny has a brilliant mind, really. Enormously brilliant, actually. Arguably, one of the most clever men we have on our faculty. Sadly, he doesn't quite have the depth that it takes to be as good as Congreve. Essentially he is not quite serious enough, if you know what I mean."

"Interesting, very interesting."

"Why do you have to make everything a joke?" Mona had demanded when she told him that she was leaving him.

"Because most things are a joke," he had replied. "Like a mother deserting her children so she can become a person."

It was, actually, very funny.

Oh well.

"You hide behind your laugh," Connie O'Rourke, a girl he almost married, had once told him. "It's a mask."

Connie was right. Mona was right. His mother was right. The university was right.

But if he wasn't incorrigibly playful, he would never have won the Nobel. And Congreve, for all his heavy erudition, would never win the prize, precisely because he was not playful enough.

Oh well.

More footsteps. Not to worry, my guardian angel is with me tonight.

His imagination, where his comic demon resided, began to play with the image of a guardian angel lugging along a Nobel Prize certificate.

Then suddenly and without warning, his theory of "periods of punctuation in the evolutionary process"—itself a pun which not everyone caught—converged with the image of a guardian angel singing wearily at the end of a long hard day the hymns on Stacey's tape player.

"I'll be damned." Sean stopped dead in his tracks, oblivious to whether the footsteps on the deserted streets had stopped.

Carefully, as he had learned to do, he examined the images bubbling, like freshly opened champagne, inside his brain.

Where had he read the troubling quote?

Von Ditfurth!

It would take a couple of days to dig it out, but he was pretty sure he could remember what it said.

Outrageous!

He grinned. Indeed!

Impossible!

Certainly.

But fun.

Oh boy!

True?

Well . . .

For the moment it didn't matter.

They couldn't take the prize away from him.

He imagined the solemn faces of the Royal Swedish Academy distorted in pain.

Why the hell not?

He ran the rest of the way home, not because he was afraid of muggers but because he wanted to hunt for von Ditfurth.

And interview his daughters.

3

"What do the Jebs teach these days about angels?" he asked the solemn-faced young women who looked up from their American literature textbooks to consider their father with a mixture of affection (bordering on worship) and amusement (bordering on disrespect).

"Angels!" They spoke in chorus, not unlike Stacey's aliens.

"Angels," he repeated.

"Daddy!" Fionna, aged fifteen and a half, protested.

"Really!" Deirdre, aged fourteen and a quarter, agreed with her sister.

By his own admission, Sean Seamus Desmond worshiped his daughters. Fragile as Belleek china, bright as an August moon over Galway Bay, loyal as an Irish wolfhound, strong as an Aran sweater. . . .

All images offered without the benefit of ever visiting Ireland.

Unlike most teenage siblings they were always together, even studying in the same room (always Fionna's) even though they had rooms of their own.

"Don't angels exist anymore?" he asked. As always, the Catholic Church was not around to help you when you needed it.

Fionna, the elder, always began their recitations. "Father Lyons says that angels are God's messengers, but that God really doesn't need messengers because He can do it all Himself. Like totally."

"So," Deirdre took up the baton, "like, when you read, I mean, in the book of Genesis about the angels visiting Abraham or wrestling with Jacob, it's totally not some geek with wings, but God, Who totally does not need a geek with wings to do His work for Him."

Sean had not gone to church regularly since he graduated from Notre Dame, a school which he had despised. Mona had been a dedicated early-nineteen-fifties Catholic who turned against the Church on the birth control issue, then returned in a Catholic charismatic group, then moved to a Pentecostal charismatic group, then back into the Church with a group of Catholic feminists (including nuns who said Mass, despite the fact that no one had ordained them), then into femtherapy, and then out of their marriage. At latest report she was involved in a conservative, very conservative, political action group.

So their children were fiercely dedicated Catholics—of the new, postconciliar Jesuit variety perhaps, but still as intensely loyal as the Ryan sisters had been in St. Praxides when they were growing up.

A certain kind of Irish Catholic you can't drive away from the Church even if you try your best to do so.

"But can't they exist anyway?"

"Who knows? Really."

"Who cares? Really."

"I mean, like isn't God enough?"

"And the Blessed Mother?"

"She's still in fashion?"

"Daddy!"—in chorus.

The two winsome little elves were grimly determined to recall their erring father to the practice of his faith. "Not because you need it, Daddy," they had argued recently, "but because the Church needs you."

Which was an interesting approach, to say the least.

So they constantly nudged him to visit his friend the Rector of the cathedral. Or to invite him for supper. "We'd love to cook for that adorable little Monsignor you went to school with. Really."

"Really."

They were polite and respectful to their mother, never criticizing her either to her face or to him when they came home from their Saturday visits.

Still, there was no doubt on whose side they were. They had even recently urged him to remarry, doubtless after long discussion and careful preparation of their lines. "Like, Daddy, you're too young—"

"—and too good-looking—"

Chorus of giggles.

"—to go through life alone."

Solemn high silence.

How do children acquire such wisdom?

Probably by growing up in a family where your mother is a well-meaning but shallow child and your father a slightly flaky—no, considerably flaky—genius who wants to make up for all his failures as a husband and father by winning a silly prize.

"So we don't have guardian angels anymore?"

"If you want to have one—"

"—there's nothing wrong with it."

"But what's wrong with praying to Jesus—"

"—and to God the Father?—"

"—and to St. Ignatius?"

"Really!"

"Why don't you go—" Fionna grinned like a little gombeen man.

"—and ask Monsignor Ryan?" Deirdre finished for her.

"You guys have one-track minds." He tried to laugh them off.

"Really!" they both huffed.

Mona had been pretty and awed by the attention of a Notre Dame graduate who was studying biology at the University of Illinois. She had not gone to college and was not from the neighborhood—and hence, looking back on it, not much of a threat to his insecure male ego. She loved to neck and pet. She wanted to marry. After all, his mother had said, had she not, we're poor people. We don't move in the country club set.

Nonetheless his mother did not approve of the marriage. And neither did Mona's parents. By the wedding day, no one was speaking to anyone else, a not uncharacteristic condition for the merger of two Irish families, especially when both think their child is marrying down.

It soon became apparent that Mona had not liked necking and petting, not really, and that she was not prepared to like sex either. Her key character trait was dissatisfaction, blended with a strong dose of self-pity. Attractive she was and continued to be, but she was a chronic complainer, a passive-aggressive person just like his mother. Nothing was ever right, nothing he did was ever good enough, nothing he ever said was kind enough. He was a loser, by her definition and in fact, from the day they were married.

Looking back on their courtship—if that's what the hasty meetings and gropings that occurred after a long ride on the Illinois Central from Urbana could be called—he realized that the traits which spoiled his marital happiness were plain enough to see. But he was young and sexually eager and busy with his studies and, as he thought, in love.

Still, he was faithful to her until she walked out.

Doubtless much of their unhappiness was his fault. The only way he knew to respond to her complaints was the way he had responded to his mother's complaints: silent withdrawal.

Occasionally he would venture the suggestion that maybe she would feel better about herself if she took some courses, maybe even got a degree (she complained daily about the "arrogant bitches" and their highfalutin degrees—meaning the wives of his colleagues and friends), or even perhaps began a career of some sort.

Her response was always an hysterical "And then who will take care of *your* daughters?"

He never replied that most of the time the kids took care of themselves.

So Sean lost himself in his work and Mona lost herself in her complaints. When she departed—with two hours notice while two of her femtherapy friends waited impatiently—she blamed him for preventing her from having a career. Foolishly he tried to defend himself.

That was when the femtherapy people led her out of the apartment.

"When their self-hatred becomes unbearable," a psychiatrist on the staff of the university hospital had told him at lunch one day, "they must blame someone else. The spouse is the first available target."

So it went. Now he had won the Nobel Prize, a dream come true. And he had no one with whom to share it.

And the dream was pretty hollow.

"Well," he said to his daughters the night the prize was announced, "maybe I will do just that. Maybe I will have a little talk with the small Monsignor. I bet *he* believes in angels."

Much later Sean would wonder why angels were so much on his mind that night. Maybe his daughters had planted the idea in his head.

"Daddy," Fionna began hesitantly.

"Yeah?" He was still thinking about angels, evolutionary ones, not daughter types.

"We're so proud of our dad the Nobel Prize winner," Deirdre finished.

They both hugged him fiercely. All three of them wept like the sentimental Irish fools they were.

And Sean Seamus Desmond fell asleep that night thinking that perhaps the world was not such a bad place after all.

His dreams were peaceful too, filled with music that, he told himself the next morning, his subconscious remembered from Stacey's tapes.

Wonderful, lyrical, seductive music.

4

s she put his room in order, the woman was humming music that sounded familiar to Sean Desmond.

"You really ought to keep your room neat," she said, hanging up his overcoat, "and buy yourself a new overcoat. We can't have a Nobel laureate who looks unfashionable."

You could buy a lot of fashionable overcoats with the silver she was wearing—impeccably tasteful earrings, bracelet, and pendant, simple and costly.

"Mozart trumpet concerto?" he said.

"Telemann, actually, Concerto in D."

She brushed off his suit coat as she hung it up.

"Your name is really Gabriella?" He studied the smooth lines of her backside. Women this beautiful exist only in dreams.

"Hebrew name . . . it means, well, *gabor* means strength in Hebrew." She had adopted the dry pedantic tones of the round table, a schoolmarm with a slow pupil. "So you could interpret the name as Strong One of God. . . ."

"I can respect that." Seamus shivered slightly.

"Now let's see what we can do about straightening up your

bathroom. It's an extra service guardian angels provide for certain of their clients. Then we'll see about a bite to eat. I will not have the waitress be embarrassed by a messy room."

"It's *your* name." He followed her into the bathroom.

"Well," she pondered as with deft movements—so quick that Sean hardly saw them—she rearranged the tubes and bottles on the wash basin table, "it's *one* of my names. Actually, I rather like it. You might think of it as the name for phenomena that your species has come to associate with my presence."

"Uh-huh . . . does that mean you play the trumpet?"

She strode briskly back into the parlor of his suite, dusting off her hands to indicate a cleaning job completed. "Superstitious folklore."

"That doesn't answer my question." He trailed after her, still convinced that he was dreaming.

She patted her hair to make sure that every strand was in place. "I don't have to answer your questions. I must tell you the truth because we angels tell the truth, which is more than your species does. But you have no right to my knowledge."

"You won't tell me when the Last Judgment will be?" He eased himself toward the doorway, thinking that he might break for the corridor.

"Did not your Teacher say that even He did not know?" Her hand rested imperiously on the phone. "If He didn't know, how would I know?"

There seemed to be a nimbus of red dots swirling around her head. Or were they only in his imagination?

"You don't play the trumpet, then?"

She hesitated. "I have some skill on a musical instrument that might be thought of as an analog to your trumpet. However, I am not assigned to sound it for your mythological Day of Wrath."

In the background he thought he heard, faint but lovely, the sweet piercing notes of a trumpet playing a concerto that he knew did not exist.

"Which does not mean that you couldn't be assigned to blow the trumpet?"

She shrugged her lovely shoulders indifferently. "We try to accommodate the Other's requests. They are infrequent, you know."

"Could you wake up the dead with the trumpetlike thing of yours?"

She put down the phone and walked over to him. Her breasts, lavish yet somehow delicate, offered an invitation to endless peace and rest. Challenging yet reassuring. Strong yet somehow vulnerable. Definitely a woman in a dream.

She tilted his chin back and absorbed him in the mystery of her deep brown eyes. The trumpet music seemed to grow louder, a waterfall of sound pouring into a rushing river.

"Jackie Jim"—she smiled affectionately—"I could wake up all the dead in the cosmos with my horn."

As the trumpet notes soared toward a crescendo, Sean Desmond found himself sinking into the soothing marshland of her eyes. "Quite an alarm clock," he murmured.

5

"**M**ay I read a quote, Monsignor?" Sean Desmond had asked in the Rector's suite in the cathedral before he flew to New York.

"Certainly, Professor."

"Hoimar von Ditfurth, professor of physics at Tübingen ... I quote:

> There must be many places in the cosmos ... where evolution for various reasons has made more headway than here on earth, many places where it has by now pressed its efforts beyond generating life, consciousness, and knowledge to new heights, enlarging the realm of subjectivity by annexing regions of which we are still ignorant. ... These creatures would be equipped with brains which would help their owners to a much larger share of that mind which has just now begun to shed some light, though as yet a relatively faint one, on our own heads. ... We ourselves may have descendants as genetically distant from us as we are from *Homo habilis*. ... We might constitute a bridge to nonbiological descendants of an entirely different sort. ..."

"Interesting," whispered Blackie Ryan. "Sounds not unlike your periodic punctuation theory, great leap forward."

"Into angels?"

"Arguably. Did you not yourself suggest as much to the venerable *New York Times?*"

"I was joking."

"We both know better."

Sean could never figure out whether his priest friend deliberately used academic buzzwords to tease him or because he was himself an academic of a sort—Ph.D. in process philosophy and with a book on criteria of truth in William James.

With Blackie Ryan you could never be quite sure where the leg pulling began and ended.

Which, arguably, was the reason why they were friends.

"St. Augustine"—Blackie sighed as if he were about to experience an enormous asthma attack—"held that angels had spiritual bodies. He was constrained to do so by his philosophical presuppositions, but given his convictions about evolution, he would not, we may assume, be completely offended by your suggestion."

Johnny Desmond and Johnny Ryan had not been close friends at St. Praxides. The former was always in trouble, the latter never in trouble. Moreover, the "little Ryan boy" was from what Johnny Desmond's mother called "country club Irish" while the Desmonds were poor but hardworking "ordinary people."

A city building inspector, Sean Desmond would conclude many years later, ought not to live in Beverly, not even on Vanderpoel Avenue in the east end of the parish in what might have been the smallest bungalow in the neighborhood.

And the Ryans lived in the biggest house on Longwood Drive.

Johnny Ryan, Blackie to everyone, was as quiet and reflective as Johnny Desmond was loud and obnoxious. The only event that could stir Blackie out of his absentminded tranquillity was a mean word from a nun about his cousin Catherine Collins or his next-door neighbor Lisa Malone, both of whom doted on the pudgy little kid with thick glasses.

It was only in later years, after Blackie had been ordained and Sean had left the Church, that Sean discovered what Blackie probably already knew: they had similar minds.

Sean told himself that he should have known there was more

to the future priest than merely his opaque stare and his round head always buried in a book. If two such lovelies as Catherine and Lisa were fond of him, he must have something.

Two women like that in class and he had to marry Mona.

"If they have bodies"—Sean leaned forward confidentially— "there might be sexual differentiation, might there not? I mean male and female angels?"

It was still all a *jeu d'esprit*, a game, a flight of a Nobel laureate's fantasy, a potential joke on the Royal Swedish Academy.

"Doubtless." Blackie, with the customary heavy hand, refilled his guest's Waterford tumbler with Bushmill's Black Label. "Though I don't think the inestimable Augustine would have approved. He didn't quite hold with sexual differentiation. As though the Almighty had made an artistic mistake in ordaining the mechanics and dynamics of human procreation and of the nurturance of human young."

The aforementioned Rector, wearing a Chicago Bears' windbreaker over his clerical shirt (*sans* collar), was sprawled on an enormous easy chair. On the wall behind him were posters of what he liked to call "the three Johns of our adolescence: the pope, the president, and the Baltimore quarterback."

Next to Johnny Unitas there was a pedestal from which reigned a saucy medieval ivory madonna and her equally saucy kid. Blackie had told Sean once that the statue was a gift from his father, Ned Ryan, who claimed that the madonna looked like Blackie's mother as a young woman. Blackie had been in grammar school when Kate Collins Ryan had died of cancer at the family's Grand Beach home. It was the first wake that Sean Desmond had ever attended. He came away from it terrified by death, a terror that had never left him.

So they wonder why I joke? You either laugh at death or you sob hysterically.

And now he and Blackie were the same age as Kate Ryan when she died.

"Angels, then, might be the result of an evolutionary process in another solar system?"

"Or galaxy. Or, arguably"—the priest gestured with his tumbler, a hint of fun in his pale blue eyes—"another cosmos. Perhaps they have evolved to such a state of perfection that they can leap over Planck's wall, that barrier set up in the minute fraction of a second when there was only one force in the nascent universe."

"One could be burned at the stake out at the university for such a thought."

"Doubtless." Blackie looked at his empty tumbler as though he suspected that a throne or a domination had stolen some of its precious contents. "Would you care for some chocolate ice cream?"

"Why else would I come?"

"Indeed."

The Ryan clan were all chocolate freaks. None of them thought it strange to consume ice cream after Irish whiskey.

In their infrequent conversations, the priest and the professor always pretended to speak first about their academic interests, then about theology, then about Sean's marital problems, then, finally, about God.

Blackie dug liberal scoops of ice cream out of a container he had found somewhere in a freezer hidden in his closet. "You propose to suggest this possibility to those marking your reception of the Nobel Prize? Angels as a punctuation, perhaps even an exclamation point in the evolutionary process?"

"Can they eat chocolate ice cream?"

The priest considered the plate he had filled. "With God all things are possible ... but surely that will cause a sensation?"

"Why not?"

"Indeed."

"Maybe your buddy Teilhard de Garden was right."

"Chardin, Professor, although your invariable and invariant mistake, we both know, is deliberate. But consider: if we are really moving toward Point Omega, the ultimate goal of everything, and if the angels are really one step, or perhaps several steps ... pardon, punctuation points ... closer to Point Omega than we are, does it not follow"—he extended the calorie-laden dish to Sean—"that we ought to be concerned about the nature of Point Omega, about who She is and what She wants of us? ..."

"And then it follows that I should get an annulment of my marriage to Mona, find some nice Irish Catholic woman who finds my odd humor funny, return to the Church, and perhaps sire more children like Deirdre and Fionna? Consider it all said and tell me about angels."

"A world which can produce such persons as your admirable

daughters," the priest said as he spooned a giant chunk of chocolate into his tiny mouth, "need not have angels to be filled with
wonder. However, let us leave aside such poetic exclamation
points and consider other angels...."

God, the little bastard was clever.

"The Jebs tell them there are no angels. They represent God's
work in the world. So we don't have to believe in guardian angels
anymore. Sister Intemerata would die if she hadn't died already."

The priest continued to wolf down his ice cream. "There is
some debate among theologians as to whether the scriptures constrain us to believe in angels. I think the weight of opinion is with
the excellent Jesuits at St. Ignatius. Surely in the scriptures the angel is a function rather than a person. Yet the issue remains open as
to whether they in fact exist even if we need not accept them as a
matter of faith." He sighed again. "It is not an issue that much
occupies theologians, who now are principally interested in politics while science fiction writers and filmmakers are interested in
theology. Spielberg, for example, obviously believes in creatures
of light, the cherubic characters in *Close Encounters*, the forces of
good in *Poltergeist*, even perhaps the admirable ET."

"Creatures of light?"

"I like to think of them," Blackie added, "as creatures of fire,
passionate fire even."

"Interesting." Sean nodded his head. "But hardly to my point.
Might they really be lurking around, singing Palestrina or maybe
Orlando Lassus for my friend Stacey?"

"If they lurk—and I would rather think they do—it would
take more than artifacts as puny as a fifth-generation computer to
capture them." Blackie's normally soft eyes glinted. "And one
would be ill advised to mess with them. Passionate light, fireballs
of love might be very dangerous creatures."

"You think they might lurk?"

"I wouldn't write off the folklore completely."

"Well ..." Sean Desmond felt a shiver run through his body.
"Presumably they would not be angry with me if I suggested that
they too were part of the evolutionary process."

"I hardly think that likely."

"Good"—the Professor rose from his couch—"I think I have
enough for a talk at the Royal Swedish Academy. Pure speculation,
of course."

"Indeed ..." Blackie was preoccupied.

"Nothing to worry about, is there? I mean it's mostly a joke."

"Half fun and full earnest."

"Comic speculation."

The priest considered the professor very carefully. "Fireballs of love can be dangerous, Sean Seamus Desmond, if you get caught in one of them."

"A guardian angel is worse than a wife," Sean complained, "especially when she is a woman guardian angel."

Gaby's laugh was warm and rich, a mezzo-soprano in the angelic choirs.

"The trouble with you, Sean Seamus Desmond, academic immortal, is that you have a weakness for passive-aggressive women. So you think a suggestion is a demand. My species doesn't nag. It suggests. It leaves you all your freedom to resist with no threat of withdrawal of love."

"How many times do you suggest?" He did not want to deal with the hint of love.

"Until you do what you're supposed to do"—she laughed again—"or until you tell me to shut up."

"Which you will do?"

"Which I will do."

"So . . ."

"The problem," she said crisply, "is that you are so burdened with guilt about your failures as a husband and father that you don't realize how much your daughters love you. So you don't phone them every day, making yourself feel even more guilty."

"Is that any of my guardian angel's business?"

"Everything, Professor Desmond"—she arched her eyebrows—"is a guardian angel's business."

He wasn't sure that she was telling the whole truth. Even after a few minutes' conversation, he had concluded that angels—well, this angel at any rate—were very clever with words. Somehow he had to get a list of ground rules for this game.

"But if I say forget it, you'll forget it."

"We may be a little devious with words." She walked to the window and glanced out of it. "But we don't take away the freedom of other species, as I have told you several times already. If you tell me not to mention a phone call to your daughters ever again, I'll do what I'm told."

Despite the lovely shape of her posterior as she stood at the window, Sean doubted her pledge. Oh, the woman would never bring it up directly, but there'd be lots of hints. However, she probably wouldn't sulk.

"Okay," he said, "that subject is off limits from now on."

"You're the boss," she said evenly. "Now, about the press conference tomorrow morning..."

"What press conference?"

She returned to the dresser opposite his bed and pulled a crumpled piece of paper out of his cloth briefcase. "The one at the American mission to the U.N. The one for which you've written notes"—she reversed the paper—"about the goals of the evolutionary process."

"Oh." Sean felt sheepish. "*That* press conference."

How quickly, he thought, the impossible becomes commonplace. Yes, I have a guardian angel who takes the form of a gorgeous woman and proposes to administer my life for me.

Better than I can.

And how quickly the alleged guardian angel's personality had emerged. She was efficient, prickly, at times bossy; on the other hand, she was also witty, considerate, and—Sean hesitated at the word—sweet.

Before their fight about the phone call to his kids, she had ordered "tea" from room service, told them that Professor Desmond would like the same tea that was being served downstairs. Earl Grey tea, scones, clotted butter, sandwiches, and pastry. For two.

"What kind of sandwich? Professor Desmond has an enormous appetite. Three of every kind."

"They don't normally send tea up from the Gold Room, do they?" he asked.

"For special people, like Nobel Prize winners, they do."

"If the tea is ordered by their guardian angel."

"That helps, of course."

"Will they send up one of those pretty college girls who serve tea?"

"More likely graduate students or young actresses. I suppose they'll do that too. And you'll charm her, like you always charm women until they get too close."

"Touché," he admitted ruefully.

"The trouble with you, Sean Seamus Desmond, is that you have yet to make peace with the feminine side of your character." She had put on her aloof, judgmental expression, which included shrewd brown eyes that cut through the outer walls of his soul. On judgment day the Lord God would not be more dispassionate.

"Huh?"

"You are acutely sensitive to other people, especially women; you feel their fears and their hopes, their anxieties and their needs. You respond to these signals with care and even tenderness. When a woman is treated that way, she is prepared to unveil herself to such a man in trust. Can't help it. Then you run. Watch this young woman who is about to knock on our door with tea."

The brown-haired young person in the red jacket and long skirt who did indeed knock on the door was happily flustered and embarrassed by Sean's grave gratitude. She was even more pleasantly abashed when he asked her if her graduate work was in English. She admitted that she was "into" comparative lit at NYU. After she had served the tea with flushed face and averted eyes, she asked him for his autograph.

Gaby treated her like she was at least an archduchess. "My dear, the man will be insufferable if every pretty young woman between here and Stockholm asks him for his autograph."

The girl smiled admiringly. "You only win a Nobel Prize once in your life."

"Who says so?" Sean demanded.

Gaby and the waitress both laughed, making common cause against him as women usually did.

"Well, the next time I stop in New York on the way to confront the Royal Swedish Academy, I'll come here."

They laughed again. Gaby signed the check, reached in her purse—which Sean had not noticed on the dresser before—and pulled out a crisp bill for the girl.

From where he sat, it looked like a fifty.

I know the purse wasn't there. She made it appear. The money too.

"See what I mean," she demanded when the girl, still confused and happy, had retreated. "You made her day. She felt like she was naked in the presence of a very gentle lover who cared for her profoundly. So naturally her self-esteem soared. Not a profound encounter, but a nice one."

"I didn't run."

"In five minutes you would have."

"Does my feminine side have the same effect on females of other species?" he asked innocently.

"That"—she glared at him—"is an unbelievably impertinent question." She turned to the tea trays. "You drink your tea black, don't you?"

"You know very well I do." Sean was still engaged in trying to keep the blasted woman on the defensive. "Is your job to protect me or to remake me?"

She looked up from her ministrations to the teapot and shook her head patiently. "You never can tell what a guardian angel will do, can you?"

"I don't have that influence on other species, do I?"

"That's an impertinent question which I will not deign to answer.... Tea, master?" She handed him a teacup. "And sandwiches? And a glass of sherry?"

She hadn't ordered the bottle of sherry. It had materialized too, a very old bottle whose label was so blurred that Sean could not read it.

"The best sherry I've tasted in all my life!"

She beamed happily. "We aim to please."

"It cost too much here?"

"They don't have it here. Or anywhere in New York either."

Oh.

It was all a dream, a projection of his already travel-weary unconscious. She was not real. The sherry was not real. The men with the guns were not real.

The bullet hole in the wall was real, however. Wasn't it?

Except that the neat little hole had disappeared. The woman doesn't miss a trick.

Might as well enjoy it. He sipped more sherry and wolfed down a salmon sandwich.

Gaby's eyes twinkled at him over her sherry glass.

"You're eating?" He put his glass down and watched her devour one of his salmon sandwiches.

"You object?"

"You said you didn't have a real body. What I'm looking at is an, uh, analog. How can analogs eat salmon sandwiches and sip the greatest sherry in all the world?"

"And drink Earl Grey tea." She lifted her teacup.

"Yeah, that too."

"I didn't say that we lacked bodies—eat your scones before they get cold, the sherry will keep. On the contrary, I insisted that we do have them. They're different from yours, that's all." She turned up her nose at a cucumber sandwich and took instead a cheese sandwich.

"Superior."

"Different," she said sharply.

"Further along on the evolutionary scale."

"Different. If we have bodies, does it not follow that we take nourishment? And would it not be logical that when we generate analogs, we could, through such wave patterns, consume and even enjoy your foods. Do not dogs, for example, like an occasional sip of beer?"

"Uh-huh. . . . Is this your sherry or our sherry?"

"Oh, it's yours . . . not until you eat another of those delicious scones." She removed the sherry bottle from his reach. "I assure you, Professor Desmond, that a sip of one of our intoxicants would deprive you, for the rest of your life, of the remnants of sanity you still possess."

Braggart.

He dutifully consumed two scones and then extended his glass.

"Have you forgotten that I like my sherry on the rocks?"

She blushed and bit her lip. "I did not notice. I suppose I should have assumed that, shanty Irishman which you are, you'd want to spoil this liquid with ice."

"Ah, so angels make mistakes?"

Instantly she was serious. "Indeed we do; sometimes very serious mistakes. As I've tried to tell you, we are creatures just like you. Our mixture of mind and energy patterns is a bit different from yours. . . . Now let's not get into the argument about superiority again. That's your hang-up, not mine. We can do a few things you can't, which imposes on us somewhat, ah, different responsibilities, but we're still finite beings."

"I don't believe in infinite beings."

"Nonsense. Of course you do. You're what we call in my species 'other-haunted.' God-haunted in your terms."

I'm not going to touch that one, he thought.

"Well, you made a mistake on the ice, and I guess you can't correct that, for all your clever tricks."

"Oh? Why don't you look in your glass?"

Tiny blocks of ice had appeared in the glass with his sherry.

Sean Seamus Desmond began to shiver. This dream was turning into a nightmare.

"Don't be afraid, Jackie Jim," she pleaded, tears apparent in her eyes. "I won't hurt you. I'm here to help you. Forgive my silly little trick."

"It's a good trick," he agreed.

"I promise that I won't do anything like that again."

"Ah, woman, if you know me at all, you know I like tricks."

Her cheer returned. "Well, maybe not quite that sudden. I"—she hesitated—"have a reputation among my friends of being a trickster. My—but we won't discuss that."

She walked over to the window and glanced out again. The side view of her was outstanding too, Sean noted—flat belly, solid haunches, outstanding legs. His imagination began to picture her without clothes and then stopped instantly. What he was watching was not a real woman, only an analog. Right?

And what won't we discuss? I'd better not ask.

"Looking for something?"

"More or less."

He returned to his fantasy. She was tall, about his height. Five-ten or so. In heels, that made her six feet. I'll have to stand on my tiptoes.

And legs that compared with the sherry: cool, classic, elegant, intoxicating.

As for her rear end, it was classical. Well, maybe neoclassical.

Not Venus surely. And not Juno either. No way. Diana? Could be. Or maybe Maeve. Who was no better than she had to be.

Only an analog.

"If I had listened to your—"

"You should always listen to me."

"And not opened the door, those men would still be alive, wouldn't they?"

He buttered another scone and poured raspberry jam into it. The supply of scones did not seem to diminish.

"Now we see the tender side of Professor Desmond. Don't feel guilty about them. They were destined for destruction in any case. As the Teacher said, they who live by the sword will perish by the sword."

So that's what they called Himself. Teacher. Well, He sure was that.

"That seems kind of heartless."

"Pity is not the appropriate reaction." She drew her lips together primly.

"Sister Intemerata would have said that I ought to pray for them."

"A much better reaction. As the Teacher also said, nothing ever lives except in the Father's love."

"Where did He say that?"

"It never was written down, alas." She poured herself another half cup of tea. "But He meant that no one, not even the most apparent evil ones, ever lives in vain."

"Leave them to heaven, huh?"

"Along with Hamlet's mother."

"Did you hear the Teacher say those words?"

"That question"—prim lips again—"is irrelevant."

"May I have another wee drop of sherry? We can't let it go to waste, now can we?"

"Of course not." She filled his glass. "Though it wouldn't go to waste."

"It's making me kind of sleepy," he admitted.

"You've had a hard afternoon." She rose from her chair. "You need a bit of a nap."

"I do not!" he contended stubbornly.

She stood over him, smiling benignly. "Be fair to your colleagues in chronobiology. All your dozens of clocks are askew and you haven't even flown to England for your lecture at Cambridge.

You're at one of the sleep thresholds now. Take advantage of it."

She touched his forehead lightly.

So, willy-nilly, he slept peacefully.

When he awoke, rested and refreshed, he hesitated before he opened his eyes.

The dream is over now. When I open my eyes, she won't be here.

The thought must have been clearly written on his face.

"I haven't disappeared, Jackie Jim. Still here."

"A dream within a dream." He opened his eyes. Sure enough, she was still there.

"It's a serious conference tomorrow." She ticked off comments on her fingers, hardly needing a notebook. "Science writers from the national magazines and the networks. *The New York Times*, of course. It's up to you, naturally, but you might want to take the opportunity to be a little bit less the freckle-faced, kinky-haired, green-eyed leprechaun tomorrow morning. It's an opportunity to raise some important questions that will interest a lot of people."

"Yes ma'am."

"Don't patronize me, Sean Seamus Desmond. Angels have tempers too."

"No ma'am ... what I mean is that I might be able to get in some serious licks against the fundamentalists who are hassling me."

"Without mentioning them explicitly?"

"Sure."

She wants to remake me. Not the first woman to try that. First woman angel to try it, however.

"Okay." He pointed at the phone. "You're supposed to be my assistant. *You* call my daughters."

"May I talk to them?" She clapped her hands, momentarily herself a teenaged hoyden.

"Why not? They'll see you near me on TV tomorrow and wonder who you are."

As far as Sean could tell, she didn't bother to punch in the numbers.

"Fionna? I'm Gaby, your father's assistant. He asked me to place the call for you. Why don't you ask Dee to take the other phone?"

"Dee" was strictly a personal nickname between the two girls.

"Like I said, I'm Gaby. Some important persons hired me to make sure he doesn't get into too much trouble during the trip . . . kind of a guardian angel." She winked at Sean. "Hard work, Dee? . . . Tell me about it." Giggle, just one of the kids. "Anyway, I'll make him call you every day. . . . Oh, he's fine, just ate too many scones for tea. . . . Really! . . . Here he is."

"Daddy!" Chorus.

"Is she as pretty as she sounds?" Fionna.

"How old is she?" Deirdre.

"She's attractive enough, if you don't mind gray hair. And she's *really* old. Like *totally*, you know?" He put his hand over the phone. "Like a couple thousand years anyway."

The alleged guardian angel blushed furiously.

"Daddy." Fionna.

"There were men here." Deirdre.

"Asking questions." Fionna.

"About you and Ms. Reed." Deirdre.

"They said they were from the government." Fionna.

"Real geeks."

"What did they want to know about Stacey?"

"Like about her work, you know?" Chorus.

Sean felt his stomach clutch and unclutch. Gaby's face was grim, intent. Obviously she didn't need a phone to listen to both ends of the conversation.

"Listen very carefully, girls. I'm going to call Monsignor Ryan, you know, Father Blackie. He'll call you. He has lots of friends in the government. Like Senator Cronin, the Cardinal's sister. You tell him what you told me. Maybe Mr. Casey from the police department will come see you. There's nothing to be afraid of."

"Yes, Daddy." Huge sighs of relief.

"Father Blackie is cute." Dee.

"So is Mr. Casey." Fee.

They talked about New York and the press conference tomorrow and about some totally gross boys at Ignatius and about how much they loved one another.

Gaby listened to the love between father and daughters, it seemed to Sean, with glistening eyes.

"You win that one," Sean admitted as, limp and drained, he slumped in his chair. "I hope you guys are taking care of them too."

"If we are protecting you"—Gaby was still grim faced—"Sean Seamus Desmond, with all your faults and failings, would we not certainly be protecting them too, little angels that they are?"

"Angels?"

"Metaphor."

"Can you do it from here or do you have some of the guys hanging out in Chicago?"

She was looking out the window again. "That question is not appropriately worded. It suffices to say that my, uh, associates and I can manage."

"Are the men from the same group as our friends this afternoon?"

"Hardly. The other side, I would rather imagine."

"Our side?"

"Your side, not mine. We're neutral in the East-West foolishness."

"Neutral in our favor."

"Presumably."

"You'll forgive me, but I want to call Blackie too."

"Certainly. The presence of Chicago's finest will reassure the girls. It is by the way a very rare exception that my kind are permitted to let themselves be seen. Should I place the call?"

"Why not? It's quicker than punching the little buttons."

She didn't bat an eye at that comment.

"Monsignor Ryan? I'm Gabriella, Doctor Desmond's guide on his pilgrimage to Stockholm," she said, adjusting her manner to suit Blackie's personality. Even sounding like him.

"Doctor Desmond ... Sean Desmond ... Jackie Jim...." She rolled her eyes, hand over the phone. "Sleeping, of course, poor dear.... Yes, *that* Doctor Desmond. He wants me to tell you that some men claiming to be from the government have been harassing his daughters. CIA probably. You know how they are. He wondered if you could have a quiet word with perhaps Senator Cronin and the admirable Mike Casey the Cop. ... And your good father too, naturally.... Oh, that would be capital, Monsignor.... Yes, I'm sure they'd love to sleep over at your sister Nancy's. Fee is a classmate of her daughter's...."

Blackie was obviously not expressing any doubts. Why don't I ask him about a guardian angel when she lets me talk to him?

"And one other thing, Monsignor.... You know that application for an annulment he sent you before he left with the note to hold it? . . . Well, perhaps it will arrive in today's mail. . . . Yes, well, he asked me to tell you to send it on to the matrimonial tribunal."

"You would never have said that," she argued defensively after she had hung up, "but you want to say it. So I really did nothing more than you wanted. Right?"

Sean was quite incapable of replying. No one else knew about the application. Not even Blackie, who could not have received it yet.

How did she know?

He wished the dream would end.

Right now.

In search of an angel, the week after his award was announced, Sean Desmond had wandered into the new John Crerar Library in the med school/biology quadrangle on the northwest corner of the campus. As a theoretical biologist, he avoided both the med school and the library. But someone had remarked at lunch that a Chicago writer had compared the sculpture in the atrium of the library to an angel.

"A woman angel, Sean? Can you imagine that? Do Catholics still have to believe in angels?"

"Only if they're science fiction writers." He had smiled his most leprechaunish smile. "And, by the way, did you know that St. Augustine held that angels had spiritual bodies, which raises the question of sexual differentiation in the angelic choirs?"

"I'm not surprised," the law school professor had replied—a typical academic response to almost any new information that someone else has proposed.

"Would you think now that angels screw?" he had asked, with a bluntness no more appropriate for a round table than it would have been in a lunchroom of elderly nuns.

He had weighed the possibilities carefully. "Screw" would cause marginally more dismay than "fuck."

He then rushed into the shocked silence with another one of the gaucheries that made Congreve the local favorite for the Nobel Prize: "Would they do it more quickly than we, do you think, or less quickly? And can they fuck humans, do you think?"

"Well, the Greek gods did." A red-faced classicist tried to get the conversation back on its path.

"Did they now? I'm not surprised to hear it."

So after lunch Sean inspected the four-story sculpture called *Crystara*. This man Mooney was good, he decided, damn good. Long, graceful, rounded aluminum struts bound together by solid bars of Waterford crystal—think of how many bottles of Black Bush or Jameson's Special Reserve that much crystal might hold. Multi-colored lights playing on it as it hung, free and independent, in the center of the library.

Too good for us physical scientists.

He glanced at the brochure. M.A., Notre Dame.

The artist must really be something else if this university is willing to take something from a Notre Dame alumnus. And admit he went there.

I bet they don't have anything of his down there.

And if Congreve won the Nobel, they'd give him an honorary degree.

I mustn't let my self-pity interfere with enjoying this.

Well, enjoy them both.

He climbed up the stairs of the library, circling the atrium all the way to the fourth floor. At every level and from each angle at a level, *Crystara* looked different, a graceful, elegant, colorful work—light yet solid, dainty yet massive, intricate yet simple, incorporeal yet preempting all the space in the atrium.

Was it an image of an angel?

Could be, Sean decided. Why not? Could he work it into the draft he was preparing for the Royal Swedes? Maybe.

On the top floor, facing the statue, Sean concluded that, angel or not, *Crystara*'s shape from this perspective was definitely womanly, a woman graciously and generously opening herself up so that a man might enter her.

What a wonderful idea for the round table tomorrow.

They might take the sculpture down if he suggested that.

Probably not, they wouldn't want to be accused of accepting censorship. He could imagine the headlines:

University Sculpture
Called Pornographic

Feminists Denounce
Abstract Statue
as Obscene

Work by Notre Dame Grad
Said To Be Exploitive

Wonderful!

Then he thought of the women over whose bodies he had poised before entering them.

That ruined his day.

There hadn't been that many. He had been faithful to Mona until she left him. Not that there weren't opportunities. A full professor with some distinction was a favored customer, as the mail-order catalogues would say, in the flesh market of graduate students and junior faculty.

A market that, all over the academic world, operated on the same principles of supply and demand as in pagan Rome—"classical antiquity," his colleague at the round table would have called it—and with the same rights and privileges accorded to senior professors as to Roman senators in days of yore.

The market had recently been expanded by the addition of women assistant professors, perfect targets for a baron who promised to return a tenure vote for sexual favors.

A new crop of captives—first-year graduate students and assistant professors—were not paraded naked on a block to be offered to the highest and most prestigious bidder. Not quite.

But they were evaluated just as carefully and in as much detail as if such a parade had occurred.

Not that all of them were either unaware or displeased by the process. Or unwilling to become the temporary slave of a powerful faculty baron.

The market would continue as long as there were powerful men who felt they had special rights to the more attractive women, and women who did not mind belonging temporarily and perhaps permanently to powerful men.

As long as there were men and women, with only the rules and the rhetoric changing?

Maybe. As the father of two daughters, Sean hoped not.

The university, stuffy about most things, was stuffy about sex. So there was rather less sexual exploitation than at most other institutions.

So Sean abstained from the market. Being human and male, he noted the new intake and fantasized a little.

His restraint was not necessarily a sign of virtue. Maybe he was shy. Maybe he had a hard time believing that women would find him attractive. Maybe his sense of the comic prevented him from making a fool out of himself as many of his colleagues did. Maybe he had a low hormone count in his bloodstream.

He was respectful to his women students and colleagues. In return, they came to him with their problems, academic and personal (They think I'm a celibate priest, he told himself wryly), and laughed at his jokes, which was all that was really required of any of his students.

Some of them even seemed to like him, a phenomenon that always surprised Sean Desmond. He was invariably astonished that anyone would like him.

He walked out of the Crerar into the barren university campus—as dull and drab and as unproductive as his own life.

Two beautiful kids and a Nobel Prize?

Mostly luck in both cases.

When Mona walked out and his code on the Availability Scale was shifted, as the university community saw it, from "0" to "1."

he was astonished to find that there was a plentiful supply of women who were prepared to offer themselves to him. The mobility of academic life, the uncertainty of academic marriages, the principles of ideological feminism had notably expanded the slave market despite his inattention.

Sean felt in his gut that women were more likely to be deeply hurt than men. So he avoided first-year graduate students and untenured faculty.

Yet he hardly lacked for companionship either in or out of bed. Some of the relationships went badly, only one went well for a time. Nonetheless, Sean Desmond experienced a postdoctoral course in academic sex, discovered that he had hormones after all and that some women enjoyed making love with him, and was no happier than when he and Mona were sleeping in separate bedrooms in their apartment in the Cloisters.

Blanche was the exception, a gorgeous, full-bodied Ph.D. candidate from Oregon who frankly set out to seduce him, by her own admission, and was spectacularly successful.

"I give myself two weeks to get myself in bed with you, Mr. Desmond," she informed him. "So if you want to run away, start running."

You proposition a man and call him "Mister" as the university protocol requires when you are addressing senior faculty.

"Why?" he had asked. "Times are not that bad, are they?"

"First of all"—she counted on her fingers—"I want to be able to tell my grandchildren that I slept with a Nobel Prize winner, and secondly I think you'll be a marvelous fuck, and thirdly I kind of like you: you're funny and you're one of the few gentlemen around here. Fourthly, if I'm not sleeping with someone, I'll have to fend off all the vultures. You'll never chase me, so I guess I'll just have to chase you."

It had never occurred to Sean that the rumors he might be a laureate would make him an attractive sexual prize. So that's why they were after me, he told himself.

He thought about running but never quite got around to it.

Blanche seduced him, bedded him, taught him about sex, made him a skillful lover, and captured his heart.

When she left for her first teaching job at Emory, he discovered, to his dismay, she didn't want his heart.

"If I was going to Circle or even Bloomington or some place like that, sure I'd say let's keep up the fun," she told him. "But it had to end sometime, didn't it?"

"Did it?" he had asked glumly.

"Don't tell me you're into permanence?" She was astonished. "Are you *really*?"

"More or less."

"But that only makes it hard to end a relationship. All relationships have to end, don't they?"

"Do they?"

"Sure. Everyone knows that."

Yet she sobbed hysterically in his arms just before she boarded the plane for Atlanta.

He had wanted to marry her. The kids seemed to like her, and she them. Sixteen years was not all that much difference, was it?

Yeah, it was. He'd been a fool.

But so had she. If enough relationships end, each of them taking away a little of you, then afterward you have nothing left.

He sounded like a Christian ethics teacher at Notre Dame.

He hoped that while there was still some of her left, she learned that permanence, more or less, was not so absurd.

He had proposed marriage before she left. She had replied that she was flattered and that he was sweet and the finest man that she ever knew and she would always love him but it wouldn't work out.

Hurt and confused, Sean didn't ask why it wouldn't work out.

Later he thought that perhaps he ought to have pursued her with greater determination. Carried her off, psychologically speaking.

He realized that his wounded pride and injured sensibilities made such a response impossible. So he settled down to cautious, safe, and unsatisfying relationships with women like Stacey.

Who got him to thinking about this crazy angel business anyway.

He turned up his coat collar and bent his head against the hostile wind sweeping in off the lake. Damnit, that statue did look like a beautiful angel offering herself in love.

What would they have said at that press conference if they knew I was thinking such thoughts, heretical to the university and blasphemous to most Christians.

What if Stacey is right? What if there are aliens we can't see? And what if my suggestion is right that such a model would explain a lot of data in the religious traditions?

Should I dump that on the Swedes?

Why not?

Blanche had called him right before the first press conference at the university, with tearful congratulations. No, she was sorry, it wouldn't work out for her to go to Stockholm with him.

She didn't sound too positive, however. Perhaps she was learning how much of you is taken away by a relationship. Or perhaps she was only tempted by the thought that she could tell her grandchildren that she had slept with a laureate the night he received his prize.

He did not push the invitation.

The first press conference was for the local media, a half-hearted attempt by the university's PR staff to pretend that they were proud of him.

He emphasized his debt to Barbara McClintock, whose earlier work on directional evolution in maize had won her the Nobel Prize a few years before—when the rest of the profession had finally caught up with her.

"I was lucky," he said truthfully. "I read her stuff before most of my generation did and had a head start on some of the others."

Poor Congreve had dismissed her as unimportant ten years ago when Sean had first discovered the woman's prophetic work.

"Will this help to find a cure for AIDS?" was the first question.

Dumb Sean Desmond didn't realize that it was the only biological issue on the minds of reporters these days.

"That was not the intent of the project," he said, stumbling over his words, "when we started. It will certainly not make a direct contribution to such a goal."

"Mr. Desmond"—the university's flack cut in—rather nastily Sean thought—"is not part of our infectious disease program at the hospital. Nonetheless, his theory has very important implications for that program, does it not, Mr. Desmond?"

"Well," the reporter persisted, accusation dripping from her shrill voice, "what good is it if it doesn't help find a cure for AIDS?"

"Isn't that like asking"—mistakenly Sean tried to be cute—"what good a breakthrough is in astronomy that doesn't prevent another space shuttle disaster?"

"Okay," said the reporter, "so what good is such a discovery if it doesn't help anyone?"

"The Nobel Prize"—the flack was now miserably unhappy—"exists to award distinguished scientific effort whose pragmatic and programmatic implications may take generations to uncover."

"Truth doesn't always have to be practical," Sean added.

"Yeah, but then what good is it?"

The flack steered the questions to other subjects. Yes, Sean and his wife were separated. No, they had not yet discussed the prize.

Dear God, what will Mona say when these idiots get to her?

"Do you think the marriage broke up because of your ambition to win the prize?" Another angry woman's voice assailed him.

"I hope not. All the prizes in the world would not be worth the termination of a marriage."

"Do your kids give a shit about the prize?" This from a bearded fellow who worked for *The Leader*, a pompous, "free" weekly.

"You'd have to ask them."

I feel like a criminal, Sean thought.

"What do you think they feel?"

"They woke me up with the news, screaming joyously. They went off to St. Ignatius very proudly, it seemed to me."

Needle this crowd about Ignatius.

Mistake. Never introduce religion at a press conference.

"Do you believe in God, Professor Desmond?"

"I'm not sure."

"Don't you think your prize will offend millions of American Christians?"

"I beg your pardon?"

"All those Christians who don't believe in evolution?"

"I'm only talking about a process, not the origin or the end."

"But do you believe that God directly created man?"

"Humans."

"All right."

"The evidence seems to indicate that the process was different."

"So won't your prize offend all those who believe differently?"

Sean felt that maybe it would be a good idea to give the prize back.

"I was raised a Catholic; as I understand it, Catholicism has no problem with evolution. Even St. Augustine"—God bless you Blackie Ryan—"seems essentially to have supported such a theory."

"Yeah, but what about all those who believe differently? Won't you offend them?"

"I don't want to offend anyone." Sean drew a deep breath. "I simply report the results of testing my theory. It suggests that the process of development of human organisms moves smoothly and regularly most of the time, but then leaps forward dramatically at certain critical turning points."

"God causes the leap?"

"If you're a theist," he tried to keep his voice even, "you could certainly say, if I remember my philosophy courses from Notre Dame properly"—got that jab in anyway—"that God originates and sustains the process, but the process has its own internal dynamism."

"God didn't cause your punctuation marks?"

Now a big mistake for Sean Desmond's big Irish mouth.

"If He did, I didn't see Her in my laboratory."

The lead paragraphs in the AP wire story that day:

Chicago. Nobel Prize winner, Dr. Sean J. Desmond dismissed the possibility that God might be involved in the evolutionary process. "I didn't see Her in my laboratory," Doctor Desmond said at a news conference today at the University of Cook County.

Doctor Desmond dismissed the possibility that the granting of the coveted prize to someone who ruled out a role for God in creation might offend millions of Christians who believe otherwise. "I simply report the truth," he said. "If they're offended that's their problem."

They got his middle initial wrong and quoted him inaccurately.

The next day, like a lamb to the slaughter he went to his second news conference, the music of Stacey's aliens still ringing in his head.

Jerry Falwell, Oral Roberts, and Jimmy Swaggart had denounced him as godless. A ministerial group in Dallas had demanded that the prize be revoked. A federation of churches in Oklahoma said that he was an instrument of Satan if not Satan himself. In tones appropriate for his fellow rear admiral David Farragut damning the torpedoes, Cardinal O'Connor said that only a fool excluded God from nature. Cardinal Louis Gabardine told the press that some people praised Professor Desmond's work and others condemned it and that he had heard from both sides.

The second conference—now on national network cameras—was an even worse disaster than the first. The principal issues were whether biology forced one to believe in God and why Sean did not believe in God.

Did he think that science disproved the existence of God?

"No."

"Then why don't you believe in Him?"

"Science leaves Her existence an open question. I am a scientist."

"Can you have morality, Professor Desmond, without religion?"

Not at this university, he thought.

"I'm not certain," he said. "I am a biologist, not an ethician."

"Does biology teach morality?"

"It may give us some hints, but it is not an ethical system."

"What will happen to the family if scientists like you destroy religion?"

"The family has remarkable durability, and I am not out to destroy religion."

"But isn't that the conclusion that can be drawn from your work?"

And so it went.

Only a few of the journalists were fundamentalists, Blackie Ryan explained later on the phone. "They cite the fundamentalist objections because they have to ask something to fill time on the screen and space in the paper and because it gives them a chance to crucify a celebrity, which is what the media are about."

"Indeed."

"Arguably, you should give it back."

"And we have yet to hear from Mona."

"Libera nos, Domine."

"How do I protect myself?"

"Distract them with an issue more outrageous than the one they pressed on you."

That's when Sean S. Desmond began to think seriously about raising the angel issue before the Royal Swedes.

Mona contributed her share to the fateful decision. She had

finally given an interview to the *Trib* in which she blamed his "obscene" desire to win the Nobel Prize as the "rocks on which our marriage ended, causing untold harm to our poor little kiddies." Neither she nor the feature writer bothered to note that Sean had been granted custody of the "kiddies." Uncontested.

As he crossed Woodlawn at 58th Street, Sean made up his mind. He would work materials about the evolution toward greater mind into his Nobel acceptance speech. The mass media would forget about creationism, they would forget about Mona. They would, truth to tell, forget about the bearded Jesuit revolutionary who had won the peace prize.

How proud of him Sister Mary Intemerata, R.S.M, would be. Was she still alive? She seemed old in 1954, but then so did everyone else over twenty-five. A wispy little woman with a long ruler, a fanatic's glowing eyes, and a piercing voice.

Sisters of Mercy, what a wondrously inappropriate name!

Sister Intemerata was high on Poor Guardian Angel. A good boy or girl sat on the left side of his schoolroom seat to leave room for Poor Guardian Angel, slept on the left side of the bed, walked a little to the left on the sidewalk, and tried to find an empty seat on the right when he went to a movie.

"Your Guardian Angel sees everything you do, hears your most secret thoughts, watches you every day of your life," Sister I. thundered. "You can never escape from him. He counts every one of your sins, so God can enter them into His Book of Life. You can never escape from your Guardian Angel!"

Well, maybe Sister Mary I. would not like his speech. Still, it would be an acceptance speech they would remember for a long time.

The Royal Swedes *et al.* would gape just as did his colleagues at the round table lunch. He chortled to himself. Another Desmond outrage!

The leprechaun of Dorchester Avenue rides again!

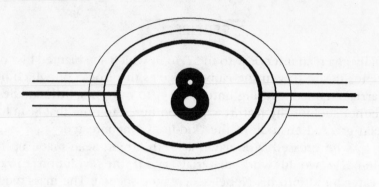

"Did you folks really sing at Bethlehem?" Sean asked, half in fun and full earnest.

They were eating in the rose and silver Trianon Room of the old Villard house, onto which the Helmsley had been grafted. It was Stanford White at his most baroque. Gaby had informed him that real baroque homes were not nearly so comfortable when they were first constructed.

Gaby, dressed in an attractive black cocktail dress with thin shoulder straps, frowned at his question about Bethlehem. "If you insist on asking questions like that, you will have to learn to whisper, Dr. Desmond."

She was wearing an emerald brooch around her neck, a large and memorable stone, as the breasts below it were large and memorable, black net stockings (pantyhose, he assumed, though you could never be sure about your women angels), and a discreetly powerful scent, Fendi's was it? La Passione di Roma? If you made it up yourself, why not the best? Every eye in the lobby turned to watch her when they exited from the elevator. Every head in the Trianon Room swiveled when she entered. Sean thought that was fine. She was worth looking at. And I get credit for having such a woman in tow.

If they only knew who she was.

Whom she claimed to be, he corrected his thought.

She was also wearing spiked heels. But somehow she was no taller than he.

Our angels come in expanding sizes.

As far as Sean could tell from a discreet peek into her adjoining room, she traveled without any luggage. Her closet was empty, no dresses, no coat, nothing.

The cocktail dress, with its low neckline and its ruffled miniskirt, probably came from the same place where she had found his ice cubes.

There was no denying the fact that, angel or not, she had more than a touch of vanity about her.

Angels vain? Could that be? Well, if you have physical bodies, it seemed logical that you should be concerned about your physical appearance.

She was a number of different women—a prim and impatient executive (fingers drumming on the arms of chairs, eyes stern); affectionate mother (soft smile, warm eyes); merry imp (jaw tilted upward, eyes dancing). Had they deliberately designed her body and character to disarm him—the kind of woman he worshiped and avoided?

So it seemed then. Later he would have reason to suspect a much more convoluted scheme.

"I think we're attracting attention," he had said to her when they entered the dining room.

"Oh?" She smiled complacently.

"People have never seen so much of an angel analog's tits before."

"Don't be vulgar," she reproved him. Then, after a significant pause, she added with a chuckle, "Or thighs, as far as that goes."

"You're vain." He made his accusation explicit.

"Not without some reason, wouldn't you say, Dr. Desmond?"

Now he was "Dr. Desmond." Riding down the elevator, a Chinese red and gilt box that looked like a closet from Versailles, he had become "Seano," his nickname among graduate students.

"Well, did you?" he said in what he thought was a whisper.

"And not a stage whisper either," she said impatiently. "That couple at the table in the corner are from the Other Side . . . and *please*, don't stare at them."

He restrained the muscles in his neck. Gaby's alabaster shoulders, throat, and chest, undeniably attractive, had about as much impact on him as would a statue in the Vatican museum. She had not created a suntan for herself, he noted.

Nonetheless, he filed the images away for future reference.

Out of the corner of his eye he caught a quick glimpse of a man and woman in their middle thirties at the corner table. They looked like prosperous tourists from Topeka.

"Not the KGB type," he muttered.

"Who said KGB?"

"Nor CIA."

"Who said CIA?"

"So you won't answer that question? Okay, what about Bethlehem?"

Gaby shrugged her shapely shoulders. "It was a night on which there was reason to sing, was it not? Do not misunderstand. Despite your religious superstitions about us, we do not act as messengers for Anyone, at least not regularly. Although there are times when there are special missions that we feel we must take on, we are as ultimately uncertain about the existence of Anyone as you are. Yet we do have certain insights that on occasion we feel we must share with those who live on this planet. Sometimes we sing."

"Will you sing for me?"

"Perhaps." She sipped the seventy-five-dollar Côte de Rhône red he had ordered. He bet it meant nothing to her.

Do angels drink wine?

"Is it necessary to stare at me?" Her large brown eyes regarded him severely.

Incredibly long lashes.

"I'm a scientist"—he found his quick Irish tongue—"I can't help but wonder if it's really you sitting across the table from me."

"What else would it be?" she said briskly, like a senior professor dealing with a dull first-year graduate student. "I appear to you in the form of an analog: that is, what I would look like if I were in your species and at your stage of the evolutionary process. The energy patterns that constitute my body are not perceptible to your sensing mechanisms"—she shrugged those damn ivory shoulders again—"so I alter my energy patterns that you may perceive me."

"We can't do that."

She smiled, a patient mother with a spoiled little boy. "When your species evolves into its next phase, we presume that you will develop that power. It is not particularly remarkable. Watching your evolutionary process is one of our interests on this planet. It will facilitate our understanding of our own past."

Again he felt like a chimp in a laboratory. Or the wolfhound panting worshipfully next to his mistress.

"Where's your planet and what's it like?"

"Those are irrelevant questions." She drew her lips together primly. "And planet is not exactly the appropriate word for the region of our ancestors."

"Why don't you appear like one of your damn ancestors?" he said irritably.

She threw back her head and laughed, the first time she'd done that. She was so heart-stoppingly gorgeous when she laughed that Sean had to hang on to the table.

"Our predecessors were not ugly creatures with six feet and whirling antennae and yucky scales, as your daughters would say. Nor were they cuddly little adorables like ET. You would doubtless recognize them as fellow rational beings, and graceful ones at that. But this overdecorated dining room would empty in a fraction of one of your seconds should I produce an analog of your phase in our evolutionary process. . . . Incidentally, your friends at the corner table are asking for their check."

"How many angels can dance on the head of a pin?" As long as he asked questions, she couldn't return to his relationships with women.

"A very stupid question." She filled his wineglass. "Typical of your species. What do you think the answer is?"

"At Notre Dame they told us in response to that question that angels don't dance."

"Calumny," she snapped. "You can do better than that."

"Well . . ." He pondered the question. "You are energy patterns with some biological base. So I'd guess"—he grinned wickedly—"that all of you could probably focus some of your energies on the head of a pin. But that it wouldn't be much fun."

She nodded approvingly. "You *are* clever. No wonder you won the Nobel Prize."

"You really dance?"

"Really."

"Will you dance for me?"

"Certainly not."

"Why not?"

"It would be inappropriate." Her chin shot up.

"Please. I mean, I never saw an angel dance."

"*Istar Variations* as background, I suppose."

How did she know he was thinking of d'Indy's music?

"If you wanted to."

"Certainly not." She dismissed him and his ideas with a wave of her hand.

"Any dance you want."

The executive was replaced by the imp. "I'll think about it."

He pursued his catechism. "Are you really a woman?"

She was watching the couple from Topeka intently. And her answer was preoccupied. "Am I the source of life? . . . No, you mean do we have sexual reproduction, don't you? You don't follow your own hunches rigorously enough, Professor Desmond. You say in your Nobel Prize talk that once there are biopolymers, then the emergence of life, organic structures, and memory and intellect—first unconscious, then conscious—are inevitable. Do you not find bisexual reproduction as inevitable?"

Out of the corner of his eye again, Sean saw the man from Topeka give the maitre d' an American Express card. Gold, of course.

"Angels screw?" he murmured.

Her brown eyes flicked back to him, like impatient bumblebees. "Your species' ability to use distasteful language for important functions is not attractive. But the answer is yes, we do join our energy fields as part of the reproductive process and we enjoy it far more than you. And we do it for weeks and weeks of your time too. Feel inferior now, Professor Desmond?"

So now I know I can offend mothers in two evolutionary processes.

"You're a mother and a wife?" he asked, trying to cover his confusion.

"I am here to protect you because, despite you're obnoxiousness, you are especially important to us," she snapped at him. "I have not come to discuss my personal life."

"Sorry," he mumbled.

"No, I'm sorry." She smiled apologetically. "I am unduly sensi-

tive.... Do go on with your questions about our, ah, comple-
menting processes, to use a word that approximates our own."

"So you feel, analogously, lust?"

"You'd better believe it." She actually winked. "We are rigorously pair-bonded, male and female linked by biological ties that
cannot be violated. We are essentially"—she winked again at the
buzzword—"like those cute pairs of birds in Arizona, the Gambel
quail. Apparently that is an evolutionary development. In a million
years or so, your species may be pair-bonded too, though as I've
insisted repeatedly, the processes are at best analogous, so we cannot actually predict what your species will be like after the next,
ah ... *punctuation* is I believe your word?"

"Stuck with Mona for the rest of my life?"

"As it moves toward pair bonding, evolution apparently selects for those reproductive information patterns—genes, in your
species—that produce much greater skill in complement selection."

"I wouldn't have chosen her?"

"Decidedly not." She shook her head vigorously. "Or most of
the others with whom you have more casually coupled."

"I think I feel embarrassed."

She smiled again. "Arguably, your problem is not the women
you select—on the slave block, as your male fantasy puts it—but
the ones you don't select."

"Huh?"

"You run from the women, like our little friend this afternoon,
who are ready to collapse in response to your charm, and you pur-
sue those who reject your ability to reduce them to willing emotional nakedness. You fear any woman who will permit you to become close to her."

"I do?" he asked dubiously.

Her analysis was reducing him to emotional nakedness—
which was probably what it was intended to do.

"We can discuss that later." She put down her wineglass.
"Right now I am too busy watching your friends over there who
are preparing to leave and are extremely curious about us."

"Do you lady, uh, woman angels suckle your young?"

"Do you mean to ask whether I possess an analog system comparable to these boobs at which you stare so fixedly?"

"I don't mean to be too personal."

"Yes, you do." She smiled affectionately at him, nice doggy. "But it's all right. At least you don't hide your curiosity. But what do you think the answer is? After all, you're the biological theorist and I am only a temporary messenger."

"Well, when evolution selects for sexual differentiation, the one who produces the egg is usually the nurturing one, if only, as in the case of birds or fish or insects, through proteins included in the egg. Once we get to mammals, as the very name suggests, we have suckling, so . . ."

"What makes you think we are mammals?"

"Well." Sean poured himself some more wine, wondering if she carried hangover medicine in her bag of tricks. "I suppose you don't have to be mammals. Maybe I'm a mammalian chauvinist. But I bet that you are, analogously, of course."

"Okay." She toasted him with her wineglass. "You win that one. And speaking of breast feeding . . ." She turned to the pink-jacketed waiter. "Professor Desmond will have chocolate ice cream with chocolate sauce, and I'll have raspberries with the sauce. . . . Where was I? Oh, yes, you were wondering whether I have breasts in my reality as well as in my analog. And I had been baiting you."

"Teasing the chimp."

"And now you are baiting me. The answer is that in our species as in yours the ones who bear the offspring also nurse them, by energy arrangements that our opposite numbers find attractive as we do ourselves, if the truth be admitted. Indeed, if I may say so, our male partners seem to be even more attracted to these, uh, systems than you are to their counterparts in your species. Satisfied?"

"There are degrees of physical attractiveness in these and similar matters?"

"You're getting as good at circumlocution, Jackie Jim, as I am. But yes, of course, why would there not be?"

"And I'm sure"—he wound up for a fast pitch—"that you are rated as one of the most attractive women seraphs around."

She blushed deeply. "Woman seraph is an irrelevant title, and yes, some of my associates make that judgment."

"I thought they might."

Impulsively she touched his cheek with two fingers of her

right hand. "You're sweet, Seano." Her eyes glowed. "A nuisance sometimes, but still a good and kind man. I'm glad I was assigned to be your guardian."

For a brief and delirious instant, Sean Seamus Desmond felt that he was filled with all the peace and goodness and beauty of the universe. Sexual pleasure? No, something that transcended sex in the same degree that sex transcended chocolate ice cream.

Fireball of love, the little Monsignor had said.

"I am too," he managed to say eternities later when he returned to earth and the Trianon Room of the Helmsley Palace Hotel.

"Any more questions?"

"I suppose you have two girl kids?"

"Now you're reading my mind."

"Only your face when you talked to my brats. You've been there before."

"I have born two bearers of life." She nodded solemnly. "Yes, they are perhaps a bit older in our framework than the delightful Fee and Dee."

"And that ring I see on your left hand sometimes. And sometimes not, like you're not sure whether it ought to appear?"

"You are an observant little man, aren't you?" She considered him with steady eye and pursed lips.

"Clever little chimp."

"Clever enough to win a Nobel." She smiled her sweetest of smiles, and the thunderclouds on her brow disappeared. "Yes, I have . . . I had a . . . spouse, to use your word. He is no longer . . . We are mortal too, like all energy patterns. We live much longer than you do, relatively speaking. Yet it does not seem long enough. . . ."

Her voice trailed off. Her ring finger was now definitely free of a ring.

"And you do not go gentle into that good night either?"

"We are no more certain than you that there is Anyone waiting in that good night. There are excellent reasons. . . . When we play our messenger role, we seem to be working for someone and yet . . . we cannot be sure."

"Angels are vulnerable, then?" To his astonishment he had touched her fingers as they rested on the stem of her wineglass.

"Surely." She sighed. "The more one is mind and love, the more that— They are coming over here."

Gaby stiffened, presumably preparing again for her Wonder Woman routine.

But the tourists from Topeka seemed eminently friendly.

"Doctor Desmond, isn't it?" said the man, overweight, balding, and genial. "We don't often see red-haired, freckle-faced leprechauns on the cover of *Time*. Congratulations on your prize, we're all proud of you."

Their name, appropriately, was Jones, and they were from Toledo, not from Topeka.

"My assistant . . ." He began to introduce Gaby and realized he didn't know what name she was using.

"Doctor Gabriella Light," she said, smiling easily.

"We hope you have a wonderful time in Stockholm," said Mrs. Jones, a dumpy, pleasant woman.

"They seem like nice, ordinary people," Sean said after they left.

"Don't they?" She watched them intently as they walked out of the dining room. "Nevertheless, they are on the other side. Yet I do not understand . . ."

"Maybe they're more interested in you than in me."

Her head turned quickly. "A possibility, surely. Though it would not make much sense. . . . Still . . ."

He wanted to finish tonight's lesson on the anthropology (probably the wrong word) of angels.

"Do . . . uh, I mean, widows . . . remarry in your culture?"

"I suppose you are going to insist that I find myself another complement and settle down," she said hotly. "I will not accept such importune suggestions from my own species and certainly not from another."

"I'm importuned the same way," he said, trying to sound wry and whimsical.

"But I chose well. I did not combine with a bitch merely to anger my family. . . ." She drew a deep breath. "I am sorry, Seano, you have touched a sensitive . . ." She smiled winningly. "You do have a record of making members of the opposite sex angry, don't you?"

"Only in two evolutionary processes, though," he replied,

feeling now like an adorable golden retriever who had made a mess on the parlor floor.

"And I don't consider you to be either a chimp or an Irish setter," she insisted, touching his hand. "Rather, a fellow pilgrim, a companion on the journey."

He decided that he would do his part to ease the tension. "Well, I guess I may have paid too much attention to Sister Intemerata when she said that the only sin the angels could commit was pride."

She relaxed, accepting his offer of truce. "We are victims of all seven of your cardinal sins and a few others besides."

"So you don't do only the sin of Lucifer, refusing to serve even God?"

Gaby exploded from her chair, like a rocket racing for orbit.

"You shanty-Irish bastard ... I don't care whether they kill you or not."

She stormed out of the dining room, a Fury in retreat.

Sean emptied the Côte de Rhône into his wineglass and drank it thoughtfully.

He then withdrew to the oak-paneled bar, the former dining room of the Villard house, ordered two glasses of Napoleon Special Reserve, and strolled to the Gold Room, a gilt mausoleum with LaFarge paintings at either end and a live harpist playing on the balcony beneath one of the LaFarges.

The couple from Toledo was in the next room, the Madison Room, just visible through the door. They were sipping a dark, misty liquor.

Gaby had said that the place was a poor imitation of the real Renaissance palaces in their prime. Implying that she had been in them in their prime.

He then dispatched with equal thoughtfulness the two glasses of cognac.

What did I say?

He was not particularly worried that anyone would attempt to kill him. Gaby was not the sort of ... of guardian angel that would leave him unguarded.

Could she bilocate? Was that one of the other easy things at their stage in the evolutionary process?

Irish setter indeed. I thought "golden retriever."

I should be an Irish wolfhound: lordly, charming, gentle.

The tourist couple drifted through the Gold Room, nodded in his direction, and then returned to the lobby.

They do look a mite suspicious, he thought. I suppose the damn angel woman knows what she's talking about.

Angel woman, indeed. Absurd. It had all been a dream.

All his life Sean had been "cute," not impressive, an adorable if neurotic Irish setter. That's probably what they would think at the Royal Swedish Academy.

He sighed as his grandmother would, a long, low, County Kerry sigh, indistinguishable from the first phase of a serious asthma attack, and signaled for the check.

"Madame has taken care of *l'addition*," said the maitre d', "in cash."

Probably counterfeit.

A tall, blond linebacker type in tuxedo followed him out of the dining room and past the pink Saint-Gaudens fireplace. Gestapo, Sean thought. He ducked around a corner and ran down the chandelier-lighted steps that joined the old brownstone mansion to the ornate Helmsley lobby. Through the arched glass doors, he saw the grim gray mansion of the Cardinal, huddled like a puppy with its mother to the vast bulk of St. Paddy's.

Maybe I should take sanctuary there.

He made it to his elevator just as the blond muscle man appeared in the lobby, from the other direction. How the hell did he do that? Or is that one of Gabby's?

I should ask him if his name is Michael.

Except, before this is over, I might find that Mike's real name is Michelle.

He leaned against the wall, waiting for an elevator. The lobby was empty. No blond giant Luftwaffe pilot, no dowdy tourists from Ohio, no one at all.

He leaned around the corner to look in either direction. Totally empty ... that's strange for this time of night, isn't it?

At that moment the heavy, life-sized Saint-Gaudens nude on the wall of the lobby began to tilt in his direction. There was a quick movement behind it, a tuxedo vanishing into the next rank of elevators. Brained by a naked woman, Sean thought as the statue fell straight toward his head. I ought to run, but it's too late. Where the hell is that damn angel woman when I really need her?

The statue paused in midflight, as though it had changed its mind, and with the same slow motion with which its bust had approached Sean's head, it returned to its place, shuddered once like a woman in an aftershock of orgasm, and settled down for its long night-watch of the Helmsley lobby.

I'm not frightened. I sweat like this every night after supper and a couple of drinks.

The lobby was filled with people again, none of them in tuxedos. An elevator door opened and Sean jumped in. By the time the door opened at his floor, even though he was still trembling, he had decided that the whole experience had been an illusion, a fancy trick that the damn angel woman used to impress me with her power.

Like the phony money she carries around.

Well, I won't say a word about it unless she does.

Even if the cash is phony, the treasurer of the United States wouldn't be able to tell the difference.

"Gaby ..." He knocked tentatively on the connecting door, which he was absolutely certain hadn't been there when he checked in.

"Come in, Seano," she said, contrition in her voice.

She was sitting on the edge of her bed, huddled in a satiny beige robe. Expensive. No sign of the black dress. I bet she makes them up and throws them away as she needs them. The net stockings were still on her glorious legs, part of which peered from under the robe. Definitely pantyhose. Probably all that's underneath the robe, not that it makes any difference to my extinguished lust.

"I am very sorry," she began immediately, "my behavior was disgraceful. There was no excuse. You meant no harm." She grinned shyly. "At least you know that angels are capable of many different sins."

"Not pure spirits," he said lightly.

"Neither pure nor spirits, I'm afraid."

"But not without virtues, like picking up the check."

"I will take care of the bills on the trip." She dismissed her generosity. "It will be easier that way."

"Do you have a crowd around here? There was a big blond guy in the lobby."

"Oh no, we are relatively few in number and have ... far-reaching, let us say, responsibilities. I am the only one in charge of you."

"Was the big blond guy Michael?"

She laughed, some of her joy returning. "Michael would find that suggestion most amusing."

"He is not a Michelle?"

"Most definitely not."

"The blond was on our side?"

"I think that's a fair assumption. It was silly of you to run from him. You really can't get away from an angel, Seano."

But you didn't deny that you were the big blond guy in the lobby. Might you be so big that you can be the blond in the lobby and yourself up here at the same time.

A creature forty-seven stories high? A fireball of light and love that big?

Enormous tits, he thought irreverently.

"What did I say wrong?" He sat next to her on the bed, though as far away as he could.

"Nothing, really, except your species' mixture of Christianity and Iranian mythology has always infuriated me by its inaccuracy and its arrogance. There is no need for devils to persuade you to do evil. You are quite capable of it on your own. And, Professor Desmond, as far as we can ascertain, there are no demons in this cosmos. There are certainly some evil forces and energies and they are not without power, Most High knows, but they are not personalized like your Satan." Her voice rose again. "And if you would read the Book of Job, which you haven't, like most of the rest of the Bible, and if you ignored that vile"—she searched for a word—"that vile *puritan* John Milton, you would know that even Satan at that time was considered to be one of Yahweh's court and not a rival prince of darkness."

"No Satan?" he said, kind of disappointed.

"Didn't Monsignor Ryan tell you that Satan was Yahweh's jester? Not a bad angel. And Lucifer was not a demon, he was a good spirit, he never defied the Most High, he was brilliant and kind." She clutched both fists tightly. "And deeply devout."

Gabriella Light ... Oh my God ...

"And your, uh ... complement?"

She bowed her head and nodded.

Angels, he told himself resolutely, are not supposed to cry.

ow about the press confer-
ence ..." Gaby Light was all business this morning, the grief of
the previous night firmly suppressed. "The trick is to impose your
own agenda on them instead of permitting them to set the
agenda."

"Why do you care about my press conferences?" he demanded crossly.

So she was in a good mood. Well, he was in a bad mood.

"We angels"—she grinned at him most attractively, he might
even say seductively—"offer a full and comprehensive range of
services."

"Seraphic Kelly Girls?"

"With certain extra skills ... After all, since 1951 I'm the
patron saint of those engaged in electronic communication."

"Who decided that?"

"The Pope. Who else decides about patron saints?"

"On his own?"

"I might have whispered in his ear!"

No way he could resist that impish grin. He always fled impish women because they overwhelmed him instantly. Talk about psychological nakedness.

"Can I finish my pancakes and bacon first?"

"Surely a Nobel Prize winner can do two things at once."

"Well, I can chew gum and walk."

"So you can eat breakfast and talk about the press conference."

Sean had been awakened from a tranquil sleep—his most tranquil night in years—with an abundant breakfast served in bed.

The sleep had been no less tranquil because it had been inhabited by a woman, in various stages of undress (never quite total), who looked like Gabriella. The inhibitor mechanism that prevented him from sustaining erotic thoughts about her did not work on his unconscious. Did she know about his delicious dreams? Did she care?

"Guardian angels," he had said sleepily, "are protectors and messengers, not servants."

Gaby had stared daggers at him. "One part of protecting you, Professor Desmond, is to make sure that you sleep off your hangovers. And, just to be clear about it, I am no one's servant."

"Except the Most High's." He swallowed his grapefruit juice. Naturally she knew that he liked grapefruit juice. What else?

"Of course."

"Will I receive this kind of protection every morning even if I don't have a hangover?"

"If you're a good little boy." Her prim visage was devastated by a resurgent comic smile.

There's a strain of the outrageous comic in you too, my dear. Very close to the surface, despite all your attempts to be austere. A thousand expressions chasing each other across that mobile, hauntingly lovely face. They chose well, I guess. Whoever they are.

She was wearing a tan wool gabardine dress, no collar, long sleeves, big buttons in front, little buttons on the sleeves. Redingote style. Pockets in the skirt. All cool and competent and understated. Seven hundred dollars at least. What the rich research assistant wears on a trip to pick up the Nobel Prize.

Why not send her and let her bring it back? he asked himself irritably.

The dress was designed to appear to create the impression of self-effacement and discretion, without in fact doing so at all.

Nothing Gaby might wear would make her part of the background, not with that statuesque body and alluring face.

Why don't I feel any desire for her? Am I afraid of aliens who claim to be angels?

Or have they put my hormones on hold?

They could do it if they wanted to, no doubt about that.

The thought that he need not feel desire for this sumptuous "bearer of life" both angered him (How dare they mess with my hormonal balance!) and relieved him (Well, I don't have to worry about that, anyway).

Admire, but don't touch. Remember you got burned the first time you did touch her.

The woman in his dreams seemed less distant, but then that was always the way with women in dreams, wasn't it?

The dream woman was also less analog and more human. Maybe the unconscious didn't know about analogs.

"Well, what about the press conference?" He slopped up the last pool of maple syrup on his plate and popped the enormous chunk of soggy pancake into his mouth.

"It will be an opportunity for you to be quoted saying something serious and important." She sat on the edge of the bed, dismayingly close. Different scent this morning too. "I won't promise it will exorcise the previous image, but it will help to create a new one."

"Is 'exorcise' the appropriate word, all things considered?"

She sighed in resignation. "I can see that this will be one of those days. Now, the point is that the science editor of *The New York Times*—"

"In this city they call it simply the *Times*."

"*Will* you be quiet for a minute. . . . Here, give me that tray . . . you can keep the coffee cup. . . . The man from the *Times* will ask you the first question. It will be about the major problems facing evolutionary biology and you—"

"How do you know what he will ask?"

Sean was being difficult in part because he was embarrassed. If he had known that his guardian angel would burst into his room with breakfast and a day full of plans, he would have worn pajamas. Or at least shorts. As it was, he found it no easy task to devour breakfast and maintain a semblance of modesty.

Not that he ate any less of the breakfast.

"I think you can safely rely on my prediction that he will speak first and that he will ask you about the challenges of evolutionary biology."

"Did you eat breakfast?"

"PLEASE." She rose from the bed, furious at him. "Listen to me. No more interruptions. Understand?"

"Yes ma'am."

The docile chimp again.

"You will tell him your thoughts about the dynamics and the direction of the evolutionary process. That will set the tone for the rest of the conference. No matter what anyone asks, you return to your primary thoughts on the subject. Your answers, not their questions, will set the tone for the conference. Moreover, you should be your sweet, charming"—she smiled benignly—"affectionate self. No jokes, no wisecracks, no smart-mouthed jabs, understand?"

"Can I talk to say, 'Yes ma'am'?"

"You are a serious scholar who has done important work," she said, ignoring his interruption, "work that answers some crucial questions but which leads to even more crucial questions. The most you can do is try to ask the questions right. Understand the image?"

"Why is the image important?"

"Because it is. Now hurry up and take your shower and shave. We don't want to keep *The New York Times* waiting, do we?"

"*Times.*"

She made a face at him and flounced out of the room and into her own room, noisily slamming the door.

I think I won that one, Sean Desmond told himself as the waters of the shower beat reassuringly on his skin. She is kind of fun. She understands the game and plays it well.

Better than I do, damn her.

Again he doubted the whole business. There was not a woman in the adjoining room. Certainly not a woman claiming to be a guardian angel. In fact, there was no adjoining room. It was all a slight mental aberration brought on by the shock of winning the Nobel Prize and his preoccupation with angels since he had heard the choirs on Stacey's tape player.

Right?

Right.

She was a figment of an Irishman's fantasy, a pure creature of imagination.

As he was shaving, clad in his shorts, the figment burst into the bathroom.

"Sean ..."

"You might have asked if I were decent."

"If I didn't know you were decent, I wouldn't have come in." She paused and appraised him critically. "I must say for a male of your species at your age"—her eyes moved from his head to his feet—"you are not an unpresentable specimen."

Sean felt his face flame. "Leave my clothes on," he begged, not completely unhappy with her assessment.

"They're irrelevant, as I'm sure you must know." She continued her careful inspection. "A little too thin and not enough muscle tone. We'll have to see you eat the right kind of food and resume your exercises. Swim in London; there's a pool at the Grosvenor. Jog in Stockholm and in Dublin on the way back."

"Why bother?"

She smiled archly. "Oh, there's no telling who you might meet on this trip."

"Whom. Now if you're finished evaluating me, can I finish shaving?"

"Go ahead." She continued to contemplate him. "Posture leaves a little bit to be desired too ... and don't pretend to be offended. You do it to women all the time. Turnabout is fair play."

"What is sauce for the gander is sauce for the guardian angel?" He flicked on his shaver.

"Something of the sort. Incidentally, there's a new blade for that on your dresser. Put it in today sometime."

"Yes ma'am."

"Ass muscles will need some exercise too." Her voice was momentarily critical. In the mirror he could see she was examining him again. He tried to pretend that he was not embarrassed. "By the way, you will enjoy the article in the *Times*"—giggle—"about your friend Jim McMahon of the Bears."

"You didn't read the *Times*."

"Sure I did."

"Not in the paper. It hadn't been touched when I opened it up."

In the mirror he saw her impish grin. I'm not only a chimp I'm a straight man. "There are other ways of reading it."

"In the computer?"

She waved her hand in dismissal. "Possible but too much work."

"As it is transmitted to satellite?"

"Ah," she said, beaming, "you Nobel Prize winners are smart."

"Even if our asses leave something to be desired?"

"Well . . ." She evaluated him again. "Not too much." She started to leave. "Oh yes . . ." She paused. "There was something I wanted to tell you before you distracted me with your foolish modesty."

She sounded worried.

"Bad news?"

"Not terribly bad . . ." She hesitated again, not looking at him. "I'm afraid your former wife gave an interview to the *National Enquirer*."

"Oh no!"

"You don't want to read it. I'll talk to the girls and settle them down. Then the best thing to do is to forget it."

"I suppose." The day, enjoyable thus far, now seemed ruined.

"Poor woman needs help." Gabriella spoke without much conviction.

"Same old stuff? How I traded her in on the Nobel?"

"Pretty much. I would imagine that it might come up in the press conference. You simply don't want to comment on it. Then someone will ask who has the custody of the children. You will say very quietly that you have—the *Enquirer* doesn't go into such mundane matters. Then someone else will ask if custody was contested, and you will say no. That will end the discussion. If anything goes out on the wires or the networks about your marriage, it will be that fact. All right?"

Her vast eyes were filled with sympathy.

"Thanks," he said, his voice husky. "You will talk to the girls?"

"Right away." She left the bathroom and then turned around at the door. "Oh yes, one might even say that you are a more than presentable male of your species." She leaned in the door and touched his shoulder with her fingers. "Stand up straight, Jackie Jim. Slouching is bad for your posture."

Something creaked inside him and he indeed stood up straight.

He had been evaluated the way the wife of an Irish landlord would evaluate a male wolfhound that she was thinking of adding to her kennel.

Except that the wolfhound had more privacy.

On the other hand, they don't have their posture problems cured instantly and painlessly.

He glanced at himself in the mirror. More than presentable, she had said. Angels don't lie. I never thought of myself that way.

What am I going to be like when this is all over? Will the infernal woman remake me completely?

And I had better not even think the word infernal in association with her.

Gaby decided that they would walk from Madison Avenue to the U.N., despite the subfreezing weather. "You definitely need the exercise."

She was wearing a tactful cashmere coat, not the mink he assumed she would. She knew when restraint was appropriate.

She kept a careful eye on the people near them on the street. How would she dispose of any would-be killers in public? Would they turn to jelly too?

"The girls were fine—stop shivering, you're not that cold—as I thought they would be. They're remarkably resilient young women."

"They don't get it from me."

"The hell they don't." She chuckled. "You should excuse the expression."

The auditorium at the Mission of the United States of America to the United Nations was Edward Stone modern, somewhat deteriorated as was appropriate in a time of budget cutbacks—glass and aluminum functional, with acoustics that were not functional. Sean Desmond was astonished at the crowd, almost a hundred people, dozens of cameras and microphones.

Gaby surveyed the crowd. "It looks all right," she murmured.

"Looks," he said uneasily.

"Like I said," she snapped back, "angels aren't perfect."

"Damn near, you should excuse the expression."

"You are cute, Jackie Jim." She smiled at him. "A nuisance but cute ... and forget that Irish setter line."

"Wolfhound."

She sat in the first row, cashmere coat neatly folded on the seat beside her. The man next to her was a slim, handsome Irishman, blue suit and tie. Priest, Sean decided. I can smell one a mile away. Gaby faded into the background as the conference began.

Well, that was not true. A woman like Gabriella Light could never really fade into the background.

Sure enough, the man from the *Times* asked the first question: "What would you say is the most important issue facing evolutionary biology today?"

"The one which interests me the most is the directionality of evolution. My own work has refined a little our knowledge of how the process works, but it forces on us some very difficult questions as to how it works and, more interesting, *why* it works and *for what ends* it works. We do not even begin to know why or how this seemingly random process acquires directionality. We understand the engine, if you will, but we don't know where it gets the map it is following. How does randomness produce purpose?"

"Could there be an, uh, divine power at work?"

"That's theology, not biology. As a biologist, I don't know. Note, however, that theoretical physicists are as puzzled as are we theoretical biologists about the apparent directionality of the cosmos."

"Some biologists object to your use of the word 'intelligent' to describe the transpositions of genetic codes. How do you reply to them?"

"If they have a better word to describe a process that is purposive, I'll be happy to use it."

Sean was enjoying himself. He was giving intelligent (and, yes, he thought charming) answers to intelligent questions. Cameras were whirring, pencils were scribbling, Gaby was nodding her head. I'm doing okay, finally.

She's a pretty good flack, among other things.

"Do you think it is possible for us to discover the direction of our own evolutionary process and, uh, facilitate it? To produce superman, just as you produced superfly?"

Sean felt his stomach turn. It was almost a blasphemous question.

"I think it would be very dangerous to try. We would almost certainly make a mess out of such interventions. By the way I didn't produce superfly, I merely predicted it. The 'intelligence' in our organism that presides over genetic transposition ought not be confused with discursive intellect and is probably unavailable to it. I think the best we can do is not get in the way of our species' development."

Gaby was frowning, somehow displeased. What did I say wrong?

"On the other hand," he continued, hoping that he still sounded smooth, suave, and reasonably serious, "it seems to me that when they find themselves in new ecological niches, organisms make choices about evolutionary leaps. If the 'intelligence' decides wrongly, makes an evolutionary mistake, it simply disappears. With the spread of our species to the whole planet, scientific progress, and of course the bomb, we are in a niche different from any our species has ever occupied. I am confident that our biological intelligence is capable of making the proper choice—unless other levels of our intelligence intervene to prevent that choice."

Gaby's frown was replaced by a faint smile—her pet wolfhound had performed well.

The priest next to Gaby raised his hand.

"What would you call this new ecological niche, Professor Desmond?"

I might as well set up this guy, Sean decided. Gaby inclined her head slightly.

"Noosphere is as good a word as any, Father."

The clergyman colored faintly. "And you wouldn't mind calling the direction..."

"... Le Pointe Omega? Why not? So long as I don't have to accept Father Teilhard's theology."

"You are aware"—the priest was enjoying the game—"that some physicists, Dr. Hawkings of Cambridge for example, suggest that even before creation there existed the laws of physics."

"And perhaps the outline of my 'intelligent' evolution too?"

The priest grinned. "It sounds like *logos* to me."

"You're a Jesuit, aren't you, Father?"

"George Hunt." The priest grinned again. "From *America*."

"*Logos* is a Greek word. I know because some of your confreres taught me Greek. The younger ones don't teach it to my daughters." Gaby was grinning again. "If you spell it with a small lambda, Father, I'll buy your *logos*."

Gaby guffawed. Proudly, he thought.

Another woman reporter—network news, Sean thought—took over the questioning: "Professor Desmond, have you seen the article about your wife in the *National Enquirer*?"

"No, I have not."

"She says that your lust for the Nobel Prize spoiled your marriage and ruined the life of your daughters. Would you care to comment."

"No."

"You won't comment?"

"That's right."

"You do have custody of your daughters, don't you, Doctor Desmond?"

"Yes."

"That custody was not contested, was it?"

Good old Gaby. If only she didn't look so satisfied with herself.

"No, it was not."

"How would you characterize your daughters, Doctor Desmond?"

That question wasn't in the script.

"Fee and Dee—Fionna and Deirdre? Utterly delightful young women!"

There was a smatter of applause. So much for the *National Enquirer*.

"Let's go back to biology, Doctor Desmond."

"Fine."

More laughter. And more head-nodding from herself.

"How does your work increase the evidence that evolution has direction?"

"Well, the ordinary process of evolution goes along at a very slow rate of progress for a long time—in the case of *Homo sapiens sapiens*, for millions of years; in the case of my fruit flies in a much shorter time span. Then there is a leap, indeed caused by natural selection but not explained by it. It's the leaps that seem to point. I don't think we know yet where they're pointing. You can see in retrospect, but not in prospect."

A man two-thirds of the way toward the back was twisting and turning in his seat, like he was having a seizure.

Epileptic fit? Or heart attack? Only those immediately around him seemed to notice.

"You see a future for humankind."

"I see our species pointing in a direction. Whether we will permit ourselves to survive to continue in that direction remains to be seen."

The man was struggling out of his row of seats. Why didn't someone help him?

"Are we groping toward a greater consciousness, a planetary consciousness perhaps?"

The man was running down the aisle toward the front. Odd.

"Some would say so, most notably Teilhard de Chardin, whose vision I take to be more mystical than scientific. Of course, greater consciousness means different things to different people...." What was the matter with that wild-eyed nut? "I would resist some of the more popular interpretations, drawn from parapsychology, for example—though that is a discipline which in its best manifestations ought to be respected."

The sick man, tall, lean, bespectacled, with stringy blond hair, pulled a massive gun from his coat, the sort of six-shooter Wyatt Earp or Matt Dillon wore on television. No tiny .22 for this killer. Where's Gaby? How will she handle this one? Or is it too late?

Once again, for the second time in two days, Sean S. Desmond prepared with commendable academic objectivity for the end of his life.

"Filthy Satan!" screamed the killer.

He began to fire. Curiously Sean watched the flashes belch from the muzzle of the gun.

Somewhere a bugle sounded "Charge!"

The killer emptied all six bullets into Gabriella Light, who had jumped between him and Sean Desmond at the last second.

"It's easier," said Sean Desmond, gesturing mentally at the solemn darkness in the general vicinity of the main altar to St. Paddy's, "to believe in you than to believe in her. What the hell are you people trying to do to me?"

If there was Anyone lurking up there near the altar or faintly glowing red sanctuary light, that Anyone did not think it was appropriate or necessary to answer.

"Hell," the Nobel laureate continued, "you didn't give me a chance to finish the response to that question, and it would have been the biggest help for your image in this whole nutty business. I was going to say that there could be no doubt that in some sense we were essentially evolving toward greater mind, even if you spell it with a capital letter. Point Omega, I was maybe going to say—hadn't quite made up my mind—seems to be out there waiting, perhaps impatiently. Can you imagine what that would have done for you?

" 'Course, I suppose you don't have to worry about images, do you?"

Whoever might be in charge was no more ready to comment than Sean had been ready to comment on his family life.

"I suppose I can work that into my acceptance speech, but there's already too many good quotes in that. Why didn't you let me finish before you unleashed that crazy nut?"

The *Daily News* headline said it all:

Crazy Tries To
Kill Nobel Prof

"But no, you let him fire all six shots into poor Gaby."

Who was not fazed by them in the slightest.

The sub-head told that story:

Woman Aide Subdues
Would-be Killer

That was putting it mildly. After she had absorbed the six shots—six in the belly as Brian Donleavy had said in *Beau Geste*—Gaby had calmly taken the nutcake's arm, twisted the gun out of his hand, and quite firmly pushed him to the floor, where she held him until New York's Finest arrived and took charge.

The man, it turned out, was a "radical fundamentalist" who was convinced, according to his family, that Satan had taken possession of the Nobel Prize winner.

"If he were not on the side of Satan," he had screamed, "my bullets would have killed him."

"The asshole couldn't shoot straight," the Police Captain, a short, bald, rubicund mick from Brooklyn, had muttered after they had watched the "attempted assassination" on videotape. "My guys are digging all the bullets out of the wall. Nice circle all around you. Damn good thing he couldn't shoot straight, Doctor Light, or you would have taken all those bullets. It was a brave thing you did."

"I didn't stop to think about it, Captain McNamee," she had said demurely.

Not only had she diverted the six bullets, or maybe refracted them as they went through her "energy fields," she had corrected the images on video tape so that it did not seem that the bullets were entering her.

"*Very* clever," Sean informed the putative deity.

Through all the confusion after the attempted kill and the long conversations with the police and questions from the frantic press, Gaby would not look at him. She was clearly very unhappy with herself.

"Well," Captain McNamee had said finally, "that about wraps it up, Doctor Light; I don't suppose you or Doctor Desmond will object to the NYPD keeping an eye on you until you leave for . . . Stockholm, is it?"

Sure, ask her the questions, God knows she is in charge.

"Not in the least, Captain," she had replied smoothly. "We both are very grateful for your efficiency and concern."

Who the hell, Sean had wondered, was responsible for the security that let that loony in?

But he let Gaby do the talking since she would anyway.

"You were the heroine, Doctor Light," the Captain had continued. "He was trying to reload when you hit him. No telling what he would have done if he'd got a second chance. If you ever get tired of teaching biology, we might use you on the force."

"Just a few tricks I picked up while earning my black belt, Captain," she had said meekly.

Black belt! And I thought angels didn't lie. I know, she'll say it was an analogy. Everything is a goddamn analogy.

He repeated that complaint to the sacred emptiness of St. Paddy's.

"Everything is a goddamn analogy." Then shocked by his blasphemy, he added, "You should excuse the expression."

They had been driven back to the Helmsley in a U.N. mission limousine with bulletproof windows. A NYPD squad car preceded them and another one followed.

"Sorry, Sean," she had whispered contritely as soon as they were inside the limo. "I almost blew that one."

"I'm still alive," he had noted, reasonably enough he thought.

Sometime this would all catch up with him. But now he was more astonished by her performance than by the danger to his life. Yesterday's act might have been a dream or a nightmare. Today's took place before TV cameras. It would be seen on the evening news by millions of Americans—and would include the beautiful silver-haired woman ripping the gun out of a would-be killer's hand.

Great footage, one TV journalist had told him.

"There's that," she had agreed, still not looking at him. "You are still alive, but"—her excuses had tumbled out—"I was expecting the same crowd as yesterday or maybe even your friends from Langley. I know what they all look like. I wasn't expecting a crazy fundamentalist who confused you," she had choked, half laughing, half crying, "with my poor spouse. I should have been ready."

"Angels aren't perfect?"

"No, not perfect. We make mistakes, but that was a bad one."

If she were any different from a perfectionist woman graduate student who had made a mistake, Sean didn't know what the difference would be.

"Hey, you saved me, you captured the guy, you fiddled with the TV tapes, you impressed everyone, don't be a perfectionist first-year graduate student."

She had not been ready to be laughed out of her dissatisfaction with her own performance, but some of the tension did seem to slip out of her wondrous shoulders. "Captain McNamee was suspicious about the neat circle of those bullets in the wall. If he measures them he'll find a perfect circle. That will make him wonder. I should have thought to deflect them irregularly, but we have this obsession with balance and harmony."

Yes, that would indeed have baffled the poor Captain, for the rest of his life. He was too cute a mick to take the chance of that happening by actually measuring the distances among the bullet holes.

"You know damn well he won't measure them."

She had nodded. "Right, he doesn't want to know any more than he has to know. Poor man, he was in the back of the room and he thought he saw the bullets go through me too."

"Well, you sure moved fast enough."

"Speed of light." A smile.

"Really?"

"Well, almost. We can't quite get up to it, but we come pretty close."

Sure. Naturally. Of course.

Sean had found his hands sweating.

"Lucky for me. So you actually caught up with the bullets?"

"Right." She had nodded briskly. "It's not such a difficult trick when you know how to do it."

"And when you have the speed."

The bullets must have seemed like a tortoise racing the proverbial hare.

"On the video tapes you don't even see me move in. I was too quick for the camera. Captain McNamee, poor dear man, noticed that too. But, like you say, he doesn't want to think about it."

Sean didn't want to think about it either.

"What's going on, Gaby?" he had asked, sinking deeper into the comfortable limo seat. "What's it all about? Why are people trying to kill me? I'm not worth the trouble. When is all this craziness going to stop?"

"This was a deviant event." The smile had faded, she was still angry at herself. "We deal with patterns. Deviant events throw us, probably one of the costs of our evolution. That poor sick man is not part of the pattern we're fighting."

Well, that explains everything, now doesn't it?

"How does a broken-down biologist who has wasted most of his life fit into your patterns?"

"First of all, Jackie Jim," she had said, absorbing him in her affectionate smile, "I'll not be taken in by your self-hatred. You're important, more important than you can possibly understand now." She touched his arm gently, but with no ecstasy charge this time. "I wouldn't be here unless it was patent to us that for all your blarney and your quirkiness, you were enormously"—she winked as she always seemed to at one of the buzzwords—"important. My associates would not have insisted that I become perceptible to you—we do this very rarely—unless we were all convinced that we had to protect you."

"I'm flattered but I don't think I understand."

Sounds like bullshit to me.

"And I don't think I can explain." She had frowned. "Not that it's a secret exactly, but it's so hard to translate into your language and thought paradigms. There are patterns in the cosmos that we see very clearly and which, because we are what we are, compel us, well, almost compel us to act.... That doesn't make much sense, does it?"

"Something like how I've been compelled to solve scientific puzzles?"

"A little bit." Her frown had deepened. "But it's a lot more than curiosity or the elegance of your models that constrains us. There's beauty and goodness too.... We are pattern-obsessed creatures. There are some patterns that almost demand our intervention. In that sense we might be called messengers of God. Heralds of the pattern anyway."

"Nazareth?"

She had glanced at him, surprised and a little suspicious. "Very clever, Jackie Jim. You catch on quickly."

Later in St. Paddy's, Sean glared at the pregnant emptiness in front of him. "You realize what the woman was saying, don't you? She was claiming to be the angel of Nazareth, that's what she was claiming. If she's really Gabriel, and she's as much as said she is, then that was her all right. I wonder what she thinks of all those paintings down through the centuries. Anyway, why is the *Angelus* angel—or should I say *Angela* angel—messing with a dummy like me?

"And if you're laughing, I want you to know that I'm not amused."

In the limo he had pressed his advantage. "And I suppose that some of you see the patterns, in all their goodness and beauty, more clearly than others, and they are the ones who are said to stand before the face of God?"

She had considered him intently. "You really do deserve that Nobel Prize. What is it Joshua Hechter said to the *Sun Times* about you ...?"

Hechter was a gifted professor at Northwestern whose early work on proteins in the brain had always fascinated—and dazzled—Sean. So the woman was reading his press clippings, was she?

"'A brilliance of insight,'" Sean had said, flushed with pleasure, "'matched only by his dazzling flair.' You remembered that?"

"Naturally. But you have it a little inaccurately. One character trait for which the evolutionary process selected on our pilgrimage to mind—capital *M* or not, as you said just before you were cut off—is a passion for the beauty and goodness of a pattern. When the beauty and goodness is there, we enjoy it, oh, how we enjoy it. When it's incomplete, we are pushed by the essence of our nature to try to eliminate that which is threatening its completion. Am I too obscure?"

"Scary but not obscure."

"Don't be afraid of me, Jackie Jim, I said I wouldn't hurt you."

"Can you give me an example?"

After some consideration, she replied, "I can tell you about one of our tragic failures. August 1914."

"World War I?"

"The end of the modern world. It's difficult for those of you who view the last half of the nineteenth century and the first decade of this one from the perspective of the world after 1920 to realize how impressive that era was. It was a lot more than Proustian decadence."

"Oh, I've always thought the Edwardian era was kind of quaint, *The Importance of Being Earnest* and that sort of thing."

There he had been, a brand-new potential Nobel laureate in a bulletproof Lincoln trapped in a midtown Manhattan traffic jam listening to a history lecture by a beautiful woman who claimed to be an angel.

The dream would end soon. It had to end.

Didn't it?

"That's the way the generations born since August of 1914 have to think about it. The possibilities that were destroyed were so great that you can't face the tragedy." Gaby had warmed to her lecture. "Life expectancy had doubled since 1800. Science, medicine, engineering, technology had made enormous progress. For example, the streets of the cities were lighted at night for the first time in human history. The pattern that we saw was a world in which prosperity and peace were spreading, unevenly and awkwardly to be sure, over a whole planet. It all died in August and September of 1914. Your species has never recovered the confidence it lost in the forty years of war that followed. Your technology improved, but you lost your faith in your ability to control it and so in fact you didn't control it. As I said, the Modern World, the Enlightenment, the Renaissance—call it whatever you want—was over."

"It was only a four-year war."

Outside, snow flurries were beginning to sweep 42nd Street. The driver turned on the windshield wiper.

"One war, Seano, from 1914 to 1945, with a period of truce. Two hundred million people died, more than your species had produced in the years from the time it had acquired language to 1700."

"Two hundred million?"

"Counting the famines in India and Russia, the purges in Russia, and the victims of the Spanish influenza, all of which were the result of the war. Sixty million in Russia, forty million in India from flu and famine, thirty-five million in China, twenty-five million in Germany, eighteen million in Poland, six million of them Jews. Is it any wonder that your species has lost its nerve?"

"You tried to stop it?"

She had nodded vigorously, seemingly quite unaware of the dirty gray snow and the traffic jam in the slush in front of Grand Central Station. She was back in August of 1914.

"We saw the pattern of peace and progress, uncertain peace and uneven progress, admittedly, but still more than your species had ever known. And we saw the pattern of evil rising to meet it." She had paused thoughtfully, her delicate facial figures troubled. "In any event, during that beautiful summer of 1914, the most beautiful in a thousand years, by the way, we did everything we could to protect the pattern of beauty and goodness we saw developing and to frustrate the mindless evil that threatened it. Mindless is the right word. It made no sense at all. Its very randomness was its greatest power. A tiny splinter group of Serbian nationalists? Sarajevo, a town no one had ever heard of? Franz Ferdinand, a nice man, but his death causing two hundred million more deaths? We did all we could to stop them. It was too late. In your words, Seano," she had said, falling back into the cushions, "we blew it."

"Oh," he had said quietly. "Isn't that a little hard on yourselves?"

"It was our task to prevent the war and we failed."

"Pretty high standards."

"If your species can judge itself harshly," she had snapped at him, "so can we. Patterns are our business. We saw the pattern and we lost it."

This woman is blaming herself for two hundred million deaths. I want out of the car. Now.

The car had started to move again, inching toward Madison Avenue.

"How did you know that the *Times* man was going to ask the first question and not know about the man with the gun?"

"I whispered in the reporter's ear," she had replied with a sigh. "I didn't look closely enough in the crazy's eye. So you were in unnecessary danger." She had touched his arm. "I'm sorry."

"Well, what didn't happen today can hardly be compared to Sarajevo."

"There's that." She had relaxed and beamed at him, a bit possessively he thought—cute little puppy dog. "We did save you this time. Barely."

"Were you on the case in Sarajevo?"

"I was, how would you say it, a consultant. My principal responsibilities were elsewhere. I would have blown it too if I had been directly involved."

Sean had waited to be sure she was finished. The limo had turned at last on to Madison Avenue.

"It wasn't all your fault."

"I know that."

" 'God, should She exist,' to quote Blackie, 'draws straight with crooked lines.' "

"Two hundred million deaths?"

"I don't believe in Her, you do."

"I know." She had sighed wearily. "I know."

"You don't think you, er, sinned do you?"

"Certainly not! We did our best."

"It wasn't good enough."

"That's right, it wasn't good enough. If some of your species can be perfectionists—"

"Why can't yours? And because you're so good at patterns, your standards for perfection are high?"

"That's right," she had replied listlessly. "And we blew it."

"You win some?"

"*Certainly* we win some."

"You personally?"

"*Certainly* I personally."

"Tell me about one."

"*Well*, back in 1962—" She had stopped and glared at him. "I'm the guardian angel, Sean Seamus Desmond. I am not a silly first-year graduate student to be patronized."

"Tell me about it anyway."

"Cuban missile crisis, remember?"

"Sure, I was in college. We were scared stiff. The papers said some of them were aimed at Chicago."

"Absurd." She had waved her hand, dismissing childish nonsense. "They weren't aimed at anything that early. Anyway"—now smiling complacently—"President Kennedy's advisers had virtually agreed on a surprise air attack on the missile sites. Russians would have been killed and the world would be on the same slide it was in 1914."

"World War III?"

"Probably. The Kennedys had learned something at the Bay of Pigs fiasco, and that was not to trust their advisers, especially the military advisers. Bobby had doubts. He kept saying that it wasn't in the American tradition to launch surprise attacks. You can imagine how far that went with Dean Acheson and all the old-timers. So," she was glowing now, "so I got the idea of whispering into his ear, 'Your brother will be the General Tojo of the nineteen sixties.'"

"Tojo?"

"The Japanese prime minister who gave the order for the Pearl Harbor attack. I couldn't force him to try to veto the plans"—smiling happily—"any more than I can force you to say intelligent things at a news conference. But I could suggest and I did, and with a little more help from us the world avoided a war, and it looked like maybe there would be negotiation and a slow return to the world of the first half of 1914."

"And?"

"And we blew it again in Dallas a few months later. Exit Camelot and all it promised. Instead of peace, your species got Vietnam. And Watergate. Random idiocy again."

"Did the Kennedys see you like I do?"

The car had been only a block away from the Helmsley, creeping ahead in the snow and the hasty December dusk, like it had entered a forbidden and dangerous forest.

"You *must* be joking!" Now she was irate. "Those men were satyrs. They would bed anyone who seemed even remotely like a human female, angel or not. Not their fault, maybe—their father was even worse. They were good leaders, but despicable human beings. We don't get to choose the people who are important."

"Or you wouldn't have chosen me."

"I didn't say that," she had shot back at him.

"You could have always deadened their libido like you deadened mine."

She had glared at him again. "My, aren't you the clever little wolfhound!" They had both laughed together. Somehow Gaby had turned his feeling that he was a member of an inferior species into a joke they both shared. "Well, their libidos were much more vigorous than yours and they were much less principled than you are. Besides, our plan didn't require that they see me. I would have probably scared them to death, with all they had on their consciences."

"You would have killed them if they were fresh, like those men yesterday."

"I wouldn't have had to go that far. Anyway, we won that one. We lose more than we win and the ones we win we often lose later. We still are not skilled at anticipating random lunacy. But we try. And the Most High doesn't seem to be completely displeased with our efforts."

"I'm glad."

The car had slithered to a halt and was waiting patiently for room in front of the entrance to the hotel.

"By the way"—she smiled her maternal approval—"you were quite good today before—"

"Before I was so rudely interrupted."

They had laughed together, companionably. Fellow survivors of the holocaust at Masurian Lakes in September 1914.

I bet you didn't know I was at the Battle of Masurian Lakes, did you? he imagined himself saying to the doorman as Gaby tipped him with what looked like a brand-new twenty-dollar bill.

He had told her that he was going over to St. Patrick's for a few moments. God, she had thought, would be surprised. A New York cop in the squad car behind was assigned to guard him. Gaby didn't seem concerned.

Forty-seven floors and a block were no great problem, it seemed, for an angel veteran of Masurian Lakes.

He'd have to ask her sometime whether Constantine really saw a cross in the sky before the battle of Melvian Bridge.

"A hundred and seventy?" he had asked as he turned to slosh through the snow over to the cathedral.

"What? Oh, you mean miles per second. No, no, much faster than that."

She seemed disappointed that his estimate was so low. Wolf-hound puppy loses points.

"How much?"

"*Well* ..." She had colored faintly. "A few miles under the speed limit."

A hundred and eighty-six thousand miles a second minus ... what? Two or three miles? Or even a hundred?

He was reasonably safe in the lace-curtain-Irish piety of St. Paddy's.

"It's bad enough"—he was winding down on his complaints to the deity—"that you get me messed up in all this foolishness. Why do you have to send a woman angel to plague me? And worse still, a woman angel with problems of her own that I'm supposed to solve, like I solve the problems of some of the kids in my class who think I'm some sort of a priest."

He let that one sink in.

No one said that he was supposed to help Gaby.

He knew, however, that it was expected of him, if not by her.

"At least, she's not the weepy, clingy kind I usually get mixed up with.

"Sorry. With whom I usually get mixed up.

"She hinted that she loves me. I suppose that goes with the territory. I'm beginning to love her too. Is this your idea of a fun game? Because if it is, I want you to know I don't like it one bit."

He thought about it a little more. Like maybe 185,997 miles a second?

You're still alive, aren't you?

There's that ... and stop laughing.

It was time, Sean Seamus Desmond decided, to get out of the cathedral. It was haunted.

He stopped at the news stand in the lobby of the hotel to see whether the *Daily News* headline had changed. It hadn't.

On a hunch he picked up *Harper's Bazaar* and thumbed through it.

Sure enough, there were both the gabardine dress and the cashmere coat. *Vogue* had the miniskirted cocktail dress from the previous night.

She was producing her clothes out of the current fashion magazines.

I need a long nap, he thought.

The suite—it had been transformed again into two bedrooms

with an intervening parlor—was empty. Maybe she was in another galaxy.

Sean Desmond had a long and pleasant nap, unaided by angelic intervention.

His dreams, as he remembered them, were amusing. No random lunacy. Only patterns.

When he woke up, he told himself that the random crazies were in the real world, the patterns in his dreams.

Gabriella Light daintily buttered her hot scone. "As I have indicated before, Professor Desmond, the problem with you is not so much the women you couple with as those whom you don't couple with."

"With whom I don't couple," he corrected her English. Rarely do you catch an angel in a grammatical error.

She threw back her head and laughed heartily.

"You are more fun," she continued to laugh, "than any *Homo sapiens sapiens* to whom I have ever been assigned."

"We try." He felt himself blushing.

The young person who was presiding over their tea in the Gold Room returned to the table to ply them with more Earl Grey tea and sherry (Helmsley variety, not angelic) and another plate of scones. She smiled happily at Gaby. "Anything else, Doctor Light?"

"Not just now, my dear."

Maybe she had learned her charm in St. Petersburg before the battles in East Prussia.

Almost everyone seemed to like Gaby. When she turned on the charm, even New Yorkers smiled back, some of whom Sean would have been willing to wager hadn't smiled in twenty years.

Those who did not respond to her smile were fixed with a hard glare that seemed to occasion immediate reaction. Sean called it her "Gaby look" and rejoiced that it had never been aimed in his direction. It lowered the wind-chill factor, he was certain, by at least ten degrees.

There had been no further attempts on his life. They had walked the bitter-cold, sun-drenched streets of New York with confident serenity. Gaby assured him that they were leading a procession of shadows.

"In order, Seano, there are the NYPD, the FBI, the CIA, the Mossad, the other side—"

"Why the Mossad?"

"Overachievers. They follow anyone whom others are following. And, to finish my list, three random loonies!"

"What!" He had jumped almost a half foot in the air, or so it seemed.

"Only joking." She poked his arm; no ecstatic current this time either. She turns it on and off when she wants to.

He was still standing up straight too.

The two girls were taking everything in stride. Mommy's article was "gross"; the press conference at the U.N. was "awesome, even if you did wear that old suit"; the shoot-out at the end was "really cool."

Yeah? You should have been at Sarajevo.

Fee: "Gaby is totally bitchin'."

Dee: "I mean out of sight."

Fee: "Is she really black belt?"

Dee: "Does she have any kids?"

"Three teenage daughters," he said.

Gaby rolled her eyes at that exaggeration.

Solemn chorus: "Out of sight!"

As they left the hotel in the morning, Gaby announced, "In the morning we will deal with your body, Professor Desmond, and in the afternoon your soul."

"Comprehensive."

"With your body by constraining you to walk a couple of miles—"

"In this cold?"

"—and by purchasing the kind of clothes that are suitable for a Nobel Prize winner."

"I don't have any money."

"We'll not worry about that small detail. I promised your daughters I would see that you look 'totally cool' in Stockholm, and I intend to honor that promise. You'll note I'm wearing a mink this morning. It facilitates service in the stores."

"I'm sure it does."

Her coat would not have cost a penny under twenty thousand, if she paid for it, which he very much doubted.

So they visited Paul Stuart and Barney's and purchased a doubled-breasted dark blue three-piece suit with light pinstripes, made-to-order shirts (with French cuffs), and socks and ties that were color coordinated with the suit and shirts.

At first they were told that alterations would require two weeks. Then Gaby favored the assistant manager with her "look," and all alterations were promised for the morrow.

Sean had to admit, grudgingly, that the suit made him look both academic and well dressed. An *Esquire* Nobel laureate.

"You show up at the round table with this on," Gaby insisted cheerfully, "and you'll own your university."

And she added in a whisper into his ear, "You're now a notably more than presentable male of your species."

"With an ass that needs work, nonetheless."

She chuckled and patted his arm.

Okay, woman, have the time of your life at my expense.

They also purchased cologne and shaving lotion that were both too expensive and too strong. So he claimed.

"Nonsense. You have to smell like a Nobel Prize winner."

"Whorehouse."

"You've never been in one and they don't smell that way."

She also selected new underwear for him, far too skimpy and "youthful" for his age, he argued.

"Never can tell whom you might meet in Stockholm. Some agreeable buxom Swede perhaps."

"I doubt it."

"You fear it, you mean. Come on, we have to make the museums this afternoon, Metropolitan, Guggenheim, and Frick. MoMA if we have time."

"All-purpose guardianship."

"Definitely." She laughed again. She was laughing all the time, the witch.

Nothing was purchased in quantity. "We've got to fit into your Gucci flight bags. Air travel is light travel. We can always buy more in London or Sweden."

"As long as your money supply holds out."

"Never fear."

She paid with crisp new bills from her shoulder bag—not the same one she had worn the day before. For his suit, she had pulled two $500 bills off the bottom of her wad. The clerk seemed a bit surprised but glanced at the bills and at her mink and gave her the change.

"Is it counterfeit?" he whispered as they left Barney's.

"Angels cheat? Don't be insulting, Professor Desmond."

"Stolen?"

"Certainly not."

"How did you get it?"

"We earned it."

"Do those who paid you know you earned it? Or even that they have paid you?"

She pursed her lips thoughtfully. "Let's say that if they knew all the circumstances of our service, they would pay us a lot more. I mean how much is it worth to the United States Mint to prevent World War III?"

He was not about to argue that.

At the Frick that afternoon he asked her about the "Gaby look."

"Do you ever stare at me the way you stared at that waitress at the Russian Tea Room?"

"How did I stare?" She was considering some Limoges cloisonné about which she had lectured to him intelligently—whether because she had read the guidebook or because she had actually seen the stuff made he did not want to ask.

"Your Gaby stare, which got our lulu-kebab delivered almost at the speed of light."

He tried to imitate the Gaby look.

She responded with hilarious laughter, much to the displeasure of one of the attendants, who began to approach them. She fixed her Gaby look on him and he drifted away.

"It doesn't really take away freedom, it merely, ah, enhances motivation."

"Cattle prod."

Instead of contesting his consistent complaint about being a member of an inferior species, she simply laughed again.

This time the attendant made no move to intervene.

"I can imagine how hard our procession of shadows," she chortled when they finally reached the Gold Room of the Helmsley, "will struggle over their reports tonight and how hard the analysts in their respective offices will work trying to make sense out of it."

Sean Seamus Desmond was exhausted. To be taken on a whirlwind cultural tour and shopping exposition by a woman angel, he had complained, was like hiking a hundred miles in the Amazon jungle.

"You wouldn't say that," she countered, eyes dancing mischievously, "if you had ever hiked in the Amazon."

Top that, inferior species.

Gaby insisted sharply that they would have their tea in the Gold Room, not the Madison Room.

"How come?"

"No windows. I don't want you to be an easy target."

"Couldn't you just turn on the power and outrun the bullets?"

"It's the first step that's important"—she signaled the hostess with two fingers—"like in your football. If the bullets were too close to you, like coming through a window, I might not have time."

"Wonder Woman has limitations?"

"Sit down!" She laughed. "I don't wear swimsuits around all day like she does."

"You're better built than she is."

"Impossible."

A young woman in a gold gown that matched the fabric on the walls was playing the harp again, on the tiny balcony at the north end of the room.

Gaby, Sean Desmond remarked—only to himself for the sake of delicacy—never seemed to have to go to the bathroom. Either her energy patterns disposed of waste in some other, doubtless neater fashion, or arguably she exercised her apparent ability to be in two places at the same time.

"Are you that good on the harp?" he asked.

Gaby was slipping out of her mink, revealing a white wool winter suit and matching sweater—the kind of suit that made you look both warm and hopeful on a cold day. Eight hundred dollars according to *Bazaar*.

"As good as her?" She listened to the harpist for a moment. "Actually she is quite good. For a member of your species, that is. Probably plays in one of the local symphonies. I'll do a little concert for you tonight. If you wish."

"I certainly wish. I was fascinated by the sounds on Stacey's tapes."

She smiled confidentially. "We'll see if I do any better."

No doubt about that, is there?

Then she launched her critical review of his love life.

"What do you mean, the women with whom I didn't couple?"

"You have a remarkable ability to overlook women with whom you might be happy and choose the women with whom you certainly won't be happy."

"Like?" He felt his face turn hot again.

"Lisa Malone."

"She's a movie actress and producer, and I'm a stuffy college professor."

"Whom did she marry?"

"George the Bean Counter."

"And?" Her butter knife paused above a scone.

"He's an accountant, thought by most to be stuffy . . . but she wasn't interested in me back in grammar-school and high-school days."

"Certainly she was." She piled clotted cream on top of the butter. "Everyone knew that, even you did, but you pretended not to because she scared you. Any woman who is not a whining, clinging dishrag scares you."

"Who else scared me away?" He pushed aside his sherry glass. Even drink wouldn't help now.

"In high school, Anne Finn and Maureen Keegan; in college, Mary Ward and Linda Boyle and Connie O'Rourke."

"I should have married one of them?"

She shrugged her lovely shoulders and reached for a salmon sandwich. "These are really good—for Earth, that is." She grinned wickedly. "An inferior world peopled by cute but dense wolf-hounds. . . . You *could* have married any of them and not made the mistake you did by coupling with that terrible Moaning Mona you did marry."

"You don't think much of Mona?"

"Not for you."

There was no arguing that point. He lifted the sherry glass and then put it down again. "So what do they have in common other than I apparently didn't notice that they liked me?"

"That should be obvious. Drink your sherry, it's not poisoned. They were all strong, intelligent women, with a sense of fun and a need to be both aroused and protected by someone like you. Perfect."

"Who recently? Blanche?"

"Probably not." Her eyes scanned the room looking for trouble. "But maybe. She was kind of young. Still, you learned a lot from her, didn't you? You certainly didn't try very hard at the end, did you? . . . But what about Mrs. Taylor? You had her on the block, to use your fantasy images, ready to be acquired, and you let her get away."

"Who?"

"Mind you"—she munched enthusiastically on yet another sandwich—"sexual attraction is not enough to cement complements together. But it's a good beginning, especially when both partners sense that there is more in the chemistry than merely mutual desire. Oh yes, she liked being on your slave block, though her fantasy was, as I'm sure you'd admit, somewhat different."

"*Who?*"

"You had disarmed her, and if I may say so, also disrobed her emotionally with your mixture of sensitivity, gentleness, and charm. Then you fled to the ineffable Stacey Reid."

"Damnit, *Gaby, who* are you talking about?"

"Whom?" she simpered.

"WHOM?" he bellowed.

"Shush, everyone's looking. . . . Laura Taylor, the receptionist in your office building last year. The one with the lovely laugh and the sweet smile. Don't tell me you don't remember her? You certainly had enough lustful thoughts about her."

"I don't think I ever caught her name," he said sheepishly. "Anyway, she wasn't interested in me."

"She was too." Gaby poured both of them more tea. "Very interested. You're not unattractive, as I've said before, and since Blanche, you radiate a certain sexual competence as well as gentleness, which you always exude. She was yours to overwhelm and carry off as you yourself describe it, in terms more appropriate for your species' immediate predecessors."

"Laura Taylor?"

"Too late now. She's already happily married. She's good in bed too. See what you missed."

"Oh."

"It's not your fault, Jackie Jim." Her hand touched his quickly. His spirits soared immediately. "Strong women scare you, weak women make you unhappy. You knew only the second kind when you were growing up, mother and sisters; the point is that now you have to change."

"Overwhelm them with my charm and carry them off?"

"Charm and sensitivity and tenderness." She nodded briskly. "I guess I don't have to add the last. You're always tender with women, even women of superior species!"

"Nobility buying a dog for their kennels!"

They both laughed.

Sean Desmond's heart was pounding. Life might not be empty after all.

"And don't grieve too much for Laura Taylor." Gaby signaled for the check. "There will be others. And if you'd married her, I wouldn't be here because you wouldn't have thought up your crazy idea of hinting at our existence in your acceptance speech."

"That's what started it all, then?"

"Certainly." She placed a fifty-dollar bill, new and crisp, on top of the check. "Haven't I said that already?"

"I guess. . . . Are you guys upset because I blew your cover?"

"Blew our cover?" She rose from her chair. "Sean Seamus Desmond, most human beings take our existence for granted. You're merely reminding the academic community of what most of them learned as kids. We're delighted, but that's not the reason we're protecting you."

He followed her out of the tea room. The lobby was crowded with Japanese tourists hauling luggage that looked bigger than they.

"Must travel light," Gaby murmured.

"They're good at making things, but not as good as you are." She giggled.

They stepped into one of the lacquer-box elevators. Two men were already there, stout blond men with heavy mustaches dressed in expensive dinner jackets.

Foreigners, Sean thought, exercising the Irishman's right to resent everyone who came to the country after his family.

One of the foreigners stuffed a snub-nosed gun into his belly. "Ve vill not make a sound, vill we?"

"Und ve will push the button for thirty-seven, von't ve?" said the other, his gun buried in Gabriella Light's belly.

Her face was an impassive mask. Okay, they couldn't kill her. But could she get a quick enough first step to intercept a bullet aimed at his small intestines?

Probably not.

He pushed the button for thirty-seven.

"What are you guys planning?"
Sean asked, figuring that he might disconcert their captors by making light and pleasant conversation. "You're not going to get away with this, you know. The NYPD is protecting us. They're on the next elevator, disguised as Japanese tourists."

Neither man moved a muscle. Their hard, empty eyes stared at him coldly.

"You don't have to jab me with that thing," he continued. "I'm not about to run, not as long as you can hurt herself."

Gaby seemed to smile faintly. Ah, good, the woman likes my sense of humor.

After several long eternities, the elevator stopped at the thirty-seventh floor.

"I think we can get out here, Seano," Gaby said easily. "Our friends probably won't want to come with us."

She slipped away from the man with the gun in her belly and held the door for Sean.

The gunman continued to point his snub-nosed pistol at the wall of the elevator.

"Come, Seano, we don't have all day. Your friend is in no condition to do anything to you just now."

Gingerly Sean Desmond eased away from the muzzle of the gun. Sure enough, his hard-eyed "friend" did not bat an eye. Sean backed farther away, still prepared to see flame leap out of the gun and tear a hole in his gut.

"Hurry up," Gaby growled impatiently. "We'll have a hard time explaining this if someone else shows up."

Still expecting the gun to explode, Sean backed toward the door of the elevator.

"I said hurry up." Gaby pulled him through the door.

The gunman continued to point his weapon toward the empty space where Sean had been standing.

Gaby turned him so that he was pointing at his companion; the two mute weapons were almost muzzle to muzzle. Then she pushed a floor button and jumped out of the elevator.

"That's that," she said with a sigh of relief.

"Random violence?"

"No, patterned craziness."

There were two sharp snaps of sound, like loud firecrackers, a few floors up.

"What was that?" Sean demanded.

"In, Seano." She shoved him through an elevator door that had opened on the opposite side of the hallway. "We will want to be peacefully in our rooms when the NYPD does finally catch up."

"What was it?"

She pushed forty-seven and relaxed against the red lacquered wall.

"I think our two would-be assassins may have eliminated one another."

"You killed them, Gaby!"

"Quite the contrary." She smiled placidly. "They killed themselves with the same squeeze of the trigger with which they had intended to kill us. Poetic justice if you will."

"But—"

"Save your liberal guilt for some other time. I told you no life was wasted, didn't I?" She pushed him out of the elevator and shoved him toward their suite-which-was-not-supposed-to-be-a-suite. "You're not really tough enough to survive, are you? No wonder you were not strong enough to stand up to that witch you married. And by the way, when she tries to come back to you—and count on it, she will try—you had better be tough enough to say 'No way.' Most High does not like people who waste Her second chances."

"Yes ma'am," he said docilely when she shoved him through the door. "Anything you say, ma'am."

"I'm sorry, Jackie Jim," she apologized after the door had slammed itself firmly shut. "I didn't blow that one, but I'm still nervous after yesterday."

"You spotted those two in the lobby?"

"Right. Same gang as day before yesterday. And I still can't figure— Anyway, no one's death should be taken lightly, not even professional killers. I hope I didn't seem callous. My first concern, of course"—she wrapped him in her maternal smile—"was you."

"Why?" Sean slumped into a chair. "I don't get it. Why do they want to kill me?"

"Isn't that obvious?"

"It sure isn't." He began to quiver, as if he were coming down with the flu. "What did I do?"

"You've been talking for the last six months about superflies and evolutionary leaps and angels. There are men in the world who are interested in supermen. Despite what you said at the press conference yesterday, they're confident that they can intervene in the process of transposition, rearrange the coding of the human genetic lines, and produce superman."

"Good God!"

"Indeed." She sat on the arm of his chair and touched his forehead with her fingers. "You know about Stacey's work, you have theories about evolutionary leaps; these men see you as a threat to their own plans to take control of the next leap for humans. They think they can push the species, or some of its members to be precise, on a leap in the direction of angels. You apparently are seen as an obstacle."

"They're mad!"

"Oh yes. You know that and we know that, but they don't know that."

"Nazis? Those two sounded like—"

"Like the villains on old TV films? Every guttural accent is not necessarily German, Seano."

"Who's involved in this stuff?" The gentleness of her fingers brought peace to his body and soul. A lot better than Valium.

"Just about every major government in the world and, in this reign of Margaret Thatcher, a private company in England—the so-called Project Archangel."

"And they think I'm an obstacle? Why?"

She hesitated. "We're not sure. Maybe just on general principles that you know too much."

"Nice people. . . . Anyway," he said with a sigh as quiet oozed through his bones, "thanks. Sorry I fell apart. It's just that I'm kind of new at all this."

"And I'm sorry"—a bottle of Black Bush had materialized in one hand and a tumbler filled with ice in the other—"that I was nasty about Mona. Here, drink this, it will help your nap."

"Thank you." He didn't know that a nap was scheduled. "You're right about Mona, by the way; she'll be back and I'll have to force myself to say no."

"The kids might help." She was looking out the window. "Ah, the inestimable Captain Michael Patrick McNamee. Poor dear man, he'll need a vacation before we get out of town."

Only as he began to sip the potent whiskey did Sean Seamus Desmond realize how badly he was trembling and how weak his muscles had become. Great hero. Stick a gun in his stomach and he folds up.

"Is this advice to the lovelorn part of remaking my body or my soul?"

"Both." She turned around and sighed. "And truly, Professor Sean Seamus Desmond, you'd try the patience of an angel, to coin a phrase." She grinned and then caught herself. "How many times do I have to tell you that I do not and cannot deprive you of your freedom."

"Even by being right all the time?"

They both laughed together, good companions again.

"The trick is to force yourself to see the opportunities. Once that happens, you'll do the rest on the strength of your instincts and your hormones."

"Like Laura Taylor." He now remembered the lovely woman very clearly.

"There'll be others. Now take your nap and maybe, just maybe, when you wake up, I'll sing a little for you."

She's going to try to back down on her promise, Sean told himself, as he drifted off into the peaceful sleep that had become a habit since Gabriella Light had intruded into his life. She doesn't want to sing for me. An exhibitionist but a shy exhibitionist.

So he was determined to make her sing. Win at least one encounter from your nosy, pushy, tender guardian angel.

As sleep completed the calming of his nerves that the drink had begun, he heard Gaby—a long way off, it seemed—talking on the phone.

"Captain McNamee, how nice to hear from you again. . . . Oh, we went shopping, as I'm sure your subordinates told you, and then had some tea. Professor Desmond is resting just now, in the other room I might add. . . . *What?* A double murder in the hotel? This is a dangerous city, isn't it? Two foreign agents . . . from what country? . . . I understand that it must be a secret, of course. U.N. missions, I suppose. . . . Yes, that place must make it harder for you and your aides. . . . Killed each other, my heavens how strange! . . . Single bullets to the hearts fired at the same instant? Remarkable. . . . No, I don't see either how it could have anything to do with the attempt on Professor Desmond's life yesterday. That man was a religious fanatic, wasn't he, not a foreign agent. . . . No, I won't alarm him unduly. We leave on the night plane for London tomorrow. . . . He's too poor to fly the Concorde. . . . Yes, thank you very much for calling, Captain."

Right.

He was awakened later from pleasantly but obscurely erotic dreams by the smell of a swissburger drenched in mustard and onions.

He was tucked in bed, dressed only in his shorts. Damn woman thinks she's a nurse.

"Damn sensate paradise," he murmured, "food, drink, and a beautiful woman. It'll spoil me for the real world."

"Be quiet and eat your swissburger."

Her white suit had been replaced by the familiar beige robe.

"What kind of wine do you have this time?"

"Neirsteiner Glock Eiswein, 1976?"

"Fine." He had no idea what the name meant.

"Try some." She offered him a wineglass he had not seen before.

"Oh boy!"

"Like it?"

"Something this good has to be sinful."

"Only venial."

They both laughed together again. Good friends.

"How long does this cruise last?"

"Eager to get rid of me?" She tilted her head to one side.

"No, just eager to get rid of folks like our two friends this afternoon.... Anything on TV about them?"

"Not a word. If people don't exist, they can't be killed, can they?"

"We're covering up?"

"Your government is covering up. I don't identify with them."

She leaned over him to fill his wineglass, revealing a snowfall of white lace under her robe. A couple of hundred dollars of lingerie for one quick glance.

No, she makes them or steals them or buys them with her phony money that isn't phony and then probably sends them back. And like women of our species she dresses more for herself than for me.

"Nice lace."

"Thought you'd like it. Better than the wine?"

"Greatest wine in all the world. Really!"

"Totally?"

"Out of sight bitchin'!"

More laughter.

"Are you still going to sing for me tonight?"

She sat on the chair opposite his bed and drew her robe tightly around her.

"Do you want me to?"

"Sure. I need some entertainment after a hard day—new clothes, long walk, difficult museums, painful lecture, gun in my belly...."

"My songs are *not* entertainment."

"Is Mozart?"

"All right, maybe a little bit entertaining, in an intellectual sort of a way.... I'm not sure you'll like them."

Truly a shy angel.

"I liked the music on Stacey's tapes."

"Poor imitation." She snapped her fingers.

"Is she a threat?"

"Stacey? To whom?"

"To you? To me?"

"She's irrelevant." Gaby waved her hand and bounced out of the chair. "Her sponsors are another problem."

"Will they break your code?"

She looked at him startled. "Figure out what our communications mean? You must be joking, Sean. What is her computer support? Fifth generation? When you get to the two hundredth generation, maybe you'll understand a few of our verbs."

"Stacey won't get anything out of her work?"

"Full professor.... Concert in a half hour. In the parlor. Dress up. Suit, tie, fresh shave, everything."

"Heavy duty!"

"When was the last time an angel sang for you?"

"Gabriella!" he called as she bounded out the door, eager to prepare for a concert he was sure she was dying to give.

"What?" She was back in the bedroom, frowning impatiently.

"Sit down."

"An order?"

"And from an inferior species too. I'm practicing for dealing with strong women."

Her frown deepened. "Wolfhound ordering the nobility around?"

"Gentry. Now sit down like I said."

"All right"—she smiled—"I'll let you win this one. What do you want?"

"Is your species happy?"

She sighed and her shoulders sagged. "What makes you ask *that?*"

"All this energetic running around. I mean for me, sure, but for all these patterns you want to protect."

"That's a fair question." She bowed her head and lowered her eyes. "You're no one's fool, Seano Jaymo, no one's fool at all at all. Do I seem unhappy?"

"Driven, sometimes."

"I may not be typical."

"I'm sure you're not."

She breathed deeply. "We're fellow pilgrims of the absolute, as I've said before. What can I tell you? I sound like a New Yorker, don't I? After a species achieves reflectivity, is there really any difference in the average level of happiness?"

"You tell me."

"We have a lot more fun." She would not look up at him. "Running around the universe all the time. And a lot more interests and a lot longer life...."

"And higher expectations and responsibilities, or these patterns of goodness and beauty that seem to obsess your kind?"

"So it cancels out, I suppose." She stood up, tightening the belt on her robe. "Your Augustine, a terrible man in a lot of ways, said our hearts are restless till they rest in Most High. All reflective species, I suspect. Fellow voyagers through the mysteries and surprises of the universe."

"Uh-huh."

"Answer your question?" She walked much more slowly toward the parlor.

"I guess."

"It really doesn't, you know." She leaned against the door frame. "You wanted to know if I were happy, didn't you?"

"Illegitimate questions to a guardian angel?"

"No."

"Well?"

She winked at him. "I like my work. Now get dressed for the concert."

Damn clever answer.

And, to whoever or Whoever might be lurking across the street in St. Paddy's, I don't like the deck you've dealt me this time, fella. Not one bit.

Not that whether I like it makes any difference.

He didn't have his new suit yet or the made-to-order shirts, but he did don one of the color-coordinated ties and splash himself liberally with the scent she had chosen. Does too smell like a whorehouse, even if I have never been in one.

He sat next to the massive TV set in the parlor, which he hadn't dared turn on because he didn't believe in his heart of hearts that it really existed. Any more than he believed that Gabriella Light existed.

The lights in the parlor dimmed; an aroma of incense—he could call it nothing but heavenly—wafted across the room. A bright beam, from no discernible source, illumined an ornately carved ivory stool that had materialized on the other side of the room.

Solemn high, he thought.

Then Gabriella appeared. Wow! he did not dare say the word aloud. It would be like talking at the consecration of the Mass. He applauded lightly.

She bowed solemnly in response and seated herself on the stool. Then she began fiddling with the strings on her ancient Celtic harp, the way harpists always do.

She was dressed in a glittering white gown, long sleeves, clenched at the waist and flowing to the floor, with a deep V neck that plunged almost to her navel. At least. An elaborate jeweled choker circled her neck, and in her silver gray hair, done in a new wave for the event, she wore a tiara that would have made the Queen of England envious.

No paste either, he was willing to bet. Not that they were stolen from anyone permanently.

Probably the harp had been borrowed for the moment from a safe in Trinity College in Dublin.

This crowd had class when they engaged in larceny.

"Irish harp," he murmured, wondering if Sister Intemerata would slap his wrists for talking in church.

"When in Rome," she sniggered nervously.

She's worried about pleasing her audience! Well, I suppose all performers are, once their species reaches—what was her word?—reflectivity.

All fellow pilgrims of the absolute do worry about how they are about to perform before an audience. Even angels.

Desmond's First Law.

Then she began to play and sing, first in one voice, then in many voices, her notes running the full range from deep bass to high soprano and sometimes deeper and higher. She was often a pure and lonely voice gliding over the water, and then a mighty choir of eight parts dancing back and forth in intricate harmonies.

Her first song was to Stacey's tapes what a Handel oratorio is to a kindergarten ditty.

And she got better.

Her overture reminded him of water, trickling brooks, bubbling creeks, rushing streams, rolling rivers, surging oceans, pounding rain storms, crushing waterfalls, glistening dew, a drop of water on a thirsty tongue.

Then silence.

He forgot to applaud.

"Too much, Seano?"

"Oh no."

"Sure?"

"Who's clinging now?"

Rich laughter. Then a song about laughter—no, a song of laughter—no again, a song like laughter. All the joy and merriment, all the comedy and delight, all the jollity and mirth in the world—no, in the universe—merged into one wild, hilarious ecstasy.

"Not bad." He sighed appreciatively when she had finished. "With a little practice you might be the Spike Jones of your generation."

"Humf," she sniffed. "More?"

"Oh yes."

There were no words in her songs, not as he knew words; rather, sounds which said more than words.

The next piece was dirge, so sad, so melancholy, so bittersweet that tears poured down his cheeks. A funeral march for her spouse? Most likely but he would not ask. No way. Then so subtly, so imperceptibly that he hardly knew what was happening the dirge turned into a triumphal hymn of hope and glory.

"Analog sounds, I suppose," he said at the end of the melody, for want of courage to make direct comment.

"Certainly, the sound patterns we hear are translated into waves that your ear can perceive."

"What if you sang them in the original sound patterns and didn't modify the waves, would they be too much for me?"

"Oh no, Jackie Jim"—she chuckled—"you wouldn't hear anything at all. I have to translate them. One more?"

"As many as you want. It beats Johnny Carson."

"One more will be enough. This is hard work. Let me see . . . I know!"

The final song seemed to combine all the others and add something more—it was funny, sad, impertinent, angry, outraged and outrageous, saucy, implacable, crazy. It ended with a nutty little fillip that seemed to say, not without affection, "To hell with you."

"Bravo, bravo!" Sean stood up and applauded.

"Not so loud!" She bowed complacently, her face and chest flushed with pleasure. "You'll wake up our neighbors."

"Wake them up, why it's only"—he glanced at his watch—"midnight? You've been singing for three hours?"

"And nine minutes."

"The last was a self-portrait."

"Fresh!" She strummed a protest chord on the harp.

"It was too."

"All right."

"You wrote them all, I bet?" The Eiswein bottle, replenished, was at his side with two goblets; he filled them both.

"We wouldn't put it that way." She accepted a goblet from him. "We are a bit more communal than your species, but in your terms that statement contains the truth."

"I suppose that anyone of your gang can do the same." He toasted her.

She acknowledged the toast. "Certainly not. Some have some talents, others have others. My, this is good wine."

"You made it. You ought to know."

"I did not make it." She sipped it again. Perspiration was running down her face and neck. Hard work indeed. "Not exactly anyway."

"I would assume that you are one of the better, uh, composers in your gang?"

"A fair assumption," she said, nodding politely.

"So why don't you spend all your time composing instead of flitting around the universe, meddling in the affairs of other species?"

She disappeared from view for a moment. Where there had been a woman in white with an Irish harp in one hand and a glass of wine in the other, there was nothing at all. Indeed, the whole parlor vanished and Sean was back in his own bedroom.

I think I am in real trouble.

Then everything twinkled back into view. He expected to see an angel analog in a white dress with deep cleavage at the height of cherubic fury. Instead, she was sitting on the ivory stool laughing hilariously.

"Wonderful, Seano, absolutely wonderful." She chortled. "Put the nosy, pushy angel woman in her place. Touché and again I say touché." She lifted the wineglass for more.

"You won't get drunk on me?"

"On this stuff?" She gulped the Neirsteiner. "Don't be absurd."

"You're not angry anymore?"

"How can I be angry at my sweet little wolfhound?" More laughter.

And she evaded my point quite nicely.

"I'm just practicing on how to deal with the next nosy, pushy, vulnerable earth woman, I meet."

"Of course. Hoisting me on my own petard, I believe is your saying. All right, Jackie Jim. It's late and you have a long day before we catch our plane tomorrow night. To bed!"

"Anything you say, lady. No, wait a minute." He emptied the wine bottle. "One for the road . . . I have one more question before this most interesting day is over."

"Ask." She had found a towel somewhere and was wiping her face and neck and chest.

"What was she really like, the kid I mean."

"What kid?"

"Mary of Nazareth."

The movement of the towel stopped. Gaby's big eyes grew even bigger.

"She was wonderful, Jackie Jim, dazzling. My songs made you think of her?"

"I guess. I don't know why else the question came up."

She sighed. "Your species says all the right words about her, but you don't know what they really mean. I've never met anyone quite like her. In any species. . . . You know what she is really like? Monsignor Blackie's ivory statue."

"Saucy?"

"And cute and funny and adorable and smart and respectful and tough as they come. God knows she had to be. And I've already said too much."

"Fair enough. . . ."

"The pictures," she said, as she removed the tiara from her hair, "are terrible, mostly anyway. They're almost as bad—"

"As the pictures of you?" He finished for her.

"I didn't say that." She unfastened the choker. "And I won't be tricked into saying anything more. Now go to bed, I have work to do."

"I just want to go on record as saying that the pictures don't do you justice."

"To *bed*!"

"Yes ma'am!"

Work, he thought as he fell to sleep. She can conjure up a tiara that would sink an aircraft carrier and an Irish harp that's at least fifteen hundred years old and a gown that's worth five big ones at least, and she still has to work.

His last sensations were of an argument being conducted in melodic angel voices. He could pick Gaby out. She was, he was certain, trying to resign from her responsibility for him. He was, she seemed to be saying, too much of a handful altogether.

Well, I'll drink to that.

The others, gentle, soothing, reassuring, were telling her that she was doing just fine. No problem.

Gradually the Gaby voice calmed down. All right, I'll keep on trying.

He didn't know whether to be glad or sad.

On the whole, he whispered to no one in particular, I think she's right. Send someone else. I don't deserve the first team.

Maybe I need it.

Sean Desmond could not sleep.
No sweetly sexy dreams about surrogate Gabys tranquilized his
nervous system.

He turned over in the bed, wished he had not given up smoking and tried to review the data like a good scientist should.

There was someone in the room beyond the parlor—which
didn't really exist—who claimed to be an angel, indeed hinted that
she was the angel Gabriel and that she had sung at Bethlehem on
Christmas night. She had also announced to Mary the coming of
her child. She had been present at Masurian Lakes and during the
Cuban missile crisis. She was Lucifer's mate before that good spirit
had died. She was, if her story was to be believed, still mourning
him. She had, apparently, saved Sean's life, by disposing of two
would-be assassins, quite abruptly and with chilling efficiency. She
had also captured a fundamentalist loony, after intercepting his
bullets by the rather simple ("easy when you know how to do it")
trick of catching up with them. At a speed marginally shorter than
the speed of light. She had frozen two hit men into a position in
which they would kill each other, with single shots mind you, the
moment she unfroze them.

Without so much as a "by your leave" she had instructed the "adorable" Blackie Ryan to process his application for a marriage annulment.

She was engaged in remaking him, body and soul—fixing his posture, outfitting him with new clothes, advising him about attracting women.

She argued that she was not taking away his freedom, but her demands, instructions, suggestions, requests, opinions, and recommendations were almost irresistible.

No, totally irresistible.

She said she was protecting him from mysterious enemies and that he was part of some important and apparently gracious pattern at work in the world. But she wouldn't tell him who the enemies were or why he, of all people, was so important.

She was also a strangely vulnerable sort of angel who seemed almost to need his help and who responded positively—sometimes—to his attempts to reassure her.

Even docilely.

And sometimes with robust laugher.

She was gorgeous. And she seemed to think that he was "more than presentable" and, for a member of an inferior species, perhaps even deserving of love.

By a woman seraph? Because that's what I think she is, one who stands before the face of the Most High (her title for God, not mine, because I'm not sure you're even there) in the sense that she sees the patterns with special clarity.

She claimed not to be the pure spirit of Sister Intemerata's religion class but a corporeal being whose energy patterns were not perceptible by human senses, though she seemed to admit that most of the phenomena which had been attributed to angels were the work of herself and her friends.

They are interested in the world and in some ways protective of it because it aids them in a comparative study of their own evolutionary process, one which is more mature than ours but not totally dissimilar from it. And even more because they seemed to have been programmed by their evolution to seek out and protect emerging patterns of beauty and goodness, even when the task of protecting them seems well-nigh impossible.

She is one of their better composers; no, bet she's among the best. But she flits about the cosmos when she should be home writing more music. Claims that she likes her work, but I don't think she does, not anymore.

She even wants to get out of the Desmond Project.

Desmond Sanction?

Desmond Caper?

Desmond Conspiracy?

Desmond Diversion?

That's probably the best. Alliterative.

She asserts that she is in fact the precise kind of creature about whose existence I speculate, mostly as a put-on, in my acceptance speech. And has more in common with such creatures than she does with Sister Intemerata's angelic spirits.

She sings the most wonderfully appealing and seductive melodies.

Obviously, patently, clearly—choose your own academic buzzword—she doesn't exist.

Can't exist.

Let us consider the possibilities.

Rationally and scientifically like the good scholar that I am:

1. I am in a deep coma in some New York hospital after a terrible auto accident.

2. I am drunk and have been drunk for weeks. A long celebration of my Nobel Prize.

3. I have lost my mind, arguably the loss is permanent.

4. This is a brief dream that seems like several days because I'm still in it.

Check one.

Or as many as apply.

Why not?

On the other hand, why?

Why should anyone want to kill me? I'm a harmless academic, a phony Irishman who has failed at everything in life except biology.

And the science of biology at that.

I don't believe any of this.

And yet I sit at a dinner table, eating roast beef with her and drinking Côte de Rhône for which she pays as though it were perfectly natural to have an ice goddess guardian angel protecting me.

I listen, quite calmly, while she discusses her responsibility for the end of the modern world in August of 1914. I am enthralled by her singing. Despite myself, I take careful note of her wisdom on how to improve my love life. I drink a toast to her in white wine that is almost as good as sex.

Better than a lot of the sex I've had.

Someone is playing a trick. It's all illusion, a very clever game.

Lucifer's woman, indeed.

He threw aside his blanket; despite the fact that he was wearing shorts—in itself a disturbing datum—he put on his battered robe, and strode to the connecting door.

It had not been there when he checked in. Yet it must have been there. Doors do not appear suddenly in the walls of modern luxury hotels.

Hypnotism, that's what it was.

Nonetheless, he pushed the door open very gently.

Sure enough a large and comfortable parlor—on a floor on which, his directory of the hotel assured him—there were no suites. Nor should there be an ivory stool, lifted probably from the Greek rooms of the British Museum.

He tiptoed across the manifestly nonexistent parlor, its soft carpet caressing his feet, and carefully pushed farther open the door to what must be an adjoining bedroom—left invitingly ajar.

There was enough glow from Manhattan to see that she was not in the room. The bedclothes had been arranged to make it look like someone had slept there, but there was no one in it.

And no sign of either the white gown or the beige robe she sometimes wore. No harp.

No pantyhose or lingerie, not that there was much under that gown.

No jeweled choker or tiara.

No Giorgio scent.

Indeed, no sign in the room or the closets or the bathroom that anyone had been there.

Well, he said decisively to himself, that settles it.

He was not quite sure, however, what it settled.

He touched the mattress of the bed. No trace of warmth.

Illusion. Clever illusion. Now I must figure out who is behind it.

He turned and walked back to the door of the parlor.

"You really ought to get some rest, Professor Desmond," she said sleepily, as he was slipping through the door back to his own room. "Since you won't fly on the Concorde, it will be an overnight flight tomorrow. You know how you act on airplanes."

He knew what he would see even before he turned around.

Gaby in her bed, the covers pulled up to her waist, silver hair shining in the Manhattan glow. She was wearing a dark blue sleep T-shirt with red trim and white letters—rather inelegant covering for such a splendid torso.

"Yes ma'am," he said, like the dutiful chimp he was. "Flight's today, though."

He slipped back into the parlor and stumbled to his own room.

He shut the door and made sure that it was closed tight, though he did not lock it.

Why bother?

Then he became aware of the words on the fabric against which her sumptuous breasts and firm nipples pressed:

OUR LADY OF ANGELS.

A Catholic school some place.

And a very nice touch.

Comic.

Go Lady of Angels! Beat Sacred Heart!

Yes, this illusion was a comic illusion.

Shivering with a sudden chill, he jumped into his bed and pulled the blanket up to his neck.

Tomorrow, I'll find a religious goods store and buy a rosary.

And maybe a St. Christopher medal too.

Maybe every medal they have in the fucking store.

"Don't be so jumpy," Gaby snapped irritably. "You certainly must know that I can prevent the plane from crashing."

"You admitted that your kind make mistakes. Remember Sarajevo."

"Keeping an airplane in the sky is a lot simpler than preventing a war. And I see I shouldn't have told you about that mistake."

"If you're not infallible," he pointed out, hoisting his traveling bag nervously on his shoulder as they waited in the first-class check-in line, "and you admit that you're not, the plane could still crash."

"Nonsense," she said crisply.

They were waiting, with very little patience, to check in for the TWA flight to London. They had first-class tickets but the first-class counter was closed.

"Typical of a capitalist airline," she sniffed.

"Your idea to fly first class," he whined.

The first-class tickets were the beginning of their long day of bickering. Gaby pleaded with him to change to the Concorde. It would be a quicker and more restful trip.

Absolutely not. I can't afford it.

I'm paying the expenses, I told you that.

I could use the money for my children's college education.

They'll win scholarships and don't worry about them anyway.

No Concorde and that's final. I thought you folks respected the freedom of your pet chimps.

All right, no Concorde.

So she went over to TWA and changed their tickets to first class. I am not going to have you complaining all night about a Turkish baby vomiting in your lap.

Then they fought about packing.

In her view he would wear his new suit and cashmere coat, pack his three shirts, three extremely brief undershorts, a swim-suit (that he thought was too skimpy, a protest which she found greatly amusing), three pairs of socks, three ties, assorted sundries, pictures of his daughters, books and papers, all in his two Gucci bags: one over the shoulder and the other in his hand, with plenty of room left in the handbag.

A formal suit for the awarding of the prize. Shirts to wear with the suit, black ties, sport clothes, sweaters to wear in Cambridge—everyone wore sweaters in Cambridge because central heating was a rarity—umbrella, raincoat, extra shirts and underwear.

They have stores in London and Stockholm.

You won't buy them, you'll make them, like you make your own clothes.

I do *not* make them.

A likely story. What about the clothes I've packed?

Packed badly, I might say. You don't need them. Sensible people travel light. Remember how long you had to wait for this enormous old suitcase at La Guardia.

How did you know Laura Taylor was good in bed?

It's obvious. Why are you still thinking about that?

You guys are voyeurs, that's what you are.

We are *not*. Your coupling is of no more interest to us than that of...

Irish setters?

You're being difficult because you're afraid of airplanes.

You don't have to be my guardian angel to figure that out.

He lost the argument—ungraciously, of course. His old luggage and clothes simply vanished.

If you really want that crap back, I'll get it when you come home. Not the tux, however; I'll be a laughingstock among all the other guardian angels if I permit you to ever wear that again.

Crap is not a nice word for an angel to use.

It happens to be the only appropriate word in your unimaginative language.

Well, it was one way to take your mind off the prospect of sealing yourself in an aluminum tube for seven or eight hours and permitting some idiots to propel you through space at the rate of approximately half a thousand miles per hour.

There was not, he told himself, anything to *really* worry about. She could surely hold a plane up in the air indefinitely if she chose to do so. And, since on the basis of proven performance, she could move at a rate only slightly less than the speed of light, she could surely catch him a fraction of a second before he tumbled into the hungry Atlantic.

But . . .

But what?

Just but; that's all.

He had to wear his new suit, of which he had become inordinately proud, because a Nobel Prize winner had to look like a Nobel Prize winner when he disembarked in London. She dressed comfortably if expensively in black T-shirt and black jeans and a yellow cotton-and-silk long jacket that looked like an oversized windbreaker and was priced at $700 on the page of *Bazaar* from which she copied it or stole it, however she produced it.

It was a crowd-stopping ensemble.

What will they think of a would-be laureate that gets off the plane with that in tow?

They'll think he has good taste in women.

Expensive taste.

Grudging laughter from both of them.

If she was his wife, or better, his mistress, he reflected, he would have fucked her four or five times that day, partly out of aggravation and partly out of affection and admiration.

Instead, she was his guardian angel. Thank God.

I guess.

If you're there to thank.

Isn't that the way to keep such a woman in line? I mean if she's a human woman, not an angel?

Likely to make her worse.

A point.

The phone rang off the wall. Congratulations, farewells, names to look up, Fee and Dee bursting with pride because there had been a whole day in his honor at St. Ignatius, requests for interviews from magazines and newspapers, lecture invitations, a rumor that *The Leader* was going to do an exposé on him.

"Do you think they really will?" he asked anxiously.

"So what's to expose? Your sex life?"

"That's nasty."

"It is and I'm sorry. Don't worry about them. They're useful only for the bathroom."

"For me, not for you."

Much laughter. "Got you baffled, don't I?"

The lecture invitations were turned down. You don't like to fly, you have work to do, and Fee and Dee will need help with their homework when you come back.

People was politely refused. It will give Moaning Mona another chance, and they are merchants of envy anyway.

Ditto for *USA Today.* The McDonald's of journalism, and that's probably not fair to Big Mac. And innocent of ethical restraint.

Good sports page.

Fine. When you're elected to the NFL Hall of Fame you can give them an interview.

Yes, Mother.

So it went.

If I am supposed to search out a wife who is like her after this game is over—and I gather that's the game plan—there's going to have be a lot of fucking to protect my male ego.

Well, nothing wrong with that.

I hope.

So finally they arrived at the check-in counter. The bored woman clerk demanded their passports.

"Doctor Desmond and Doctor Light?" She glanced from one to the other.

"That's right."

Gaby, he noticed, was wearing her ring again. It would suggest to those who saw it either that she had other commitments or that she and Sean were seriously involved.

Well, she knows best.

"Upgraded to first class?" She typed their names into the computer terminal.

"That's right."

He let Gaby deal with the ticket agent, because she would do so anyway.

"Yes, I see." The woman searched the screen uneasily. "Any luggage?"

"Carry-on." Gaby gestured to the four small bags.

"Believe in traveling light, I see."

"Goes with the name."

The woman nodded, either ignoring the pun or not catching it. "One moment please."

She walked away from the desk and through a door behind her.

"What's that about?" Sean answered.

"Trouble," Gaby said glumly.

The ticket agent returned with two tall, lean men in business suits, one brown, the other dark blue: look-alikes with closely cropped dark hair and receding hairlines.

"Spooks," Sean whispered.

"Your spooks," Gaby nodded agreement. "Ollie North types."

"Doctor Desmond?" Brown Suit pretended not to be sure which was which, even though their pictures were on the passports.

"Yes."

"I'm afraid we have a little problem with passport formalities. Might we have a word in private?"

"What's wrong?" Sean demanded uneasily.

"Nothing serious I assure you, sir." Blue Suit smiled agreeably. "Nothing that should interfere with you catching your plane if you will bear with us for a few moments. Just follow me please."

"Certainly," Gaby replied for both of them.

"It won't be necessary for you to accompany us, Doctor Light," Brown Suit said, "your passport is in perfect order."

"I'll come anyway."

"I *said*"—Blue Suit being tough—"that it won't be necessary."

He was favored with a Gaby "look" and, despite considerable pained resistance, managed to say, "Very well."

They were conducted into a small windowless room behind the ticket counter. A gray metal table stood in the middle of the room, two chairs on one side of it, one chair on the other. A telephone and two briefcases rested on the table.

Both men sat behind the table.

"I'm agent Spence," said Blue Suit.

"And I'm agent Cliff," said Brown Suit.

"Please sit down, Dr. Desmond." Spence glanced up at Gaby, as if trying to figure out how she had managed to get into the room. "I'm sorry, Doctor Light. . . ."

"I'm quite capable of standing, Agent Spence."

The temperature in the room went down ten degrees.

"We're going to miss our plane," Sean protested nervously.

"I don't think that will be necessary," Cliff waved his hand, "if we can obtain a little cooperation. The problem is, Doctor Desmond, that you seemed to have neglected to renew your passport. It expired two weeks ago." He showed the book to Sean. "See, it says November fifteen of this year as the expiration date."

Sean glanced at the passport in astonishment. The permit had another year to run, of that he was sure. But the date had been smudged so that the last number of the year was hard to read.

"No," he said carefully, "I think you've made a mistake, Agent Cliff. It's the date of next year."

"I'm sure not." Spence pulled a stack of papers from one of the briefcases on the table. "We checked in our files and it is certain that your passport expired. You can always apply for a new one, but that takes time and I assume that you don't have time now."

He removed the passport from Sean's hand and laid it on the desk in front of him.

"Doctor Desmond," Gaby said icily, "has a lecture in Cambridge the day after tomorrow and then must go on to Stockholm to receive his Nobel Prize."

"So we understand." Cliff withdrew another stack of papers

from the second briefcase. "That's why we would like to work something out. I'm sure you both understand that the laws of the United States are very strict on passport matters."

"You smudged it," Sean shouted, "you fucking bastards smudged it."

"Very well, sir." Spence pushed his papers back into his briefcase. "If that's the way you feel about it, I would suggest you apply for another passport. Perhaps the Agency can get it to you in time for your Nobel Prize."

He stood up. Cliff lifted Sean's passport from the steel table, put it in his briefcase, zipped up the briefcase and stood up too. "Sorry we could not have worked something out."

"May we see your IDs?" Gaby asked, her hands jammed into the pockets of her expensive jacket.

"If you wish." In one motion the men produced plastic cards from their jacket pockets.

"Passport Agency." Gaby glanced at the cards with scarcely veiled contempt. "May we have Doctor Desmond's passport back?"

"Sorry, ma'am, that won't be possible." Agent Spence smiled thinly.

"Come on, Spence, we both know better than that. You have no right to his passport."

Reluctantly Cliff removed the disputed passport from his briefcase and laid it on the desk again.

Gaby picked it up. "Why doesn't everyone sit down? You too, Dr. Desmond."

Sean was not even aware that he had risen at the same time the two government agents had risen.

Tapping her chin lightly with the passport, Gaby sat at the corner of the desk. "Langley, I presume?"

"Certainly not!" Spence flushed brightly.

"Sure." Gaby grinned. "Let's put the cards on the table because we very much want to catch our plane. What do the spooks out at Langley want to know?"

"We are not spooks," Cliff barked.

"Sure and I'm Oliver North." Gaby put the passport back on the table. "Let's have it guys; what are your questions?"

"We want to know about Doctor Desmond's involvement with Doctor Stacey Reid."

"We want to see a copy of his Nobel acceptance speech."

"We want him to agree, in writing"—Spence pulled a long document from his briefcase—"to ask certain questions for us and to observe certain phenomena for us when he is in Europe."

"Only minor matters," Cliff cooed reassuringly.

"Project Archangel, I assume?"

"We don't know what you're talking about." Spence had begun to twitch, first a muscle in his neck, then one above his right eye.

"Doctor Desmond?" Gaby cocked an eyebrow.

"My relationship with Dr. Reid is my own affair." No one laughed, though Gaby rolled her eyes. "I will not submit my acceptance speech to the government, and I'd sign a pack with the devil before I put my name on this crock of bullshit."

He winced after he had said "devil," thinking what it would mean to Gaby. She only rolled her eyes again.

And winked.

"So I'm afraid you have your answer, gentlemen."

"Then Doctor Desmond"—both agents stood up as if on signal—"will not be able to leave on this flight," said Spence.

"And, I can confidently predict," Cliff added, "he will not be able to go to Stockholm to receive his award. Perhaps"—he leered faintly—"you can accept it for him, Dr. Light."

"Why not?" Gaby asked innocently. "This passport is brand new. It was issued only last week."

She offered the little book to Spence. He flipped open the cover, glanced at it, did a double take, and seemed to unfold like a wet newspaper.

"What the hell!"

Cliff grabbed the document, looked at it, and crumpled into his chair.

"This is impossible!"

"Look in your computer output." Gaby pointed at a sheaf of papers sticking out of one of the briefcases.

Fingers quivering, Spence pulled out the continuous feed packet and began to thumb through it.

"Give it to me," Cliff barked, "you've got the shakes."

But he was not much better at finding the right page.

Finally he pointed at a name toward the bottom of a sheet.

"My God, she's right!"

"But it couldn't be. Only a few minutes ago . . ."

"May we go now?" Gaby was most demure.

"NO!"

"Why not?"

"There's fraud here someplace!" Cliff jerked open his tie.

"Or witchcraft, maybe?" Sean had begun to enjoy himself.

Gaby frowned her disapproval, but her eyes were dancing.

"You can't leave, that's final."

Gaby retrieved the passport and gave it to Sean. "I think we're going to walk out of this room, find a New York police officer, put in a call to my good friend Captain McNamee, and tell him that we are being harassed by two men impersonating State Department employees."

"Don't leave this room." Spence reached for what Sean feared might be a shoulder holster.

Don't do it, fella, or your wife will be a widow. My assistant doesn't like kids who play with guns.

"Why don't you answer your telephone?" Gaby pointed at the silent black phone.

It rang.

Spence, one hand pressed against his forehead, grabbed it.

"Spence here. . . . Yes sir. . . . No sir. . . . Nothing sir. Following orders, sir. . . . Senator Cronin, sir? . . . No, of course we don't want to explain the project to her subcommittee, sir. How did she find out, sir? . . . I know that it's none of my business, sir. . . . Yes sir, right away sir. . . . Yes sir."

"Toodle-loo, Agents Spence and Cliff." Gabby entwined her arm with Sean's. "Pleasant dreams!"

"But, sir"—Spence was babbling—"the passport changed its date while they were here in the room!"

"Let's go to the boarding gate." Gaby tugged at his arm. "You'll have a minute or two to call Monsignor Ryan and thank him for the quick action the Cardinal's sister-in-law obtained for us."

"We have to retrieve our tickets and get boarding passes."

Gaby reached in her purse and produced both tickets and passes.

"And our bags."

"Right there." She gestured at the foot of an escalator where four Gucci bags waited patiently.

"I'm getting a headache."

"We'll get you an aspirin or something once we're on board. Do hurry, we have to call that adorable little priest."

"Who needs a phone? You didn't use one in there."

"Of course I did. Do you think I shouted?"

"There was only one phone in the room—I'm walking as fast as I can—and you never left the room."

"Didn't I now? Here we are." She waved the tickets at a cabin attendant. "Does Doctor Desmond have a minute to make a phone call?"

"Two." The young woman beamed. "We're honored to have him aboard."

"Don't spoil him worse than he already is. Here, darling, let me make the call."

She shoved the phone into Sean's hands, naturally without pressing any of the buttons. The witch was having the time of her life.

No wonder she said she enjoyed her work.

"Father Ryan."

"Blackie, Johnny Desmond, a minute to get on the plane, I'm calling to thank you for turning Senator Nora loose on the spooks."

"Indeed."

"It was just in the nick of time."

"The inestimable senator, to say nothing of my noble Lord Cronin, has a distinct distaste for spooks. As I told your admirable aide, the good Doctor Light, when she called an hour ago, the assignment would give pleasure all around."

"An hour ago?"

"Indeed. Bon voyage, Johnny. The annulment document has been filed, by the way, and is making progress."

"Huh? Oh yes, sure."

"Mike the Cop continues to supervise your worthy daughters, the esteemed Dee and Fee."

"Thanks, they're waving me on board. Gotta run."

"Indeed."

Dazed, no longer sure where he was or why he was there, Sean Seamus Desmond permitted himself to be led on board and to be seated with the attention appropriate for a reigning monarch.

"Blackie said you talked to him an hour ago. Before we met those two spooks. Did you know they were laying for us."

"Not really." She was totally satisfied with herself.

"But how . . . ?"

"Oh, I played a few little simple tricks with time."

"With TIME!"

She nodded. "Nothing really very difficult when you know how to do it. Relativity, that sort of thing. You're too frazzled to understand it now. Poor Jackie Jim has had such a hard day. He should have a nice sleep before the big old mean airplane thing takes off and scares him to death. He won't even"—her finger touched his chin—"know it's taking off, bad old airplane thing."

Jackie Jim did indeed fall into sound sleep, a sleep as usual populated by images of Gaby's breasts and belly and thighs.

But not before he wondered how anyone, even an angel, could mess with time.

"That crowd isn't waiting for me, is it?" Sean Desmond pointed at a knot of twenty men and women, some with cameras and others with microphones and recorders, beyond the passport checkpoint at Heathrow's new Terminal Four. "After my pleasant and restful flight across the Atlantic, do I have to face them?"

"Pleasant, restful, and *safe*," she corrected him. "Unless there was a rock star on the plane, which I doubt, they *are* waiting for you. You'd better get used to it, Seano, you're a celebrity."

She handed the two passports to the rather dour British immigration inspector and smiled. He stamped both of them without even glancing through and smiled back.

"You love every second of this, don't you?" he accused her.

"I told you that I enjoyed my work." She led him away from the passport control toward the waiting band of journalists.

"And you're an imp."

"So long"—she giggled—"for you to figure that out."

"I bet you embarrass your kids with your antics."

"Sometimes." She poked him affectionately in the ribs. "They're proud of me just the same. . . . This is not Professor Sean

Seamus Desmond, the Nobel Prize nominee, ladies and gentlemen, this is his twin brother Liam Brendan Desmond. He'll answer all your questions, however."

He was asked about his wife's comments in the *Enquirer*, about his daughters' reaction to the prize, about the attempted assassination (with difficulty he resisted the temptation to ask in response: "Which one?"), about the conflict in Northern Ireland, about what he thought of the United Kingdom, and about AIDS.

On the last three questions he opposed violence, praised the U.K. (with fingers crossed), and hoped for a cure and a vaccine against AIDS. He was pushed as to whether he thought AIDS was a divine judgment on homosexuals.

"I'm not sure there is a God." He gave his standard answer, although he was less and less sure since one of those who stand before the face of God had intruded herself into his life. "But I presume that, should She be, Her aim is more accurate. He would not have hit innocent children with hemophilia, for example."

"Is that all, ladies and gentlemen?" Gaby asked authoritatively. She had smiled and nodded her head in approval at his answers, proud of her handiwork in having remade him into an artful celebrity.

"One more question, if you don't mind, sir," begged a large man who looked just like G. K. Chesterton. "In your remarks at the American mission to the United Nations, which we saw here, you were discussing a possible evolution toward mind. Some have said that the psychic and occult phenomena that are of so much concern to many today are a harbinger of such evolution. Would you care to comment?"

"It may take several more leaps—over millions of years, I would suppose—before we are able to clearly distinguish between what are fashionable epiphenomena and what are central to the underlying directionality."

Figure that out, friend.

"Do you believe there are channeling spirits among us, or even aliens?"

"I never met one." Which was, he realized after he had said it, an outright lie.

"Would you approve, sir, of the attempts of some governments to enlist such aliens in their military effort?"

Beside him Gaby stiffened.

"I was unaware that such efforts were being made."

"They are, sir, even here in the U.K. Private initiative in Mrs. Thatcher's era. A scheme [he pronounced it "sheem"] to establish contact with aliens for purposes of military and political intelligence, and for information about how to accelerate our own evolutionary progress. It's called Project Archangel, I'm told."

"Such matters," he said, groping for the right words, "are far beyond my competency as a scholar. As a citizen, I find them offensive and would oppose them. I also suspect that the aliens, should there be any, might well resist a draft. Finally, Superman exists only in a comic strip that is older than I am and in one of your Mr. Bernard Shaw's plays."

"Thank you, Doctor Desmond."

Gaby guided him through the crowd to the taxi stand in front of Terminal Four.

"Was that an accident? That last set of questions?"

"What do you think?"

"I'm beginning to believe that nothing is accidental. British intelligence?"

"More likely someone with sources inside."

"I'm not sure I believe in angels"—they climbed into a taxi—"saving Your Reverence, of course. I know most of my colleagues will think I've lost my own mind if I hint about such beings in my talk. Yet all the intelligence services in the world are trying to recruit you folk."

"It would seem so." Gaby was withdrawn in deep thought.

"Are you somehow dependent on us, like that guy suggested?"

"Hardly." She patted his arm, a now familiar gesture. "That doesn't mean wishful thinking would not make it so."

"Do you think they might have caught on to you?"

"Could anyone seem more earthy?"

"I guess not."

The rest of the trip into central London was conducted in silence as Gaby continued her deep thinking and Sean gawked at the city, drab and unfriendly in the dim light of a brief December day.

Their suite in the Grosvenor House on Park Lane seemed an authentic suite, not one put together on the spur of the moment by angelic powers.

Their bags were deposited by a grinning black bellman in the middle of the parlor. "These two sure are light," he said.

They ought to be, Sean noted to himself, the woman carries hardly anything at all with her.

Still lost in thought, Gaby produced a ten-pound note for the young man—her wad had been transmuted from crisp new American bills to crisp new British bills. Sean was not even surprised anymore about this sort of trick. Strictly minor league.

"Off to the Reform Club for a luncheon address." He looked at the typed schedule she had produced for him—without any obvious access to a typewriter.

"You go by yourself this time, I think." She doffed her costly yellow jacket and pulled her T-shirt over her head, a wife casually undressing after a long trip. "I think I better fade into the background for a while to see what happens."

"I'm not sure I like that idea."

"Becoming attached to me, Seano?" She grinned crookedly as she kicked off her jeans.

She was wearing black underwear, of course, probably no more than a hundred and fifty dollars' worth of lace tap pants and bra. The latter was solid and businesslike as was appropriate for her large breasts.

"I feel safer when you're around." Sean tried not to stare.

"I didn't say I wouldn't be around." She was oblivious to his fascination. "If you need me, merely say, 'Please, Gaby,' and I'll swing into action."

She scooped up her shirt and jeans and strolled toward her bedroom.

"Would pretty please be better?"

"With sugar on it." The door to her room closed, leaving Sean Desmond alone in the parlor with four flight bags, two of them empty.

If I opened that door, he thought to himself, the bedroom would be empty. I bet she's gone into consultation with her buddies. Something odd is happening. She is not the bashful, retiring type.

He glanced at his watch, which someone, not he surely, had

updated to London time. He should get his suit, his only suit, pressed before leaving for the Reform Club.

Then he looked at the trousers of the suit. Already pressed. She was not so preoccupied as to forget the little niceties of angelic behavior. Life without Gaby would be difficult.

In the taxi on the way to the Reform Club, he pondered two undeniable and contradictory truths:

1. He still did not believe any of it. She didn't really exist. She wasn't an angel sent to protect him from an odd assortment of characters who wanted to kill him.

2. Their relationship had become so casual as to be taken for granted. They were of different species, millions of years separated on the evolutionary process, but still, male and female; they had settled down to an intimacy which was not quite easy but certainly matter-of-fact.

There might be a hint of some law of evolutionary directionality in that latter truth, some clue to a basic truth that would apply to all species in which reflectivity and sexual differentiation had developed.

He had better not mention that theory in his talk to the Royal Swedes. He would surely be locked up.

How could it be phrased?

Once reflectivity has been achieved, males and females, of whatever species, tend to like one another and fear one another.

Desmond's Fourth Law.

Well, he pondered on his mighty insight, you won't win a Nobel for that one.

Something at the impromptu press conference must have bugged her. She was giddy and cheerful when we got off the plane and abstracted and worried since the conference. It must have been the question about aliens depending on humans. She dismissed the possibility and she doesn't lie. But still, something is worrying her.

Outside, the rain was pouring down. He was glad he was wearing the London Fog trench coat which had materialized in his closet. A London Fog in a London fog. Maybe I can write a haiku about that.

Lunch at the Reform Club—where Daniel O'Connell himself

presided at the door in a full-length portrait—was for the upper brass of the British scientific establishment. It was something like a round table back at the university, as self-important and narcissistic, but less pompous and more witty. His cleverness, a liability at the university, was an asset with these men.

So he had a good time and, in the camaraderie of a group of men who liked and admired him, forgot about his lovely and absent assistant.

Maybe she was only a figment of his imagination.

Hastings, who was to be his host the next day at Cambridge, had come down for the lunch. He was an elderly, tweedy man with long hair, a discouraged mustache, and sparkling eyes, a Nobel laureate of fifteen years before.

"Rather miss your charming assistant, old chap."

"Doctor Light? Oh, she thought she might be out of place at an all-male lunch."

"Quite discreet, eh? I saw her on the telly, you know. I do hope she will join you tomorrow."

"I presume she will. . . . You saw her on TV at the airport this morning?"

"Yes, indeed, on the midday news upstairs before you arrived. Quite striking in that yellow jacket, don't you know?"

"I suppose. . . . Did they show that odd question about recruiting aliens, I mean from other worlds, for military purposes?"

"I believe they did," he whispered back, glancing around the table.

"What was that all about?" Sean had lowered his voice to a whisper too.

"This is not quite the place to talk about it, old chap." He continued to glance about nervously. "Perhaps tomorrow."

"Classified stuff?"

"And, it would seem"—Hastings stabbed anxiously at a slab of roast beef—"dangerous. Very dangerous."

They were swimming in the pool of the Grosvenor House Hotel, Park Lane, London SW1.

Gaby was sumptuous in a skintight white maillot, high-cut thigh, naturally. One of the models in the *Sports Illustrated* swim-suit issue had worn it, he was sure. Angelic white, he presumed. Every head in the pool area turned when she walked in. Which is what they were supposed to do.

The high-thigh suits left little of the model's ass to your imagi-nation. So you risked wearing one only if your flesh was both am-ple and solid. Naturally, Gaby could run the risk. Her firm figure and silver hair were a devastating combination.

Which, again, is what they were supposed to be.

Her hair was always perfectly groomed without any effort. And she never did seem to need a shower. She did, however, keep the rules of the pool and head for the shower room before they swam.

"Gorgeous ass," he observed when she reappeared.

"Vulgar man," she replied, both displeased and flattered. Con-siderably more flattered than displeased.

"Sumptuous, I might add."

"Classical." She was the old contentious, cheerful Gaby again. Whatever her problems had been, she must have straightened them out with her buddies.

"Only a half inch too broad. Maybe three-quarters."

"It is *not*!" She turned on him furiously, then grinned, knowing she was being baited.

"I won't ask what it's an analog of."

"Of what it's an analog," she corrected his grammar. "And you'd better not."

"You get high on wearing the most expensive human fashions, don't you?"

"Putting them on my analog," she corrected him. "Why shouldn't I? It's fun. We're not prudes."

"I noticed. . . . The analog is not you, but then it's not not you either. Right?"

"That's one way of putting it."

"Then I repeat my comment: it's a great ass."

He playfully swatted that delicious part of her analog's anatomy.

"Sean Seamus Desmond," she pretended to be furious. "How dare you do that to"—she lowered her voice—"an angel."

She then picked him up and, like he was a bathtub toy, heaved him into the pool. Before the attendant at the other end could turn to see what had caused the noise, she dove in after him.

"If we play that game," she whispered in his ear, "I'll win."

"I don't doubt it for a moment." He swam rapidly away from her.

Dangerous woman. Person. Whatever.

The perfect assistant to a Nobel laureate.

Does she sleep with him? he imagined one reporter asking another.

I'm sure she does, the other (female) would reply, though I can't imagine what she sees in him.

If you punks only knew what she really was, Sean said defensively to the imaginary journalists.

Sexually she continued to affect him as much as "Venus" dug up from a Stone Age cave, though she was much better put together. How do you get horny over an angel?

But he had become dependent on her and, in a weird sort of way, fond of her. It was more pleasant to have her around than not.

And she certainly precluded the possibility of his chasing after women.

An angelic function with which Sister Intemerata would have been quite happy.

So, despite the disapproving stare of the cockney lifeguard, she shoved his head under the water at the deep end of the long, narrow, low-ceilinged pool, an English hotel architect's idea of masculine luxury. Women had been admitted by cultural norms which the artist who painted the half-naked Chinese women on the side wall could not have imagined.

Sean, an old hand at dunking women, fought back. He pushed her head into the water and held it there, wondering if you could drown an angel.

You couldn't, it turned out. Mostly because they were as strong as a Patton tank. She broke his grip with a quick, deft movement and came up sputtering and laughing.

"Angels can breathe underwater," she chortled.

The lifeguard walked in their direction, like an English bobby approaching two undisciplined kids on his beat.

" 'Tis the woman that's to blame, Officer," Sean said in his Irish brogue.

"I can see that, sir." He was admiring the woman and wondering how to reprimand her effectively.

Gaby produced one of her "Gaby" stares. The lifeguard seemed content that somehow—he didn't quite know how—his problem had been solved. He paused and then walked back to his chair at the other end of the pool. He continued to admire her.

"That should take care of him." Gaby smiled benignly.

"Stupid Limey," he muttered.

"Please, don't use the brogue here," she pleaded. "They don't like the Irish all that much ... and he's a nice boy."

She shoved his head under the water again. He ducked away and tackled her. She kicked at him, but not very hard. Handicapping herself to give the cute little chimp a chance.

So they frolicked like two teenagers without any worries in the world.

Except that most teenagers were burdened with what they thought were horrendous worries.

"Enough." Panting for breath and hanging on the side of the pool, Sean finally struck his colors. "You win."

"Draw." She pretended to be exhausted too. "Now do your lengths."

"What?" he protested. "I've already had enough exercise."

"Jackie Jim," she said sternly, "swim!"

"Yes ma'am."

So he swam. She was, after all, the boss, draw in their wrestling match or not.

Like Jacob, he had wrestled with an angel. And he had not been smote on his thigh yet.

"How do angels die?" he demanded, after he had swum the half mile she had ordered.

Sitting above him on the side of the pool, a towel around her shoulders, she hesitated as she always did when he probed for information about her species.

"Second law of thermodynamics mostly. We grow old and begin to fall apart. We have managed to control most infectious diseases that harm us, though occasionally a microbe appears that causes problems. . . . Accidents, of course."

"Accidents?"

"Which one would encounter in certain places. There are some disadvantages in our complex and intricate energy patterns. When they are disrupted by such intrusions, they do not easily reactivate."

"You die?" he asked, wrapping a towel around his shivering shoulders.

"Indeed we do," she said somberly. "Now hurry with your shower, we will barely have enough time for the noon train to Cambridge."

Like all things English, the shower arrangements were quaint; Gaby had to go up a flight of stairs and Sean down a flight. It took a long time for the water to warm up. So-and-so's believe in cold showers.

As he luxuriated in the warm water and covered himself with soap suds, Sean wondered about proton blasts. Angels ought to stay away from cyclotrons. They probably knew that.

Another male entered the shower room, a strong-man type with bulging muscles and a thick black beard. Sean, embarrassed as always by his puny physique, turned his back.

Could have gone back to the room for a shower, but herself doesn't want me to catch cold.

Chills don't cause colds. Well, maybe she knows something I don't.

A vise closed on his neck and a huge paw covered his mouth. His breathing stopped as though someone had turned off the switch.

The bearded bastard is killing me.

He fought, as successfully as would a rag doll in the hands of an angry three-year-old.

This time his life did rush by. Fiona and Deirdre ... no one at all to take care of them, except Mona. Dear God, no.

Where was Gaby? What was the magic phrase that was supposed to draw her back?

He couldn't remember.

The act of contrition from Sister Intemerata's class came back to his mind, as consciousness faded. He couldn't quite remember how it went....

He was on the slippery floor of the shower room. The hot water was beating down on him. Fool must have bumped into the shower knob. A hideous bearded face loomed above him. The last sight he would see.

Where was his damn guardian angel when he really need her?

I am hardly sorry— No, damnit.... Heartily ... never could keep it straight. Throat on fire, chest collapsing, heart about to explode.

Then he heard the sound of a trumpet, loud, angry, violent. Suddenly he was free, desperately gulping for air.

A naked Gaby was swinging the giant through the air, her hands holding his feet, as effortlessly as he used to swing a yo-yo.

God, she is beautiful.

The killer's head cracked against the shower wall and split in half. Blood smeared the shower wall and rushed down to the floor, mixed with the hot water, and poured over him. Roll away from the water, you damn fool.

Then the bearded man's blood and body disappeared, just as had the killers in New York. Heavenly garbage disposal.

Gaby wrapped him in her arms, like he was a boy child with a scraped knee. On the whole, a consoling place to be.

"Thank the Most High you are still alive."

He tried to say "I'll drink to that," but the only sounds to come from his mouth were inarticulate gurgles.

Then they were in his hotel room and he was under the covers of his bed.

We didn't take the elevator, I swear we didn't take the elevator. She's able to move instantly from one place to another. A little less than the speed of light. And carry me with her. Why did we have to fly the Atlantic in that damn airplane?

Gaby was still becomingly unclothed. So was he. Too sick to be embarrassed. Probably didn't mean anything to her anyway.

Her hand touched his throat, her large brown eyes were soft and gentle. The pain went away.

Then her hand moved to his chest. Pain there ceased too.

She's healing me.

"Why didn't you call?"

"Forgot the magic words."

Now his hand was in hers. Terror left him. Shock effect too. It's as though it never happened.

"Nice trick," he said, his voice almost normal.

"Special treatment for Irish wolfhounds." She smiled, a loving mother replacing an angel of death. "Now sleep for an hour. We'll take a later train."

She folded him into her arms and held him like a baby against her chest.

Wonderful, he thought. Protected by the best mama in all the world. Nothing to worry about.

She touched his head and he sunk into restful sleep.

None of it really happened, he told himself as the lovely body, now quite naked, appeared to grace his dreams once more. Not as perfect as the nude Gaby. Human flaws and hence human. He did not worry about the dreams anymore.

He knew that all doubts were over. Gaby was real. So were those who had determined to kill him.

Only on the train to Cambridge did he begin to wonder about what had happened in the shower room.

They were alone in a first-class compartment. He was pondering his notes for the talk that evening before a late supper at high table. The college was alleged to have the best claret in western Europe.

Gaby was listlessly watching the barren countryside under a cold December sun that was racing rapidly for the warmth and comfort of the horizon.

"Was there anyone else in the woman's shower with you?" he asked as they sped through the waterlogged East Anglian countryside.

"Two American teenagers. Plagued by silly adolescent modesty, I might add. Wanted to stare at me without being caught at it. And most embarrassed when I stared back. Typical of the prudery of your species, especially its females. Actually, they had rather cute little bodies." She smiled approvingly. "Pert young tits. Not the kind which would appeal to you save as a momentary curiosity. I made a few changes to enhance and preserve their appeal."

"Like my posture?"

"Except in such matters it is not even necessary to touch them. They will spend a fair amount of time in front of mirrors for the next week trying to figure out"—she chuckled—"whether they've really changed."

"They must have been surprised when you disappeared."

She turned away from the window. "I didn't actually disappear."

"You were in two places at once?"

"Not exactly."

"Don't I rate an explanation?"

She considered him thoughtfully. "You should discover us through doing the appropriate scholarly research instead of playing on my sympathies. . . . In any event, it would be a mistake to conclude that I am confined to that portion of my energy field that creates the analog. Our size is not the same as yours."

There were giants in those days, the scriptures said.

"So you can give the impression of being in one place while you're mostly in another, messing with the mammary glands of children you find transiently attractive?"

"Something like that." She turned back to her examination of the East Anglian countryside. "I was not," she added as an afterthought, "messing around. There was excellent reason for preserving the attractiveness of those young persons. No law against killing two birds with one stone . . . to use your folk wisdom."

I'm still not convinced that it's all not a damn clever illusion.

Yes, I am. She's real all right. I'd like her not to be real, but she's real.

"Do you mind if I ask why that man, now safely reduced to chemicals, wanted to kill me? Is it impertinent to wonder what this is all about?"

"Not impertinent"—she turned wearily to face him again—"just a waste of time. As I have said with all the clarity at my command, there are certain people who want to dispose of you. We cannot ascertain their reasons. Not quite random violence, but the next thing to it. We intend to take care of you until we find out. Is that enough?"

"No."

"Well." She turned away impatiently. "For the present it will have to do."

He considered the handsome woman next to him. She was wearing brown leather slacks and a sand brown suede jacket and carrying a matching midcalf raincoat. Undergraduate garb, fit right into the Cambridge scene. Till you looked at the price tags and realized that no motorcycle punk could afford the four-figure costs.

Beautiful, timelessly beautiful. With a thousand moods and faces, all of them attractive.

No, I don't want you to be an illusion. I don't want her ever to go away.

Only please make those other people go away.

He put his hand in his pocket and clutched the rosary he had purchased in the religious goods store at St. Paddy's. He decided that he would do something he had thought of before but never tried. Superstitiously, he pointed the cross at Gaby.

It didn't make her disappear. He didn't think it would.

"Gaby ..." he began tentatively.

"Yes?" She turned on him impatiently.

"I don't mean to be a nuisance."

"You're never a nuisance, Jackie Jim. Always sweet and cute. Sometimes..." She smiled her maternal smile.

"... A bit of a pest?"

"I was going to say a bit too curious. But then you're a scholar, aren't you? A Nobel Prize winner, which is why I'm here. Anyway, what is it?"

"You were magnificent with your clothes off."

"You were able to notice, were you?"

"You know damn well I was!"

"All right." She colored as she did when a compliment broke through her defenses. "I'm glad you liked me. To tell the truth, I figured you might. But it's only an analog body, as you know."

"A faint shadow?"

"A pale hint." She grinned crookedly. "You should see what I'm really like. Only, of course, you can't see what I'm really like, can you? That's what this whole crazy adventure is about—a species which has evolved so far that it is imperceptible to human senses."

"Mostly."

"Right," she agreed. "Mostly."

"But you guys don't wear clothes like we do?"

"That is hardly necessary or possible."

"So there's no comparison in your species for nakedness in ours?"

"A prurient question, Professor Desmond, if I ever heard one."

"We're a prurient species. I gather you're not."

That was, he had learned, an excellent way to get to her. All you had to do was suggest that they were lacking in something that humans had, and she became very defensive.

"We are too prurient," she said hotly, "more powerfully and more effectively than you are."

"But differently?"

"That's what I've been saying."

"So it's all right for me to ask my prurient question."

"Maybe it would be better for you to read your *Financial Times*." She gestured at the paper on the seat opposite them. "Its pink color is mildly prurient, I should think."

"Yes ma'am."

"That devoted wolfhound expression will get you nowhere."

"Yes ma'am."

"Besides, I have probably told you too much about us as it is."

"I don't think your friends told you that when you had your big confab yesterday. They told you you were doing fine and you should continue to follow your instincts."

She considered him cautiously, suspiciously. "In an earlier age you would have been burned at the stake as a wizard. But"—she shrugged—"my hat, if I were wearing one, is off to you, Professor Desmond. That was remarkably accurate."

"Hangdog but ingenious wolfhound, huh?"

"To answer your question, as you probably have surmised already, we do have a way of disclosing the inner self to those with whom we are intimate, and it is not totally dissimilar to your custom—interesting, I will admit—of undressing for the other. A way of revealing our depths that is both an invitation to love and a reward for it. Does that answer your question?"

"The possibility drives you guys up the wall?"

"It sure does!" She laughed happily. "What would be the point in it if it did not?"

"I'm not surprised." He settled into his round table omniscience mode.

"Beast!" She swung her fist at him, deliberately missing. "You are too surprised. Everything about me surprises you and delights you."

"If you say so."

They laughed together, friendship and fun restored at the same time.

"So you want to know how it works?"

"I'm curious."

She pondered. "Well, strictly speaking, you couldn't see it at all. I mean, if I were to attempt to lure an unattached angel to combine with me—a very serious procedure given what I've told you about our propensity to pair-bond—and I were to do it while I am watching over you, you would not even know it was happening."

"I could see your mood change, couldn't I?"

"Probably not. If I want to hide my emotions from you, I can do it very effectively. By the way"—she winked—"I am not engaged in such behavior at the present."

"Uh-huh."

"The closest I can come to you seeing me as I am was the pattern of lights you witnessed in the hotel room in New York. That did not seem to amuse you."

"It was lovely, but I wanted to see a person who went with the voice."

"The lights are a person," she said with a sigh, "but I understand you. Which would you prefer?" The woman next to him was replaced briefly by an enchanting drama of lights. Then the woman returned.

"I like them both, but it's a lot easier to travel with you the way you are now."

"I thought as much." She stopped, thinking hard. "Well, I can demonstrate a not-too-distant reflection of our self-disclosure, one you can see, more or less, from my other mode. If you want."

"Of course I want."

"Some cautions?"

"Sure."

"First of all"—she was counting on her fingers, obviously intrigued by the experiment—"you should not expect the result to be erotic in your sense of that word."

"I've given that up."

"I bet. Secondly, it may be too much for you, too much color and light. It may scare you terribly. I'll stop before it does any harm, but I should warn you."

"No problem." His heart was pounding.

"Thirdly . . ."

"Your friends advised against it?"

"On the contrary, they advised in favor of it. They argued that it would make my work easier because it would bind you to me for the rest of your life. Not as a mate, but as someone who was strongly linked to me. Do you want to risk that?"

"Let's not kid each other, Gabriella Light, you'll always be part of my life if I survive whatever these enemies are up to."

"Oh"—she waved her hand in dismissal—"don't worry about them."

"You want to bind me that way, don't you."

"Very much indeed. I . . . can't help but be, ah, emotionally invested in you."

"So what are we waiting for?"

"You're sure?"

"Absolutely."

The woman next to him vanished and the intricate and exquisite light patterns returned, dancing, bubbling, frothing, whirling. Red, green, and blue mostly, with a restless variety of combinations of patterns.

Yep, that was Gaby all right.

The dance became more intense, more excitable, more challenging. The colors flashed on and off, at one moment almost invisible and then at another moment so bright that he was forced to close his eyes.

He felt himself soaring out of the old railway carriage and into the stars. This was not a good idea after all. I am out of control now. Maybe we should stop.

It was too late to stop. The color points vanished and were quickly replaced by a massive waterfall of gold and silver that seemed to fill the whole of creation, sweeping everything before it, absorbing, caressing, drinking in, destroying.

Too much beauty, too much goodness, too much grace. All the beauty there ever was and there ever would be and still more. That was the real Gaby, stripped of all protection and all veils, infinitely vulnerable and infinitely appealing. The waterfall continued to flow, its power growing in intensity. He belonged to it forever. But so it belonged to him. There would be no turning back. Not ever.

God was noting this strange nuptial and writing it down forever in His book.

God?

No longer, in the face of so much beauty, could he doubt.

Tears were streaming down his face. He thought he would die of so much beauty. Then the waterfall became dimmer and slowly faded away.

He was back in the railroad carriage, sobbing in his guardian angel's arms.

"Are you all right, Jackie Jim?" she asked anxiously.

"Sure. . . ." He searched for his voice. "It was real nice, kind of like a fireworks display on the Fourth of July."

"Brat." She released him.

"It was the real you, Gaby," he said softly. "I'm happy to meet you."

"I'm glad you liked me."

No doubt about it, Seano, you're in for it now. You're bound to that one forever. It'll be nothing but trouble.

So what happens next?

19

"I'll leave you two to your laureates' conversation." Gaby placed her sherry glass on the stained antique table in John Hasting's "digs" and stood up. "I'll drift around town, look at the Cam River in the dark and do all the things a tourist in Cambridge is supposed to do."

"Must you really leave, my dear?" Hastings was being polite. It had been made clear that Dr. Light was invited to the lecture of course (as was anyone who might walk in off the streets of Cambridge), and to a glass of sherry with Professor Hastings beforehand, but that Hastings expected some time alone with Professor Desmond before the lecture and that high table was for Professor Desmond alone.

"I really must." Gaby blew a kiss at Sean. "I'll see you both at the lecture. Remember to stand up straight."

"Do I have any choice?"

She rolled her eyes, which in this case meant that, no, since she had touched his shoulder, he had no choice at all. It would take years of effort to recover his old familiar slouch.

They both watched through Hastings' first-floor window as

Gaby, hands jammed into her jacket pockets, sauntered off into the early dusk.

"Heh-heh, a remarkably attractive woman." Hastings devoured her with the privilege of the old.

"As a matter of fact, yes." Sean had discovered that "matter of fact" was a fashionable English academic buzz-phrase, especially when uttered in a tone of surprise, indicating that one was "quite astonished" (another approved colloquialism) to discover something that was apparently obvious to others. "Quite intelligent too. One of the finest of her generation. Great future."

"Naked, heh-heh, she would, I think, look like a Rubens nude."

Sean had also discovered that there was no way to explain Gaby. If he insisted that he was not sleeping with her, he would be accorded the same credibility as if he had told the truth—that she was a guardian angel and, arguably, a seraph. One of those who stood before the face of God.

Lucky God, he thought, marking the cautious renewal of diplomatic relations between him and the Deity, a renewal which had yet to generate any signs of delight on the part of the Deity.

"Not quite as much flab," he said thoughtfully, "but then Rubens models didn't have torture instruments such as the Nautilus available for conditioning."

"Quite." Hastings sighed.

Doesn't know what the Nautilus is, Sean decided.

"How old is she?" Hastings did not want to change the subject even though Gaby had by now disappeared into the gloom.

"Older than she would seem, actually," which was as true as anything he ever said. "Still and all," he added even more truth, "she's useful to have around."

Hastings was a nice old man and very clever. Sean didn't mind anyone admiring his Gabriella. Nonetheless, unlike his Jewish or WASP colleagues from the university, he was neither charmed nor awed by the ceremony of the great Oxbridge colleges. If this place had really good claret, as it was alleged, he would certainly drink it. Beyond that, his latent Irish nationalism was rubbed the wrong way by the stuffy, fusty antique gentility of the college. Moreover, he suspected that his Irish origins made him the object of very subtle patronizing; no, he hoped that he was being patronized, so that he could be both offended and outrageous.

"There is no need," Gaby had instructed him when they left their guest room at the corner of the inner quadrangle of the college, "to play the role of the militant Irish nationalist with these people."

"Sure there is," he replied.

"Save it for Stockholm," she ordered.

"Yes ma'am."

They laughed together. Sean was sure that the epiphany on the train would never be mentioned again. Their relationship had entered into a new phase of casual trust that required very little discussion.

"And try not to spill any of Professor Hastings' sherry on your dinner jacket; you don't want these people to think you are a shanty-Irish drunk."

"Hide the truth at all costs."

They laughed in chorus again.

He had been offended by the room—twin beds for Doctors Light and Desmond.

"What if I wasn't sleeping with you?"

"You're not," she said with a giggle.

"I know that, but they don't. And if I were, twin beds?"

"Strange people, the English," she agreed.

"How can you stay warm in twin beds without central heating," he demanded.

"Bring a guardian angel"—she pulled a brown beret out of her shoulder bag and adjusted it on her head in front of the cracked mirror—"who can modify the energy waves."

"Excellent idea."

They had laughed all the way to Hastings' "digs."

"Wonderful breasts," the old man said, sighing as he replenished Sean's sherry glass. "Heh-heh, marvelous."

They probably drank as much as they did around a place like this to stay warm.

"Pretty good ass too," he added. And you should see her when she does her solid gold waterfall act.

"Well, I suppose we must talk a little serious business before we face the rest of the college?"

The schedule allotted a certain amount of time to womanly anatomy, and then it demanded more serious conversation.

"I think Gabriella is serious business," Sean said, breaking one of the rules and loving it, "but of course I am very interested at the present in your reaction to my work."

"My dear boy," the old man purred, "it is simply brilliant. I've spoken with Hawkings, the physicist, you know. He will be present tonight. Hard to understand him because of his affliction, but he thinks that you're about the same sort of work he is."

"High praise indeed, but we're a long way from a unified field theory in biology."

"Of course, of course, but it is the mystery of purpose you see. Both you and Hawkings have been driven to it by your theories and your findings; that's why everyone is so excited with your work. My generation had—foolishly and prematurely, it now appears—written off purpose, and now your generation has recaptured it."

"Directionality isn't quite purpose." Sean sipped his sherry. It was too good to gulp, though he was tempted to be a bog Irishman and do just that.

"But it is the next best thing, my boy, the next best thing."

"It seems to me that much of the interest—which, candidly, astonishes me—in my work is based on interpretations that go far beyond where I am prepared to go."

How about that for mock humility!

"That's true old chap"—the man's bleary brown eyes twinkled momentarily—"of any good work. There are, as I'm sure you see, two levels of reaction to your work. Among serious scientists you have touched a sensitive nerve: the feeling, if I may say so, that we have been too busy, heh-heh, with the trees to see the forest. You appear at just the right time, when we were almost prepared to consider that possibility, and then with elegance and grace, heh-heh, you force us to do so. Ten years ago no one would have listened to you. Ten years from now no one will believe that your work was not self-evident."

"Wonderful, I think." He wished Gaby were back. He missed her.

"On another level," the old man rambled on, making much sense as he raved, "you appeal to a more popular concern, which in its worst moments is represented by this occult and mystical nonsense but in its better moments also seeks desperately for purpose, although it is not likely to be found, is it?"

"And then there is Project Archangel," Sean said the name easily, as if he were quite familiar with the project.

"Stuff and nonsense," Hastings sputtered. "Damnable non-sense, I would add. I'm surprised"—the old man's eyes, suddenly sharp and penetrating—"that you'd have anything to do with them."

"I certainly don't," Sean replied heatedly. "Even if there were alien intelligences among us, what reason is there to think that we could force them against their will to do our bidding for us?"

"And for private enterprise, at that. I'm Labour of course, but even the Tories around here are shocked at the audacity of the scheme. I'm not surprised they're interested in you, however. Your name is a big attraction and your theory does provide some remote grounds for their plans."

Let me see, there's our side and the other side, and now the private sector. The guys in the hotel were the other side, the two nerds at Kennedy Airport were our side. Was the guy in the shower yesterday the private sector? How can you tell the players without a program?

"Only very remotely, sir." He cradled the sherry glass in his hands. "I have discovered punctuation points in evolution, times of great leaps; my bacteria, under controlled conditions—well, reasonably controlled conditions—leap forward at these points like *Homo sapiens* did perhaps a hundred thousand years ago when suddenly and apparently without warning men with fully de-veloped voice boxes appeared on the scene and soon dominated the world, after four or five million years of our ancestors commu-nicating with various kinds of grunts and snarls and clicks. To say that the next leap or perhaps the ninth or tenth next leap down the line will produce creatures like the aliens that are postulated, for no very good reason I can see, to be among us, is to go far, far beyond the data. Moreover, I think that any attempt to constrain more developed species to do our bidding is foolish and insane."

"Bravo!" The old man applauded. "And I beg you, heh-heh, to say the same thing tonight during the question period and at high table."

"The next thing such fools will try to do," he repeated the thought he had in Chicago after watching Stacey's experiments, "is to constrain God to enlist in their intelligence services. The whole idea of attempting to dominate superior species is blasphemous."

"I wouldn't, heh-heh, use that word at high table, if I were you."

"Naturally not."

It's all absolutely true and I don't believe a word of it. I'm going to come out foursquare for angels in Stockholm. Moreover, I may be the only one on this planet, but I have empirical data to support my theory.

What empirical data!

And I miss her!

"And if there were invisible and intelligent beings on the loose," Sean continued heatedly, "to try to mess around with them ... excuse my American slang, sir ... to try to turn them into our slaves would make Prometheus look like a hidebound conservative!"

"Bravo again! Come now, we must finish this bottle of sherry. It will go to waste if we don't. Waste not, want not, as my mother used to say." He filled Sean's glass again, carefully leaving the dregs in the bottom of the bottle. "The difficulty, as you and I both know well, is that it is very likely that there are other intelligent life forms in the universe and not totally out of the question that some of them may be from worlds rather proximate to ours."

"Possible, of course, sir, but the odds are very small." I'll be drunk when I talk, but what the hell, I have a manuscript.

"I for one think your man Sagan goes too far, but if we agree with Hawkings and others that the raw stuff of life emerged"— Hastings folded his hands and began to talk like an old Anglican bishop, at least the way Sean imagined an old Anglican bishop would talk—"in the tiniest minisecond of the singularity's explosion and that these raw elements of life seemed even to demand rationality"—he shrugged—"and like you I don't believe in God or any of that rubbish—it seems quite gratuitous to suppose that we are the only life process evolving or even the most advanced."

"What do you think the chances are that the life forms would be like us—reflectivity, sexual differentiation, that sort of thing?"

"Don't quote me"—the old man looked around uneasily—"but I very much doubt that the other forms would be all that different from us. None of your vegetables with antennae, heh-heh, if you follow me. If the biopolymers are the same, I would say that there would be a bell curve—that seems to be a constant in the galaxy—with a very narrow standard deviation. I'm not altogether sure that those who say we would not recognize *Homo sapiens neanderthalensis* in a business suit have the best of the argument. But if one of your alien intelligences should appear, I think he would be quite easily recognizable as, well, perhaps one should say a cousin?"

The old man had pretty well figured it out. Had the Project Archangel folks tried to sign him on?

"With or without a business suit." In or out of a brown suede jacket and expensive leather slacks. "This is all interesting speculation, sir, but even if they could perhaps travel close to the speed of light, the difficulty with all such speculation is that these other beings are not likely to exist in our part of the universe, much less lurking around earth where we can eavesdrop on their conversations with sensitive tape recorders."

And surely not likely to appear gloriously naked in the showers of the Grosvenor swimming pool. Right?

Right.

"Bravo! Again I say bravo! Well, we must toddle off to the Great Hall. Can't keep the audience waiting, can we? Your admirers await you. Heh-heh."

Hastings was in the chair for the talk. Two more junior men, Clark and Morely, were the respondents. A young woman, Arden Devoy, was to give the "vote of thanks" at the end. More creepy English ceremony.

Arden Devoy was not creepy, however, Sean concluded as Hastings rambled through an introduction that was supposed to be clever and witty but was actually close to senile. His "heh-heh" produced responses of the same dry, rasping noise from men of his generation in the audience, not unlike the "oh yeah"s at Baptist religious ceremonies.

She was in her late twenties, thin and tiny, with a striking oval face, jet black hair piled on top of her head, and a hint of great sexual energy in her tense body.

It had been too long, he told himself, since he had had a woman, and he wanted this one. From the first second of their introduction, he sensed that she responded in kind.

Why not? Gaby had said he had the right to a private life.

His presentation went smoothly enough, considering that he was well on his way to being plastered. He searched for Gaby in the packed hall, but it was now quite dark outside and the lights in the hall were dim.

Maybe she was having another conversation with her buddies.

The talk itself went well enough. He stuck closely to his technical work and suggested areas of further investigation well within the boundaries of the discipline. The two commentators were pointed but respectful. His reply was modest and charming. The questions from the audience were polite and mostly technical.

One woman shouted at the end of the proceedings, "What about the aliens, Professor? The others among us? Are we alone in the universe?"

"It's not my area, ma'am." He smiled gently. "I don't really know."

"What do you think?"

"I think we are probably not alone, but the data are too thin for us to be confident either way."

Thin, huh? And where is she anyway? I want her to be proud of how smoothly I talked even if I am half-plowed.

Arden Devoy cut in quickly with a skillful and gracious "vote of thanks," which included a quote from an English poet of whom Sean had never heard.

"Wonderful presentation, Professor Desmond." Her eyes were shining as she shook his hand. "Dazzling!"

"Thank you very much, Ms. Devoy."

Hawkings, despite the devastating effects of lateral sclerosis, was a charming and vibrant man. Through his wife, he offered Sean warm congratulations. "Keep it up," he added, with a smile.

"You keep it up too, sir," Sean replied warmly.

"A remarkable man, isn't he?" Arden Devoy was standing so close to him that her shoulder brushed his elbow.

"The Einstein of the second half of the century."

Her eyes flashed appreciatively. "I suppose you're right. Shall we go over to high table?"

"Fine. I'm starved. Which way is it?"

"Come with me, please," she said softly.

Anything you say, lady.

A man should be prepared to take the good that comes from a Nobel Prize along with the bad.

What harm would there be in a small one-night stand. She'd cherish the memory of screwing a Nobel Prize winner, and he'd prove that he was still capable of sex.

Even if he had a hard time walking a straight line across the commons to the refectory.

No one put on raincoats. Macs, as they would call them. Probably just not done, old chap. It was bitter cold and a touch of drizzle was in the air. Not cold enough to snow maybe, but still too cold to spend the night in a room heated by a stove that was old when Victoria was a virgin.

Gaby had promised to modify the energy waves but where was Gaby?

The claret at high table was as good as it had been predicted to be. And his glass was filled as soon as it was emptied. By the time the evening was over, Sean Seamus Desmond, *né* John James Desmond, cultural Irish nationalist and hater of all things British, was prepared to defend all the customs of the old Cambridge colleges—dinner jackets, high table, roast beef and claret, even votes of thanks.

Especially, looking at the color in Arden Devoy's face, especially votes of thanks.

Right?

Right.

Gaby?

Gaby who?

Besides, she was an angel, a guardian angel in fact. Not a spouse. His wife was Mona, Moaning Mona, who was probably in bed with her hairdresser (female), perhaps even now contemplating a return to his bed. But the marriage was to be annulled. Maybe annulled already. He had clout. So, since there was no ring on Arden's finger, it would only be a bit of fornication at the most. Some medieval theologians, he had read somewhere, argued that fornication was only a venial sin.

A generous and benign opinion.

Especially after all that claret.

After dinner and a couple of toasts, he was invited to adjourn to the common room for coffee and port. Arden led him to common room.

"Everyone is pretty well soused by now," she whispered. "The old boys will be asleep in a few minutes. Look at Hastings trying to figure out where the gents is. A sip of port and you can pop out if you want to."

"Thank you, ma'am."

At least he was able to find the gents for himself.

After the first glass of port he and Arden did slip out. He bid good-bye to the men still in the room, but most of them were already asleep. That's what Eliot meant by not with a bang but with a whimper, the end of an evening in a Cambridge common room. Everyone blind drunk.

Gentlemen, the Queen Empress!

Everyone drunk but Sean Desmond and this lovely young creature who was holding the umbrella over his head.

You don't have to be beautiful to be sexy, not even pretty.

Well, even Sean Desmond was a little drunk. But the Irish could hold their liquor better than the English any day—and any night too.

This Arden woman had drunk very little. A woman can't be too careful with her virtue these days.

"Would you care to pop into my flat for a bit of coffee? I'm just down the street."

"Fine. Black coffee, as black as it comes."

"Of course."

Good of her to let him lean on her shoulder. Cambridge provided everything for its guests.

Arden Devoy's flat was indeed just down the street and up a tiny alley and around to the back of a building that looked, to Sean's eyes in the driving rain, like fourteenth century.

"Bit of lightning and thunder too," she said as she guided him up the steps on the outside of the house.

"I noticed."

He hadn't. I'm not that drunk.

Lightning cracked across the sky and was followed some moments later by a distant roll of thunder.

"A long way from us."

"Coming our way, I should think. It's warm and dry inside and I'll have that coffee, black, in a jiff."

"Great." He collapsed into an old chair.

It was a small apartment, neat and colorless, no pictures on the wall, no books. Smell of burnt cabbage, and another, sweeter smell.

A place where a woman slept and ate, not where she lived. Bedroom, parlor, kitchen alcove. Bedroom door closed. Will we make love on that couch or in the bedroom? Will I stay awake long enough to make love?

"Here we go." She poured a cup of coffee for him. "This

should do the trick. Those drinking bouts are bloody bores, especially if you're not used to them. Come, sit on the couch, it's more
comfy."

He stumbled toward the couch and began to sip his coffee. He
knew in his sober moments that coffee does not remove alcohol
from your bloodstream. It does not create sobriety but only the
illusion of sobriety, enough of an illusion that if you are in the presence of an apparently admiring young woman you begin to lecture
while she listens with adoring eyes.

When she offers you a "wee tad" of port and a "bit of cheese"
to go with the coffee, you accept because that's the courteous
thing to do and it facilitates your lecture—mostly about the jerks
at the round table at your university.

And the dummy, Moaning Mona, to whom you were once
married.

Lightning was still leaping across the sky, visible through the
single window in Arden Devoy's parlor, and thunder exploding
ever closer.

With the cheese and the port—much inferior to that in the
common room—came sex, direct, simple, furious sex.

Arden put her arms around him, pushed her body up against
his, and kissed him frantically, like it was going out of fashion. Her
hands sought his hands, drew them under her sweater and against
her bare flesh. Not a whole lot there, but hot and pleasurable just
the same.

I am being attacked, I am being raped, Sean told himself, and
isn't it wonderful. Now all I have to do is to work myself into the
mood. It shouldn't take long.

Has that damn woman angel made me impotent?

Then the whole world went blurry.

"Out so soon?" Arden's kisses continued. "Pity, I thought we
might have had another romp before I made my call. Ah, well,
maybe there will be a chance at the big house."

She slipped away.

What was the big house?

She picked up the phone next to the couch on which she had
been more or less devouring him, and dialed a number.

"Henry? Arden. Well, we have him. No, no one saw us leave.
Yes, he's rather good in bed actually. We had a round of it before
the chemical in my port knocked him out. Another chance when

you lads are finished with him? Oh, that would be jolly! No, I don't
mind if he's a bit bloodied. Make it more interesting. The woman?
Haven't seen her since she left old Hastings' digs. I don't think she
matters much. They still want her, eh? Couldn't find her on the
streets? Pity. Probably can drag her out of the guest room tonight.
Yes, I know you want to avoid that if possible. The question is, do
you want her enough? We have the man as it is and he's the important one, isn't he now? All right, pop on over and we'll collect him
and go off to the big house. Promise you won't hurt him too much?
Remember you said I could watch?"

A trap. Aren't I the clever one to figure that out.

Arden rushed into her kitchen nook and returned with a saucer and a bit of wire. She dipped the wire into the saucer and
breathed deeply.

"That's better now, isn't it? Nothing like a quick snort to settle
the nerves. Care for some, luv?"

I didn't have as much of the drug as she thought. But I can't
move, so what good does it do that I know what she's up to?

"Sure you do, I knew you would." She held the snifter against
his nostril and clamped her hand over his mouth. Sean's body
caught fire and soared into space like a space shuttle rocket; he
rode the lightning bolts that were crashing around him, higher and
higher and higher.

He was filled with peace and joy and contentment. What need
was there to worry? Everything would be all right, wouldn't it
now?

"See, luv, isn't that better than booze? It'll keep you happy till
Henry and his boys come to pick you up. Don't go 'way. I'll be
right back."

Suddenly the rocket engine stopped firing. The space shuttle
lurched over and plunged toward the ocean below. Terrible nau-
sea combined with elation. He wanted to vomit, but he was too
happy to try.

Arden Devoy returned to the couch, her hard eyes shining
brightly. "It'll be a bit rough for a while, darling, but you'll be sensible and tell them all they want and then you and I'll play before
they take you away. Let's play now, shall we?"

She returned to her assault on him with ferocious intensity.
Wild with joy and pleasure, Sean tried to respond, but he could no
more kiss her than he could vomit.

I'm in trouble. I feel wonderful but I am in deep trouble.

There's a code I'm supposed to remember. If I can just say it or even think it, they won't pop over to take me to the big house.

He wanted to fight off the monster who was assaulting his lips. Sadist. He also wanted to devour her with his serenity. Death and love, how could they be separated?

Waterfalls of gold and silver cascading all around him.

Let me see, what was that angel's name?

Angel? Who needs an angel when they have angel dust?

A crack of lightning and a role of thunder very close. Thor? No, that was a Teutonic god.

I'll never drink again.

Then the name came as another gash of lightning seemed to cut through the tiny alley.

PLEASE, GABY!

The doorbell rang.

A little less than the speed of light.

"Oh, damn, just when I was beginning to get on to it. Just a minute, Henry, you're early, damn you!"

"Good evening," said a blessedly familiar voice, "I'm Doctor Gabriella Light, Doctor Desmond's assistant. I wonder if he might be here."

"Ah, do come in Doctor Light," Arden sneered. "We've been half expecting you. I'm afraid your precious Nobel laureate is bombed out of his mind. Pity, eh? I was just trying to have some fun with him."

Another flash of lightning and an immediate drumroll of thunder.

"Here she is, boys," Arden crowed. "The one we've been waiting for. The mysterious Doctor Light!"

Three huge men, bearded and in black jackets, emerged from the bedroom door. "Pleased to meet you, Doctor Light," the first one sneered, pinning Gaby's arms to her side. "I think we're going to be real good friends."

The second man grabbed her legs and the third began to bind her with a thick rope.

"It won't do you any good to scream," Arden said. "No one can hear you up here."

Gaby was not, however, screaming.

Trumpets blared somewhere outside, an urgent call to battle.

Then lightning struck the house.

The lightning bolt crackled through the apartment, bathing it in blue light and filling it with the smell of burning sulphur.

That's what hell smells like, Sean thought as the pungent odor assailed his nose.

It's all happening in slow motion. Isn't it nice I had some coke to help me watch the show.

The thick blue light flowed through the small rooms like a stream in flood coursing through a forest. It swept away furniture, destroyed lamps, brushed over bookshelves, wiped out carpets. Its movements were lazy, indifferent, careless, a monster roaring toward the sea of electricity that awaited it in the sky.

Then the blue flood crashed into Gaby like a filing drawn to a magnet. It abruptly halted its progress, a river at flood level hitting a dam, assaulting it, gathering strength for another attack, hurling all its furious power at the unexpected obstacle.

For a moment Gaby captured the lightning bolt and it captured her. She turned into a wildly dancing pattern of blue lights, reeling, jumping, diving, cavorting, buzzing furiously. Then the surging electricity became her docile servant, ready for her slightest command. Little sparks of blue light buzzed around her energy patterns, now mostly glorious crimson.

Angry bees rushing out of a hive.

Then the blue light leapt from her crimson patterns to the men who were clutching the space where she had been. It surged from her like floodwaters released through a sluice gate. The men who had tried to bind a seraph were hugging a thunderbolt.

Too bad for them!

Their skeletons glowed beneath their flesh, like luminous dials in the dark. Hideous screams of agony rent the room. The skeletons turned red, then purple, then incandescent white. The skin and muscles seared away from their bones; then the bones themselves disappeared like a Roman candle going out at the end of its wild spin on the Fourth of July.

The lights went on in the room. There was only Gaby, calm and cool, hands in her jacket pockets. She removed her hands, dusted them one against another, and looked around the room. "No fuss, no mess, no trace. I always like a neat and clean job."

She reached out and touched Sean's forehead. "You'll never make much of a drug addict, Jackie Jim," she said affectionately.

Some, not all, of the devils who had been pounding hammers against his skull suspended their work.

A woman was still screaming somewhere in the room.

Oh yes, what was her name? Arden something.

She was cowering against the wall, most of her clothes torn away, ugly and degraded in her terror.

Gaby picked up the decanter of port, sniffed it, and put it into the screaming woman's hands. "Drink it," she ordered.

"It'll kill me," Arden pleaded.

Gaby's eyes were hard. "Drink it!"

Arden began to drink, throat convulsing hysterically.

"Please," she begged.

"Give her another chance," Sean murmured hoarsely.

"I fully intend to." Gaby cocked an amused eye at him.

"That's nice." We're both softies.

"Keep drinking," Gaby's finger pointed at her, "until I say stop."

Abjectly Arden continued to gulp down her own poison.

"That's enough." Gaby took the decanter from her hand. "You'll have a nice long sleep and wake up very sick, and"—her eyes bored into Arden's—"you won't remember a thing that happened tonight."

Arden fell slowly toward the floor. Gaby caught her and eased the fall. Then she lifted the limp body on to the couch, like a mother lifting a sick child. "Poor dumb little bitch child."

"That's nice," Sean repeated.

"It's one way to cure cocaine addiction," she said. "A lesson she won't soon forget. Why don't I add to it? Stomach pumping is a good negative reinforcement." She reached for the phone. "Good evening"—suddenly a very "upper" British accent—"I'm dreadfully sorry to bother you, but there is a young woman at number 3B Convent Street who has attempted suicide. If you hurry, you might be rather successful at saving her life. Thank you very much."

In the distance Sean heard fire alarms, frantic, worried, insistent.

She hung up the phone and smiled contentedly. "Just a minute, Seano. I must see what I can do about this smell of burning flesh. Rather sickish, isn't it?"

She inhaled deeply and then exhaled slowly. The room was filled with the scent of citrus blossoms.

"There, that should do it, we'll leave the door ajar so that the smell will dissipate before the fuzz arrive. Coming, darling?"

"The men from the big house?" His mouth still felt like heavy leather.

"Henry, you mean? I'm afraid that Henry and his friends had a dreadful accident on the way over. Car was hit by a bolt of lightning, careened off the road, and into an old oak tree. The tree was not badly damaged. And oddly enough at the very same instant another bolt hit the 'big house' itself. The fire engines you hear in the distance represent the shire's ineffectual attempts to save it. I'm afraid Project Archangel is rather short of personnel at the moment. We really must be going, darling. How do you feel?"

"Terrible."

"There are some hangovers"—she sighed—"that even angels can't cure."

As they left the apartment, lightning was still flashing in the east. The whole sky to the south was lighted with a rosy glow. Yet more fire equipment was rushing toward it with frenzied wailing. The big house doubtless caught in seraph fire.

On the rain-drenched outdoor landing, Gaby turned back toward the parlor and extended her hand like a priest at the end of Mass. "God bless, poor dumb little bitch child. Now listen to me and listen carefully." Her eyes glowed with maternal affection. "I will tolerate no more foolishness from you. Understand? When you are released from hospital, you will settle down and act like a decent and intelligent young woman. Whatever you may think about yourself, you are worth loving. Or I wouldn't waste my time with you. Again I say, God bless you, you poor stupid little ninny."

Almost as solemn, Sean thought, as an ordination ceremony.

When these seraphs loved, they really loved—even if no one else could see anything particularly lovable about the object of their love.

Much later in the cramped quarters of the guest room, Sean Desmond began to recover his health and his sanity.

"You spared Arden's life?"

He was lying under two blankets, an ice pack (produced on demand) above his forehead. Gaby had, as promised, modified the temperature of the room so that it was, as she said, quite toasty.

"She was the only one where I had an option." Gaby shrugged her shoulders. "Now, I suppose, I'm responsible for her. It is possible that the traumas of the night will jar her out of the condition into which she has sunk. She may prove useful in later years."

Cynical as she sounded, she did not fool Sean S. Desmond for one minute. He had seen the maternal love in her eyes as she blessed the poor stupid little ninny. You're as soft-hearted as I am.

Gaby was lying on top of her blanket, wearing a silver and gray sleep teddy that seemed to match her hair. Three hundred dollars, Sean estimated. "I assume," she had said when she emerged from the bathroom in it, "that this will be more satisfactory than my Queen of Angels T-shirt?"

"The way my head feels," he had moaned, "you could be wearing a mumu."

"That will be the day, Jackie Jim." She had reclined on the bed with a note pad and began to jot on it.

She had never needed notes before, but Sean had asked enough questions for one day.

"It was still gracious to let her live."

"We don't get into these fights lightly," Gaby said as she continued to scrawl on the pad, "and we have strict rules. In the early days in this world, long before I came to be, we did some terrible things, partly out of ignorance, partly out of exuberance. You remember 'the sons of God' and 'the daughters of man' lines in Genesis? Most High was greatly displeased, I'm sure. So we made rules. And established review boards. Among the rules, we can't destroy until the other is attacking, even after our review board has given approval. I'm sorry that the rule constrained me to use you as bait—which I'm sure you've figured out was what was happening."

He had just barely thought of that. "We're in this together, Gaby, and you're the boss."

She put down her ballpoint pen and looked at him. "Thanks, Jackie Jim. I knew you'd understand, but I'm glad you do. You never were in any danger. I did not anticipate the cocaine, but we got it out of your blood very quickly. I don't think"—she grinned impishly—"you'll ever be tempted by it in the future."

"Fersure."

No bawling out for the booze or for his flirtation with Arden. This woman was different all right. No guilting.

"Was the man at the Grosvenor from Project Archangel?"

"No, he seems to have been with the same group that annoyed us in New York. We have temporarily depleted their resources, I think. They will be back. Project Archangel, on the other hand, is not likely to rise from the dust. How are you feeling? Any better? . . . Still hurts."

She unfolded herself from the bed. "Hmm . . . I'll admit that I have no experience with a mixture of cocaine and the amount of drink you consumed. . . . The claret was as good as predicted?"

"I'll never touch another drop in all my life."

"A likely story." She held her hand on the back of his head and pressed. "Does that help?"

Sean considered. The pain seemed to ooze out of his head. His stomach sighed with relief. Only the backs of his eyeballs hurt from the blue hell that had torn through Arden's apartment.

"Much better, thank you, mummy."

"Hard times, these past few days," she said sadly. "I'm sorry."

"Exciting times too."

"What's that in your hand?" She stared in disbelief.

"This?" He held up his rosary. "Nothing, only a medieval Catholic devotional device."

"You're *praying*?"

"After the beauty I saw on the train this afternoon—was it only this afternoon—there's no point in pretending anymore."

Gaby's eyes filled with tears. "I'm so happy, Jackie Jim."

"For me or for God?"

"For God. I'm sure it's a load off Her mind."

They both laughed. Only Sean wasn't altogether sure Gaby had been joking.

"So your friends were right."

"I guess they were." She lay back on her bed and took up the note pad.

The woman looked tired. Angels aren't supposed to look tired, are they? Only us fragile humans.

Rubens nude? Some resemblance. Much flatter belly. How do angels exercise?

"One thing I still don't understand."

"Hmm?"

"Why do all these people—the other side, the folks from Langley, Project Archangel—think they can control angels. They can't, can they?"

"Certainly not," she said briskly. "Did you see what I did with that lightning bolt?"

"But they all seem to assume they can. Don't seem to have any doubt. Scientific hubris?"

"Hubris all right." She glanced up from her notes. "But modern science is not the first human system to think it can command the spirits and force them to obey."

"Who before?"

"You've heard of sorcerers? We are dealing with modern sorcerers. Arrogant men who think that they can find secret formulae that will bring the spirit world under their sway. Like all other sorcerers, they are confident that one more spell, one more potion, one more incantation, and all the world of mind and spirit will be theirs to command."

"Fools."

"You'd better believe it."

So they were fighting sorcerers, were they? Well, that was nice to know.

And he had the magic spell that defeated all sorcery: "Please, Gaby."

All was well in God's world.

As he would later realize both he and his shapely guardian angel, happy with their triumph over the forces of darkness, had missed the most important lesson of their battle with Project Archangel.

21

"You look even more lovely to-
day than usual," Sean Desmond remarked as Gabriella lifted her
flight bag to the rack over their first-class seats on the SAS DC-10.
Indeed she did. "I'd whistle if it were not disrespectful."

He was beginning his flight-to-Stockholm agenda. There was
no point, after all, in having a guardian angel around if you couldn't
pick his, oops, her brain for advice.

The theme color today was red—trench coat, cotton knit
sweater and walking shorts (with a big red buckle), and shoes.
From the page in *Bazaar* next to the one where she had obtained
her transatlantic black and yellow. Fifteen hundred dollars.

"Why, thank you, Seano, that's very sweet of you," she replied.
"Give me your bag, I'll put it up next to mine."

"I've got it." He lifted his own bag up to the rack.

He had long since given up any efforts to play the gentleman
with her luggage. The flight bag was almost empty to begin with;
she was as tall as he was (sometimes); arguably, even in her human
analog she was stronger than he; in her angel mode she could
probably decompose the bag and make it reappear in the rack

without any effort at all; and finally, it would have been worth his life, he suspected, to suggest that she was dependent on his help.

But no woman was going to take care of his luggage, even a woman angel.

You had to draw the line somewhere, didn't you?

"A limit to how much a servant"—her eyes waltzed—"the woman guardian angel can be?"

"Sit down," he ordered her, "and let me finish my compliment."

"Yes, noble master." She took the window seat and looked up at him expectantly.

Superior species always got the window seat.

"You are especially overwhelming in red," he continued his carefully prepared recitation, "because it fits the energy and flamboyance of your character and the passion of your enthusiasms. I suspect that when you're doing your other thing, red is your color too. After all"—he was on overdrive now—"seraph means love and red is the color of love."

Her face had turned the color of the sweater. "I never said I was a seraph. And where did you learn that the word meant love?"

"I remembered from Sister Intemerata's class. She didn't talk about love much, I think she kind of disapproved of it."

"Am I going to be complimented this way every day?"

"Maybe." He buckled his seat belt. "It's kind of fun when you know the compliment will be accepted."

As it never was in either of his families. At home his mother would dismiss a word of praise with a remark such as "Well, will you look who thinks he's a poet."

And on their wedding when he had saluted Mona's naked radiance, she snarled, "Stop the blather and get on with it."

Defenses, he understood, against the vulnerability that a compliment creates. His daughters always thanked him solemnly, which was an improvement. Still . . .

Still what?

Still, with Gaby you knew there'd be a response.

"There are times with you, Sean Seamus Desmond, when I think I understand the sentiments of the late Doctor Frankenstein."

"Or Pygmalion or Henry Higgins?"

"I'll stay with my own myth," she said tersely.

I hope I haven't said anything wrong. I must get her opinion on the acceptance speech.

From the moment of their arrival at Heathrow Terminal One, Gaby had scanned every face they encountered. Often her eyes jumped to the balcony above them or the clusters of people twenty yards away. Heathrow was a melting pot of faces and skin colors and languages. You could easily persuade yourself that any dark-skinned person worked for Colonel Qadaffi and any light-skinned person for the IRA.

"Expecting something?" He tried to sound cool and composed.

"Not necessarily." Her eyes continued to roam, swiftly, systematically. "They're all around us, of course, and I don't think they'll try anything before we arrive in Sweden. But better safe than sorry, huh, Seano?"

"Definitely." His stomach did a number of slow and lazy swan dives. He was not cut out for this gumshoe stuff. No way.

On the plane, seat buckle firmly fastened, compliment successfully delivered, he began to relax as the icy voice of the chief cabin attendant advised in the language from the Ingmar Bergman movies about the trip. Eventually, she would say the same things in real language—English, that is.

Gaby's eyes continued to sweep the tarmac as their plane inched its way in the fog and rain towards the number-one slot in the takeoff runway.

His fear of terrorists was quickly replaced by his older and more powerful fear of airplanes.

"Don't worry, Jackie Jim." Her hand somehow was holding his though her eyes were still glued to the window. "It's all right."

The DC-10 roared into life and hurtled itself down the runway and into the dense clouds. His fear of flying evaporated. Definitively. It might not, he speculated, ever return. Oh yes, guardian angels are useful.

"Can we both relax now?" he asked plaintively.

"Why not?" They both laughed together. She released his hand.

When the snow maiden brought them their orange juice, Sean decided it was time to ask her about the talk.

"I'm thinking of cutting the angel section from my talk," he said bluntly.

"Oh?" She raised an eyebrow. "Why?"

"What if it's not true?"

"There's that," she admitted. "But you more than anyone alive today has reason to know that it probably is true."

"Inconclusive evidence." He laughed. "I guess I'm reluctant to stir up the sorcerers again. Or worse create new sorcerers. Maybe it would be better if we kept the possible existence of, uh, entities like you secret till the species is ready for it."

"Whatever I am, Jackie Jim, I am not an entity. Creature, being, even person will do."

"Woman?"

"By analogy"—she nodded vigorously—"sure."

"A woman who delights in fancy human fashions out of the pages of *Bazaar*?"

"The lingerie was from *Vogue*." She was unimpressed by his discovery of her secret. "No one would believe *that*, however, even if you did try to explain."

"Just the same, you see my point?"

"Certainly." She relaxed against the headrest and shut her eyes. "Right now this issue could stand to be cooled down. Project Archangel is obliterated. The others may be more cautious. No new crazies are looking for spells to put us to work on their goals. The scientific and bureaucratic world in general really doesn't believe in us. In your own case, a sensible acceptance speech that touches lightly on the question of directionality would suggest that you are not, after all, the mad Irishman which the world media suspects you may be."

"Calumny."

She opened her eyes to make sure he was grinning. Satisfied, she closed them again.

"So you think I should give that kind of a speech."

"Don't put words in my mouth, Jackie Jim." She opened her eyes again. "I'm not making your decision for you. Guardian angels are not into that."

"But . . ."

"No way, as your kids would say."

A woman who wouldn't tell him what to do. It wasn't fair.

"You gotta have some opinions."

"How long have you known me?" She closed her eyes.

"Long enough to know that a Gabriella without strong opinions is impossible."

"Fine. So I have opinions. Strong opinions. Contradictory opinions. Do you want to hear them?"

"Yes ma'am."

"You're impossible, Seano. Sweet, cute, sometimes even adorable. But impossible. . . . Anyway, on one side of the contradiction is the same argument you advanced: Let's cool it on angels."

"On the other side?"

"Two points. First"—she raised and lowered her forefinger— "science must be playful and a little mad if it's going to achieve breakthrough discoveries. But science normally takes itself much too seriously to be playful. Therefore, it needs the occasional wild man—Irish or not—to stir things up, to make the defenders of the status quo furious, to challenge the paradigms. At this reading, there are few men in the world better qualified to make your colleagues furious."

"Thank you, I think."

"Secondly"—her index finger shot up again briefly—"most people believe in us anyway." She opened her eyes and shrugged her shoulders. "Once you get beyond the thin academic and professionally trained veneer, human kind knows there are angels and devils. Like I said . . . excuse me, my language is deteriorating . . . *as* I said before, they're wrong about the devils, as far as we can tell, but they're right about the angels, up to a point. They've seen us by the tens of thousands."

"Really?"

She waved her hand, dismissing the question. "They think they have. You're not the only one who has solid evidence to back up the experience. Your talk won't surprise them at all. God's secret agents, why, certainly."

"Who calls you that?"

"Doctor Billy Graham."

"I don't pay any attention to him."

"Typical Irish Catholic bigot." She closed her eyes.

The plane thrust out of the cloud layer into the sun-drenched blue sky.

"So it wouldn't embarrass you?"

"Not at all, and it would please Doctor Graham if you quoted him."

Now that was an impish thought if there ever was one. Ah, the woman was dangerous.

"What else did he say?"

"He half suspects that we may be responsible for flying saucers. There are some ancient carvings of cherubs with wheels next to them. The wheels are not dissimilar from the descriptions of UFOs."

"Really?"

"That's what he says."

"I mean, are you guys really behind the UFOs?"

She hesitated. "Not in the ordinary sense of the word, no."

"Come on, Gabriella, don't give me the runaround."

She giggled. "I fear I am becoming transparent, Seano.... All right. There are some light phenomena that have been observed in which we may have been involved. Most UFO sightings, so-called, are not the result of our activity."

"Or any other activity?"

"Other than that internal to the human imagination. Now take that delicious breakfast which the lovely young woman is offering you."

The ice maiden had been staring stonily at Gaby, resenting, no doubt, her expensive clothes. Now she melted in the light of Gaby's smile.

"We can't permit the Nobel Prize winner to arrive at Stockholm looking hungry, can we?"

"He always looks hungry, Ingrid." Gaby's smile turned more dazzling. "That comes from being Irish. But I suspect that he's really mostly Dane, way, way back, like you."

"Then we must feed him two breakfasts." The young woman was quite captivated.

"And that's a lovely diamond you're wearing."

"Thank you very much." She poured coffee for both of them. "Karl and I will be married after Christmas."

"God grant you happiness and excitement and good children to love you."

"Thank you very much." Tears of joy rose in the girl's eyes. She turned away in happy embarrassment.

"Wow!" Sean said softly.

"I liked her." Gaby shrugged. "She needed a kind word, and you were too stubborn to give it to her."

"I'll get in trouble if I compliment every nice-looking cabin attendant I see."

"Not if you do it right."

Never satisfied. Never. They want to remake you completely.

"What about Grigio?"

"Who?" She smiled slyly.

"Saint John Bosco's gray dog who saved his life from thugs at three widely separated times. He thought it might be his guardian angel."

"Where did you hear that story?"

"From Sister Intemerata."

"You believed everything she said."

"That was a great story." He began to eat the SAS sliced ham. Not bad.

"What would the saint have done if I had appeared in my present analog?"

"Dressed in red? Run like hell, I'm sure. Maybe not a bad idea, all things considered."

"So if we intervene in certain special circumstances, we do so in forms that the one with whom we are working can accept."

"Bitch?"

"I beg your pardon?"

"Grigio or Grigia?"

"I have absolutely no comment. And please lower your voice. We don't want poor Ingrid to hear you talking about angels. She already knows all Irish are mad."

"Saint Gina Galante?"

"Gemma Galganni. What about her?"

"She saw her guardian angel all the time, according to Sister Mary I. Helped her with housework. Taught her to pray. Sang with her. Once, when an evil man uttered a terrible blasphemy, she fainted and would have fallen to the ground if the angel hadn't caught her."

"Really?" She smiled at him over her coffee cup.

"S'ter said."

"We all know that children make up imaginary playmates, even cross-sex ones as in this case."

"Maybe it was a little girl angel and she was afraid to tell people."

"Maybe."

"You're dodging answers."

"You've noticed."

"Well ... let me see. ... How often do you folks actually appear, you secret agents of God, as Doctor Graham called you?"

"Wondering how special you are?"

"A scholar looking for facts. I mean, as winged giants or little kids or playmates or she-wolves or as gorgeous matrons or in any way?"

She considered carefully. "Let's put it this way: our physical manifestations are rather rare, much more rare than most devout or superstitious people believe, but not nearly so rare as scientific skeptics would like to think."

He pondered the response. It told him exactly nothing. One more try.

"Would Saint John Bosco have been killed by the thugs if Grigia had not intervened?"

"The third time, definitely."

Aha. I don't think I wanted to know that much.

"Well, if it's all the same to those who make decisions in these matters, I'd just as soon continue with you instead of a gray wolf."

"A prudent choice." She chuckled. "Now finish your breakfast. You won't want to hurt poor Ingrid's feelings."

When he had disposed of his breakfast, he excused himself. "I lack the efficient waste disposal systems your species seems to have developed."

Her melodic laughter followed him down the corridor of the plane.

There is, he concluded, no good reason for making my talk a comedy. Better for all concerned to play it serious. I don't want to embarrass my daughters.

One less decision to worry about.

When he returned, Gaby and Ingrid were whispering, thick as

thieves. The cabin attendant, flustered and blushing furiously, ducked away.

"What was that about?" he demanded suspiciously.

"Girl talk. Buckle your seat belt."

"About me, I assume?" He did as he was told.

"Most girl talk is about men."

"So?"

"I see no reason to flatter your already excessive ego, Professor Sean Seamus Desmond. I worry about the future of womankind. Invariably they dissolve into helpless worship when you show them the slightest attention."

"What did she want to know?"

"Ought that not to be obvious? She wanted to know whether you were as good in bed as you seemed to hint you were."

"Gaby!"

"Perfectly legitimate question. A woman finds a man attractive, he responds with a winning smile. Some part of their brain, however secret and however quiet, raises the question. Our Scandinavian friends are simply more direct in asking about it."

"Well," he said, sulking, "I'm glad you didn't essay an answer."

"*Of course* I did. She loves her Karl desperately. She wouldn't sleep with you for anything. Still, it is a perfectly reasonable question."

"What did you tell her?" he demanded.

"That for an Irishman"—she winked—"you showed some promise."

"Gaby!" he shouted again.

"I didn't add—because the poor girl would not understand—that my comments were based on observation and speculation and not direct experience."

"Observation!"

"You showed distinct possibilities with Blanche."

"You people are voyeurs." He was now genuinely angry. "You have no right—"

"When we become involved in a pattern situation"—she smoothed her skirt—"we collect all the data that are necessary for our planning. Surely, as a research scholar, you can understand the necessity for data collection. In the case where a human personality is important—and (I hate to give your ego another boost) this is one such case—we certainly have to learn about our, ah, subject's sexual behavior and self-esteem. We do not find such matters particularly erotic. We have, after all, our own coupling practices and entertainments."

"Watching two chimps screw."

"Oh, a little more amusing than that."

"What have you against the Irish?" He changed the subject, still angry.

"Nothing much." She was enjoying herself enormously, the bitch. "Besides the usual complaints—too much drink, too much talk, too much self-pity."

"Oh."

"On the other hand"—she beamed kindly—"I will have to say that of all the varieties of your species I have had occasion to know, they are the most comic, sometimes even intentionally."

"Yeah? Well, woman, that's a nice thing to say, considering that yourself is Irish."

"Me?" She threw back her head and roared with laughter. "Oh, Seano, that's silly! How could an angel belong to an ethnic group?"

"You act Irish anyway."

"I'm flattered again, I think."

"Bossy, nosy, pushy, opinionated, always have the last word. Terrible altogether."

"Naturally. . . . Well, on your trip to Ireland you can decide for yourself whether any of my redeeming characteristics are Irish too."

"Such as they may be . . . and I don't think I'll go. Probably cancel the talk in Dublin."

"Why?" The word rang out like the crack of a rifle.

"I've never been there and I really have no interest in going. Besides they'll be resentful of an Irish American that won the prize instead of one of their own. And I have to get home to the kids anyway."

"You should go." Sharp, definitive. No qualification. Go, damn you.

"Could I ask why?"

She frowned. "It's not fair to play the Irish game as much as you do and not know the country. You run the risk of caricature."

Poor reason.

"It's not fair to be away from the kids."

"A couple of days won't make any difference. I told you they were all right, didn't I?"

"You seem pretty insistent."

"I assumed you wouldn't pass up a chance to visit the land of your ancestors. That's what you said when you received the joint invitation of the two universities in Dublin. They were delighted with your response. You'll disappoint them terribly."

"You seem to feel very strongly about it."

"I certainly do. You can't go through life making promises and then breaking them."

Why is it so important to her?

"Well, I'll think about it, but I won't promise."

"I certainly hope you think very seriously about your response to those poor people who are counting on you."

Well, if you're so determined that I should go, I won't go, just to show I'm independent. So there.

They were silent for the remainder of the flight, Sean sulking, Gaby upset.

He did take time to smile at Ingrid, to ask about Karl, and to tell her what a lucky man Karl was. The ice maiden was all teary slush.

"About her," Gaby said as the no smoking signs went on and Ingrid returned to her station.

"What about her?"

"I'll be candid. . . ."

"Please do."

"She is so enamored of you that if she didn't love Karl and even if you weren't a Nobel laureate, she'd be yours for the taking. Right off the slave block on which your fantasy has tentatively placed her. Is she attractive, by the way, with her clothes off?"

"Very." He felt his face grow warm as his imagination was so quickly read. "I wouldn't take her, Gaby. I'm not that kind of man."

"I know you're not." She patted his hand. "For all your faults, you are not a predator. Even your fantasies are gentle. The first thing you do to your newly purchased slaves is wrap a warm cloak around them to protect their violated modesty."

"Gaby, get out of my head."

"I'm *not* in your head." She glared at him. "Only in your eyes."

"That transparent, huh?"

"Certainly. You ought nevertheless to know what impact you have on women, especially in your present state of development."

Transformed by the prize and by you?

"I'll take your word for it."

"It could be useful in the proper circumstances."

"I suppose."

She wanted to be friends again and he wasn't quite ready.

Nevertheless, he turned on all the charm for the slush maiden on the way off the plane.

"I have two things to say to you, young woman."

"Yes, Doctor Desmond." She bowed her head meekly.

"The first is that you should be sure to tell Karl that he is an enormously lucky man and that he should take very good care of you."

"Yes, Doctor Desmond."

Gaby was already rolling her eyes.

"And the second is that you should take special care of him. A woman with your charm and intelligence, without realizing what she's doing, promises so much happiness to her man that sometimes she finds it hard work to live up to the promises he thinks he's heard. Believe me, Ingrid, it's worth the work."

"Yes, Doctor Desmond." She pondered the implication of his wisdom, smiled happily, and then dissolved into tears and hugged him fiercely. "I will be very, very good to the poor man."

"God bless you both."

"All the holy saints and angels protect and preserve us," Gaby observed as they walked down the jetway.

"Thinking about Doctor Frankenstein, Doctor Light?"

He had made two important decisions as the plane approached Arlanda Airport. He would not go to Ireland, and he would give a sober and serious acceptance speech.

The second decision was challenged as soon as they passed through passport control in Stockholm.

The Nobel laureates, thought Sean Desmond, were a pretty bedraggled crew: an opaque Chinese physicist from Cal Berkeley, a bearded Marxist priest/poet from Latin America who looked like he was carrying a bomb (and who refused to don the usually mandatory formal evening clothes), a deaf-mute chemist from Liverpool, a nervous M.D. from Harvard who scribbled notes for his next scholarly article throughout the ceremonies, and the mandatory conservative American economist who was more concerned about the closing soybean price on the Board of Trade than he was about meeting the young King of Sweden.

In such a group a red-haired, clean-shaven Irish-American leprechaun looked almost normal.

Even if he was no longer the center of attention.

And that despite the fact that his lovely mistress, as everyone assumed, was the most beautiful woman in the room. For the first reception in the two days of hectic socializing before the award ceremony itself, Gaby had dressed in a very light gray two-piece dress with thick gold zig-zag bands at the waist, on the end of the short sleeves, and at the bottom of the skirt. And gold shoes.

"That dress isn't in *Bazaar* or *Vogue*," he had observed as she was putting it on.

"Town and Country. I'm ahead of you. However, I left a copy on the table next to your bed in case you wanted to check the price."

"Spoilsport."

"By the way, did you notice that the President's daughter, I mean *your* President's daughter was the model in those pictures in *Bazaar*?"

"Maureen?"

"No, silly, Eleanor."

"Eleanor?"

"Eleanor Mondale."

He studied her face in the mirror. She wasn't joking.

"I may be losing my mind, Gabriella, but I think Ronald Reagan won the election."

She turned and stared at him thoughtfully, hands on her opulent bare hips. "Really? ... Yes, of course. Sometimes it's hard to keep the scenarios straight."

"I imagine so."

"Well"—she brushed away her mistake with a wave of both hands—"even angels make an occasional, very occasional mistake."

Nonetheless, she looked puzzled for a few moments while she sorted out scenarios.

What, he wondered, was the other scenario?

They were assigned to an enormous suite, double bedroom (the Swedes being properly cautious), on the top floor of the waterfront Grand Hotel with a view of the Old City, the Royal Palace (where the royal family no longer lived), the docks and the Archipelago (also called the Garden of Skerries) in the distance.

Despite the size of the suite, Gabriella had developed the custom of striding around the rooms in various stages of dress and undress while she went through lists of instructions that were reeling off the computer inside her head.

Or inside the energy pattern for which the carefully coiffed skull was an analog.

Starting with Givenchy bra and pantyhose. Black, naturally.

The images were memorable, and he planned to treasure

them for later times when his capacity to experience erotic sensations returned.

"You sure do look luscious in that outfit," he observed. "Such as it is, and it isn't much, mind you, save in its impact."

"We have too many things to think about, Professor Desmond, for you to waste time gawking.... Oh, I'm sorry, Seano. Thank you very much for admiring. I'm a terribly vain creature actually. I want to be admired by males in both species." She pulled the top of the dress over her head and put her arms in the sleeves. "Would you zip me up please."

"So long as I can admire while I'm doing it."

"How could I stop you?"

They laughed together.

"Pretty flimsy bra today," he murmured. It was in fact little more than a lace symbol.

"Just to change your mind about what my boobs—my analog's boobs, that is—need."

"I didn't—"

"Don't try to lie to me, Seano." She snickered. "I saw you looking at the one I wore on the Atlantic flight."

"My eyes again?"

"Naturally. You don't hide your reactions very well—which is part of your not inconsiderable appeal."

Since he saw the gold and silver waterfalls in the train to Cambridge, their relationship had become both more relaxed and more prickly. Gaby had thrown herself into the work of making him a proper laureate, for which he was quite grateful; he reacted by slowing down so that his nervous anxieties wouldn't turn him into a babbling idiot.

Gaby continued to scan the crowds, looking always for the hit men.

"Are they still around?"

"Yes, indeed, but it seems that they will hold back until the awards, probably till after the ceremony."

"That's reassuring."

"Have I failed you yet?"

"No."

"So don't worry."

"I'll try." He zipped up her dress, and wondered if that action would recur in his dreams. The dreams had become part of his ordinary environment too, so much that he hardly noticed them anymore: pleasant, reassuring, entertaining. High-class soft-core, which is what the unconscious is about, isn't it?

"It won't be much longer, Jackie Jim." She glanced at him sadly. "Soon it'll be over and you'll be rid of me."

"I'll miss you," he said honestly enough.

He was told that he was sweet.

Which didn't make his fear of the gunmen go away completely.

Definitely he would give a sober acceptance speech. Why stir them up. Maybe if he didn't talk about angels, they'd lose interest in him.

Every eye turned when he and Gabriella entered the reception room at the Royal Academy. Sean had come to take such attention for granted. And the whispers confirming that, naturally, she's his mistress. And the inner satisfaction of knowing the consternation he would have been able to cause if he replied, "Oh, no, Doctor Light is merely my guardian angel."

What he had not come to accept and what he didn't like one bit was that the eyes would then turn back to Don Martino, the bearded little Jesuit poet with the thick spectacles and the high-pitched voice, who not only wore his combat fatigues instead of formal dress, but who, judging from the smell that radiated several yards out from him, cooked chickens in his hotel room.

"I have no right to be the center of attention," he had said to Gaby at Arlanda Airport when he had discovered that the media had gathered for Don Martino and not for him.

"Yes, you do," she had replied.

"But I hate to see that little phony receiving so much attention. Despite the fatigues, he's never been in combat anywhere. He writes his love letters to Fidel in a perfectly safe teaching job at a Catholic school in Costa Rica. And it's lousy poetry."

"But it's anti-gringo and that's what counts, isn't it?"

Gaby didn't seem to like him any more than Sean did. Well, we agree on that anyway.

And I'm still not going to Ireland.

"I accept the prize in the name of all the oppressed workers in the world, particularly those who suffer from Yankee oppression,"

Don Martino had shouted at the cameras in the airport arrival area. "I accept the money of a capitalist merchant of death as a symbol of the death the working people of the world will bring to all capitalist oppression."

Cheers from a gaggle of young and bearded admirers who had gathered at the fringes of the media folk.

"I denounce all capitalism, especially North American capitalism. I also denounced Swedish capitalism, which has exported guns and ammunition all over the world to arm the oppressors of the people."

The Swedes, Sean had argued to Gaby on the ride in from the airport, always seemed to him to be a smug and self-satisfied people until someone dared to criticize them for anything, especially for their long denial of citizenship to the Italian immigrants who had for several generations done much of the dirty work in the country. It was a point that Sean, as a matter of strict principle, had always brought up when the round table was honoring a Swedish guest who would boast about how wonderfully just and equitable Swedish society was.

"So they should turn against this Jebby jerk, but he gets away with attacking them, the phony hypocrites."

"Stop being a shanty-Irish bigot, Professor Desmond. They are being consistent if they applaud him when he criticizes both the United States and Sweden."

"They don't mean it in the second case," he growled.

"Besides your political views are rather leftist aren't they?" She raised that dangerous eyebrow, a she-falcon ready to pounce.

"Round table blather, as you well know, unless you stopped your research with my mating habits."

"You vote straight organization every time out of pure cussedness."

He grumbled something incoherent, in a thoroughly bad mood by now.

His mood had not much improved the next day at the official reception, where Don Martino was still the center of attention.

"Yah, he is a stupid little pig, isn't he?" The words came in a thick German accent from a short, bald man standing next to him. "In a real socialist country we would clean up refuse like that, quick, quick."

The man, who had been poured into evening dress that was two sizes too small, rubbed his tiny pudgy hands as if brushing dirt from them.

"He's a capitalist parasite, isn't he?"

"Riffraff, nothing but riffraff." He extended a paw. "Helmstadt, Honecker Center, Leipzig. Congratulations. Your work is the most important in many years."

"Thank you." Sean felt himself smiling proudly. "I'm glad you find it helpful."

"Yah, why don't you come wisit us after. See our institute. See true socialism, yah?"

"That would be very interesting."

Leipzig was in East Germany. Honecker was some sort of government honcho over there. Probably all a bunch of Nazis. But it would be informative to see how they work.

Socialism might not be the future and it certainly didn't work, but it might be interesting to visit. Better than a trip to soggy, backward Ireland.

"Yah," Helmstadt continued, obviously relishing the prospect, "ve take care of dat kind, chop, chop."

"I'm not surprised," Sean agreed. "Candidly, I'm not surprised at all."

He then spent the next half hour fending off two lissome blond matrons who, with zero encouragement from him, indicated by all nonverbal signs possible that they were perfectly prepared to add him to the collection of Nobel laureates with whom they had slept.

In Gaby's temporary absence his hormones began functioning again and with a vigor that startled him. Both women, beyond doubt, would be excellent temporary bedmates, fully prepared—nay, determined—to take over the major responsibilities in the *pas de deux*.

Sean's antipathy for Sweden was stronger than his lust. He did, however, resist successfully the temptation to suggest that they might like to fuck with Don Martino.

"The available women too available, Professor Desmond?" Gabriella, amused and insufferable, to the rescue.

"It doesn't follow," he returned to one of his favorite themes, "that I should go to a country where the available women are not really available at all."

"You might be surprised." Her eyes glinted. "Quite sur-prised."

She had adapted the strategy of not arguing with him.

"And what really offends me," he continued to rage, "is how tasteless of them to proposition me with my putative mistress in the very same room."

"Such matters would not trouble those two poor women, I think."

"And my said putative mistress a thousand times more lovely than they."

"Impossible, Jackie Jim, impossible. And terribly funny too when you're worried about stage fright."

"If you keep reading me that accurately," he grumbled, "I'll trade you in on another putative mistress."

"I insist," she said primly, "that you are entitled to your free-dom and privacy. If you want an ... ah ... roll in the hay..."

"How likely do you think that is in this country?"

"And in your advanced state of anxiety? Oh, about one over the number of miles to the most recent supernova."

At the formal ball later in the evening—Gaby in strapless, pale green gown with two chains of pearls around her neck—he con-tinued his tirade about Sweden.

"They're so liberal and peace-loving and superior to us. That Palme character who was reelected for twenty years on an anti-American ticket got himself shot one night apparently by an Iraqi or Iranian terrorist according to the American ambassador. They bring roses to the place where he died every day, even in Decem-ber. But no one in the government really wants to find out the whole story because it might blow up in the truth about how this country sells arms to both sides. There was even an admiral who was in on the deal and whom they pushed in front of a train a cou-ple of weeks after Palme was shot. Better to hide the truth than destroy your precious illusions about your country. They're worse than the Limeys," he ranted on. "The Limeys don't pretend they're not hypocrites."

"Relax, Jackie Jim"—she took his hand—"they seem to be dancing."

"I don't dance." The touch of her hand cooled some of his fears.

"I'm sure you do." She smiled affectionately. "Just follow me."

So he danced very well and relaxed even more.

"I forgot to tell you," he muttered, "that you look wonderful, though I'm not sure bare shoulders are a good idea in this frigid place. Anyway, you'd stop an army of archangels."

"We call them legions."

"You're a wonderful dancer, Gabriella," he admitted.

"Thank you, Sean." She was very close to him, warm, reassuring, confident. "I've had a long time to practice."

"I asked you once before if you would dance for me. I mean, like you sang for me."

"I've thought about it."

"And?" The perfume in her silver gray hair soothed and relaxed him. All part of the game, but still nice.

"I'm still thinking about it. I'm not sure I can do it."

"Break the rules?"

"No. Technical reasons. I've sung for humans before. I've never tried to dance. I'm not sure how the energy patterns might be translated. I'll keep thinking about it."

That's nice. At least she *wants* to perform for me.

The next night a performance of *Cosi Fan Tutte* was scheduled for the laureates, their families, and members of the Swedish Academy at the Drottningholm Theater. Sean did not want to go. He always fell asleep at operas.

"I'll keep you awake. Your friend Don Martino, S.J., isn't going. He says Mozart was a bourgeois capitalist. Do you want the Operat company to think you are as rude as he is?"

So they went. Naturally.

Gaby wore a black dress and a double string of pearls.

"Those pearls are not bad for fakes," he remarked as the launch carried them through the winter darkness to the island castle.

"They're not fakes," she snorted. "Angels don't do fakes."

"Did an oyster make them?"

"There are other ways to produce authentic pearls." She used the tone of voice that indicated she had absolutely no intention of offering an explanation.

He changed the subject. "Do you folks call yourselves angels?"

"Certainly not; that's a human word. We accept it as useful for our purposes."

The boat slowed and inched its way toward the dock of the castle.

"So how do you refer to yourselves?"

"These are pointless questions, Professor Desmond." She accepted his help in stepping down to the dock, as if she really needed it. "I suppose your word *person* would come reasonably close. God is the Other Person—"

"And us?"

"I will not comment."

"Irish setters?"

"Not quite."

Ah, the woman is testy tonight.

Not so testy that she didn't hum the arias as they were sung by tall, handsome Swedish blonds.

"Did Salieri kill Mozart?" he asked her as they sipped champagne between acts.

"Don't be ridiculous." Her eyes scanned the exquisite little lobby. "Not that he wasn't tempted. Mozart died of what you would call the flu, with pulmonary complications. Poor, dear man."

"This opera is pretty silly," he said tentatively. "Heavenly—you should excuse the expression—music and silly lyrics."

"He had to earn a living." The bell rang for the second act. Gaby deftly placed both their glasses on a passing tray.

"I suppose," he said as he trailed her back to their seats in the front row, "that you were present at the premiere of this opera in Vienna?"

"Prague, actually.

That shut Sean Seamus Desmond up.

Only in the launch returning to the center of town, did he dare resume the conversation.

"By the way, that little man from East Germany wants us to come over on the way home and look at his place. It would give me a chance to focus my Irish-bigot babble on Germans."

"Hardly necessary after you have liberated yourself—as Father Martino, poor man, would say—from your speech."

"What do you think about going over there?"

They could visit East Germany for a day or two and still honor his commitment in Dublin, which he would cancel anyway.

"It's up to you." Her shoulders moved up slightly. "If you want to go, then we will go. It might prove very interesting."

He didn't quite like the sound of that last sentence. On the late night World War II films, were not the next words "Ve haf our vays"?

His furious scribbling had covered four pages of paper when Gabriella came into his room. The statement he was preparing would blast his enemies to the farthest parts of the universe. He'd show them all.

"Like my hat?"

Defying the weather, she had turned now to strapless dresses at all formal times, short miniskirts for the receptions, dark and tightly belted, and flowing pastel gowns for the balls. She had added large and outlandish hats to her late-afternoon wardrobe—as if to deliberately challenge the Swedes to figure out where a woman who traveled with a flight bag and a shoulder purse could possibly have carried such a huge hat.

"Monumental." His statement, now the most important thing in his life, could afford to wait for a second or two. No more.

"More décolletage than last night?"

"Only a little." She winked. "Maybe it will keep the blond vultures away this afternoon. What are you up to?"

"Responding to this." He pushed the *Leader* article at her.

"The *Tribune* reporter brought it over an hour ago."

"Oh boy."

"You know about it?"

"I hoped you wouldn't see it before tomorrow."

The headline on the front page of the "free" paper proclaimed:

DESMOND INVESTIGATION DEMANDED

The lead paragraphs reported that:

Chicago. Many Chicago scientists are demanding an academic investigation of the work of Nobel Prize winner John J. Desmond. Unanswered questions about the quality and quantity of his work, one prominent scholar told *The Leader*, make such an investigation imperative if the reputation of American science is not going to be permanently sullied.

It is unlikely that the Nobel Prize would be revoked. The Royal Swedish Academy has never reversed itself before. "Like the pope," a distinguished scientist told *The Leader*, "the academy doesn't make mistakes. But if an investigation here reveals that Desmond is a fraud, the Nobel won't be worth much to him."

The article continued with a broadside attack on his work, his character, his family life. Students had performed all his experiments. Other students were responsible for his theoretical innovations. Yet others had actually written his articles. He never acknowledged their help. His wife, it was said, had left him because of drunken beatings. There were a number of sexual harassment charges pending. Minority students were certain that he was a racist. Others said he had frequently been guilty of anti-Semitic remarks. His colleagues found him impossible to work with. Some faculty members were contemplating a petition to the faculty senate suggesting that his tenure be revoked.

There was no discussion of the substance of his work. The quotes were almost entirely anonymous. Only Rene Menon, an Indian graduate student, Congreve, and Mona were quoted for attribution. The Mona quote was lifted, without credit, from the *National Enquirer.*

Rene had left after her second quarter of graduate school after a psychotic interlude in the university hospital.

Congreve claimed to be a friend and admirer of Desmond, but one who found himself often hurt and betrayed by his colleague: "He's charming at first, but then you realize how much raw ambition drives him, surely the result of the emotionally starved Irish Catholic family in which he was raised."

It was not clear who exactly was going to do the investigating—the university, the appropriate professional societies, or possibly the State's Attorney. *The Leader* was unable to quote anyone who said that their group would definitely launch an investigation, which meant that no one was telling their reporter that there was a case against him.

Silently Gaby gave the article back to him.

"Sexual harassment," he moaned. "I should have been so lucky."

"Probably someone who remembers Blanche."

"She harassed me!"

"Everyone knows that. I'd say they had Congreve and one dissatisfied graduate student, probably someone who has flunked out. He—I say 'he' because it sounds like the kind of thing a man would do—gave them the poor Indian girl's name. They left out her quotes about the demons who spoke to her during your class. There's nothing else to the story. There won't be any investigation. Congreve made a fool of himself. He was a little too petulant. His friends will congratulate him on getting his story told, but in a few months all anyone will remember is that he dug his own grave in *The Leader.* He'll never win a Nobel of his own now."

"Bastards." Sean pounded the desk. "I'll get them all."

He began to scribble again, large angry words.

"Sean Seamus Desmond."

"Yes?"

"Cool it."

"An order?"

"Powerful advice."

"Thin distinction when it's coming from your guardian angel." He felt a grin crack his angry face. "Especially one as ravish-ingly lovely as you."

She took the sheets of paper out of his unprotesting fingers. "Don't give them any publicity. Don't dignify this crap—you should excuse the expression—with a denial. The whole thing was done to get a rise out of you and provide them with some atten-tion. You don't take these sorts of articles seriously when you read them"—she tore up his statement—"and neither does any other fair-minded person. Right?"

"I suppose." He was discouraged at a good fight lost.

"What about Joshua Hechter?"

"What about him?"

"What did he say?"

" 'Brilliance of insight matched only by spectacular flair.' "

"And you worry about this . . ."

". . . Horseshit?"

"Your words"—she sniggered—"not mine."

Damn angels are always right.

"Let's get the man from the *Trib* on the phone and give him two sentences. Okay?"

"Okay."

She picked up the phone and, ignoring the dial as always, seemed to obtain the reporter's hotel room instantly.

"I'm calling for Dr. Desmond," she cooed. "Do you have time to take a statement from him? Good."

She handed the phone to Sean and whispered the first sen-tence into his ear.

"The charges are all false, absurd, and anonymous."

He added a sentence of his own. "Why didn't they quote what Joshua Hechter said."

Gaby nodded vigorously.

Pause while the reporter wrote it down.

"And I quite agree with my good friend Mister Congreve that the Royal Swedish Academy made a mistake when it awarded me the prize instead of him."

They laughed all the way to the reception at the Foreign Min-istry.

I don't know what I'm laughing about, he told himself, people are still trying to kill me. Okay, she's managed to protect me so far.

But what if she makes a mistake. Even she admits that angels make mistakes.

In his arms at the ball, Gabriella nodded her head thoughtfully. "All right, I think I can swing it. I'm afraid it might be a little crude, but it's time someone in our species tried it."

"Tried what?" he asked uneasily.

"Tried to dance for a human."

Now don't you dare laugh."
Gabriella was standing by the thick drapes, which shut out the
Northern midwinter darkness, dressed in leotard and tights whose
color could only be described as discreet crimsons. "I've never
tried this before."

"When have I laughed at you?" Sean demanded.

"All the time," she snapped irritably.

"You laugh at me all the time."

"That's different."

"What are you worried about? Didn't your friends urge you to
do this?"

"My friends are irrelevant. They'll say they like it because they
have to."

"They're here?" Sean looked around nervously.

"They wouldn't miss it." She frowned grimly. "Always eager
to see crazy Gabriella make a fool out of herself again."

"I bet that's not what they'd say."

"I don't think it's funny. And remember, this is not a strip-
tease. I do not do erotic dances. So banish Vincent d'Indy from
your dirty mind."

"I wasn't thinking of the *Istar Variations*, but now that you mentioned them—"

"QUIET!"

"Yes ma'am."

Music began, soft, peaceful music at first, played on instruments Sean had never heard, never even imagined. Their parlor filled with mists, and they were in a vast forest of tall trees, dim light, and thick shadows. Gaby was a *Swan Lake* ballerina, but the music and the dance were not at all like *Swan Lake*. She spun through the forest like a wild, manic, graceful wood nymph, swinging from the trees, cartwheeling through the ferns, tiptoeing over the wild flowers, skipping across the creeks and brooks, diving into the tiny lakes, climbing up the sunbeams, sliding down the moonbeams. Her body was sometimes a spring breeze slipping through the forest, sometimes a winter wind shaking the trees, sometimes an almost invisible zephyr barely stirring the air.

We could make a lot of money with this act.

Then they were in the richest ballroom in all the world with a mighty symphony orchestra and scores of dancing couples. Vienna. Franz Joseph. Johann Strauss. Except that the waltz was both wilder and more comic than Strauss, the setting richer than the Hapsburgs at their most powerful could have produced, and the instruments sweeter and more melodic than any instruments known to humankind.

Gaby appeared in a free-flowing white gown, shoulders bare, and took center stage, bowing modestly to all around. Then she began her own waltz, part respectable eighteenth-century dance and part madcap acrobatic display in which her long white legs, skirt spinning and billowing around her, cut across the dance floor like thoroughbreds racing down the homestretch.

Sean began to lose his breath. It was too much, too fast, too crazy.

Next he was carried off to an ice cap in the arctic where she did a *pas de deux* to Stravinsky-like sound with a charming and polite polar bear, perhaps fourteen feet tall. The bear was soon joined by a chorus line of his fellows, all tap dancing behind the lead duo. Bob Fosse would have loved it, though he probably would never be able to find the polar bears.

This is all for me, Sean thought. She wants to calm me down for tomorrow.

Don't kid yourself: she loves every second of it.

From a larger-than-life Vienna, he was carried back to their parlor at the Grand Hotel, a parlor flooded with misty, multicolored lights. The other dances had been modulations in space across which Gabriella's body had moved. Now, there was not space, only her body, most likely nude, pirouetting gracefully in the dense mists. No Istar or Salomé, Gaby's fluid movements displayed the dignity and the charm of human body (female) in motion, whirling and spiraling, bending and stretching, sweeping and mesmerizing in the rapidly changing lights as flutelike music urged her on.

I'm dizzy, he thought, why doesn't she stop?

Stop she did, as the flute was replaced by a mechanical sound, melodic and yet harsh. Modern dance now—Gabriella in factory work clothes leaping wildly from smokestack to smokestack, charging up and down assembly lines, plunging dizzily into coal mines, clinging to the caboose of a railroad train, hanging on to the tail of a 747.

Not bad, not bad at all.

Then the lights went on and they were back in their parlor at the Grand, Gaby in her dress from the ball. She reached out her hand to Sean, inviting him to dance.

"No, thank you," he responded. "No way, José."

You don't say no to an angel.

They whirled off into space, dancing across the cosmos, sliding down the tails of comets, tapping on asteroids, skipping from spoke to spoke of galaxy wheels, drinking in the Milky Way, doing the polka on the moon, riding up on solar winds, frolicking on the rings of Saturn, waltzing across the canals of Mars, jitterbugging in the fog of Venus.

Time to stop.

No, not quite. The last act was a merry prance across the blue waters of Lake Michigan on a quiet summer day to music that sounded like Copland's *Appalachian Spring.*

Only, Gaby seemed to be singing "Lord of the Dance."

When they came to the line, "They cut me down and I jumped up high!" the two of them skipped up to the sky and then bounced down on the Oak Street Beach.

Somehow he thought they may have passed a cemetery on the way down.

With an open tomb.

Open and empty.

At last he was back in his chair in the Grand Hotel. Gaby, drenched in perspiration and breathing heavily, was sitting next to him, wrapped in a huge terry-cloth robe.

"Pretty hard to do all that on the head of a pin," he observed.

She laughed between gasps. "Hard work," she said, "even for an angel. Did you like it?"

"Take it on the road." He clapped enthusiastically. "Sure commercial success."

"I'm so glad." She beamed happily. "It was the first time I tried it."

"What about your friends?"

She dismissed them with a brief flip of her hand. "Angels tend to like anything other angels do. . . . Now, Jackie Jim, a shower and bed for you. Show's over and tomorrow is an important day."

"Can we do that Lake Michigan fling again?"

"No way." She pointed at the bedroom door. "BED!"

"Yes, Mother."

Later that night Sean woke from his sleep with total illumination.

There's no point, the illumination said, in not being who and what you are. She dances because she's a dancer.

Right?

Right.

So I should do tomorrow what I do best. Right?

Right.

He crept through the parlor to the other bedroom and peeked through the door. As he had expected, Gaby's bed was empty. No sign of the gown she'd worn to the ball or her red leotard or any other clothes.

Where did she go at night?

Well, it didn't matter. He would do what he intended. She said he was free, didn't she?

The awards ceremony, solemn, high, pontifical, Sean remembered the words from his altar boy days, had begun at three in the afternoon in the concert hall with the presentation of the diplomas and medals by Karl Gustav and the reading of the citations by representatives of the academy, followed by fanfares from the Royal Swedish Symphony Orchestra. The other laureates all seemed awkward and embarrassed, even the arrogant monetarist.

Don Martino chewed on his Havana cigar. Poor man, Gaby had said, he overreached. Now everyone is avoiding him.

Gaby was sitting next to Sean, looking even more like a queen in her white gown than the young queen did.

Not that the queen was at all difficult to look at, sweet, wide-eyed, pretty little thing.

"Is it me they're talking about up there?" he whispered to Gaby when his citation was being read.

"Shush, this is serious."

"No, it's not," he insisted, "and you of all people, uh, persons here ought to know that."

"You didn't need me," she said with a sigh, "to keep you cool."

He felt a touch of anxiety when the time came to rise from the plush chair in the front row and walk up to the dais. He remembered Paul Newman at the motion picture academy dinner and resolved he would bounce up, bright and smiling, the same way.

No point in being solemn, this is a fun event. Let them see by the smile on your face and the glint in your eye that you love every second of it.

That'll show the bastards.

What bastards?

All of them, whoever and wherever they may be.

Sean Seamus Desmond did indeed love every minute of it, as he strolled up to the throne and received his prize. He even said "Thank you, Your Reverence" to the handsome young King and winked at his pretty wife.

She blushed and, delighted, winked back. The three of them laughed.

The King held his hand a little longer. "You are a delight, Professor Desmond. It is so wonderful to have someone who is not pompous."

"We Irish Americans react to fear differently than some other folks do," he said honestly enough.

"My wife and I," the King whispered, "would like to have a private and off-the-record cup of tea with you before you leave, if that be possible. You and your beautiful companion, naturally."

"We'd be delighted." And he pumped the King's hand again.

And the Queen's. Which was not part of the ceremony but which earned him an extra round of applause. He thought about kissing her cheek and concluded that he wasn't sure how Lutherans would react to that. Instead, he kissed her hand.

Tumultuous cheers.

It was the least a man with a long history of republicanism behind him could do.

Gaby's smile of amusement as he returned to his chair was as wide as the Baltic Sea.

Then the festivities adjourned to the new Town Hall, which rose over Lake Mälar like the Doge's palace did over the Grand Canal in Venice (at least like it seemed to do in the pictures Sean had seen).

There were more trumpets, more ceremonies, more royalty, and then the traditional, candlelight dinner featuring *potage aux champignons, filet de boeuf Béarnaise* (washed down with *monopole rouge*), and a spectacular ice cream dessert.

Gaby, absolutely stunning in a strapless white evening dress, was in close attendance, despite his weak protests.

"Brilliant, Seano, I knew you'd be perfect and you were."

"Sister Mary Intemerata said that only God and the angels are perfect."

"Now you know she was wrong on one count."

Her keen eyes, alert like vast brown searchlights, swept the crowds. How big was she really? he wondered. The column of lights in the Helmsley had reached to the ceiling of his room. Was the real Gaby somewhere at the top of the giant hall, looking at every face to see if it revealed a potential killer?

He found it hard to believe that there had been four attempts on his life. They had happened so quickly and the traces swept away so briskly that they seemed like brief nightmares.

And maybe that's all they were.

He was the last of the speakers. The others were incredibly dull; even King Carl seemed a bit bored by the bitter denunciation of American capitalism by the Jesuit poet.

Indeed, the poor man had overreached. It was no longer the nineteen sixties.

Sean decided that he preferred Father Higgins, the priest of his childhood, denouncing birth control every Sunday morning as he sunk deeper into the pleasant swamp of senility.

I'll twit the Jebs at Ignatius when I get back about this guy.

He was suddenly lonesome for his daughters, all that he really had left in his life, he thought sentimentally. The sooner I get home to them and Chicago the better.

Single-parent Christmas was no fun. Still, he'd be with them.

Right home from here. No, damnit, I have to go to Leipzig with that pest What's-his-name. Well, straight home from there.

Will Gaby come with me? Or does her assignment end when I leave Europe?

I will miss her. She's special. Probably has changed my whole life, even if I haven't quite figured out all the implications.

The Jesuit finally ended with a *"¡Viva la Liberación!"* that woke up some of the sleeping audience.

Well, I won't put them to sleep, he thought rather smugly.

"The Irish are accustomed to being last," he began with more than a trace of the brogue. Gaby winced.

At first his remarks were standard: chain of biological knowledge like the chain of life itself. Gratitude and praise for other scholars and colleagues. The expected hypocrisy.

Then astonishment that some religionists thought evolution took the mystery out of life. Actually science brought more mystery into life. The more we know the more we know that we don't know. Many dynamisms that we have yet to discover. And others of whose existence we can only guess but which we know that we will never discover. Modern science reveals not a closed, explicable universe, but an open and mysterious one, which even hints at transcendence.

Some restless stirring in the audience, like they thought they were listening to someone halfway through a dirty joke.

From the very first minute fraction of a second when the "singularity" exploded in its "big bang," the cosmos was biotic, oriented toward the production of life. The biopolymers were fated before the first second of the explosion was over and with them a universe teeming with life. It was inevitable that memory, intellect, organic structure, sexual reproduction (a wink at Gaby), and eventually consciousness, at first rudimentary, then advanced, would emerge.

And with consciousness, eventually Mind, which, despite all the attempts to reduce it to biology and chemistry, seemed not so much to emerge from evolution as to merge with it.

The deaf-mute chemist whose wife was scribbling a translation as he talked, look at Sean as though he had lost his mind.

Much stirring from the antidualist forces.

No one would dare to say he was wrong, however.

Gaby tense and white. What's she worrying about?

Has not von Weizsacker said that matter is mind submitting to objectification? As evolution progresses, will not that objectification become more and more elaborate, subtle, and Mind serving?

Others have suggested this, von Ditfurth, Vollmer, for example (always useful to quote Krauts, no one thinks they're comedians). It is necessary to say it explicitly even though there is great resistance in the scientific community to what our research seems to be suggesting: Such elaborate, sophisticated, and efficient brain/

mind composites might very well consist of matter and energy patterns that would be quite beyond our powers to record, rational corporeal creatures whom we could not possibly see unless they chose to reveal themselves to us.

Increasing restlessness and dismay in the crowd.

You haven't seen anything yet, little brothers.

"If such unperceivable creatures should exist—and I do not, to repeat myself, say anything more than that they are a distinct evolutionary possibility—they might well someday come among us. There is no reason to think their modes of transport would impact on our senses any more than they themselves would.

"And if they could come among us, perhaps they already have, perhaps they are even present at this august occasion, perhaps amused by our dim probings, much as we would be amused by the doings of chimpanzees or Irish wolfhounds."

Gaby's eyes closed in dismayed amusement. She wasn't ready for that ad lib.

"Is it not possible that the stories of spiritual beings which are to be found in every cultural tradition in the world are hints of the presence of such corporeal intelligences whom our sense mechanisms do not record? May not such beings, for example, have appeared to the maid of Nazareth, sung on the hillside at Bethlehem, waited at the empty tomb very early in the morning on the first day of the week?—"

Cries of protest from the audience. Call for the Inquisition, guys, the crazy mick dared to hint at God.

Gaby was still there, but she looked like she wished she wasn't. What's the matter, woman? I put that ad lib in especially for you?

"I do not insist that any of these hypotheses are true, or that there is sufficient evidence to make them any more than interesting questions. But I do insist that we now know enough about the mysteries of life and the mysteries of evolution to make them not merely interesting questions, but questions that must be asked not in the name of religion, which I do not take seriously—at least for the purposes of my biology—but in the name of pure science. To say that they should not be asked or cannot be asked is to abandon science to dogmatism, to replace inquiry with obscurantism, to ignore the demands of our data, and to side with those who locked Galileo in a cell and burned Giordano Bruno at the stake!

"Finally, I have been labeled in my own country, mostly through my own fault, as the discoverer of superfly. I do not propose to suggest here that Superman is an angel, though clearly he has angelic powers. I do wish to insist, however, that long before we reach such a phase of our evolutionary process, we must first develop a higher degree of skills at peaceful cooperation. We cannot accelerate that process. The 'intelligence' that governs our evolution cannot be short-circuited. But, unlike all other species, we in the species *Homo sapiens sapiens*—a redundant if not inaccurate label—have the capacity of blocking the directionality of our organisms. We can stand in the way of our pilgrimage in the direction of what someone once called the Point Omega. Unless our culture and social structure acquire more skills at cooperation, the organisms that bear our endlessly transpositioning genetic codes will not survive to make the big leap in the angelic direction.

"Or even a small leap toward peace."

Wild applause as the leprechaun departed the podium.

Nothing succeeds nearly so well as failure.

With the exception of martyrdom.

The pretty Queen, it turned out, was a devout Lutheran and had read Luther's work on angels, a body of literature about which Sean Desmond knew nothing at all.

With the help, however, of an occasional word or sentence from Gabriella Light and memories of Sister Intemerata, Fee and Dee, and Blackie Ryan, he managed to hold his own in the conversation.

The King listened politely, proud of his wife and fascinated by the mad Irishman who came to tea.

"Well," he said finally, "I am perhaps not as devout as my wife, though she says I am more religious." He beamed at her and she smiled back. "I am a bit of a scientist, though only as an amateur."

"Your work on forestry"—Gaby jumped in smoothly—"suggests far more than that."

"Why, thank you very much." The young monarch was pleased as punch at the compliment. One more for Gaby. "But to speak about angels, I am not sure we have to believe in them anymore, but it would be a shame, it seems to me, if there were not, somewhere in creation, creatures like them. It would, how shall I say, be less complete a universe."

"And less beautiful," Sean added.

Gaby bit her lip to hold back laughter. She was charming, reserved (a devout Lutheran queen might be uneasy about a mistress, a putative mistress, that is), and weary. So angels show the effects of stress too.

The night before, she had hugged him briefly after his talk, an encounter that made him feel like he had been launched for a quick trip to the new supernova.

"You were wonderful," she whispered. "I'm so proud of you."

"A guy doesn't hear that often from his guardian angel."

"Shush."

Then the reporters and scholars were all over him.

"You looked worried at the end of the talk," he said to her later during a brief interlude of peace.

"Sometimes even angels have self-doubts. Tiny, tiny ones. You were yourself, which is what you should have been and what I always knew you would be."

A fair number of those who swarmed around him were hostile. Two greatly different men were favorable.

The first was Bishop Stendahl of Stockholm, who had been the dean of the Harvard Divinity School, a tall handsome man with a rich voice and a happy smile, and with a purple vest and a pectoral that, added to his roman collar, made him look more like a cardinal than Chicago's raffish Sean Cronin.

"You would make a very good theologian, Professor Desmond. I'm sure the divinity school would give you a chair after today's talk."

"You mean the *Harvard* Divinity School."

The bishop laughed heartily. "Yes, I forget that at the University of Cook County, no modifier is needed. Strange, is it not, theologians are preoccupied with politics, ethicians can talk only about sex, we bishops worry unduly about money, and physicists and biologists think about creation and purpose."

"And filmmakers like Spielberg portray creatures of light?"

He winked at Gaby, who had the good grace to appear mildly embarrassed.

The next man was Herr Doktor Professor Heinz-Johann Helmstadt. "Ya, Desmond," the ugly little man crowed, "you make good Marxist. Contradictions, nein? Thesis, antithesis, bang! synthesis, is so?"

"I guess."

"Damn good Marxist. Socialism admires creative thinkers. Does not allow press idiots to bother them, nein?"

"If you say so."

"Creep," Sean said to Gaby.

She nodded grimly.

Before they went to bed there were two phone calls, one from Fee and Dee.

"Daddy—"

"—You were wonderful."

"All our friends—we had a Nobel Prize party—thought you were really excellent."

"Truly outstanding."

"Totally bitchin'?" he asked.

"Daddy!"

"Really!"

"Gaby looked really super!"

"Outstanding!"

"Where does she buy her clothes?"

"Out of *Vogue* and *Town and Country*."

"Daddy!"

"Say hello to her for us."

" 'Bye, Daddy."

"Love you, Daddy."

"What man can need any more than to know that he's like totally super?"

By now he took it for granted that Gaby did not have to pick up the phone to hear a conversation.

"No sermons, angel lass.... Do they think I'm sleeping with you?"

"No."

"How do you know?"

"I know."

"They don't think I'm capable of it?" His feelings were hurt.

"Not at all. They had a long discussion and came to a correct if incomplete conclusion. And I won't violate their privacy by reporting it."

"Would they have minded if they thought I were?"

"I will like totally not answer that question."

Before they could settle that one the phone rang again.

"Johnny? Johnny."

"Blackie!"

Gaby started to guffaw.

"Well yes, what was it you wanted?"

"You called me."

"So I did. Where are you?"

"Sweden."

"Indeed, remarkable.... Ah, yes, for the prize. Indeed. You were quite typical, if I may be so bold, on TV. My Lord Cronin was pleased to comment that you were a real shit-kicker."

"Takes one to know one."

"Arguably. The local media are very positive about it all. You have become an enormous folk hero. Actually, I'm not surprised to hear it at all. As a matter of fact, the worthy *Leader* is in full re-treat."

All the buzzwords in one paragraph. 'Ray, Blackie!

"Wonderful of you to call."

"You seemed to have learned an astonishing amount about angels."

"My guardian angel is a good teacher."

"Sister Intemerata, God be good to her, will doubtless be pleased."

"Not often," Gaby said, trying to control her laughter, "when you are one up on him."

"First time since second grade."

The next day after tea, as the King, with some show of reluctance, was leading them to the door of the royal apartment, he said, "It would seem, Doctor Desmond, that the world has divided in half on your speech."

"Without, most of them, having read it."

"How true! Well, my wife and I are on your side. We must never be too solemn at these gatherings. We are very glad you came and said what you did. Men and women will read your work for many years. Maybe centuries."

"But what we will remember," the Queen added, "is that you are not only a good scientist but a good man. That is more impor-tant."

"I'm flustered for the first time in the last twenty-four hours," Sean admitted, kissing her hand again, "but thank you very much."

"Flustered indeed," Gaby sniffed when the two of them

emerged from the palace into the cold sunlight. "That poor child is one more conquest. I don't know what we're going to do about you."

She was obviously pleased that there was a need to do something.

The wolfhound loves and worships his owner, but he doesn't desire her. He desires wolfhound bitches.

So I have to find my own wolfhound bitch. I'm a good man, it turns out, and women think me "adorable." Shouldn't be hard to find my own female wolfhound with those credentials.

But what was this good man bit? The pretty Queen said it unselfconsciously. Her husband loves her too much to disagree with her, but he didn't seem surprised. And Gaby? Well, she didn't make one of her smart ass comments, so she must agree.

"I don't think of myself as a good man," he pleaded, as they approached the launch that would take them back across Lake Mälar to Stockholm from the Palace on Drottningholm Island. "What the hell's happening to me?"

"Angelic influences, I suppose."

"Is it all over, Gaby?"

"Not quite, Seano, our big battles are still ahead of us."

"When? Where?"

"Soon."

"I want to go home."

"You know," she said, sighing, "I do too."

If Sean Desmond were not sleepy and hung over, he would have seen the big trawler bearing down on them as soon as it had rounded the corner of the island.

He didn't know what Gaby's excuse was. And there wasn't time to ask her.

Gaby did not approve of the cruise in the Skärgården archipelago. Despite the mild weather and the sunny skies, it was December. Moreover, she insisted, Sean did not realize how short were the daylight hours this far north.

Neither did the officials of the Royal Academy or the staff of the American embassy. But Sean was adamant. He insisted that he had a powerboat on the lake at home, that he was a skilled navigator, and that he must see some of the locales of the Bergman films. He also promised to stay close to Stockholm.

The Garden of the Skerries consists of thousands of islands, large and small, some barren, some wooded, some of the larger ones cultivated. The guidebook said that until recently the small farming and fishing population had been largely unnoticed. Now the islands were a summer playground.

They'd have to play pretty quickly, summer was so short here.

The academy found a boat, the embassy equipped him with a map, and a reluctant Gaby tagged along.

He had learned early in their relationship that she would not veto any plan on which he insisted.

She had expressed some reservations about the visit to Helmstadt's institute outside of Leipzig. "The man was a Nazi," she insisted.

"My father supported Joe McCarthy."

"You're not *that* dumb."

"He's one of the few scholars to take my acceptance speech seriously."

"He's quite mad."

But she made the travel arrangements for Leipzig.

She continued to pay all bills in cash, and with fresh new bills of the local currency, which she crackled in her fingers as soon as they had gone through immigration, without a visit to the currency exchange, of course.

"We're quite good at currency speculation, you know."

She also continued the game of telling him she would meet him in the lobby as he left their suite for the elevator and then greeting him with a mischievous smile as the elevator door opened in the lobby.

"Poltergeist," he said impatiently when she pulled her little trick the morning of their trip in the archipelago.

"I am not the result of the neurosis of a pubescent female," she responded with a sniff.

"You should act your age, whatever that is."

"And you should realize that evolution is in the direction of laughter and playfulness." She linked arms with him. "In your world animal infants play, but for the most part only human adults. And of course only humans laugh. I might add that you don't play or laugh nearly enough."

"And I suppose you do play and laugh all the time," he said glumly, growing weary of her brief, schoolmarmish lectures.

"Not quite, no more than the characters in the Irish sagas, which a professional Irishman like you ought to read someday. But we have little choice in the matter. It is much more in our nature to laugh and to play than it is in yours."

Damn arrogance of a superior species.

On the whole, Sean was delighted at the press reaction to his acceptance speech. The *Chicago Sun Times* headline had rung round the world:

Did "ET" Sing at Bethlehem?

His press conference in which he had rejected religious motives for his talk had been a huge success.

The bearded Latino Jesuit denounced him as a traitor in the class war and a social parasite.

"Does God exist?" asked a supercilious English reporter.

"I'm not sure whether She does or not," he replied. "That is a question beyond biology."

The denunciations were violent. A group of biologists had formed a caucus to oust him from professional societies.

The New York Times at its grave, gray best had defended him editorially. "The attacks on Professor Desmond reveal that the antiscientific dogmatism of many scientists is as serious a problem as his brilliant satirical acceptance speech suggested that it is."

Point made.

He certainly was the center of attention at the ball in the Town Hall, the night after the presentations. Until Gaby, dressed in an off-the-shoulder Roman-style dress, which he suspected was totally authentic, insisted that they dance. She again rejected his insistence that he did not dance.

"You have forgotten already about last night?"

"That was different," he replied stubbornly.

"Remember the musical plays at St. Ignatius." She took both his hands in hers.

"You know too damn much," he grumbled as he permitted her to lead him on to the dance floor. "Your dress is stunning by the way, but it is not in any of the magazines, is it?"

"Different magazine."

Dancing with her was like being swept away on a gently flowing river, as it wound its way through Swiss mountain valleys. After
the first few moments, Sean was convinced that his feet were no
longer touching ground and that soon they would be dancing
again over Lake Michigan.

Which reminded him of a question he had yet to ask. "You
didn't say anything about my reference to the angels at the empty
tomb."

"And I'm not going to either. Be quiet and concentrate on
your feet. These lessons would cost you a lot of money anywhere
else."

"Wonderful dancers," said the economic laureate, smiling for
the first time in the week.

"Dr. Light dances like an angel," Sean replied.

His toes were promptly stepped on, gently and affectionately.
Each day, he thought, he was becoming more the lovable little
lapdog.

After the ball, however, Gaby became solemn and nervous,
apparently sensing more trouble. She would not give him any
hints. She insisted, however, that she would sleep on the couch in
the parlor of their suite, a couch which had somehow moved itself
to the door of his bedroom.

"You've had a bit too much of the Creature, Jackie Jim. Get
some rest for our little voyage tomorrow." She arranged blankets
and pillows on the couch. "And *don't worry*. Leave that to your
guardian angel."

"I won't worry," he promised. "I wish I were back in Chicago."

"We don't have to do that boat ride tomorrow." She pulled
the Roman gown over her head and laid it carefully on a chair.

"Yes, we do. I've always wanted to."

"Don't forget to say your prayers." She slipped under the blankets. "Now that you believe in God again."

He sighed his County Kerry sigh, a sound that had absolutely
no effect on her. Obviously such sighs did not represent the direction of evolution.

Later in the night, he peered through the tiny opening between the door and the door frame of his bedroom. Unlike the
other nights, she was curled up in the blanket, visibly present.
Well, in her analog.

She looked innocent and youthful, almost childlike. He felt a strong affection for this dutiful guardian angel. He wanted to go home, but he would miss her.

The next morning, in clear December sunlight a few miles outside Stockholm harbor, looking like a silver-haired Liv Ullmann in a multicolored wool jacket (produced from nowhere, of course), she seemed relaxed and at ease.

They, whoever they were, could not threaten him out here.

"You want to go home too?" he asked as he guided the boat carefully between two islands.

It was a twenty-eight-foot cruiser, notably bigger than the sixteen-foot outboard on which his kids water-skied during the summer. He had not told the whole truth about his boating skills.

A boat was a boat, wasn't it?

Would the pretty Queen think he was still a good man if she knew he had, uh, exaggerated about his boating skills?

There wasn't any danger. His guardian angel didn't seem particularly worried. She could probably drive a battleship if she had to.

"Oh yes, indeed." She leaned back against the plush leather seat in the cabin. "Does it seem strange to you that I should want to go home?"

"I didn't know that angels had a home."

"We're bodily creatures, we occupy space, though a bit differently than you do. So naturally there is a space that is our special place."

"A long way from here?"

"Uh-huh. Well, not too far away. It takes longer than flying across the Atlantic, but our time frame is different."

"A little less than the speed of light?"

"How else?" She unzipped her jacket.

"Is it a planet or something like that?"

"Something like that. It's a place. If you were there, you'd be able to see it. Quite beautiful."

"Similar to Earth?"

"Not greatly dissimilar. You would not be completely disoriented. Lots of green hills." Her eyes were far, far away. "Lakes—these islands remind me of them—and flower-filled fields."

"Sounds idyllic."

"It is."

"What do you do all the time? Sort of sit around and loaf and sleep?"

"One of our evolutionary advantages"—she tilted her nose—"is that we require much less sleep than you do. Sleep is only pleasurable for your species because your body needs it so much. Actually it is an inefficient use of time."

"And it takes weeks for you to screw, doesn't it?"

"Whatever made you think—? I told you that, didn't I? But you knew I was joking?"

"Did I?"

"You did . . . it's hard to make time comparisons across species— Don't run into that little reef, Seano."

"What little reef?"

She turned the wheel slightly to the left. "The one we just missed. . . . Naturally, we spend much time in the various aspects of love, especially when we have been separated from our complements for a time."

Her voice drifted off into melancholy. How long has he been dead? Better not ask.

"Angels get horny?"

"That's a very bad analogy." She frowned her disapproval.

"Sorry."

"We sing a lot," she went on softly, "and dance. We're pretty good dancers, aren't we? You seemed to enjoy dancing with me the last several nights."

"It was better than a visit to the dentist's office."

"Drink your hot chocolate!"

"Actually it was like floating on a cotton candy cloud." He filled her hot chocolate cup.

"I'm thought to be a very skillful dancer."

"And singer and everything else you folks do."

She waved her hand as if rejecting his praise. But she didn't deny it. "And I'm also thought to be quite vain, I fear."

"Impossible."

"We talk a lot. Well, that's not a precise word. Language for us does not require voice boxes. I should have said we communicate a lot. And argue. . . . Oh, Seano, we're such terrible arguers. We don't fight in our arguments. We just argue, on and on and on. The silly folk tale that the author of Revelation uses to illustrate the problem of good and evil . . . ?"

" 'Michael and his angels did war with—' "

"It is such an absurd misunderstanding." She pounded her thigh impatiently. "Michael and my complement were the closest of friends since they were tiny ones. So they loved to argue. Once they had an argument so big that all of us who were present were on one side or the other." She laughed like a happy young girl. "I was on the other side, which delighted my complement greatly. It is most rewarding to argue with those you love. That's where the story started."

"Who won?"

"No one wins our arguments. If someone won, then the argument would have to stop and the fun would be gone."

"Michael is kind of, well, the boss?"

"In some sense, I suppose. But not even as much as that adorable young King is the boss of this country. We need rather less coordination than you. Still we need some."

"You guys play a lot?"

"As I've said, it is in our nature." She rolled over on her belly, as relaxed as Sean had ever seen her. "One of the more difficult aspects of working on this planet is that your species is disinclined to play, even as much as its limitations permit. It is a specially burdensome trait"—she jabbed her finger at him—"in creatures like you who have strong play propensities."

He didn't think he wanted to touch that one. Better to continue with the interview about her while she was in a talkative mood.

"I'm sorry, guardian angel, ma'am. I'll try to do better."

"You will indeed." She stared at him thoughtfully. "Perhaps more than you could imagine."

"Well, I think you definitely sound Irish to me, like I said the other day."

"So?" She raised both eyebrows.

"You live in a place with green hills and lots of lakes. You lie around and loaf and do nothing except screw and sing and dance and argue and tell stories, and you probably drink a lot too."

"I didn't say we told stories."

"But you do, I know you too well to doubt it."

"Okay, we tell stories."

"And you drink a lot?"

"Only in moderation."

"So all right, angels are Irish."

"No."

"Why not?"

She hesitated, looking for a response. "Because you don't like sex enough."

"We did till the Church took over."

"And even after the Church took over, till the famine. All right, all right, I'll tell my associates. If they ever want to settle permanently on Earth, Ireland might be a congenial place."

They paused, briefly worn out by their argument. The woman could go on all night this way.

"It must be hard, then, to leave your home planet."

"Region might be a better word. . . . Yes, it is. However, we are a strange species. We are impelled to go forth and return. We do our work, messengers, secret agents, overseers—however you want to describe it—because it is in our nature to do so. We are not just altruists, Jackie Jim. We are explorers of beauty and goodness, companions on pilgrimage, as I have often told you."

"You're driven to leave home and find patterns to protect?"

"And to enjoy, don't forget that. We enjoy observing and sustaining patterns of beauty and goodness. We could not live, and I mean that literally, unless we did so. We are beauty-hungry creatures."

"My problems must not be all that satisfying," he said uneasily, "to beauty-hungry creatures."

"You said that, I didn't." She tossed her short silver hair impatiently. "I can see much more of your story than you can. . . . Anyway, we love to venture forth and we love to go home."

"When you go home—R and R, as our military calls it— someone else takes over your projects?"

"Oh no." She twisted into a more comfortable position. "Why would we do that?"

"So you go home only when your projects are finished?"

"Some projects go on for centuries of your time."

"How do you manage it, then?"

"It's hard to explain . . . the concepts are so different. Let me think. . . . Well, I'll be concrete. When you and I have solved your little problem, our little problem . . . and you're relieved of wondering every day what fashions my vanity will dictate as clothing for my analog . . . I will return to our region. But I will not be gone from you."

"Not ever?"

"Not ever," she said firmly. "You won't be able to see this clumsy analog—"

"Nothing clumsy about it, woman."

"Thank you. You will not be able to see me, exactly, but then, you won't need to see your guardian angel to know you have one."

She takes this guardian angel analogy seriously. I'm not sure that I like that.

"You'll be in your region and still around here keeping tabs on me?"

"Laughing at you." She grinned impishly. "You're such a delight, Jackie Jim. So many laughs."

"I think I should be embarrassed." He turned a corner around a large island and into a large inlet of the Baltic Sea. A long black and white tanker was steaming across it. The oil lifeline to Sweden. Fuel to keep the Bofors group turning out guns for Arabs. International trade.

"Only if praise embarrasses you, Jackie Jim."

"How do you do it? How do you go to your regions and still hang around here, laughing at me?"

"How would I sing and dance and play and argue and—your word—loaf while I'm still enjoying your presence?" She shook her head, still trying to find an explanation. "Well, I suppose you could say I leave part of myself behind."

"You WHAT?"

"We have the ability to detach some of our energy patterns, a model, a replica . . . no"—she kicked her legs up and down viciously as she struggled with the idea—"a little self, a miniature self . . . and leave it elsewhere in the cosmos."

"Oh." Sean turned down a narrow channel, which didn't seem to be on the map. He had no desire to struggle with the wake of a supertanker. "That's very interesting. You're really here now, aren't you?"

"Certainly. Where else would I be?"

"And when you cut out on me, you'll still be able to read my mind with this vest-pocket Gabriella you leave behind?"

"We don't read your minds!" She pounded the couch. "And

you're baiting me, Sean Seamus Desmond." She struggled off the couch and reached into the lunch box that had somehow appeared on the boat. "Eat a Swedish fish sandwich"—she jammed it into his mouth—"and don't be a geek all the time."

"So your spy can tell you what I'm doing"—he wolfed down the sandwich—"at the speed of light?"

"Don't be childish. It's not a spy. It's me left behind. And we're not held to the speed of light in such matters. Thought is instantaneous. If there is someone who can hear you at the farthest edges of space from where you are now, they know your thoughts—if you wish to send them—the instant you think them. My vest-pocket Gabriella and I are linked by mind. Feel better?"

"I'm not sure," he admitted. "It'll be nice having you around, mind you; the money and the food will run out if I'm left to my own. On the other hand, when and if I finally get this wolfhound bitch into bed with me, I think I'd like a little privacy."

Then the big gray boat, a water-skimming prehistoric monster, roared around the corner of the island and was upon them in seconds.

Its prow hurtled toward them like the mouth of a giant water monster, a diesel-powered Moby Dick cutting through the water, its lips open to drag them in, its teeth ready to crunch them into tiny pieces.

After what seemed light-years of terrified paralysis, Sean spun the helm of his twenty-eight-foot Volvo cruiser like it was a ski boat racing back to an injured skier.

The trawler missed them by a few yards. Its big bridge towered over them like a skyscraper. Its wake swept over the Volvo like a tidal wave, rocking it dangerously on its beam and drenching them with water.

The big boat wheeled around with astonishing agility and swept back toward them. Moby Dick, it seemed to say confidently, does not miss twice.

Bullets danced along the deck of the Volvo like fireflies on a summer night. Its engine died. The trawler loomed up again, as high as Sears Tower.

There was no time for reviewing his life or praying. Foolishly he tried to duck.

The harsh bow was only a few feet from his skull. He waited to hear the crunch of steel against fiberglass.

Their cruiser leaped ahead like a jet engine had been turned on at its stern. The trawler wallowed in the trough of a big wave.

What the hell was that? Another tanker rushing by somewhere out on the Baltic?

The other craft turned again and began to barrel toward them. This time there would be no mistake.

Then the trawler jumped out of the water as though Neptune or some such character had grabbed it in his hand and hurled it into the sky. It crashed back into the ocean with a sickening splatter.

A gigantic waterspout erupted under the big boat, and tossed it once more into the air, like a toy boat in a bathtub, and then sucked it back under the water. The trawler surfaced, propeller spinning vainly in the air, and almost immediately dove under the water again, like a swimmer from a high dive.

It did not come up.

In a few seconds, there was nothing to be seen but the placid waters of the gulf. No debris, no oil slick, no survivors. Nothing.

Sean opened his mouth to chide Gaby about the slowness of her reaction. Instead hysterical babble poured from his lips. Soaking wet, battered, terrified, he fell apart.

Gaby took him in her arms and held him tightly, murmuring soft reassuring sounds.

He did not particularly want to be reassured, but her comfort was irresistible.

"Do you love me, Gabriella?" he asked, the way he often wanted to ask his mother the same question and never could.

She held him at arm's length. Her eyes bored into his. "With greater intensity, Sean Seamus Desmond, than you can possibly imagine."

Uh-oh. The trawler might have been safer.

"How can you possibly—"

"I know, you're a miserable, vain, contentious, troublemaking shanty Irishman. But surely you understand that with Mind there comes Love? Some prerational creatures have affection for one another. Your species, because it is more mind, experiences more permanent and powerful emotional attractions. Can you not imagine what love must be in creatures that are, if not quite pure spirits as Sister Intemerata told you, nonetheless more elaborately and powerfully mind?"

"You fall in love easily?"

She nodded, not in the least embarrassed by self-revelation. "We cannot help ourselves. It is in our nature to love. Is it not evident that evolution is in the direction of love? Why are you immune to the logic of your own theories?"

"So you loved all the others you've protected the same way?" His feelings were hurt.

"No, Seano, even by my standards, you're special." She grinned like an impish and indulgent young mother with a wayward but lovable little boy.

Maybe it was blarney. It was still nice.

"All right, sing something for me again."

"What do you want me to sing?"

"Am I ever going to see your world?"

"Not ... not in the present life."

"Then can you sing some songs about what it is like."

"I can. And other songs too."

So as the boat, in working order again without his doing any repairs on the engine, chugged at slow speed back to the pier in Stockholm, she sang again for him. The songs were wordless, but they lifted him up off Earth, beyond the Milky Way to the farthest galaxies at the outer reaches of the cosmos, not as an awed and reverent pilgrim, but as a little boy cavorting and dancing in a splendid, fascinating playground, his heart filled with innocent youthful merriment. And then he was swept along on a thousand breathtaking rides in a glorious amusement park filled with spectacular roller coasters and Ferris wheels.

When they came finally to her "region," the melodies became slow and reverent, restful and meditative, mystical and serene— and were quickly and abruptly replaced by comic music, nutty, impish, manic, kindergarten children at play. There was more solemn "churchy" melody, then a song of infinite melancholy, mourning for her complement surely, and finally, leaving the "region" behind, a marching song, happy warriors on the road.

Next they were back on Earth and it was night and they were all singing of indescribable joy, joy that Sean wanted never to end and which he felt might survive forever.

Bethlehem again.

He wanted the Stockholm waterfront never to appear.

But it did. And she would not tell him whether the last song was really the same song that had been sung at Bethlehem.

"You're not *that* important," she sniffed.

It was only when he awoke in the middle of the night, Gaby's couch still at the door, that he remembered that she said that she loved him, "with more intensity than you can possibly imagine."

A cold sweat appeared on Sean Desmond's skin. What do you do when an angel, a putative seraph, a fireball of love, loves you?

After breakfast the next morning, Sean went for a long walk along the docks. Snow had fallen the night before, not much yet, the Swedes said, and not nearly as much as they would expect in mid-December. It did not seem like Chicago snow, which usually comes and goes. The snow that crunched under his feet as he strode briskly along the docks had settled in with intent to stay. He was glad that they were getting out on the noon plane from Arlanda. He wanted to be home a week before Christmas.

His nervousness about the awards ceremony and the acceptance speech over, he decided that he rather liked the Swedes. Indeed, if anyone had pressed him, he would have admitted that he even rather liked the English. Not as much as he liked Americans, naturally. But still ...

Ironically, he supposed, he would not like the Irish at all. It would serve him right for his ethnic chauvinism. He was not, however, giving the talk in Ireland. He would phone them from London and plead sickness. They would be offended, maybe even hurt, but too bad for them. They owned no rights to him or his presence.

He sensed that the game with Gaby had run its course. The challenge on the Baltic Sea was almost certainly the big battle that still had to be fought, the final chapter. She seemed relaxed and at ease in the evening, no longer scanning crowds in search of faces.

Or whatever it was for which she searched. Maybe smells.

He now no longer doubted her reality or her explanation. A good scientist accepts evidence that the impossible is true when the evidence is incontrovertible.

He made a mental note of the phrase. He would use it in class next quarter. Desmond's Law.

Nor could he question the intensity of the affection between the two of them—kennel keeper and favorite wolfhound pet. He would never forget her, even if he was not altogether convinced that a vest-pocket Gaby, invisible but watching, would follow him around the rest of his life.

After a while you forget about that which you can't see.

Desmond's Second Law.

He wished he had brought along a notebook so he could jot down these gems.

If, however, Gabriella was real and her stories basically true, the whole adventure existed in another dimension of reality than ordinary life. It was a component of the Nobel Prize and would pass into the hard disk in his brain reserved for memories—CD ROM.

It would all soon be over and on the way to being forgotten.

In their suite at the Grand Hotel, Gaby was sitting at the desk in the parlor watching the plaza in front of them and the docks beyond.

One of her thinking moods again. That usually was an indicator of more trouble to come.

"Nice walk?"

"Cleared the cobwebs out of my brain. Ready for the airplane flight. . . . White lace teddy today, huh? Nice."

"It's an appropriate garment"—she grinned crookedly—"for a Rubens nude, isn't it?"

Sean felt his face catch fire. "You eavesdropper!"

"I promised I wouldn't read your mind"—she chuckled—"not that I wouldn't listen to your conversation. Don't be embarrassed. I . . . well, my analog is flattered."

"I'm glad."

"You Catholics missed the boat on old Peter Paul, by the way." She sighed and stood up. "His glorification of human flesh represented the Catholic Reformation, a response to Luther and Calvin's dislike for the human body. The Hapsburgs funded people like him because they knew that Catholics were supposed to believe that the body is a sacrament of God. Then along came Philip II and that crazy Caraffa Pope who put loincloths on Michelangelo's paintings, and the humanists lost. The Catholic Reformation became the Counter-Reformation, and you're still trying to get over that, aren't you?"

"An interesting version of history." He tried to remember all that she said; it would come in handy at the round table, if he ever returned to the round table.

"The correct version." She was staring out the window again, usually a bad sign. "Depend on it . . . you folks messed that one up almost as badly as you did the time after the Second Vatican Council. We worked hard on both of them and the Curia beat us. Talk about random lunacy . . . you'd make a better pope than a lot of the people who've had the job, and you wouldn't be all that good at it."

She was pretty angry at the Vatican. I don't think I'll touch that.

"We were never taught that the human body was good. Sister Intemerata—"

"That's what I mean"—she turned away from the window and faced him again—"about the Counter-Reformation."

"What I said actually was Rubens without the flab; and you look sensational in white lace."

Never hurt to compliment a woman twice, even an angel woman. No, especially an angel woman. Well, anyone, human or angel, male or female—round-table folks excepted.

"Thank you. Give you an idea what to buy for your wolfhound bitch."

Plunging neckline, high-cut thigh. The wolfhound bitch would have to possess quite a figure.

Well, maybe she would at that.

"Too expensive." He threw his coat on a chair and sat down on another. "Fifty dollars at least."

"That's not too much for a beautiful woman."

"On a professor's salary and with my alimony payments."

"The last thing you will need to worry about when this is over, Jackie Jim, will be money." She turned toward him. "Don't even think about it."

"Yes ma'am."

He could not imagine a world in which he did not need to worry about money. Would she supply me with a stack of crisp new hundreds each week? Maybe I should ask before she leaves?

"The game isn't quite over yet," she said calmly.

"Your sitting there with your thinking cap on kind of made me think that was true. Are we going to win?"

"Certainly we are." Her eyes widened in surprise at a foolish question. "Never any doubt about that."

"Angels lose sometimes. Sarajevo, for example."

"I wasn't on that case and this one is different. Oh, we'll win all right. It may be a little hairy at times, but we're scheduled to be number one."

She held up her finger like Keith Smart of Indiana when he sank the winning basket at the NCAA tournament.

Knows about basketball tourneys and thinks Mondale won the election. Sometimes I'm not so sure.

"You're the boss," he said, trying to sound confident, "if you say so."

"Promise me one thing." She looked very grim indeed.

"Sure. Why not? Name it."

"No matter what happens, you must trust me. Even if it looks like all reason for trust has vanished."

"Absolutely," he said easily.

Later when the situation arose, he didn't trust her at all. Such for promises from our species.

"Okay, let's get dressed and head for the airport."

"I'm not the one flouncing around in an ounce or two of lace."

More dream material. He was still having the dreams, was he not?

No, as a matter of fact, they had stopped the night of his acceptance speech.

"Don't be vulgar." She reached for a dress in the closet, a dress that had not been there thirty seconds before.

"Exhibitionists like to be noticed."

"All species have a certain amount of exhibitionism programmed into them," she said smugly, putting on the dress—

black, V neck, gold buckle and buttons, zipper front—no help needed in zipping up today. "And both sexes in all species. Rational species either acknowledge it or suppress it, the latter at their own peril."

"Yes ma'am."

They both laughed.

She certainly had a lot to exhibit. He thought of the gold and silver waterfalls.

How could anyone think they could fight such powerful beauty. All right, the sorcerers were mad, but could they be that mad?

She smiled at the maid, the hall porter, the concierge, and the doorman and presented them with what Sean was sure were inordinately large tips, though he had yet to figure out the denominations of Swedish money. She thanked the assistant manager, for the wonderful service. He called the manager and he and Gaby exchanged a few polite words in Swedish. They both bowed respectfully to each other like high-ranking nobility.

"I didn't know you could speak Swedish?"

"I picked it up while I was here. It's not a difficult language, not when you know German."

"Now you can be in a Bergman film."

"I'm not serious enough. I couldn't keep a straight face while all that Nordic misery poured out. Incidentally, it won't be necessary to let our hosts in Leipzig know that I understand them, right?"

"Right."

Was the final battle, the *Götterdämmerung*, going to be in Leipzig? That would be appropriate, but how could a little pig like Helmstadt be taken seriously as a sorcerer?

He didn't look like a sorcerer.

But what did a sorcerer look like?

At the airport, her attention to the multilingual, multihued crowd was perfunctory.

"They all look like terrorists to me," Sean protested.

Gaby glanced up, sniffed the air, and shook her head. "More ethnic prejudice. Just workers flying home for Christmas."

They were scheduled to take the noon flight to Leipzig, the only flight of the day from Stockholm with a stop at Copenhagen.

There were only about twenty-five people on the SAS DC-9. No first-class section on the plane, much to Gaby's dismay.

"I never fly first class," he protested.

"I *always* fly first class."

"Nothing is too good for an angel."

"Naturally."

I mean if you can wend your way through the cosmos at the speed of light, you're entitled to first class on a DC-9.

Sean was surprised that she didn't create a first-class section.

The ceiling was low at the Stockholm airport, but they took off. Sean's fear of flying had indeed vanished, but he let her hold his hand just the same.

Enjoy the guardian angel in person until you have to settle for the vest-pocket edition.

They were late landing in Copenhagen because of the snow and low-lying clouds. They were told there would be an hour delay and they could enter the transit lounge at Kastrup Airport if they wished.

"I've never been in Denmark." Sean peered through the snow-dusted window. "Can we have a look around?"

"You won't be able to see the mermaid from inside the airport, but why not?"

"Have you ever been in Denmark?"

"Not since . . ." She giggled. "Well, not recently . . . we can buy a picture of the mermaid for your daughters. She really is a lovely little thing. Kind of sad and yet strong. Which is what a mermaid would have to be, wouldn't she?"

"Are there mermaids?"

"Don't be ridiculous. You're the biologist."

"They're in the same category as the *yeti* and Big Foot?"

"I didn't say that and I didn't say anything about Big Foot."

"Are there mermaidlike creatures in other worlds?"

"There are other cosmoi too."

"I'll take your word for it. Are there mermaids in other worlds or other cosmoi?"

"It would be unwise to stake one's career on the position that there are not."

As usual, she'd told him not much of anything.

They did buy some Danish sandwiches at the bar in the

lounge. Sean gobbled down a half dozen inside of two minutes.

"You'll spoil your supper."

She was sounding more like a mother with every passing hour.

"Who knows when we're going to eat supper. By the way, I've been meaning to ask you about Rafe."

"Even you must know that the story of Tobias and Raphael in the Book of Tobit is a folk tale with a spiritual theme."

"Book of Tobit?"

Gaby sighed noisily. "I suppose Sister Intemerata left it out of the scriptures because it was so sexy. You don't know the story?"

"Sex in the scriptures?"

"Don't pretend to be a puritan, it ill becomes you," she said primly. "Young Tobit or Tobias, depending on whether you're a Protestant or a Catholic, is sent on a mission by his father. A fellow named Raphael shows up and offers to act as a companion and protector for the kid, teenager probably. Off they go and come to the distant town and encounter this poor girl Sarah who has lost seven husbands on her wedding nights to a demon. So Raphael gives him a magic spell that gets rid of the demon, and Tobias takes the girl for his mate without lust and they all live happily ever afterward."

"Without lust?" Sean protested.

"Not without passion or desire. The scripture means he didn't turn her into a sex object, hence the demon could not harm their relationship. Anyway, the theme of the story is that angels are God's companions for humans on their journeys, hence the Hebrew name for us can mean 'companion.'"

"Nice story."

"Lovely story."

"Well, you're my companion on a journey. Are you Raphael too?"

"Heavens no." She blushed at the thought.

"Does he really exist?"

"I think that I could most effectively reply to that"—she was now playing her prim schoolmarm bit—"by saying that the Raphael role, helping young lovers, or even not so young lovers, with their problems is not unknown to us. Naturally, the lovers can resist our help, since we do not deprive them of their free will."

"Do they?"

"Sometimes, certainly. I will admit, however, that physical desire is one of our strongest assets, which is as Most High intended it should be."

At that moment Sean noted three well-dressed, dark-skinned men enter the lounge. Sleek, prosperous, self-satisfied. Oil company executives, he decided. Lording it over the Europeans they were ripping off. Getting even for Lepanto and Tours and Sobieski at Vienna.

He watched them more closely. They were young men, carrying expensive briefcases, hard-muscled young men. The illusion of fat was created by their perfectly cut clothes.

"Those three guys"—he nodded at them—"the ones who look like they stepped out of *Esquire* wouldn't be terrorists, now would they?"

"Which ones? Those businessmen standing by themselves over there? Of course not, they're probably—"

She stopped.

" 'Probably?' "

"Certainly."

"Certainly what?"

"Hezboallah, Lebanese Shiites, allies of Iran."

"Hijack?"

"Probably." She seemed to be thinking furiously.

"Why?"

"Guess."

"Me?"

"Fair bet." Then she relaxed and returned to the French fashion magazine she had been devouring.

"What's going to happen?"

"Just watch and see."

Gradually, so slowly that you hardly noticed it happening, people began to drift away from the three swarthy men, some to the bar, some to the ticket counter, some to the washrooms. No one seemed to be aware of the shift, including the three Lebanese, who huddled close together, talking in undertones and puffing nervously on cigarettes.

They still did not *look* like terrorists.

"How did they get through security?"

"They don't have any guns. Only tiny plastic explosive charges in their bags. New stuff."

"Are they sorcerers?"

"I doubt it, more likely another team that wants to get into the game."

An airport security guard came into the lounge, Belgian automatic weapon hanging from his shoulder and looked around casually.

"What's going to happen?"

"Wait and see. Allah is not on their side today."

The guard returned with two of his fellows. They began to check passports, quietly, routinely.

Gaby smiled at the guard who approached them as she handed over their two passports. He glanced at them, nodded, and smiled back.

"Did he recognize me?" Seamus asked.

"I'm the exhibitionist."

One of the guards walked toward the three Arabs. Easily, casually, the other two shifted their weapons ever so slightly and drifted in the same direction.

They *know*. Who told them?

Now that's a dumb question if there ever was one.

The guard gestured for their passports. Patiently the three men offered them. Then he gestured for the briefcases. One man shrugged and lifted the first case and opened it.

The other two opened their cases too. They were nervous now, sensing that they had been discovered.

The guard held up a cigar cylinder, or what looked like a cigar cylinder, and began to open it.

The other men reached in their cases, quickly pulled out two other aluminum cylinders and threw them into the crowd. The guard holding the third one fell to the floor. His two colleagues opened up with their machine pistols, quick little explosive coughs.

Women and children were screaming, the windows behind the terrorists shattered, the terrorists themselves turned very red as parts of their bodies disappeared and they slumped to the floor. In the midst of the confusion, Gaby deftly caught one of the cigar tubes.

Sean held his breath, waiting for the explosion.

That never came.

She held up the cylinder for him to see and shrugged her shoulders. "Doesn't seem to work." She giggled. "Can't imagine why."

Sean Desmond wanted to say "Neither can I," but the words didn't come out because his heart was in his throat.

The melee continued for some minutes. More guards rushed in. The passengers, kicking, screaming, and shouting, were herded toward the door. Yet more guards and some men and women who looked like they might be Danish army arrived. A couple of doctors and nurses in white pondered the remains of the would-be terrorists.

The guard who had challenged them was unhurt but stunned, probably in shock. Lucky guy that his buddies' bullets hadn't hit him. Machine pistols don't have much accuracy. They just kill real quick.

Two of the three bombs had been recovered. A white-haired Danish officer, colonel or general type, was barking orders. Gaby strolled up to him, said something in a language that Sean assumed had to be Danish, and handed him the bomb.

The man jumped about a foot and then, realizing that they all must be defective, took it from her gingerly and smiled. They both bowed to each other.

He didn't seem to be interested in learning her name. A Gaby "look" had probably quieted his curiosity.

"Close one," she said with a sigh as they were herded into another transit area. "You get credit for an assist this time."

"Which I will modestly accept." His voice was still shaky. "Nice going."

"Child's play when you have a little advance warning. Which is what I had, thanks to you, Seano."

"Not the last battle?"

"Sideshow. Unfortunately."

Was there danger in East Germany?

That was hardly likely. He was an internationally renowned scientist. A world celebrity. A Nobel Prize winner. An official state guest. The East German government, eager for acceptance in the latest twist of the party line, wouldn't permit anything to happen to him.

Was the final battle to be in Ireland? Was that why she wanted him to fly to Dublin? There would be a certain poetic justice in that sort of *denouement*.

Were the Irish into sorcery in the old days? His historical knowledge was sketchy on the subject, but he suspected that they were.

What if she insisted on the Dublin lecture as necessary for the final battle?

Well, if it came to that, he supposed he would have to go.

They were rerouted on a Hungarian plane—a rattling, uncomfortable IL-something—to East Berlin. Gaby sent a wire ahead to Helmstadt.

They were met with all due ceremony at Schoenfeldt, the East Berlin airport, which looked like it might be appropriate for handling flights into Iowa City.

There was, however, a real red carpet waiting for them, an honor guard, a woman officer to present roses to Frau Doktor Light. No band.

"Velcome to the German Democratic Republic!" Helmstadt boomed as he extended both his pudgy paws to seize Desmond's right hand. "We are honored a dousand times by your presence."

Like the dousand-year reich?

And all three words in the name of the country were lies.

In the dark light and the snow fall, Sean decided that Helmstadt did look a little like a sorcerer.

29

Professor Heinz-Johann Helmstadt's Erich Honecker Socialist Work Center huddled against a hill on the banks of the Elster in the snow-blanketed rolling country outside Leipzig. Its administrative headquarters looked like a cross between a Victorian haunted house and a castle of a mad German monarch.

"Built in 1960," said Gaby.

The "guest rooms" in which he and Gaby were spending the second night of their trip to East Germany managed to be simultaneously ornate and uncomfortable: heavy burgundy drapes, thick wine carpets, solid chairs and couches, a heating system that had two settings, too hot and too cold, walls which did not muffle the noise of the power unit next door.

And one large bed, emperor-size, in the bedroom.

"You'd have a difficult time finding your wolfhound witch in that bed." Gaby had gestured at it contemptuously.

" 'Bitch,' and I wouldn't bring her to this Nazi place anyway."

"Normally I don't approve of your ethnic stereotypes, Seano, especially since they're a game with you. But in this place"—she shivered—"I think you are absolutely right." Gaby was huddled in a chair, her hand at the top of her beige robe, as if protecting her-self from the foulness of the place.

"I know now that the Nazis won the Second World War."

"They did here anyway. Literally. Many of the government officials here in 1945 were ex-Nazis. And today there is a Nazi lineage among the younger leaders. Your friend Helmstadt was in Hitler Jugend."

"German efficiency plus Marxist philosophy equals Nazism. Don Martino should come here."

"He wouldn't last five minutes."

"So Helmstadt suggested."

"The people are all right." Gaby pulled the belt on her robe tighter. "People are people everywhere. It's the leaders in this prison who are evil."

"And," Sean concluded, "the people don't smile."

After a long and tedious feast, with too much schnapps and heavy wine, Gaby and Sean had been permitted to retire to their suite at a hotel near a main street that was still called Stalinallee even though its name had been changed long ago.

Gaby slept again at the door of his bedroom. Guardian angel working overtime.

The next morning she emerged in a plain dark blue skirt and light blue sweater. Socialism had apparently affected her vanity. The snow had stopped, and they were taken on a tour of museums, factories, shops, monuments (including an astonishingly ugly tribute to the Red Army, which had destroyed much of Berlin and raped every woman it could find).

"See how well socialism works!" Helmstadt would shout at each new triumph.

It seemed to work up to a point. There was no trace of dirt or poverty in the streets of East Berlin—and not much of anything else. The town was a dull, well-maintained prison, with sad silent people.

No drugs, no prostitution, no robbery, no gangs, no danger on the street at night, Helmstadt bragged.

And no happiness or freedom either.

In the afternoon they were bundled into a Russian-made limo that shook and rattled as it drove through the snow-covered countryside to visit a collective farm.

"Our farms are the most productive in the world," Helmstadt boasted. "The evidence shows it."

Sean had tried to avoid arguments. He wanted to get out of this place as soon as possible. It seemed to him inconceivable that with all the public attention lavished on him by his hosts that anything could go wrong in this country.

He was perfectly prepared to believe Helmstadt's boast, "Ve deal werry quickly, chop, chop, with the criminal element here in the Democratic Republic. So there is, for all practical purpose, no criminal element."

Except the government.

Then they were driven though more snow-covered fields, with hardly any living souls in evidence, to the edge of Leipzig and the Honecker work center. Seen from the distance, stark against the snow and brooding gray sky, with the hills along the unseen River Elster behind it, the center—low, cement block buildings clustered around the headquarters, high fences topped with barbed wire, guard towers, armed troops in heavy winter coats— all seemed to convey hints of Auschwitz.

Fantastical association, he told himself.

Just the same, I bet this place was some sort of prison not so long ago.

After the second huge dinner in two nights, he and Gaby were permitted to escape, the final toast having been downed, to their rooms.

"As far as I can see," he remarked to her as they sat in front of the empty fireplace, "there's nothing particularly evil around here. Just a lot of second-rate biological research that we did fifteen or twenty years ago."

"You're too charitable," Gaby said grimly. "Third rate, at best."

He had never seen her so affected by an environment. A playful spirit—and he was willing to bet one of the most playful in her particular species—was bound to be depressed by such an unplayful place.

"One more day, tonight we will be in the Berlin Hilton."

"Bristol Kempinski," she said. "Much nicer."

"The problem with this place as far as I'm concerned is that it's too neat. Any office or any lab that is perfectly neat is not a place where important work gets done."

"They'll never make any accusations of that sort about your lab or office." She grinned at him. "Not that I disagree. Come on, let's get some sleep. You take the bed."

"That's not the way it is in the movies. The guy always gives the bed to the girl."

"In the movies," she said crisply, "the girl isn't an angel."

They were routed out of bed for an early breakfast and then escorted by the Herr Kamerad Direktor through the buildings of the center. He talked in a rapid-fire, loud monotone, like an announcer calling a horse race. He hailed every project as the best in the world.

It was too hot inside and too cold outside. Sean's legs ached from trying to keep up with the stubby little man's rapid stride. He wanted the day to end, so they could return to Berlin, then Frankfurt, then Chicago.

He continued, however, to listen and to watch carefully. Nothing about the center seemed particularly ominous.

Sean summarized the place to himself: It looks like reasonably good equipment and highly regimented researchers. Pretty hard to do anything special in such an environment. Then again, maybe they didn't want anything special.

"Iss it not sensational, Herr Professor Desmond"—and with a formal bow—"Frau Professor Light?"

"Interesting," Gaby replied.

"Candidly," Sean added, "I find it fascinating."

Inside, the work center looked like a modern prison or mental institution: concrete and steel, Klieg lights, guards in Volpo uniforms, and technicians wearing stiffly starched lab coats like Helmstadt's.

Spotlessly clean, of course.

Again he thought of Auschwitz.

It was easy to believe that Helmstadt was mad, but hard to believe that such a dizzy old man had ever been a young Nazi.

"Come now, you listen to our angel tapes, nein? Werry interesting."

So the man was a sorcerer after all. A mad sorcerer.

Why didn't Gaby know that?

Ridiculous. Certainly she knew it.

I have a feeling that I'm bait again.

The angel tapes were not nearly as good as Stacey's. The research on angels at the socialist work center, into which the Democratic Republic had poured considerable amounts of money, seemed to consist entirely of tapes and slow motion pictures that purported to record the presence of "aliens."

"He says it the same way he used to say 'Jews,'" Gaby whispered in Sean's ear.

Helmstadt's assistant, a Wagnerian-heroine type called Frau Lutz, played the tapes and ran the films with a determined efficiency that would put a mother superior of the old days to shame.

Some of the tapes were a little eerie. One could almost persuade oneself that there were voices speaking on them, though why they should be speaking in German and mumbling East German—government propaganda was not at all obvious to Sean.

"Ve use computer-enhanced methods, ya? Werry good programs, best computers in the world. Better than at Frau Professor Reid's Argonne, nein?"

So they knew about Stacey? Well, why would they not?

The ill-concealed contempt on Gaby's face left little doubt about her opinion.

When trouble came for them that day, it came abruptly, without warning, which was probably why they were able to catch Gaby by surprise.

In early afternoon they were treated to a heavy lunch of schnapps and sausage in the Herr Direktor's office. And more propaganda about how the "aliens" had agreed to cooperate in the building of a socialist world order.

"No angels, there are no angels, only socialist aliens."

"Party members?" Sean asked.

"Not yet. Too soon."

Sean wanted to escape the work center as quickly as possible. The American government knew where they were, but the Volpo uniforms made him feel uncomfortably like he was in a concentration camp.

"A moment, Herr Professor, Frau Professor." Helmstadt flashed his oily, ingratiating little smile, like an innkeeper in a third-rate *gasthaus*. "If you please, Frau Lutz...."

The two Germans stepped out of the office. Then Frau Lutz appeared at the door. "Herr Professor Desmond, if you please, we have a small token of our esteem..."

Sean pushed aside his glass of the vile schnapps and walked to the door.

Frau Lutz pulled him through the doorway like he was a sack of moldy potatoes. Instantly a metal door slid into place behind him. Two Volpos took positions on either side of Helmstadt with machine pistols pointed in the general direction of Sean's chest.

"Now, Herr Professor, we will see a very interesting experiment, ja? We will see what happens to an alien walled into a cubicle of lead when it is bombarded by bursts of protons."

He opened a box on the door frame and negligently pushed several buttons, doubtless sealing the door. He did not bother to close the box.

"Gaby!" screamed Sean, leaping at the Herr Direktor's throat.

He was intercepted by two more Volpos, enormous stormtrooper types, like the one who had almost killed him in the shower room in London.

False walls were pulled down in the outer office, revealing elaborate monitoring devices and a massive control panel, a miniature Houston space center. Several technicians were leaning over CRT's and spinning dials. Thin tubing was crammed into every inch of the wall facing the room in which Gaby was imprisoned.

"A small and highly specialized mechanism with some of the properties of the cyclotron. I think you will find its operation very interesting, ja? Excellent proof of the superiority of socialist science. It generates quite powerful bursts of protons."

"Nazi pig!" Sean shouted.

"Frau Lutz," Helmstadt said, with a nod of his little head.

She jabbed a huge hypodermic needle into Sean's arm.

And the world turned to black ink for Sean Desmond.

When the effects of the hypo
wore off, they began to beat him.

He regained consciousness in total blackness. He was lying on
a cold concrete floor in a room with steel walls. He crawled
around the floor of the room, searching for furniture and found a
steel bed without a mattress, a desk, and a chair. As soon he pulled
himself up on the chair, the bright lights went on above him. Two
massive men and an equally massive woman came into the cell,
rubber truncheons in their hands. They made him take off his
clothes and then started to beat him.

They took turns, the woman first, then the men. When they
were tired, others replaced them. When he passed out, water was
thrown on him to wake him up.

The beating was an end in itself. They sought no information.
If they had, Sean would have gladly given it to them. He would
have done anything to stop the pain. But they wanted nothing except to destroy his body.

He begged, he pleaded, he prayed for mercy.

They merely laughed and continued the beating.

Finally, they stopped. "Ve vill be back."

Broken ribs, aching head, piercing pains inside his body, Sean passed out.

As he lost consciousness, he wondered how soon he would die. He tried to pray, but the words would not come. God was not in the cell with him.

Many hours later, Sean was awakened by a rude kick in his stomach and, barely conscious, dragged out of the cell into which he had been dumped. His arms and feet were bound. His head felt like a thousand little Nazis were inside it, pounding with air hammers. His mouth was dry, his tongue enormous, his stomach and chest a mass of pain.

Please, please let me die soon.

"You've slept well, ja?" said the Herr Direktor, grinning up at him from the control panel. "Let me show you some interesting film taken from our monitors. Frau Lutz ..."

Interesting they were, slides of incredibly lovely patterns of color and light, dancing and spinning, weaving textured images that suggested the sounds of a symphony orchestra whose melodies would fill the cosmos.

Gaby, no doubt about it.

"Ja, that's what our 'alien' really looks like. You will note that with the passage of time, the colors begin to fade. Our protons are slowly disengaging its energy patterns.... The most recent one, Frau Lutz. ..."

The new colors were pale, the patterns little more than straight lines.

"Gaby," he croaked.

"Herr Schmidt"—Helmstadt pointed at a grim, sandy-haired man in a white lab jacket—"is monitoring the emissions through another interesting mechanism that I will take great pleasure in explaining to you later. When the alien ceases to exist, we will be able to measure the remaining energy levels, compare them with earlier levels, and make an estimate of its composition. Unless, of course, its colleagues wish to negotiate ..."

"Negotiate?" Sean tried to clear the fog out of his head. What colleagues? Which negotiations?

"Ja ..." The little man shrugged nonchalantly. "We are civilized and cultivated humanists. If they wish to join our attempts to build a socialist world, we will spare their colleague, for a time at any rate: If not ... well, we will learn more about them from analyzing the debris of this one and will capture others. Eventually, they will come to terms."

Force angels to come to terms?

"Hitler!" Sean shouted, doing terrible things to his throat.

Frau Lutz slapped his face, hard.

"You must to the Herr Direktor speak with respect."

"Ja, it is true.... Ah, so ... Lutz, time for the latest picture."

A transparency was removed from a boxlike tube on the control panel and placed in the projector.

There were only a few thin lines.

"So, Schmidt, what discharges do you have?"

"None, Herr Direktor. All energy waves have ceased. Not gradually, but suddenly."

"*Dummkopf*, that is impossible." Helmstadt rushed to the monitor screen. Over his shoulder, Sean could see that it was completely black.

Poor Gaby. Well, she knew now whether there was Anyone else.

The Direktor was swearing a blue streak in noisy German, momentarily distracting the Volpos. Sean lunged toward the box on the door frame.

He almost made it. He jammed his shoulder against the box and pushed furiously.

But he didn't hit the right buttons.

A Volpo cracked him on the skull, and he tumbled to the floor, a whole new mass of pain crowding into his head.

"He has become unnecessary. We will say he defected and display to the world the double we have trained." Helmstadt's voice came from a great distance. "Lutz, eliminate him."

Through a thick mist, he saw the Wagnerian heroine take an AK-47 from one of the Volpos and point it at him.

"Gaby ..." was his final prayer.

The weapon in Lutz's hands melted, and her hands and arms melted with it. The Direktor's head dissolved into a messy white liquid; the control panel erupted in a series of rapid explosions. The Volpos crumbled to the floor, their uniforms covered with the same oozing cream that was flowing down the Direktor's headless lab coat. The wall with the miniature cyclotron turned bright red, like a blast furnace.

Desmond remembered the assassin in the shower room of the Grosvenor. Try to keep a typhoon in one room. Fools.

He felt himself lifted off the ground and dragged rapidly through the steel and concrete walls of the fortress and up a snow-covered hill. At the top of the hill he was unceremoniously dropped in a snow bank. The pains in his body seemed to have been healed on the way there.

Somewhere in the depths of Sean Desmond's drugged and battered brain a voice said, "This should be quite a show."

It was.

The Elster flowed on one side, a dark slash in the snow. Above him the stars watched silently. And on the other side, the administration building began to glow with the same bright red as the wall in the control room. The light flicked on and off, like a stop sign blinking on a country road. Each flicker seemed brighter than the last one.

Then little bits of green and white light slipped in and out of the sides of the building as the red glow became brighter and brighter, tiny sparks of energy creeping like an infection through the whole center. One by one the other buildings began to pulsate with crimson light. Finally even the guard towers were caught up in the ominously ticking red glow. Screams echoed briefly on the night air and then abruptly ceased. The whole center now was glowing like a rocket about to lift off or a Roman candle ready to explode.

The quarter-square-mile area pulsated, on and off, on and off, for several seconds, a solid mass of seething red light. Then the top of the headquarters exploded and soared into space.

From the absolute center of the haunted castle, a broad pillar of white light leaped into the sky, up and down, several times—dazzling, swirling, implacable light, glowing like molten plasma and turning the night into a blinding daylight.

The thunder of the accompanying explosion was like a combination of the sound tracks of films he had seen of tidal waves, hurricanes, tornadoes, nuclear blasts. Then the roar was drowned out by the peal of thousands of trumpets blaring in glorious triumph.

In the midst of the trumpet crescendos he thought he heard Aaron Copland's "Fanfare for the Common Man." Probably not, but you couldn't tell what angels would do when they started playing games on their horns.

Then the whole institute seemed to be drained into that column of incandescent daylight, absorbed into a mighty vacuum. Then the light expanded to the far edges of the barbed-wire fences, becoming a vast pole of bubbling light reaching from earth to sky.

The light then turned scarlet, a broad band of terrible red heat and light tearing at the sky. Slowly it passed through the rainbow from blazing red to somber violet. Then back again to red. Then the brightest, cleanest, most terrible white light Sean Desmond had ever seen.

Angel fire! Seraph fire!

He was aware as the light ascended to the heavens that his eyes were being shielded. The woman thinks of everything.

That's what she really looks like, a fusion reaction. A seraph, a being on fire with love, and now with love driven by anger.

There was a mighty explosion, a fireball like a hydrogen bomb, brighter than a thousand suns.

Then the light ceased, as abruptly as it had appeared.

And the Honecker work center was no more. All that remained was a large black scar in the snow. And the starry skies above.

Goddamn Nazis. Mess with my Gaby, will you?

And then he lost consciousness again.

31

The young GI with the blue scarf and the blue beret signaled them through the gate. Gaby rated a smart salute.

"Where you from, soldier?"

"Laramie, Wyoming, ma'am."

"It's colder there than here. And more snow."

"Not as weird there, ma'am."

"Tell me about it, son."

They both laughed and the kid, eyes wide with awe, saluted again.

Good taste, kid.

They went through the checkpoint and into the efficiently plowed streets of West Berlin.

Socialism was not all that good at plowing streets. So all right, it was more ugly and messy and corrupt on this, the capitalist side of the city. At least they've shoveled the snow off the streets.

"Checkpoint Charley," she said. "Feeling better?"

"You didn't need my help," he said, the words coming up from a swamp of confusion and pain.

"Will it make any difference if I say that I cherish your brave effort to help?"

"You must have kissed the blarney stone, woman."

"You *are* better."

"Don't you believe it."

"Seriously, how do you feel?"

"For some odd reason most of the aches and pains went away up there on the hill while you did your show. I'm just sort of exhausted with small hurts all over."

"Shock. You'll be all right in a day or two."

"Fine. That was some show out there. Now I know what a seraph really looks like."

"All right, you win. I am a seraph."

"Candidly, I'm not surprised. And that was really you, wasn't it? I mean the plasma column of light. Are you really that size?"

"Oh no."

"Smaller?"

"I didn't say that." They turned a corner and drove onto a broad street swarming with people, more vitality than in the all of the Democratic Republic. Kurfürstendamm, he supposed.

"Bigger? How big are you really?"

"Big enough. . . . To take a phrase from your descriptions of certain parts of my analog's anatomy: monumental."

"I can believe it."

Already they were bantering again. They had wiped out the sorcerers and they were joking as though they did it every day.

Well, as though she did it every day.

"How could those guys figure they could fight you? But give me the details, how did you do it?"

"You did not remember London?"

"Only at the end . . . the real you never went into the Honecker Center at all."

"That's one way to put it. I was there all right, but, ah, I left much of my energy pattern and resources outside. I am so sorry"—her voice choked—"that you had to suffer. I could not act, however, until they actually tried to kill you. Then"—she sighed—"it went very quickly."

"I noticed that."

"Poor fools. . . . You forgive me for permitting you to suffer?"

"Hell, Gaby, I feel fine, more or less. And they're finished."

"The horror is chained, yes, for a time."

"Tell me more about it."

"We knew that they were the ones who were trying to kill you. It seemed so absurd. There was so little danger to their work in your speech. Their attempts were so clumsy, even more inept than Project Archangel. You yourself suggested that perhaps it was me they were seeking." She eased their rented Mercedes slowly down the bustling Kur'damm. "You see, they were very serious about creating supermen. They didn't think you'd be much help, but they thought they could use you as bait to trap one of us. They presumed—quite correctly, I'll admit—that we know pretty well what the direction of your evolution is."

"They were crazy."

"Obviously. And for two reasons. First, you are right when you say that all your species can do is to stand in the way of the directionality of the organism. And secondly—"

"Secondly, never mess with seraphs."

"Angels."

"But why did they think your crowd would, ah, take me under its wings?"

They both laughed, nervously, to release tension.

"We have left traces of our interests and concerns down through the ages. Someone who studied it carefully—both the East Germans and the Project Archangel but surely not your CIA—might suspect that we would be concerned about you. They had nothing to lose by trying. And all you had to lose—"

"—was my life."

"Precisely. So when two of their hit teams vanished, they presumed that we were involved."

"They outsmarted your bunch?"

She smiled ruefully. "That's one way of putting it. But they're all dead, aren't they?"

"True enough."

He chewed on it for a time.

"Why do angels bother with people like me?"

"Figure it out yourself."

"Because I was saying something important, more important than I knew?"

"That's part of it. More important than you knew and more dangerous, as it turns out."

"As it turns out."

She pulled up in front of an elegant hotel, the Bristol Kempinski. Nothing but the most elegant hotel in Berlin for my Gaby. "I began to suspect what they were doing when you pointed out the possibility. So you can tell everyone that you beat a ser—an angel to a clue."

"No one will believe me."

"Tough." She laughed, pushing the trunk button. "But you understand that I had to find out their goals to report to the others."

"Your superiors?"

She laughed softly. "I don't think that's how they would describe themselves."

My Gaby is the boss. I bet even Mike takes orders from her. I wonder if he's the suitor. It would be kinda nice if he were. She deserves the best.

Gabriel and Michael, husband and wife—what would Sister Intemerata think? I hope God doesn't let her know. It would spoil her heaven.

"And you played the game out to the end to learn all the details?" They continued to sit in the car.

She nodded. "I am sorry that you were worried"—she hesitated—"and not unmoved by your generous heroism. Yet, in addition to being bound by my rules to do nothing until they tried to kill you, I felt I had to learn everything about their plan before destroying them. It was, after all, at least possible that they could do harm to my kind. Improbable, but not utterly impossible. Obviously that was not a major concern."

A doorman, dressed as though he were a field marshal in the army of Frederick the Great, opened the door.

"Were they going in the right direction?"

"Lock an angel—all right, I'll be precise—a seraph up in a lead room and destroy her with puny proton blasts? . . . You gotta be kidding."

"Pretty dumb, huh?"

They were silent until the doorman had carried off their luggage.

"Very dumb." She resumed the conversation. "Like all sorcerers, they underestimated our power and overestimated their own."

"So they lost."

"Rather decisively, if I do say so myself. Still, Jackie Jim, it was a bit of St. Crispin's day, wasn't it?"

"You bet. Only I won't be able to tell my grandchildren about it. They would want to lock me up."

"Oh, you can write the story down. Maybe some future generation will believe it. In the meantime, you loved almost every second of it. . . . Now we must get you up to your room and make those remaining aches and pains go away."

Then we'll both have to go home. I don't want that to happen, Gabriella. I'll miss you terribly.

In their dark maroon suite, her gentle hands made the hurt go away, mother again curing her injured little boy.

"Might I sing some more for you, Jackie Jim, softly so that the others in this somewhat vulgar place will not think we're crazy?"

"By all means. Especially that Bethlehem hymn."

"Bethlehem?"

"The last one you sang out in the Skärgården."

"You speculate too much."

However, she began with the song.

As she sang, softly and tenderly, Sean understood for the first time that she had risked her life. Helmstadt and his storm troopers *might* have had something that could harm her kind. There was no way to be sure beforehand. Unlikely but not impossible. Somehow her husband had gambled and lost.

So she risked my life too, he thought ruefully.

Well, I told her she was the boss. I can't complain if she took me literally.

Then he realized that she would not have permitted any harm to come to him.

Why not?

Because she's my guardian angel, that's why not.

After the Bethlehem songs she sang several he had never heard before, wordless songs that created images of peaceful fields and lakes, quiet sunsets, sparkling dawns, and radiant blue skies. Minnesota in the summer. The farm they used to visit before his father died.

His pain was healed, but he was still groggy from the drugs they had injected into his veins, and probably, as she had said, from shock. The world existed in a hazy but pleasant confusion, and the world was entirely Gabriella.

He loved her.

A marble statue perhaps or a pillar of white fire. It didn't matter, he still loved her.

Unthinkingly, automatically, his fingers went to the buttons on her blouse. Her big brown eyes widened, but she did not resist him. In the heat of his quickly ignited desire, there were no metaphysical or moral issues to consider. Only Gaby.

His lips moved to her breasts, her fingers tightened their grip on his head.

She was skilled in tender and prolonged foreplay. It probably takes them a couple of hundred years, Sean thought, as waves of sweetness rolled over him, like the peaceful waves of a caressing ocean.

Then, when it was time that he must enter her, their love changed. No, they don't do it that way. Sons of God and daughters of man. Other way around. But maybe the scripture was afraid to even hint at the daughters of God and the sons of man.

Their love became a fire rushing through a forest, a river plunging over a waterfall and dashing to the sea, a hurricane battering against the coast, molten lava running down a mountainside.

Gaby's fireball penetrating the sky.

ANGEL FIRE!

Laced with gold and silver waterfalls of love which swept him along irresistibly.

The sweetness, the pleasure, the joy were intolerable. Sean was drawn into a raging blast furnace, an out-of-control inferno that would devour and destroy.

He wanted to remain in the inferno for all eternity. He desired nothing but timeless union with its destructive sweetness. He knew that his own existence would end, but it didn't matter. There would be nothing but warmth. Forever.

Then he was dumped unceremoniously back into the room at the Kempinski, a room which, he noticed for the first time, was much chillier than a room at an American hotel.

"I almost destroyed you." A grief-stricken disembodied voice.

Why must I always deal with guilt-ridden women, even when they're angels.

She's going to be as bad as a first-year graduate student to whom some idiot gave the first B in all her life. Well, I owe her this, God knows. Don't you, God? You're responsible for this whole bloody mess. There had to have been better ways than sexual differentiation.

"But you didn't, now, did you?" He sighed audibly. Sure it had been quite a ride.

"I ought to have known better. I thought I could control the union. It is impossible for our two species to unite without destruction. Our love is too terrible."

" 'Tis interesting, I'll say that. Keeps a man warm in a damp hotel room, it does. . . . Now stop hiding, I don't like arguing with someone I can't see. It's hard on my imagination, if you take my meaning."

"I was a stupid fool."

So angels can sob too. She was not about to be kidded out of her self-hatred. Female types seldom were. Oh God, why me?

Because you're able to do it. And she's at least capable of forgiving herself if you push her hard enough. Unlike your mother or poor Moaning Mona.

"Ah, woman, you're a trial. When are you folks going to give up your ridiculous pride. You didn't kill me. You were able to stop. I learned a lesson about love. You learned a lesson about humility." His phony brogue grew thicker. "Sure, it was a benign experience for the two of us. No harm done at all, at all."

"There is that."

Ah, she wants to believe me. That's half the fight.

"I understand that, unlike the other seraphs . . . or should I use the Hebrew and say seraphim?"

"Either is acceptable."

"Well, like I say, you're the only one of that crowd who has to

be immune from temptation. A veritable Mary Poppins of seraphim ... I kind of like the Hebrew plural."

"Shut up."

"I won't. And I don't think you can make me. Anyway, you're
the only one in that immense choir—"

"Not all that immense."

"—who has to be totally perfect. A real Mary Poppins."

"I am not!"

"You are too! You're bound to be perfect."

"That's what the others will say. You are as bad as they are."

"Mike and the bunch."

"We always call him Michael."

"Well, I call him Mike. . . . Mickey when I'm upset."

"All three are acceptable," she whispered, like she was trying
to suppress a silly giggle.

"I'm still very much alive, after all"—now I'm going to put my
foot in it—"and convinced that I had better find myself a wife. But
stop feeling guilty that you cut it kind of close. And stop hiding."

"I'm so ashamed," she said, mostly convinced.

"Of being human? Or whatever the hell you are? You're not
Herself after all. You don't have to be perfect, seraph or not. Now
come back here."

She reappeared in the chair next to his bed, her slip clutched
modestly at her throat, a sheepish smile on her tear-stained face.

"That's better." The woman was almost the death of me.

"If there is pure Mind, Seano—and we both believe that there
is—you can imagine the power of that Love. The exploding 'singularity' that began the cosmos would be only a pale reflection."

"Terrifying," he agreed, and then the blarney put in its last
lick, "and if you're anything like the Other, I'll find meeting Him,
oops, Her, an interesting experience indeed."

She blushed to the roots of her silver hair.

"You see what I mean when I say there are no superior and
inferior species, Sean Desmond. We are merely fellow pilgrims,
companions on a journey."

Some companion. "I wouldn't trade with Tobias."

"Thank you." She stood up, still hiding, not all that successfully, behind her slip.

"You're getting ready to leave?"

"Yes, Jackie Jim. ET goes home!"

"Sit down."

"What?" Her imperial or seraphic dignity was offended.

"I said sit down; I have something to say."

And I better do it right.

"You have been in charge of this caper. You gave the orders and I went along, gracefully, right?"

"More or less gracefully." The imp in her eyes began to dance.

"Which is as it should be because you're the guardian angel and I'm the wolfhound, right?"

"Cute wolfhound, though."

"You gave me all kinds of orders about how to live the rest of my life."

"Recommendations."

"Sure . . . Now I'm giving not a recommendation, we inferior species can't afford that luxury. Turnabout is fair play, what's sauce for the goose is sauce for the gander, right?"

"Go on."

Getting a little testy.

"Well, I'll flat out say it. I'm not letting you go home until you promise me that you'll put aside your grief and find yourself another companion of somewhat greater durability than I possess."

Total quiet. She bowed her head. Her shoulders and breasts moved up and down rapidly.

"That's what your friends tell you, so now I'm making it official. Understand?"

"Yes," she whispered.

"Yes, you understand, or yes, you'll do it?"

"Yes, I'll think seriously about it."

"That won't do at all, Gabriella, and you know it."

Her shoulders sagged, her body slumped over.

"Yes . . . yes, I know it, and yes, damn you, I'll do it. Satisfied?"

"Promise?"

She looked up at him, weeping but grinning. "Angels don't lie. But yes, master, I promise."

"*All right.*"

Easier than he had expected.

"Most High's lines"—she laughed—"are not always this straight. Thank you, Sean Seamus Desmond. May I leave now?"

"Go in peace." He'd play priest to the end. "And God bless you."

"I'll never forget you."

"Candidly, I'm not surprised."

She stood up, ready to go.

"I won't ever forget you either, Gabriella Light."

"You'd better not."

They laughed together for the last time, and she took his hand in hers, her big brown eyes filled with infinite and tearful tenderness. He felt very sleepy. He wanted to say "I love you" before he lost consciousness, but he was not sure that he did.

He saw first a naked woman with a slip at her belly, graceful breasts poised over him, then a radiant pattern of crimson lights, and then, once again, nothing at all.

But not so soon that he didn't wonder why she did not extract a parallel promise from him.

When he awoke the next morning, Gaby was gone, as he knew she would be. No trace of her clothes or her luggage. His rosary was gone too.

And, of course, the door to the adjoining room had disappeared.

He found the money in Paris.

Two million dollars. In crisp new United States Treasury notes.

He had flown to Paris directly from Berlin on Air France. Jordan Bonfonte, the Paris bureau chief of *Time* and a friend of Blackie Ryan, had pleaded for an interview to follow up the *Time* cover story. What was it like to be a Nobel laureate? What were the costs and the rewards?

What can I tell you?

Well, I can't tell you everything, that's for sure.

He took the limo in to Paris from Charles de Gaulle and hiked over to the George V, which Gaby had told him was a good hotel if he didn't get a room next to a rich Arab family.

His plans were to stay the night, fly to London for a promised lunch with Hastings, and then leave on the next day for Chicago.

When he checked in, the clerk with typically Gallic courtesy told him that he was fortunate that it was December and there were some empty rooms. What sort of accommodation did *monsieur* desire?

"One in which I am not next to an Arab family."

"Oui, monsieur."

Gaby was right again. If there ever had been a Gaby.

He phoned his daughters as soon as he reached his room.

"Daddy!"

"You'd never guess what?"

"No, what?"

"We have a new stepfather."

"And is he ever a geek."

"Totally gross."

"He lives way out west."

"In Elgin."

Forty miles from Chicago.

"He's some kind of doctor."

"He has two totally gross sons."

"Mom goes we have to live with her now that we have a step-father."

The verb "to go" had replaced in the younger generation the archaic form "to say."

"And we go no way, José."

"Totally no way."

"I mean, his boys are space cadets. Really."

"Anyway, Mr. Ryan goes we don't have to live with them at all."

"No way, José."

Sean broke into the flow of adolescent outrage. "Mr. Ryan?"

"You know, like Laura O'Connor's grandpa."

"And Father Blackie's father."

"Ned Ryan?"

Senior partner of the legendary Loop law firm of Ryan, Rosner, and Ryan.

"Uh-huh. He's real old."

"But he's real cute."

"Was he really an admiral, Daddy?"

"Laura says he was, but he just laughs."

"A real admiral, with all kinds of medals."

"And he goes that we should tell you not to worry. No way we're going to have to live in Elgin."

"Did you have to go to the wedding?"

"It was a total gross-out, Daddy. Really."

"In church?"

"Oh, sure, St. Moron's or something like that."

"Really."

Trust Mona to grab the limelight. Well, no more alimony. She'd have a hard time proving that the children were neglected. If she were foolish enough to try after a little talk with Ned Ryan.

Someone told him once apropos of his colleague Steve O'Connor's in-laws that they were sort of a church-in-miniature, collecting strays and taking care of them—whether they wanted to be taken care of or not.

He was kind of glad to be on their list.

He called Blackie next.

"Johnny? Johnny."

"Ah, indeed. You have returned to our frantic pre-Christmas city?"

"I'm in Paris."

"Remarkable. No good will come from it. But nonetheless remarkable."

"The kids told me you called up the first team. Thanks to you and Ned and Nancy. The kids seem to have survived Mona's blitz pretty well."

"A gross-out." Blackie sighed. "Totally. The ineffable Old Fella says there's not a chance of the courts yielding her anything. He doubts that she will make an issue of it."

"A church marriage?"

"Apparently there was some decision in another diocese that there was no obstacle to her remarriage. They neglected to inform us, which My Lord Cronin remarks is typical. As a result, your process, should you be interested, is nearing a satisfactory conclusion. I wish the Church would abandon its role as a legal tribunal for marriages. It's relatively recent and an endless headache."

"Recent?"

"Only a thousand years, more or less."

"Very recent."

They didn't even give him time to feel guilty about leaving the kids with Nancy and Steve. The Ryans probably took better care of them in the crisis than he would have.

Gaby might have been involved. No way of telling.

If there ever had been a Gaby. Neither the kids nor Blackie had mentioned her. Which didn't prove anything in itself, did it?

He met Bonfonte in a little restaurant off the Quai d'Orsay and drank too much wine. He thought, however, that it was the kind of interview of which Gaby would be pleased.

Gaby, Gaby, Gaby ... will I ever get her out of my mind?

Jordan had brought along a stack of *Time* pictures of the awards ceremony. Sean considered them very carefully: not a trace of her. Either she had not been there or she had systematically erased all traces of herself from photographic negatives.

Probably also from people's memories.

After lunch he took a taxi to the American embassy to say hello to a Notre Dame classmate who was First Secretary. The diplomat was delighted to have a drink with a Nobel laureate and show him the *Herald-Tribune* and the *Times*. No Gaby. He even played the USIA's videotape for Sean.

No Gaby. Naturally.

Back in the George V, he forced himself to consider matters very carefully. Either she had never been there, he repeated to himself, or she had perpetrated an enormous deception on everyone else but him.

That was impossible, wasn't it?

Probably. Even a seraph couldn't be that systematic.

Then he found the money.

He removed his shaving pack from the Gucci carrying case and paused to reflect some more about *le problème Gaby*.

How would he still have his flight bags if there had been a thermonuclear explosion on the banks of the Elster?

On the other hand, he would never have purchased such expensive hand luggage himself, not even if he knew he would be released from alimony responsibility.

She might have snatched their belongings out of the work center at the same time, and with the same efficiency, that she snatched him.

Or simply reconstituted them afterward.

Easy tricks, she would say, when you've learned how to do them.

He poked around in the contents of the two bags. Well, she was right about one thing, anyway. It is easier to travel light.

Still a good pun.

Witch.

Then his fingers touched a thin leather case that ought not to have been there.

He extracted it from the flight bag. A Gucci billfold with two compartments, compact in length and width and slim in depth.

What the hell?

He opened the wallet cautiously. Four stacks of bills. At a quick glance fifty in each stack. Two hundred new notes, sealed with United States Treasury binders.

What denomination?

Franklyn Chase!

Ten thousand dollars!

Oh my God!

Ten times two hundred, two hundred thousand dollars!

No, multiply ten thousand by two hundred and you get two million dollars.

He dropped the wallet like it was on fire.

The woman had gone too far!

Now he was in real trouble.

He reached for the phone to call his friend at the embassy.

His fingers poised over the dial as he tried to imagine the conversation.

"I've found two million dollars."

"You *what?*"

"I've found two million dollars."

"Where?"

"In my flight bag."

"How did it get there?"

"I don't know."

Or alternately, "An angel put it there."

He slumped onto his bed, next to the billfold. He couldn't turn the money in. He'd certainly be in trouble with the government for the rest of his life.

They'd try to trace the money and would discover that they could not. Ah, the woman was a clever one. She'd cover her tracks well. No one could prove he shouldn't have the cash. Maybe they'd try to force the money back on him. Or maybe they would appropriate it for the government.

But did the government have a right to it?

He shoved the billfold away. I don't have a right to it. She stole it.

Angels don't steal.

How the hell do you know?

He opened the billfold again. They might be counterfeit.

Come on, she's not that clumsy.

What if they catch you carrying that much money around in your flight bag?

He didn't know much about international currency regulations, but he was certain he would be breaking numerous laws of France, the U.K., and the good old U.S.A. by just possessing that much cash. Even if they only took the money away from him, he'd never live it down. He could imagine the headlines:

Nobel Prof Arrested
with Money Cache

"Angel Gave Me
Two Million,"
Says Desmond

That would be all Mona would need to swarm into court with demands for custody. Ned Ryan would probably fight her off, but the headlines would continue.

Gabriella had told him he would need never to worry about money again. The woman meant what she said.

I'll have to worry not about not having it but about being caught with it. Can you imagine me walking into the Hyde Park bank and dropping five of these into a CD?

Or giving ten of them to Steve so that his friends down at the Board of Trade could open an account for me?

Was this supposed to be his pay for combat against sorcerers?

What had Gaby said about money? If they knew what he had done for them, they would willingly pay our fees?

Yeah, but ...

Angels don't steal.

I suppose not.

But they can escape trouble more easily than I can.

Damn it, it's not my money.

There was only one thing to do.

He tore the notes into little pieces and flushed them down the drain.

He left his room for a long, chilly walk under ugly, low skies up the Right Bank to Notre Dame and down the Left Bank back to the hotel.

He stood at the door of his room after he had entered. The billfold was still on his bed where he had left it.

With sinking heart, knowing exactly what he would find, he walked over and picked it up.

Sure enough. It was thick again.

He opened it. Four stacks of fifty. Two million dollars.

"Damn you, woman, leave me alone!"

Would you not say, Hastings old man, that the woman over there—without her clothes, of course—would look like a Rubens nude?"

"Which one?" Hastings peered over his glasses. "Where?"

"The tall blond woman standing by the table over near the wall."

"Oh yes ... indeed, heh-heh, rather hard to miss, what?"

"To say the least."

The woman was almost six feet tall, erect, shapely, self-possessed. Junoesque, a word he never would have used to describe Gabriella.

Hastings considered the problem very carefully. "As a matter of fact, I quite agree, heh-heh, just about the right amount of flab, don't you know? Quite delicious!"

"Uh-huh."

"In a sumptuous way, if you understand my meaning."

"Quite," Sean agreed.

The woman in fact could be described as delicious, but that was hardly Sean's point. If Hastings had the slightest recollection of Gaby, he would remember his own metaphor for her.

As a point of fact, the blond woman, delicious enough, was not at all comparable to his seraph. Or to be more precise, to her analog.

Still Sean looked at her much longer than was necessary to check Hastings' memory. His passions were finally acting up again.

Isn't that nice?

No one searched him when he left Charles de Gaulle for Heathrow on British Airlines. But he was nearly paralyzed by fear when they had put his flight bag on the X-ray machine.

What if they search it and open the wallet? Maybe they'll think I'm carrying cocaine in it.

Or something.

Or two million dollars. Angelic dollars.

They spot-checked him in the customs area at Heathrow.

Just my luck.

Or maybe I look guilty.

"All right, sir." The guard grinned. "Nothing in here, of course, but we have to check occasionally."

"No problem, Officer."

"And congratulations on the prize, sir."

"Thank you very much, Officer."

Now I know what they mean by cold sweat.

"Good thing you didn't go to Leipzig," Hastings remarked over coffee.

"Oh ... yes ... I guess so."

"I don't know what lunatic things that idiot Helmstadt was doing. Quite 'round the bend, if you ask me. The East Germans aren't saying a thing. But the Yank satellites apparently picked up a tremendous blast there. Maybe nuclear, the Yanks aren't talking much either. The next morning, I gather, though there's been nothing in the papers, all the pictures show is a large black hole in the ground."

"Imagine that."

"Rather."

"Any increase in radioactivity?"

"That's the strange thing, don't you know. None whatever."

"I'm not surprised."

Which wasn't exactly the right thing to say. Fortunately Hastings missed it.

So now I didn't even go to Leipzig. She certainly covers her tracks ... our tracks ... well.

"A bit of a dust-up at our shop the night of your talk. I don't suppose you heard about it?"

"Afraid not." But let me guess.

"Young woman who gave the vote of thanks, Arden Devoy, tried to kill herself. Drugs, don't you know? Quite disturbed actually, poor woman. Somehow thinks she was involved with angels."

"Really." Even the memories of Project Archangel have been erased. The woman is thorough. "I hope she's recovering?"

"As a matter of fact, she seems to be. Quite plucky little thing actually."

"I'm glad to hear it."

"Rather odd, heh-heh, but she thinks a woman angel saved her life. Feminist claptrap, don't you think?"

"Probably."

Score one for Gaby.

Back in his room at the Connaught, across the street from the Jesuit church at Farm Street, he discovered that his Gucci wallet with all the pictures of Franklyn Chase was still there. No one had stolen it yet, although he had left it in the open for all to see.

She is an illusion. I am convinced of that, he informed the Deity a few minutes later in the Jesuit church. No one could so systematically eliminate all trace of herself. I went through a psychotic interlude that lasted a week or so. Now it's over.

God was not prepared to contest the matter.

All right, Sean Desmond continued his disputation, how do You explain the two million dollars?

The Lord God was not prepared to offer any testable theories.

A priest was hearing confessions in the confessional on the left-hand side of the church—Gospel side, isn't it?

Maybe I should go to confession and ask for his advice.

What the hell would I say?

Bless me father for I have sinned. I necked and petted a naked angel.

Did you enjoy it, my son?

I thought I was going to die.

The bobbies at Heathrow figured he was an IRA gunman.

And himself a Nobel Prize winner.

He was too old to be a gunman.

As the pretty and obnoxious young blond policewoman with the cockney whine in her voice put it, "I know I've seen him on the telly."

"I'll miss my plane," Sean protested.

"I'm sure there'll be others, sir," the older cop, fat and florid, smiled cheerfully.

They were infinitely polite and respectful, but immovable. He could not leave for Dublin until he had a "word or two" with some "other officers, if you don't mind, sir."

"I do mind; there are people waiting for me at the Dublin Airport."

"Well, I'm sure they can wait a little longer, can't they now, sir?"

Sean's major worry was the nasty little blond. She seemed unable to let his Gucci billfold out of her hand. She turned it over and over curiously, as if she would like to know what was inside but somehow couldn't open it.

"I know I saw him on the telly," she repeated about once every ninety seconds.

What if the "other officers," Special Branch no doubt, were not so reluctant.

It was all his fault. He knew he should have stayed away from Ireland. But he was never quite able to work up the nerve to call the chairman of the committee, Professor N. A. Flanagan, whoever he was.

Then a telegram from Dublin requested he confirm his arrival time. It was too late to cancel out now.

So Gaby had won again. Damn the woman.

"You've searched my luggage"—Sean tried fury—"and you've searched my person and you haven't found anything. What legal right do you have to detain me?"

"Suspicion of illegal activities, sir." The blond child sneered. "I know I saw you on the telly."

They both had read his Nobel citation, but it did not seem to impress them. "Can't make head or tail out of this stuff, can you, Heather?"

"Not a blinking word. He claims to be some scientific big shot. I ask you, does he look like one? No, I'll tell you what he looks like: one of *them*!"

It was a long statement for her.

"He sure doesn't look like a professor," the third cop, a bored young man, more interested in the blond's thighs than Sean's credentials, admitted. "Yank accent and all."

The charge against him was that no great scientist could possibly look so Irish. Hence he had to be traveling with false papers. Hence he was IRA.

Sean was not worried about spending the night in jail, though the detention room at Heathrow Terminal Three might as well be a prison cell. At some point rationality would reassert itself. He was, after all, an American citizen with a blameless record. No traveling violations on his driver's license for ten years.

He *was* worried, however, about the Gucci billfold that was being probed by the policewoman's crimson fingernails.

An American citizen, indeed; and one with two million unexplained and inexplicable dollars in his flight bag.

"I want to talk to the American ambassador," he demanded.

"Come now, sir," the genial cop again, "there's no need for that, is there now? Not until you talk to the other officers. I can't imagine what is delaying them."

"Can I make a phone call to Dublin?"

The girl was flipping the wallet open and shut, but still not looking inside its compartments. How can she not see all that money?

"Right after the other officers come, sir." The man's unfailingly good-humored patience continued. As did his implacable refusals.

They all saw a promotion in the arrest. Oh boy, were they in for a surprise.

"Then I'm afraid I am forced to record your names for a complaint when this is over."

" 'Ere now," said the cockney girl, "you have no call for that."

"Oh yes, I do, Constable. Your name, please ... Heather what?"

"Better tell him, 'Eather," the genial man suggested. "He's within his rights."

"Cassidy," she said sulkily. "And I know I saw you on the telly."

"I'm sure you did, my dear. Your name, young man?"

"Me?" The cop took his eyes off of 'Eather's flanks long enough to try to remember his name. "Brian Donovan, sir."

Sean jotted down the name. Two micks. Worse luck to them for selling out to the Brits.

"And yours, Sergeant?"

"You're within your rights by asking, sir. It's Pat Murphy, sir. But I'm sure you'll have no call for complaint. It's just one or two questions the two other officers will want to be asking, sir."

"I believe you've made the point, Sergeant." He closed his notebook, crossed his legs, and waited. Were these goons any better than Spence and Cliff? More courteous maybe, except for the little bitch.

He wondered idly what she'd be like in bed. Probably quite unsatisfactory. Her kind of women are that way. Like Mona.

He was astonished that the question had arisen. Second woman that has stirred me today. On the whole, the one at the Reform Club was far more interesting. His libido, dormant most of the time—well, with one notable exception—since he had left the Helmsley Palace, seemed to be functioning normally again.

The two Special Branch men arrived forty-five minutes after his flight to Dublin had left and fifteen minutes before the next one. If these two had any intelligence and if he ran and if the flight wasn't solidly booked with a stand-by list, he might make it to Dublin only an hour late.

The Special Branch men were presented by Sergeant Murphy, not to him, but to the other cops as Superintendent Conley and Inspector Rafferty.

Naturally.

" 'Ere now," demanded the former, "what's going on 'ere?"

"A suspicious one, sir. Credentials looked a little odd. 'Eather 'ere was the first to notice it."

"I knew I'd seen him on the telly, sir."

Rafferty had taken the wallet from her and was inspecting it closely. He flipped it open.

"Let me see the passport, please." Superintendent Conley extended his hand impatiently.

"You may have seen me on the telly, too, Superintendent."

The cop considered the passport and Sean's face. "Can't say that I have, sir. However, the name does ring a bell."

Inspector Rafferty was studying the wallet very carefully.

"We found this document quite suspicious, sir," Sergeant Murphy continued. "He doesn't seem quite the type for a great scientist, if you know what I mean, sir."

"Quite true, Sergeant, quite true." The Superintendent began to read the English translation of his citation. Color drained from his face. "Oh my God!"

Rafferty slammed the wallet shut and dropped it on the table in middle of the room.

"I knew I saw his face on the telly," 'Eather crowed.

"I'm sure you did, Constable." He handed the passport back to Sean. "As a matter of fact, so did I. I'm very sorry, Doctor Desmond. This is most regrettable."

Patrol Officer Cassidy retrieved the wallet and began to study it again.

"Not nearly as sorry as these three officers are going to be when the American embassy has finished its complaint, Superintendent. I have missed my plane. The committee waiting for me in

Dublin has undoubtedly dispersed. I may miss the next plane. Both airports may close in this damnable English fog." He was rising to wondrous heights of anger. "I may miss my lecture tomorrow. Why? Because these three bigots did not believe it possible that someone as Irish-seeming as I am—three generations away from the Isle, Superintendent—could possibly be a distinguished scientist."

"Very sorry, Doctor Desmond." Conley looked like he wanted the earth to swallow him up.

'Eather Cassidy was still holding the wallet. But she had lost all interest in it.

Sean soared to new heights of outrage. "I am not a supporter of the IRA. I oppose violence as a solution to human problems"— unless it is a seraphic fireball wiping out the other side—"yet I must say that I can understand why some Irishmen would react violently after centuries of oppression by a police power as prejudiced and incompetent as this one."

"We'll try to get you a seat on the next plane, sir." Conley reached for the phone.

"Your Irish ancestors must be ashamed of the lot of you. You've sold out so completely to the bloody Brits that you've even acquired their goddamn anti-Irish prejudice ... and, young woman, do you mind if I take that wallet with which you have been amusing yourself for the last hour. It is mine, you know."

"Dear God, I'm sorry." 'Eather was crying.

He snatched the open billfold, half a picture of Mr. Chase peeking out of it, and began to run for the plane.

His anger cooled as he ran, and he knew that he wouldn't write a protest note. Too many people had died because of IRA bombs for them not to be cautious.

And they hadn't even noticed the money.

Ah, the woman works effectively, doesn't she now?

As he dashed up to the boarding gate, he wondered if Gaby might have set up the whole delay, for reasons of her own.

Goddamn guardian angel.

The flight from London to Dublin on the crowded green 737 was like a long wait in the dentist's office—its only possible merit was a reduction in time required in Purgatory.

The plane bobbed up and down like a small boat on Lake Michigan in a storm. To his surprise, Sean was not frightened. So there was something useful accomplished on the trip.

His stomach was, however, protesting. It wouldn't take many more bumps to make him sick.

Was Purgatory still a belief? He'd have to ask the kids.

Dear God, how much I miss them. What the hell am I doing in Ireland when I could be in Chicago?

It's all that seraph's fault.

The plane seemed to be lingering forever in the fog. Had they lost Ireland? Would the world be troubled if that soggy island were indeed lost?

Then through the clouds he saw the greenest landscape on which his eyes had ever rested, deeply, implausibly green.

No wonder they like the color.

Well, I'm here, I may as well enjoy it.

Then the clouds closed again and the 737 plugged doggedly on.

Maybe we're close to Long Island now.

Why doesn't that moron up front tell us something.

And why don't those babies stop crying.

Finally, when he was about to despair of ever setting foot on earth again, the plane slipped through the rain and miraculously found the runway of Dublin International Airport. Sean was exhausted from the harassment, the mad dash to the plane, and violent weather.

Well, Gaby's magic worked. I'm not afraid of flying anymore. Even on a day like this when I should be.

It was still raining. That's what it does in Ireland. It rains. All the time. What an intolerably gloomy place.

He looked around the lounge. And they all look Irish, how monotonous.

The Irish customs guard waved him through with a cheery smile.

"Welcome to Ireland, sir. *Cead mille failte!*"

"Everyone looks Irish." Sean glanced around in astonishment.

"Sure, isn't that what all you Yanks say, sir?" The guard grinned. "What else would you be after expecting?"

"On the South Side of Chicago, only half the people look that way."

"Chicago, is it?" the guard responded.

Sean realized that he could spend the rest of the night talking to the guard. He'd better not. He was already late and probably in deep, deep trouble.

Let's see . . . he was to meet . . . he fumbled for the paper . . . a Professor N. A. Flanagan from Trinity College.

A woman was waiting for him outside the door of the customs hall, a very familiar woman in raincoat and stretch slacks. She was frowning grimly, a frown to which he had grown very accustomed.

"Professor Desmond? Welcome to Dublin! Better late than never." She didn't sound very pleased with him. At all, at all.

"Gaby," he gasped.

37

"**N**o . . ." The woman was flustered. "Nora . . . Nora Flanagan from TCD, Trinity College, Dublin."

"Nora Anne Flanagan, I presume? With an *e*?"

He felt his eyes bulging from his head. What madness is going on now? Damn their trickery.

Not exactly Gaby. Her complexion was not as perfect, her clothes not as chic, her confidence not as serene, her posture not as firm. She was, as a matter of fact, rather shy and rather dowdy. No, that's not true. She's tired and angry and dressed in slacks and a heavy sweater for cold rainy weather, but she's gorgeous. A less-than-perfect but appealing human mirror-image. And the large, tender brown eyes with long lashes were indistinguishable from Gaby's.

Dear God, how appealing!

His desire for her was intense and demanding. He imagined his hands on her body, claiming, caressing, challenging.

He fantasized about her warmth in a bed on a cold rainy night. Altogether delightful.

And he was also furious at all of them. Nora Anne (with an *e*) Flanagan included. He was tired, he was sick, he was angry. He was in no mood to think about sex. Right?

Right.

She was angry too.

"Quite right, Professor Desmond," she replied curtly, in a soft, cultivated, and furious brogue. " 'Tis a shame that you did not come at the time you promised. The rest of the reception committee has already left."

Not passive aggressive anyway. Not by half. The woman in his dreams? Not quite. The opposite sex in the unconscious is always pliant. That was not a modifier appropriate for this woman with the banshee anger in her eyes.

"I was delayed; sorry, Professor Flanagan."

"Is that all your luggage now? We can order you a taxi. I'm afraid the Mercedes we hired for you has returned to Dublin. Or I'll give you a lift in my old Renault?"

He'd fix the damn conniving seraph and all her kind. She'd engineered the mess in London to leave him alone with this outraged virago, this obnoxious clone. I'll tell her that the taxi will be fine.

"If you're prepared to forgive me for being late"—the charm emerged against his will—"I'd be happy to ride with you."

"Surely you could have phoned us?" They were striding rapidly towards the entrance of the airport, her pace matching her anger. "But I suppose that we Irish are not important enough to a world celebrity, are we now?"

She's not bad looking when she's angry, not at all, at all.

"I was in the police detention room at Heathrow. They wouldn't let me use the phone. By the time they decided that I was not an IRA gunman, I didn't have time both to catch the plane and phone you. I really am sorry."

She stopped dead in her tracks. "Gunman? Jaysus!"

"You gotta admit I look like one." He savored being one up on the bitch. "They thought that no one who seems as Irish as I apparently seem could possibly be the winner of a scientific prize."

"You poor man." Her hand reached out to touch his arm. "And me playing the Irish washerwoman for you. I'm terribly, terribly sorry."

"As I said, I regret I missed the plane, but it was not the

result"—he twisted the knife—"of any lack of respect for Ireland, its universities, or its people."

"I'm so embarrassed, Professor Desmond, truly I am. It's just, well, you're much of a hero to us here."

"The clay in my feet, Professor Flanagan, is pretty soft even if this time it wasn't my fault."

It was the fault of a goddamn seraph of whom you're a clone. An appealing clone too, damnit.

How did Gaby work it out? Did she have Nora Anne Flanagan in mind all along? Did she deliberately make herself look like this woman? Or did she model herself after my fantasies? Or is Nora Flanagan really some kind of human analog—no, not that, some human counterpart?

Gaby might have messed around with time too. She was pretty good at that. Maybe she went back—what?—thirty-six, thirty-seven years when this one was conceived, and modeled her after herself.

I bet that wouldn't have been much of a trick at all, at all.

"May I report this to the press, Professor Desmond? It's an outrage. We can't allow them to do that, can we?" She pulled a notebook and ballpoint out of her raincoat. "Do you have the names of the officers?"

"I do." He reached into his jacket and then paused. "If it's all the same to you, I'd just as soon not mention their names. They're all Irish. I don't want to get them in trouble. Everyone makes mistakes."

Besides, the real villain of the piece was a certain pushy, bossy, obnoxious seraph who is a lot like you.

"Of course." She returned the notebook to her pocket and her brown eyes widened in . . . what?

Admiration, respect. And I wasn't even trying.

"Superintendent Conley was the man who finally sorted things out. He even put me on this flight or I might not have arrived here till it stops raining. And that could be months."

Pen and notebook out again, she ignored his attempt at wit. "If I may . . . I mean, so your reputation here won't suffer, not that it matters all that much to you."

"If I hear one more word of Irish self-hatred out of you, Professor Flanagan, I'll get on the first plane to New York. Is that clear?"

She nodded, close to tears. That's how women win. Like that little bitch 'Eather Cassidy. They play on our sympathies.

"Now go make your phone call."

He watched her as she rushed off to the line of phone booths. Not quite so tall as Gaby (when she was tallest) but at least five-eight and a half, maybe five-nine. Possibly a quarter inch more on the waist, but nothing that wouldn't come off with some exercise. Otherwise, a figure pretty much like that goddamn seraph.

Overworked, hassled, discouraged, terribly vulnerable for all her efficiency. A lot of pent-up passion.

I don't care. I'm not about to be railroaded into this, not by Gabriella Light or anyone else.

His imagination, operating on its own, started to undress her as she dialed the phone. Sure, it would be nice to caress those thighs and pat that ass instead of admiring them from a respectful distance like you must do when you are involved with a seraph.

He instructed his imagination to cease and desist and turned his back on her.

Nonetheless, when the aforementioned irresponsible imagination sensed that she was off the phone, it made him turn around so that it might continue its pleasurable activity with a front view. Not at all unsatisfactory from that perspective either.

She knew she was being evaluated and tried to pretend that she did not notice. She did, however, seem entirely displeased.

Women always know.

"Now," she said shyly, "I wouldn't blame you at all at all if you wanted to take a taxi."

"I said the Renault, did I not, Professor Flanagan?"

"You did." She still wouldn't look at him.

"Then the Renault it will be."

As they hurried through the rain, under her umbrella, to the "car park," she discussed the schedule for the remnants of the day. She realized that he had suffered through an exhausting schedule, compounded by the outrage at Heathrow. Surely he deserved a rest, poor man. There was nothing planned for this evening. He could go straight to his room at the Shelbourne and have a good night's sleep. Or if he wished, there was a nice restaurant in a mews down the street from the hotel.... She would be happy to buy him supper, "as a peace offering." She managed her first smile. Not unlike Gaby's at all.

"Sure you deserve a much better introduction to Irish hospitality than I've been after giving you."

"The best part of the hospitality"—he beat Gaby and all the rest of the bastards to the punch—"is the offer of some rest. I'll take a raincheck on the dinner."

She nodded sadly. Of course.

"It's not much of a car, I'm afraid." She unlocked the door of the ancient Renault and opened it for him, extending her umbrella to keep him dry.

What he should have said was that any car with so charming a driver was a wonderful car. Something like that.

What he did say was, "All I care about is my room at the Shelbourne."

"We also have a reservation for you at the Westbury. It's brand new. Quite American and far more comfortable." She was having trouble with the Renault's mechanical choke. "But without any history and it doesn't have a view of the Wicklow Hills ... 'course, that's not much good unless it stops raining, is it now?"

"The Shelbourne will be fine."

The car finally started and she eased it carefully out of its place and toward the gate.

"It was generous of you to forgive those police officers."

"We all make mistakes, don't we now?"

"You're mocking me, Professor Desmond!" She shoved the gears sharply into second, almost stripping them.

"I am not, Professor Flanagan," he blazed back as angry as she was.

"You most certainly are!" She gunned the car into the highway, skidding across a lane in the process.

"Glory be to God, woman, you'll be the death of us all!"

"There, goddamn you, you've done it again."

Ah, passion indeed.

"I guess I have," he said sheepishly, "and you must forgive me. It was neither intentional nor disrespectful. On the contrary, it was unconscious admiration for the loveliness of the Dublin Irish accent, which I agree with the experts is the most beautiful sound of English in all the world."

Not bad, not bad at all, at all.

"Oh." She seemed a little mollified. But not much.

No passive-aggressive personality here. Everything up front. In technicolor and four-channel Dolby sound.

Just like Gaby. Like Gaby and not like her.

Of course, stupid, she's not an angel. You can sleep with her and not burn up in a volcano.

"The trouble is, I'm afraid I'm a natural and unconscious mimic. My daughters too, even worse than I am, I fear. They pick up different accents and patterns in a half hour. I become fascinated by the variety of sounds and, without realizing what I'm doing, talk the way the others are talking. It's never got me in all that much trouble before. I promise I'll stop."

"No," she sounded close to tears, "please don't do that. You are rather good at it actually. I'd almost think you were from Fingal, the Danish area north of here where I was born . . . but if you don't mind a suggestion, Professor Desmond?"

"Certainly not, Professor Flanagan."

"Before the lecture tomorrow you might say exactly what you said to me. People won't think you're making fun of us."

"Will they think I'm guilty of blarney?"

She actually laughed. "Arguably. But we Irish never mind that. . . . You have daughters, do you now?"

"Two, fourteen and fifteen. Very American names."

"Which are?"

"Fionna and Deirdre, Fee and Dee to their intimates."

She laughed again. "And my two, about the same ages, actually, are Elizabeth and Anne. With an *e*."

"Naturally."

That attempt to break the ice of awkwardness in which they had been mired died aborning. Nora Flanagan peered anxiously through her windshield, the wipers of which should have been replaced long ago and were barely clearing away the sheets of rain.

"Were your parents born here, Professor Desmond?"

"Great-grandparents, actually."

"Oh? Where, if I may ask?"

"The County Kerry, a place named Dingle, I think."

"Oh, that's the most beautiful part of the whole country. We used to go there on holiday when I was young. Dennis and I went there on our honeymoon."

"I'll have to visit it sometime. What does your husband do, Professor Flanagan?"

"He was a soldier, Professor Desmond, a commandant—major, that is. He was in the Irish peace-keeping force in Lebanon. He was killed last year."

"I'm very sorry, Professor Flanagan, very sorry indeed."

"Thank you, Professor Desmond."

So they had arranged a widow woman for him, had they now? Wasn't that nice? A woman still grieving, though if I interpret the tone right, the marriage left a lot to be desired.

If I had a wife like her, I sure as hell would get out of the army. Of course, you don't anticipate you'll be sent to Lebanon.

"Do you know the Kerryman jokes, Professor Desmond?"

"I can't say that I do."

They were in the city now. In the rain, it looked like one massive, gloomy slum.

"How do you recognize the Kerryman on the oil rig?"

"I don't know, Professor Flanagan, how do you recognize the Kerryman on the oil rig?"

"He's the one shooting the bird gun at the helicopter."

It was not unfunny, but he didn't want to laugh. If they laughed together, Gaby would have carried the day.

"Indeed."

She tried again, unable to quit when she was behind. "What's the definition of a Kerry farmer?"

"You tell me."

"A man outstanding in his field."

Perversely Sean stifled his laughter.

"We have parallel jokes in Chicago," he said stuffily, "about Poles mostly. These jokes 'contage' around the world. I often wonder whether they start in Chicago. In England, I regret to say, they are Irish jokes; in France, Belgian jokes; in Germany, Friesland jokes; in Poland, Russian jokes."

How about that for academic pomposity!

"You find them offensive?"

"Not always."

Another awkward pause. Well, I showed you guys, didn't I?

"Only a few more minutes, Professor Desmond." Her voice was unsteady. "Would you like to drive down O'Connell Street? By the GPO, the General Post Office? It's where the rising began on Easter Monday 1916?"

"But it was called Sackville Street then, wasn't it, when Yeats's 'Terrible Beauty' was born."

"That's right."

That put you in your place, didn't it? Kerryman jokes, indeed!

Ah, but I may be going too far altogether. I don't like being sandbagged by Gaby and her bunch, but I do want this woman, more than I have ever wanted anyone in all my life.

Now isn't that an interesting discovery!

"You're a physicist, are you now?" His turn to be ice breaker.

"Theoretical physics, as a matter of fact. I suspect that's why I was asked to chair your presentation tomorrow."

"I met Hawkings at Cambridge."

"I was with him there, a few years behind, naturally. But I knew him and his wife. Lovely people, poor dears."

"You studied at Cambridge?"

"After I was married. While I was expecting the girls. Dennis was in Cyprus."

Impressive.

"I met a woman physicist there last week. Arden Devoy."

"She was after me. Poor woman, she's had a hard time of it lately."

"So I gathered from Hastings."

"He was one of my teachers. Nice man, a bit of an eye for the nicely turned ankle now, hasn't he? But harmless really."

So the woman was a good physicist. So what?

We are both frightened—attracted, yet frightened. The electricity began leaping back and forth as soon as we met.

They drove into O'Connell Street and found themselves caught in a traffic jam.

"Sorry, Professor Desmond."

"A few more minutes won't matter."

She pointed out the flower bed that marked the spot from which Lord Nelson's statue had been blown.

He sang the first few lines of the Clancy Brothers' song "Up Went Nelson!" then lost his nerve.

"You have a nice voice, Professor Desmond."

"Whiskey tenor."

"Not really . . . we don't actually think of the Clancy Brothers as Irish."

"Don't you now?" he snapped at her. "Well, will the Chieftains do? Or Mary O'Hara?"

"And herself, poor woman, a widow for all those years." She sighed, like she was about to be struck by an attack of asthma. "But aren't you terribly interested in Ireland for a Yank? You've been here before, have you now?"

"I have not," he said firmly.

That sounded pretty Irish, didn't it?

"So you receive a typical warm Irish reception when you get off the plane, almost as bad as your farewell from England."

"Everyone says the Irish"—he sighed back at her—"are the most hospitable people in the world, don't they now?"

She glanced at him quickly, saw that he was grinning at her, and laughed tentatively.

He laughed back, with equal caution. "Forget it, Nora Anne Flanagan."

"I will *not*." Her turn to grin. "What's the point in being Irish if you can't enjoy feeling guilty? . . . Actually"—(she pronounced it "akshully") deep, deep breath—"we may be colleagues next term."

"Really?" What devilment—or angelment—was going on now?

"I've been invited to teach at the University of Cook County during the winter and spring term. Sight unseen. I suspect they need someone to meet undergraduate classes."

"I'm not surprised. The typical professor at the university under normal circumstances isn't at the university."

It was too much altogether. A crude, devious plot. Gaby and her bunch were boxing him in. Well, they wouldn't get away with it.

"If I accept—and the decision isn't final—it has been suggested that I place my daughters in a Jesuit school there. I didn't know the Jesuits taught girls, but . . ." They crossed a river, doubtless the Liffey, the dark waters from which Dublin received its name, on a crowded bridge.

"In Chicago they do. St. Ignatius. My daughters go there. Only very bright girls are admitted. I'm sure your children will have no trouble."

Gabriella Light, you have no shame at all, at all.

I'll have no part of it.

"Just one more turn and we'll be on the Green and then down the street to the Shelbourne. St. Stephen's Green. You may remember the passage in Joyce."

" 'Crossing Stephen's, that is, my green.' "

"Yes."

Another direct hit.

Then he thought of the woman curled up next to him in his bed on a cold winter morning in January, the four kids off to school, and decided that the nonsense must stop.

How to stop it?

Well, lust finds a way. Even maybe love.

"They hired you sight unseen, did they now?"

"They did. Afterward, one of them flew over from London to vet me, I suppose."

She mentioned the name of a habitué of the round table.

"And what were you after thinking of your man, Professor Nora Anne Flanagan?"

They had stopped in front of a wedding cake building that was surely the Shelbourne.

She looked up at him, defenseless, frightened, devastating.

"I was thinking"—she hesitated—"that he was a bit of a bore and a bit of a lecher."

"A terrible thing to say, terrible altogether"—he shifted into half fun and full earnest—"and inaccurate altogether. You should be ashamed of yourself for such a mistaken judgment."

"In what way am I mistaken?" she demanded hotly.

"In three little words: 'a,' 'bit,' and 'of.' "

A minisecond while she figured it out, and they laughed together again, precisely what Gaby had planned that they do.

"You know about Eric the Red?" Sean considered her face. It was really very pretty—much like Gaby's, not as perfect perhaps, but warm and lively and appealing. He resisted a powerful impulse to reach out and touch it with gentle admiration.

"The Viking?"

"Icelander." His eyes dropped to her bust, distinctive and delicious even in the darkened car, and he felt a spasm of desire. "And himself at least half Irish on his mother's side. Well, in one of his sagas, he goes beyond Iceland and beyond Greenland and even beyond Vineland and comes to a place where there's a big monastery of Irish monks having a procession like they were wont to do." His voice took on the tone and the accent of the stage-Irish storyteller that *The New York Times* had hinted he was some of the time. "He called it Great Ireland. I figure that's the U.S.A. and rightly enough because there are ten million of us—twenty if you count the Prots—and only five million of you. You're the Mere Irish and we're the Great Irish."

Risky, but let's see how she takes it.

Pretty good thighs too, come to think of it, even if I have to imagine them in this car.

She laughed, easily and confidently, just as Gaby would.

"Sure," she said, her face lighting in an impish smile that was irresistible, "haven't I always said that you Yanks, 'scuse me, you Great Irish will be Irish long after we are indistinguishable from the frigging Belgians!"

They laughed together, establishing a tentative and still uneasy companionship.

I want you, woman, I really do. Which is what that damn seraph has had in mind all along.

This was the critical moment. The force and energies that had conspired to create repulsion between them were changing their direction. They were a man and a woman sitting in a decrepit old Renault, now quite conscious of the drives that were drawing them toward one another. What, both of them were wondering, should I do next?

"I want to say two things, Nora Anne Flanagan." He put his arm around the front seat, not around her but with a hint that such an act was not totally out of the question. "Before I enter that historic hotel and my suite from which I can see the Wicklow Hills if it ever stops raining . . ."

"Yes?" Her eyes shifted anxiously.

"The first is that my name is Sean—long ago, Johnny; more recently to my students from whom I get no respect, Seano. Understand?"

"Yes, Professor . . . Seano."

"And the second is that I feel I've betrayed the honor of the

County Kerry tonight and acted myself like a Kerryman joke ...
I've turned down an invitation to dinner from an intelligent, beautiful, and fascinating woman. I think, as an honored guest of Trinity
College and University College, I deserve a chance to reconsider
my folly."

"Tonight, is it?" There was a warmth beneath her shyness and
a mystery inside of her kindness. "Sure, I think we might be able to
arrange that. It might not be any trouble at all, at all."

38

Sean Seamus Desmond, Distinguished Professor of Biology and Nobel laureate, was hopelessly in love. Not only did he desire with furiously demanding lust to bed his woman, he adored her. Already.

She certainly seemed interested in him too.

She was no longer either drab or dowdy. Her hair was neatly combed, her makeup was skillfully applied, her shoulders were erect and confident, her stylish beige cotton-knit dress left no doubt about the allurements of her figure.

Definitely a clone of Gaby in that respect.

Her wit was delicate and subtle, her laughter warm and inviting, her conversation light and charming. And her soft brown eyes were filled with admiration for him, an expression he had seen only at the end in Gaby's eyes.

The restaurant was cozy, the food was superb, and the wine smooth and reassuring. Nora Flanagan blossomed under the influence of his smile and respect.

They engaged in the dance, ancient and new, ritualized and never the same, by which a man and a woman seek to know one another as a prelude to a decision about love. They probed and feinted, disclosed and hid, unveiled and obscured, laughed and almost cried.

The dance was in fast tempo; they both knew they had so little time to finish their mixture of waltz and reel, polka and fox-trot, before the music stopped and he was on a plane to Chicago.

Mature, intelligent, self-possessed academics that they were, with adolescence and its powerful hormonal demands far behind them, they fell in love with each other.

Hopelessly and permanently, he thought.

He knew that he not only lusted after the woman, but loved her, mysterious, fragile, efficient, shy, intelligent, comic woman/child that she was.

And the glow of worship in her eyes left no doubt that the combination of lust and love had taken possession of her too.

Her most effective step in their *pas de deux* was candor. When she said "candidly," she meant it. She told more about herself than you would expect her to tell, more than you would want her to tell, more even perhaps than she should tell—and just enough to devastate you with her honesty.

"Sure, I'm a terrible compulsive eejit about neatness." She brushed some bread crumbs into her hand and placed them in a saucer. "If you take me meaning. Aren't the wee lasses, poor things, always complaining about my obsession with neating the house up?"

"Terrible," he agreed, "altogether."

"And my office a bloody mess!"

"Hope for redemption."

She was most attractive when her slow smile—upturned lips, crinkly nose, little flecks of gold in her brown eyes—turned into a light, self-deprecating laugh in which the rain and the sun of Irish picture books seemed to merge into a rainbow sky.

Most unlike the inestimable Gabriella, as Blackie would have called her if he knew about that troublesome seraph's existence.

Yet not too different from Gabriella either. And human, thank God.

Well, thank Gaby too. A little.

"And, faith, what a sensualist I've become." She considered the color of the red wine. "Food and drink will be the end of me altogether."

"And sex?"

"Ah, sure, that's not been a problem in Ireland for the last hundred and twenty-five years!"

"So I'm told, but to be honest I don't altogether believe it."

"If I had my way"—she sipped the wine slowly, lovingly—"I'd probably have a couple of jars when I came home every afternoon and be fluthered at the end of the day."

"Why don't you?"

"Well"—she frowned in mock seriousness—"for a number of reasons."

"And they are?"

"Would I be wanting to scandalize the girls—pardon, I must keep up my part of the illusion—the wee lasses?"

"You would not."

"Would I be able to afford it?" She drained the glass and held it out to him to refill. "And meself with such expensive tastes?"

"You would not."

"With the Creature numbing my brain cells, would I have the mind to think about theoretical physics and work out the complex formulae by which I earn my living, or the will to resist sexual overtures, not that there's too many of those?"

"You would not, at all, at all."

"And would I want to be doing irreparable harm to the remnants of my figure with too much of the drink taken every day?"

"I wouldn't be saying remnants," he countered, breaking the response to her litany.

"What's that would you be saying now?" she demanded, her mobile face taking on the mask of a potentially angry mother superior.

"Classical charms?"

"Ah, that's nice now; we won't talk anymore about the subject, but those are grand words."

"Kind of like a Rubens nude, if you take my meaning. Without the flab."

"Rubens, is it now?" She was flustered, wondering whether she should be angry.

"Garden of Love."

"I know what picture you mean." She considered him, still not certain whether to lose her temper. "I'm not a complete eejit."

"I can't make a scholarly evaluation while you have your

clothes on, but on the basis of the evidence presently available to me, I'd say that such a paradigm at least merits further testing."

"You're a desperate man, Sean Seamus Desmond." She blushed, anger dismissed as utterly inappropriate, and looked like she was about to cry. "Desperate altogether."

"Desperate?" Maybe the Rubens comparison was a mistake. It drenched his brain with tasty and dangerous pictures of a naked Nora Anne. He was a little fluthered too, come to think of it.

"Too much altogether, but still nice." She touched his hand. "You're trying to melt me poor heart with your blarney, but I like it just the same. I must be fluthered already."

"You're not," he said, as he held her fingers.

"Candidly"—she was her sober, academic self again—"I hardly drink anything at all. Nothing in Advent and Lent."

"Isn't this Advent?"

"I gave myself a dispensation." She giggled. "Am I not having dinner with one of your fine, grand Nobel Prize winners?"

"You're not fluthered," he continued to hold her hand, "but if you keep up at this rate, ought you to be driving home?"

"Won't I take the train now? Isn't it only a half-hour ride on the DART? Can't I collect the car tomorrow when I take you to your grand lecture? Sure wouldn't it be a terrible sin not to enjoy this wine, and it being so dear, especially since the university is buying it for us?"

Gently she withdrew her hand.

"I'm the one that's fluthered, woman, and not on wine either."

"You shouldn't say that, Sean." She tried to be serious, afraid that the conversation was getting out of hand. "I'm just a dowdy, overweight Dublin widow with a dry academic mind. But it's very nice to hear it just the same."

Glory be to God, it ought not to be this easy.

He reached across the table with his right hand and captured her stubborn Irish chin. He caressed the flesh beneath her lips very slowly.

She lowered her eyes, frightened, but not repelled.

"No passes, Nora Anne, not tonight anyway. Just a bit of adoration."

"I don't know why." She looked up, troubled, uncertain.

"I thought we banned self-hatred."

She laughed and permitted him to hold her eyes with his own. "I suppose a woman can't stop a man from adoring, not if he has made up his mind to adore."

"He has made up his mind."

She eased her face out of his possession. "I don't want to lose my heart to you, Sean Seamus Desmond. Not at all, at all."

She was, he reasoned, a woman capable of nearly total surrender in trust. She had done it once and it had not worked out so well. She was afraid of doing it again. But she would. To someone, eventually. So why not Sean Seamus Desmond?

"Faith, woman, there's a lot more than your heart at stake. Starting with your dress, for example."

Head bowed again, she hesitated and then murmured, "God knows, I understand that. I knew that as soon as you came off the plane at the airport. That's why I was such an onchuck—female amadan"—a tiny, tiny laugh—"and worried half to death that something had happened to you. Sure, I wanted to cry for joy when I saw your wonderful Irish face."

Her eyes were closed, her face taut and anxious. Dear God, what openness. Had poor Dennis been frightened by such an awesome, passionate offering and run away from it? Was she now afraid of another such oblation, perhaps comprehending how she could terrify a man and yet not knowing how else to make a gift of herself?

God knows, woman, I would have run from you before I fell in with herself.

Now tread carefully, you amadan.

He recaptured her face, both hands now on her cheeks. "I'll make no bones about it, Nora Anne: I intend to do everything I can to lure you into my bed, and on a long-term basis. But I promise I won't hurt you. Now or ever."

She opened her eyes. "I'm not afraid of you hurting me, Sean Seamus. I trust you."

"Do you now?" He felt mildly offended that he had so quickly been rated trustworthy. "And meself talking so much blarney?"

"Och, now." She touched his cheek quickly and then pulled her hand away, looking around to see if anyone in the room had noticed her gesture; she did not try to escape his hands, however. "Isn't your blarney transparent? Even if I'll probably have a wee look at my book of Rubens when I go home. You wouldn't hurt anyone. You're a good man."

"Funny thing. That's what herself, the Queen of Sweden, said to me just the other day."

She grinned at him, somehow utterly delighted. "And were you trying to seduce her too?"

"I was not. Now that you mention the thought, it might not have been a bad idea, and her husband there all the time."

They laughed together again.

"It's meself I don't trust." She sighed, suddenly unhappy. "I don't want to hurt either meself or you."

"I won't let you do that."

She frowned and tried to pull away from him. He tightened his grip and forced her head back so she had to look at him.

"Are the terms clear, Nora Flanagan? I want you and I intend to have you."

Her face twisted in a rapid flux of emotions: fear, joy, pain, longing. She tried again to twist her head away from him. He tightened the control in his tender vise. Finally she bit her lip and then smiled. "Well, now, if a man wants to try to seduce a woman, sure, I don't suppose there's anything she can do to make him stop trying, can she?"

She ceased resistance to his possession of her face. Capitulation.

A sudden, powerful wave of desire swept through him.

I could take her back to my damp suite at the Shelbourne and make her mine before the hour is over.

Don't be a fool, that's not the way to do it. She'll feel cheap afterward and then where will you be?

Maybe she won't.

Well, don't push it tonight anyway. Sure, the day after the lecture or maybe even the next day, will she not be inviting you down to that wee cottage in south county Dublin and the girls off at their school? That'll be the right time, won't it now?

He released her face and returned to his sherry trifle.

"I know in theory"—she frowned thoughtfully—"that my body is good, but so much of my religious education suggests otherwise."

"I'll vote for the theory, if you upgrade the word from 'good' to 'superb' or even 'mind-boggling'!"

"Thank you." A blush and a soft smile and averted eyes. "You'd make a good pope."

"Not very good but better than some of them."

They laughed together. Would the rest of his life be a partial replay of discussions with that damn seraph?

"May I ask a question?" She peeked up at him, her eyes awash.

"Indeed you may."

"You're a desperate man altogether. You look at me like you know everything about me already and want me anyway. It's flattering"—she grinned self-consciously—"to be admired and wanted"—she gulped—"so intensely . . . disconcerting but not totally unpleasing. Still, why me? I acted like the blooming queen of all witches at the airport and was a terrible eejit in the car coming in. I can't see why a man would want, on such short notice, so awful a woman. And it's not self-hatred this time. I'm puzzled, honestly."

Not without reason. But how can I explain that it's all been designed by a pack of seraphs. Oh sure, we're still free, but they've pushed us into a corner from which we'd have a hard time escaping even if we wanted to.

A couple of cold and lonely middle-aged humans looking for a bit of warmth and affection.

Well, there was nothing wrong with that, God knows.

It might well be—and he didn't especially like the thought—that all along she's been the important one and that the seraph bunch has been grooming me for her.

"Well," he said, considering very carefully, "let me say that for all my life up to now I've been searching for you and that for all my life from now I'll be after explaining why I was searching for you. All right?"

It was indeed all right. She cried and laughed and dried her tears and finished her sherry trifle. His hint that he was planning more than a one-night stand did not seem to add to her confidence. She took that for granted.

I'm such a good man, it disgusts me!

"Still," she said as she finished the dessert with the cool efficiency that characterized everything she did—her plate was as clean as if it had been licked by a famished puppy—"I don't completely understand. It's not as if . . . as if you don't have any other options."

"None that I've ever found in a more attractive package. Can you live with that answer?"

"Certainly." She closed her eyes and sighed, her breasts moving sharply against the fabric of her dress. "What woman couldn't?"

He gritted his teeth to restrain the thunderbolt of passion that ignited him. She's ready to succumb, he thought. More than ready. Eager even. Why not now?

39

On the short walk back to the
Shelbourne, both of them shy and reserved again, she told him that
she was not at all sure about the University of Cook County. The
money was certainly good, better than she could have hoped for.
But the expense of crossing the Atlantic, putting the girls in
school, and food and housing in America.

Losing her nerve, she was.

Then he saw with the clear and vivid eyes of imagination a
little boy: Dermot Desmond, a possible fruit of his love for Nora
Anne Flanagan. His head turned light with affection for still improbable Dermot—and with a wrenching lustful tenderness for
the wee one's mother that was so strong he was momentarily fear-
ful that he might begin clawing at her clothes right there on the
rain-drenched street.

Dermot! Was he the one in whom the seraph crowd were
most interested? Were his parents minor actors in one of Gaby's
patterns of beauty?

"Is there something wrong, Seano?" Nora's hand rested on his
arm. "You're weaving a bit."

"Too much of the drink taken," he replied.

"Not true." Her eyes searched his face, looking for something that might or might not be there.

"Maybe just a little tired. Sure it's been a long, hard day."

"The truth, Sean Desmond." She stopped walking and her grip on his arm tightened and it was his turn to feel naked.

"Well," he hesitated, "I was thinking of my son Dermot and his mother and how much I loved them both."

"I thought you didn't have a son?"

"I don't, to tell the truth. But maybe someday I might have one."

They resumed walking toward the Shelbourne, but his arm remained in her possession.

"That's beautiful, Sean." She drew in her breath quickly and her lovely chest expanded and contracted. "Very beautiful. Dermot, is it now? Ah, sure that's a fine name."

For a moment she was utterly submissive, ready, even eager to be impregnated.

The most seductive words of the evening had been spoken without seductive intent. He made a mental note of the fact. Dermot, is it?

"Where was I now?" He fought to restrain his passionate longing for her. "Ah yes, about Chicago. Won't you be after moving in with us? There's plenty of room, even if you'll not be sharing my bed. And the four wee lasses can go to St. Ignatius together."

"I couldn't do that," she protested anxiously. "What would people say?"

"They'd say you were sleeping with that crazy man Desmond, and even if it wasn't true, it would protect you from the predators."

"The other predators."

They laughed again. She thought the suggestion was outrageous. But too interesting to reject out of hand.

"Will the wee lasses be at me lecture tomorrow?"

"Ah, would they ever forgive me if I wouldn't let them come? Sure don't they have your picture hanging on the wall in their room? Wasn't I telling you, Professor Desmond, you're a hero in this country?"

Allies.

In front of the hotel, she pointed out the plaque honoring that wee gombeen man, Oliver St. John Gogarty.

Now I'll have to kiss her.

Well, what are you waiting for, eejit?

He put one arm around her shoulders, brushed his lips against her forehead, and then very quickly against her lips.

She leaned against him. He felt her body yielding completely, her superb breasts touching his chest. For the third time a body-wrenching surge of physical need raced through his body. Mine for the taking. Why wait a few more days?

Because she had been hurt and was still fragile.

Because with a vulnerable woman a man should be very soft at the beginning. Her eventual gratitude for his restraint would pay rich dividends. She would keep. And he could wait. For a while.

"Good night, Nora Flanagan. Thanks for everything."

"Good night, Sean Desmond. Thank you for everything."

The promise in that exchange was enough for both of them. There might be some hesitations. There'd be no turning back.

Impulsively he knocked on the rain-soaked window of her old Renault.

An indulgent smile on her lips, she rolled down the window.

"I suppose you'd be after playing a musical instrument, wouldn't you now?"

She was startled. "How would you know that I play a cornet in a Dublin brass group?"

"That's one of your pint-size trumpets, isn't it now?"

"And you're the kind of man"—her forehead knotted in a frown—"who would object to a woman blowing on a horn in his apartment, are you not?"

"Ah, sure." He chuckled, despite the hollow feeling at the base of his stomach. "Have I not a great devotion to the trumpet?"

They laughed together, sharing a great joke. Nora Anne Flanagan, however, did not understand how funny it was.

On the slow ride up the problematic old cage elevator to his floor, he pondered various images of what Nora Anne Flanagan would look like with her clothes off and some of the more interesting activities in which he might engage with her, the various endearments, for example, his lips might work on her nipples and her breasts. And her belly and her loins for that matter.

So, despite hints of "Fanfare for the Common Man" in the deep recesses of the hotel, he forgot to punch the button for his floor and had to ride down from the top of the building.

Well, such images were all well and good, he advised himself. Still, his seduction of this vision of beauty should proceed very slowly. At the end, he'd let her make the first move.

Would it require self-control?

Well, now, hadn't he been told recently that he understood women perfectly?

In his suite, under a cold shower, the only kind they seemed to have at night in the hotel and not much good for all its chill at reducing his passions either, he cursed his caution in front of the hotel and then praised his wisdom and virtue.

Finally, tucked contentedly in a vast if floppy bed, he admitted sheepishly to himself that there was another reason for his care and restraint.

Maybe those were not colored lights dancing intermittently at the door of the restaurant all evening. And on the street while they walked back to the Shelbourne. All the hues of red and some green and blue with an occasional hint of gold and silver.

Maybe there were no lights at all. Maybe he was merely a little fluthered.

Right?

Wrong!

The lights were there.

Fersure.

ANGEL FIRE?

SERAPH FIRE!

As Sister Intemerata used to say, if you keep in mind that your guardian angel is always watching you, it's easy to be good.

Then, just before he fell asleep, he remembered with a mixture of dismay and elation another one of her dicta:

"Your guardian angel watches over you and protects you all your life. Whether you like it or not."

More About Angels

They give to God's relationship to man the contour and concreteness in which it can be perceived as the new Creation FOR man.

—Lisabeth Cohn

The angels mark ... (the) reaching of the incommensurable into the commensurable, of mystery into the sphere of human possibilities ... they are at the place where the speech and action of God commence in the created world.

—Karl Barth

Then a man came and wrestled with him until just before daybreak. When the man saw that he was not winning the struggle, he hit Jacob on the hip and it was thrown out of joint. The man said, "Let me go, daylight is coming."

"I won't, unless you bless me," Jacob answered.

"What is your name?" the man asked.

"Jacob," he answered.

The man said, "Your name will no longer be Jacob. You have struggled with God and with men, and you have won; so your name will be Israel."

Jacob said, "Now tell me your name."

But he answered, "Why do you want to know my name?" Then he blessed Jacob.

Jacob said, "I have seen God face-to-face and I am still alive!"

—Genesis 32/23–30

Was I the one who wrestled with Jacob? The poor dear was a patriarchalist, remember? He wouldn't have wrestled with the visitor if he thought the being was female. But if the Malik Yahweh—that's Hebrew for the Angel of Yahweh—had been a bearer of life, I don't think she would have found him all that attractive.

—Gabriella Light, Ph.D.

If we are forced to puzzle about the story we may offer interpretations, moral, psychological, or whatnot, but the interpretation cannot displace the angel of the story from his position in our phenomenological empyrean. We must cope with him somehow.

—Stephen Crites

She sung beyond the genius of the sea
The water never formed to mind or voice
Like a body wholly body, fluttering
Its empty sleeves; and yet its mimic motion
Made constant cry, caused constantly a cry
That was not ours although we understood,
Inhuman, of the veritable ocean.

—Wallace Stevens

Early successes, Creation's pampered darlings
Ranges, dawn-red ridges
of all beginning, pollen of blossoming godhead,
hinges of light, shields of felicity, tumults
of stormily rapturous feeling and suddenly, separate,
mirrors, drawing up their own
outstreamed beauty into their faces again.

—Rainer Maria Rilke

We feel that the angels in Rilke are stronger than in our own faith as we actually experience it.

—Karl Rahner

All species are sacraments of the Most High's passionate love. It's no particular virtue on our part but we happen to be more powerful sacraments than you.

—Gabriella Light, Ph.D.